BOY
FALLEN

CHRIS GILL

PRNTD

Published by PRNTD Publishing 2022

1 3 4 5 7 9 10 8 6 4 2

ISBN 9780994462084

First published in Australia in 2022 by PRNTD Publishing

Typeset in Baskerville

www.prntdpublishing.com

For my husband

Prologue

A t first, it was hard to tell if what was lying on the rock was, in fact, a corpse. Hours had passed since the weak winter sun had slipped behind the wild coastline, and the glow from the fingernail moon was faint. The night's stillness was interrupted only by the white noise of Taonga Falls and a bitter southerly wind.

The man padded towards the mystery form at the base of the waterfall, hoping it was just the moonlight playing tricks with the mist. But the feeling in his stomach's pit said something else. Something far more sinister.

He set his lips into an anxious line and slowly crouched beside the wide, flat rock. Close enough to get a better look, but far enough to keep his distress at bay. Before he had a chance to get even closer, the wind whipped north, clearing the shroud and revealing the body in its entirety.

There he was. Blonde hair sodden. One milky eye, the other

crushed inward. The once beautiful face of Evan Wiley, now a waxy-pale and putrid vision of horror.

Nausea rippled through the man, stealing his balance and causing him to tumble forward. His palms slid on the wet rock as he landed on his knees. He was now close enough to Evan's swollen face to see a crack of skull through a bloom of broken flesh.

Heaving himself upright, the man's stomach churned aloud at the realisation of what he'd discovered. But still, he couldn't look away. A photo. Oh, how they would have loved a photo last time. Now they'd get one. All thanks to him. Maybe there'd be a bidding war. The final image of the famous Wiley boy.

Sliding his phone from the pocket of his now-muddy jeans, the man tapped the camera icon. Glaring at Evan's moonlit corpse through the delay of the grainy screen, a visual played out in the man's mind as to how the teenager found his fate. Had the boy fallen? Or had he jumped? Maybe money really doesn't buy happiness. The man's eyes skipped the length of the river, and as they did, his conscience finally kicked in.

Closing the camera, he took a moment to appreciate the night's silence. The sound of rustling ferns filled the air, animated by the midnight breeze. He knew it wouldn't be quiet for long. Taking one final big breath, his shaking index finger tapped one, thrice.

Soon, the remote town was filled with news vans and reporters that would speak to anyone willing. Everyone was equipped with a story about Evan Wiley, although most weren't true. It wasn't the first time darkness had come to Taonga, and the locals were afraid it wouldn't be the last.

Chapter One

Her heart stopped as the wheels hit the tarmac. It always did when Brooke got closer to home, but this time she questioned whether it would start back up again.

'Kia ora, welcome to Christchurch.' The pilot's voice carried through the cabin. 'The local time is ten past one and the temperature is eight degrees. For those visiting, we hope you enjoy your stay. For those returning, welcome home.'

Staring out the oval window at the snow-capped peaks in the distance, Brooke wondered how many times she'd heard those same words. The last two always filled her with dread. As the plane taxied, she pulled her eyes from the threatening blanket of grey clouds coating the horizon and pushed her long mousy hair out the way of her face. She switched her phone off flight mode and braced for an influx of notifications.

The first worth reading came from her mother. *Hope your flight went ok. See you soon x.* Brooke had told her she'd take a taxi from the airport, but Barbara insisted on sending her stepdad.

The next message was from him. *Just seen you've landed. I'm at the arrival's gate. Gary.*

She read one final message – two words from her sister. *Prepare yourself.*

Still nothing from Lana. She'd last heard from her Wednesday saying she was worried Evan hadn't come home, but it had been Lana's mother who had broken the news. Called her up hysterical, informing her his body had been found at the foot of Taonga Falls. She'd asked her to get down as soon as possible. Brooke had packed her things and booked the next flight out of Auckland.

A red-lipped flight attendant tried to control her shiver as she stood next to the open door. Another handed Brooke her coat and luggage. 'Goodbye, Ms Palmer. Thank you for flying with us again.'

Brooke managed a polite nod as she wrapped up in her merino, but it wasn't enough to stop the familiar gush of Arctic air as she stepped off the plane. Drifting through the terminal like a ghost, she opened the New Zealand Herald app. *Waterfall death: Police confirm identity of Taonga teen*, the headline read. She wasn't surprised it had made the national.

Next, she would check the Greymouth Star's website. *Wealthy Wiley teen found dead at Taonga Falls*. She traced her eyes across the sentence that ran beneath a picture of Evan – his perfect smile frozen in time: *19 years after the Palmer murder in what locals fear to be a copycat crime.*

Her spine stiffened. Could that be what it was? She attempted to still her mind as she quickened her pace towards arrivals.

She knew she would be studying both stories closely later.

'Your being here will really lift your mum's spirits,' Gary said, punctuating his sentence with a reassuring smile.

Brooke's stare shifted from her chalky complexion in the wing mirror to the raindrops that had started dotting the window. 'It just doesn't feel real. I'm in shock.'

Gary flicked on the windscreen wipers while keeping his eyes on the road. 'We all are.' There was a silence before he raised a pointed finger to the dashboard. 'Mind if I turn the radio on?'

'Course not.'

'–anything more at this stage?' The woman's voice was stern through the speakers.

'No, not yet,' a man replied from the wrong end of a phone line – his accent thick and local. Brooke recognised him instantly as the town mayor. 'But we're urging the community to remain calm. Calm, but vigilant.'

'So they think it's murder?' Brooke spoke over the presenter.

Gary gave her a glance before returning his mahogany-eyed gaze to the road. 'The police are treating it as suspicious, the last I heard. So the press is jumping on that, of course.' He gestured to the radio. 'Sure we'll find out what actually happened in the next couple of days.'

Brooke looked back to the highway and thought hard, not wanting to indulge in the media's sensationalism. 'Could've been an accident, I guess. He could have been up there with his camera or something. Trying to get the perfect shot.' Her mind wandered back to the last time she'd seen Evan. It was when she had been down briefly at Christmas. He'd been so excited to show her his brand-new DSLR. He'd spoken of his plans to go travelling once the European summer rolled around. He was going to start a portfolio in an attempt to forge a career as a travel photographer. She'd told him the world was his. The memory made her chest heavy.

'Yeah, it's possible.' Gary turned down the radio which was now emitting sixties soul. He lifted his hand from the steering wheel and ran it through his hair, which had become more salt than pepper in recent years. 'Course, there's also the question about whether… you know…'

'He took his own life?' Brooke jumped in without a beat.

An eerie quiet followed, interrupted only by the surrounding traffic smacking the waterlogged road.

'Yeah.' Gary's tired eyes looked through his glasses into the rear-view mirror, then ahead again.

It wasn't as if the thought hadn't crossed Brooke's mind more than once on the flight down. There were plenty of people who had made Evan's life miserable when he was at school. Something she remembered from her own experience growing up privileged in Taonga. But he was so happy at Christmas. It didn't make sense. Suicide didn't add up.

Gary indicated left before veering off the highway and onto the road that snaked into Taonga. 'Reckon you'll do a bit of snooping while you're down?'

'Might be a bit close to home.'

Gary gave a brief nod. 'Probably best to have some time off right now anyway. Use the time to be there for your mum and sister. And Lana, of course.'

The car slowed to meet the speed limit of the road that ran into Brooke's hometown. She eyed the dated signpost, which had long ago surrendered to its surrounding flora. *Welcome to Taonga*. She didn't need to see the sign to know what the secondary script read: *The West Coast's Gateway to Gold*. Those glory days are long gone, she thought, just as she always did. The rain was really beating down now and it had grown dark.

'Missed the rain?' Gary's smirk was laced with sarcasm.

'We get our fair share.' But Brooke knew all too well the rain wasn't as bad in Auckland. That constant mist that hung over the West Coast seemed to favour Taonga the most.

Brooke watched her stepdad navigate his Range Rover through the undulating streets of what had become known as Taonga Heights. The family had lived there long before it became the place for CEOs to invest in their future coastal lifestyles. Vast mansions stood renovated and ready, waiting for the retirement of their owners. A day that would never come.

As they reached their family home, Brooke noticed a news van parked uncomfortably close. They'd love nothing more than a quote from a member of her family to pad out their reports. She doubted they would bother had the podcast not gone viral.

They pulled into the driveway and waited a few minutes to see if the rain would relent before retrieving Brooke's luggage from the boot. It didn't.

A chopper circled noisily overhead.

Brooke wheeled her suitcase along the cold polished-concrete floor, leaving a trail of wet in her wake.

'I'll let your mum know we're back,' Gary said, making his way to the kitchen.

The scent of kumara roasting offered a fleeting moment of comfort as Brooke continued to her bedroom. Everything was exactly as she'd left it. All three siblings' rooms had been kept perfectly intact, like a time capsule of their youth. But the rest of the house had undergone many updates in their three decades of living there. Its current iteration was starkly minimal and mostly white. An unconscious effort to keep up with the nearby new builds.

Brooke placed her suitcase in the corner of the room and collapsed on her neatly made bed. She shifted her focus to a photograph on the bedside table. The two girls couldn't have been much older than fifteen. Brooke's hair was tied back in a pony as it always was in school. Lana's an explosion of blonde curls. Both were covered in freckles – as if they were competing – but Lana had attempted to mask hers with makeup. Their sweeping smiles exposed bright white teeth that hid so much. Their joyful expressions a believable lie.

Brooke reached out and picked up the photograph. It had faded, but the memories hadn't. The jeering taunts. The malicious notes. The jealous eyes. They'd been lucky to have each other, at least. To look out for one another. To keep each other strong. She wished Evan could've had the same. Maybe things would have turned out differently. Maybe he would still be here now.

Evan met the boy's green-eyed stare and instantly regretted walking in. But it was too late now. He'd committed. The boy gave him a shoulder-shove en route to the sink. Evan said nothing and stood at the urinal, the boy's

8

reflection blurred in its brushed metal. He unzipped his fly and listened to the tap's rush of water, hoping it would help him to release. Nothing came.

The tap turned off, but no footsteps followed. 'What is it? Toilet not up to your standards?'

Evan kept quiet with his eyes clenched, wishing he could just let go. But still nothing. The fear had won.

An obnoxious laugh cut through the stale air. 'Thought so.'

Evan heard the door close and the release he'd been waiting for finally came. As did the tears.

A knock on the door prompted Brooke to place the picture back next to her bed.

Barbara let herself in slowly. Her eyes were glassy. Her smile, sympathetic. She embraced her daughter for an unceasing minute. The pair tried with all their willpower, for each other, to hold back the tears.

Barbara inhaled a long breath. A bid to compose herself that paid off. 'Do you want anything to eat? I've made your favourite.'

Brooke shook her head. 'I'm not hungry.'

Barbara sat next to her daughter and wiped a tear. 'Neither am I. I haven't eaten since—' She cut herself off.

Brooke looked at her mother closely. Had it really been seven months? Her bobbed hair remained the same shade of boxed chestnut, but her face was noticeably older.

'We must try and get some sleep though,' Barbara said. 'You'll need your energy for tomorrow. Have you heard from Lana yet?'

Brooke gave a shake of the head and said nothing. Rain

thrashed against the window.

'Just give her time.'

Brooke pulled out her phone. 'Look.' She flicked to the Greymouth Star tab. 'The press is framing it as a copycat crime.'

Barbara studied the screen intently. 'That's the same picture they've been using on TV. It's everywhere.' She passed Brooke back her phone. 'But we don't know what's happened yet. It might have been an accident.'

'Do you honestly believe that? You know our families have always been hated here.'

Barbara released a sigh. 'Places do change, Brooke. And horrible things happen to good people all the time.'

Brooke's face grew flushed and breath rapid. 'Not in towns like this.'

Barbara gave a gentle nod and sympathised with her eyes.

Brooke switched on the TV that hung above a chest of drawers opposite her bed. The same image of Evan that had been used on the Greymouth Star filled the screen, his blue eyes bright and alive. It was replaced with a blonde reporter clutching an oversized foam microphone. She stood pre-recorded outside the front of Lana's family home, speaking with an Australian accent. 'Evan Wiley's family have issued a statement saying they are heartbroken and lost for words. They've asked for their privacy to be respected. No further comments have been made by the family at this time.'

'Give them a moment to digest the news.' The texture of Barbara's tone cut through the room.

'That's exactly what they were like with us,' Brooke said with a wobble of breath.

Barbara kept her lips pressed tight.

The shot of the reporter was suddenly replaced with an image of Jack. The sight of her brother made Brooke flinch.

'Locals are already commenting on the parallels between the murder of fifteen-year-old Jack Palmer that took place nineteen years ago. From another of Taonga's wealthiest families, Jack's murder garnered international attention more recently when it became the subject of true-crime podcast, Envy.'

A middle-aged man appeared on screen, speaking from inside a pub. He had an unkempt beard and a ruddy complexion. 'Yeah, it's very sad. But can't say any of us 'round here are surprised. They've got everything in that family while most of us struggle just getting by. Some kid must've done it 'cause he was jealous. Just like what happened last time.'

Brooke turned to her mother, her head atilt. 'Still think places change?'

Chapter Two

The July chill bit into Brooke's bones as she climbed out the silver sedan she always drove when back home. She'd forgotten how much colder it got down south, but at least the rain had eased. Burying her chin into her coat's collar, she stalked through the fog that cloaked the town on winter mornings without fail, avoiding the hardened faces of nosy locals she recognised. She could just imagine what they were all thinking. Snobby family had it coming. Jealousy's an evil thing, she thought.

Lana's family home was situated on the town's only arterial road, an ornate stone structure built in Taonga's golden age. Brooke pushed her way through a small scrum of reporters outside the house. She noticed how they nearly all worked for overseas news outlets. Their copycat angle must have been gaining momentum. Two teenage boys murdered two decades apart. It was almost *too* perfect.

'C'est Brooke, viens vite,' a French journalist said to his cameraman, readying his microphone. Another camera flashed. Brooke bit her lip hard. She'd learned the importance of keeping quiet the first time around.

The blonde reporter Brooke had seen on the news last night surged through the crowd, pushing past her competitors. She reached out and positioned her microphone inches from Brooke's cheek. 'Ms Palmer, what do you have to say about the death of your best friend's son?'

Brooke swallowed her response as she ascended the stone steps to the front door. Even a few words uttered would be twisted before being spread all over tomorrow's papers. Or online within the hour. This time around, they had the twenty-four-hour news cycle to deal with.

One of the large black double doors opened, allowing a small gap to slide inside. Amanda Wiley appeared in part and spoke past Brooke. 'Get off my property! We asked you to respect our privacy, now sod off.' She gave the door a decisive slam and draped her arms around Brooke. 'They're relentless, aren't they?' Her sharp British accent was as intact as ever, despite having lived over half her life in New Zealand.

'They sure are.' Brooke hugged the woman who had always been like a second mother to her, breathing in her familiar flowery aroma.

'Come on then.' A reassuring pat on the back concluded the hug. 'Let me take your coat. Tea? Coffee?' Amanda's wispy, silver hair was scraped back into a bun, her angular features highlighted with intense makeup. As always, she wore bright white. A thick silver cross hung from her neck.

'I'm fine.' Brooke peeled off her coat and passed it to her. 'I'm so sorry.'

Amanda's eyes grew wet, steaming up her thick-rim glasses. She hooked the coat on an already-overloaded antique stand, causing it to tip a touch. 'I know you are.' There was a pause before she spoke again. 'Come on. Lana's in her room. Hopefully you'll get a few words out of her.'

Brooke mirrored Amanda's pace through the heavily wall-papered hallway to the living room, where a fire was burning. Its crackle and glow instantly made her relax, but its ashy smell could barely be detected. Instead, a symphony of fresh floral notes swamped the room. Extravagant bouquets took over every surface, each giving Amanda's perfume a run for its money.

At the fire's side, Frank Wiley was slumped in an armchair. His white hair, which was once the same terrific blonde his daughter and grandson had both inherited, was neatly combed. His solemn face said it all as he stood up to greet Brooke.

'Frank.' She reached out and gave him a brief but sincere hug. She noticed instantly that he'd thinned. The grief had already begun to take its toll. 'I'm so sorry.'

Frank nodded and muttered his gratitude. He'd always been a quiet man. Often deep in thought. Growing up, many of Brooke's memories of Lana's father were him spending his free time at church. He was even more religious than Amanda.

'How are *you* doing?' Amanda examined Brooke's eyes as she placed a palm on her shoulder.

'I don't know. Numb, I guess.'

Amanda dropped her lids and whispered a few words of faith beneath her breath. When her eyes reopened, they had glassed over again. 'How long are you down for?'

'At least a fortnight. I'm using my leave.'

'It'll mean the world to Lana having you here. And to me.' Amanda blinked fast to prevent her tears. She reached out a hand for Brooke to hold. Her narrow fingers were cool to the touch. Each nail painted perfectly scarlet.

Brooke offered a sad smile. 'I just can't believe this is happening.'

'I know,' Amanda said with a catch in her voice. 'It must be bringing up so many awful memories. How's your mum coping?'

A beat of silence. 'She's doing okay.'

'Your mum is strong.' Amanda lifted her glasses to wipe a tear. Her rapid blinks could only do so much. 'As are you.'

'Guess we've had to be.' Another pause. 'Thanks for calling. For thinking of me so quickly.'

Amanda flitted her fingers. 'Of course. Lana needs you right now. Come on. I'll take you to her.'

Brooke remained silent as the pair climbed the grand staircase to Lana's bedroom. Family portraits hung next to oil paintings and ornaments from overseas trips. Any space left between was filled with a crucifix. 'Stupid question, but how's she doing?'

Amanda's gaze sank to her feet. 'Not good. She's barely said a word since. She hasn't even spoken to the police.'

Brooke thought about how far removed this was from Lana's true self. She pinched the bridge of her nose to hold back her tears. Now wasn't the time to fall apart.

'It's even harder that she's going through this alone,' Amanda went on. 'Without a man in her life, I mean. And obviously *he* wants nothing to do with it. Makes you sick, doesn't it?'

Brooke knew the *he* Amanda was referring to was Evan's father, who had never been in his son's life. Lana had always struggled to hold a relationship down, her last being about a year. But that was at least a couple of years back.

When they reached Lana's bedroom, Amanda gave a gentle knock with a curled index finger. 'Brooke's here.'

Silence. Brooke and Amanda exchanged a glance.

'Let me know if you need anything.' Creases formed across Amanda's face. She gave Brooke's arm a squeeze and disappeared downstairs.

Lana was sitting on the edge of her bed, facing the wall. The room smelled musty. As if a window needed to be opened. Scrunched tissues scattered the room like wilting flowers.

'I'm so sorry, Lan.'

No response. Brooke took a seat in the chair opposite her friend. Lana's normally voluminous blonde locks were loosely bunned and understandably hadn't been washed for days. Her face was bare of makeup. Her swollen eyes a sign she'd been up all night in tears.

The first time Brooke had spoken to Lana, it had been *her* who had been crying. Perched on the grass behind a rimu tree in the school playground, Lana had found her with her face buried in her hands, sobbing. She'd only been in Taonga for a week and it was her second day at school.

'Are you okay?' Lana had said, brushing her untamed hair from her face. Her wide-set blue eyes had stared intensely at Brooke.

'I'm fine,' Brooke had lied, wiping her eyes with her sleeve.

'Leave me alone.'

Lana had crouched down next to her with the warmest smile. 'Don't worry – I'm not like them.'

Now, over twenty years on, Brooke watched Lana's vacant gaze and had to once again fight back tears.

Lana finally met Brooke's focus. 'He didn't kill himself. He wouldn't.'

Brooke opened her mouth to say something, but nothing came. She doubted her friend had been following the news much. If she had, she'd know her son's death was already being treated as suspicious. 'Do you think it could have been an accident?'

Lana's lips began to tremble – her composure caving in. Brooke fastened her arms around her friend as she gave into reality.

'What was he doing there on his own?' Lana managed through desperate sobs.

Brooke kept quiet for a beat. She had always seen Evan as a bit of a loner, so the idea of him tramping solo didn't seem so alien. She gave Lana's back a solid rub. 'Did he have his camera with him? When they found him?'

Lana reached for a tissue. She dabbed her glistening cheeks. 'No. Nothing. Not even his backpack. It's missing.'

Brooke broke into a sudden sweat. There was now no question in her mind. Someone killed Evan.

Lana closed her eyes as the tears reappeared. They fell with force. 'I just can't get my head around it. One minute he's here, the next he's gone.' Her words trailed off into a fragile whisper.

Brooke continued to smooth her friend's back. 'When did

you last see him?'

Lana's focus fell to the floor, tear tracks glossy on her cheeks. 'Tuesday afternoon.' Her words hung heavy in the air. There was a drawn-out silence that was broken by the distant sound of the doorbell.

'How did he seem?'

Lana looked up and met Brooke's stare. Her expression had changed. 'Things had been a bit... different since you were last here, Brooke. Mine and Ev's relationship had become a bit... strained.'

Brooke took back her palm. She hadn't known that. 'Strained? In what way?'

A heavy knock. 'Lana, the detective's here.' Amanda opened the bedroom door a fraction. 'He needs to speak to us. He has the results.'

Brooke knew what that meant. She flinched at the memory of being taken through Jack's post-mortem. 'I'll leave you guys to it.' She gave Lana a final embrace and stood up to face Amanda. 'Let me know if you need anything.'

Amanda curved her lips a dash, but Brooke could see the terror in her eyes. 'I'll show you out.'

As Brooke followed Amanda along the hallway, she thought back to how Evan had seemed at Christmas. She'd only seen the Wileys once on the short trip, but it had been all smiles. No signs of a tense relationship between Lana and Evan. What happened in the last seven months?

When they reached the front door, a man stood draped in a long coat. Somewhere in his forties, his dark hair was streaked with waves of grey – his eyes big and brown.

'Brooke, this is Detective Tane Collins.' Amanda mustered a polite introduction, despite herself. 'He's going to be working on Evan's case.'

Collins outstretched his hand. 'Nice to meet you.'

Brooke obliged the gesture with a shake.

'Brooke's a detective, too. Well, I suppose I should say *Palmer*.' Amanda unhooked Brooke's coat from the stand and helped her put it on. 'Up in Auckland.'

'Oh yeah?' Collins brushed the bristles on his chin with his index finger and thumb. 'How long for, Palmer?'

Brooke fastened her buttons. 'Over ten years now. Just made Sergeant.'

Collins raised a heavy eyebrow and nodded. 'Fantastic. Not far behind me then.'

'Inspector?'

'Bingo.'

Brooke glanced to the file in Collins' hand. 'Anyway, I'll leave you guys to it.' She hugged Amanda. 'Honestly, if you need anything – anything at all – call me.'

Amanda gave a knowing nod. 'Thanks.'

Brooke stepped out into the frigid wind and fished the car keys from her coat pocket. The rain had finally stopped completely, but dampness clung to the air. The mist had also cleared, but the reporters remained, albeit less cocksure with the presence of two uniformed constables at the front door. Making her way down the street, Brooke imagined the conversation that would be taking place back inside. Her heart rose to her throat as she returned to the warmth of the sedan.

Chapter Three

'Would you wear this?' Barbara held a burgundy mid-length dress up against herself.

Brooke's focus skipped past the garment, which looked like it had never even been worn. 'No.'

Barbara looked at the label inside the collar. 'It's Tom Ford?'

Brooke went to roll her eyes but closed them instead. 'You know that means nothing to me. How can you even focus on this right now?'

'It's good to focus on *something*.' Barbara folded up the dress and placed it neatly on an ottoman. 'Besides, it's for Amanda's charity event. She's organised a luncheon with the ladies, and we're all donating a few pieces to Dress for Success. Have you heard of it? They give clothes to women in need to help them thrive in the workplace. For job interviews. Things like that.' Barbara held up a dress with ornate sequin detailing down the front. 'This is a good one to donate. I don't think I'll wear it again. It's…' She checked the label. 'Valentino.'

Brooke glanced at her mother. Before she met Amanda, she probably didn't even know what Valentino was. And before meeting Gary, she definitely wouldn't have been able to afford it. 'Mum, do you honestly think anyone would wear a Valentino gown to a job interview?'

'I suppose not.' Barbara folded it up and gave it to the pile. 'But I don't want to look mean.'

Amanda religiously hosted a number of charity fundraisers each year, but Brooke somehow sensed this one wouldn't go ahead.

Barbara crouched down inside her walk-in wardrobe and began pulling out boxes. 'How was Lana?' She peeked into a beige shoebox embossed with a silver signature.

'Terrible. The detective assigned to the case turned up. He had the results from the post-mortem.'

Barbara winced, before opening the box completely. A pair of black heels lay interlocked on a bed of monogrammed tissue. She turned to face Brooke. 'I see. Well, at least we'll know soon then.'

'Lana told me Evan's backpack is missing. The one he always wore.'

Barbara said nothing. Instead, she picked the heels up to inspect their condition. Blood red outsoles glinted in the light, interrupted only by a patch of matte on each shoe.

'It's got to be murder, Mum.'

Barbara neatly returned the heels to their box and brought them over to the ottoman. 'Every woman needs a pair of these.'

'What if it's true what the media's saying?' Brooke's voice

inched louder. 'What if some kid Evan went to school with did this because he's jealous of what he had? Don't you think that's possible? Just like—' Brooke stopped short of saying her brother's name.

Barbara sat next to her daughter and clasped her hand. 'It's possible. Yes. There are a lot of people struggling in this town these days. A lot of people are angry and tensions are high. That's one of the reasons we had the new security system installed. It's a scary time and I don't need the constant reminder. Please, can you just help me sort through my wardrobe? Please.'

People had been struggling in Taonga for as long as Brooke could remember. But it was true; it had gotten worse. She'd sensed it when she was back in town at Christmas.

'Come on then,' Brooke said, giving in. Despite the task being the last thing she wanted to do, she was happy if it kept her mum distracted. She also took the chance wherever possible to encourage Barbara to let go of things she'd been holding on to. 'So, when do you guys think you'll downsize?'

Barbara had the look in her eye of a plan backfired. 'We're happy here, Brooke. It's the family home.'

'You know you're going to have to let go eventually, Mum. It's too big for just the two of you. And it's not healthy – you know –'

'What?' Barbara furrowed her brow. 'What's not healthy?'

Brooke wanted to bring up Jack's room, which still held his teenage clothes and other possessions, but she bit back her words. It wasn't the right time. Things were tense enough.

As if answering her wish for a distraction, Brooke's phone shivered in her pocket. She pulled it out to be met with an unknown number. 'Hello?'

'Palmer.' She recognised the gruff voice straight away. 'It's Collins here. Hope you don't mind Amanda giving me your number.'

'Not at all. Is everything okay?'

'Are you free to swing by the station? Have a little chat?'

Brooke eyed her mum, who now had an array of dresses over her arm. 'Sure. Be there in five.'

'Who was that?' Barbara's concerned stare was firm.

'The detective working on Evan's case. Sorry, Mum. I'll be back later.'

Outside, the rain began to fall once more.

Sitting opposite Collins under the unforgiving fluorescence of his office light, Brooke got her first proper look at the detective. He was handsome. His face was warm and worn, and the dark circles below his deep-set eyes were mirrored by the thick eyebrows above. He sat behind a would-be empty desk had it not been for a small pile of documents. An old computer sat to his right, unused in favour for the thin black laptop in front of it. Behind him, a black and white photo hung of a bygone force, standing tall and uniformed. Their moustaches placed them firmly in the eighties.

'I know you're close to the case.' Collins snapped his laptop shut and turned his attention to the documents in front. 'You're okay to see the file?'

Brooke gave a sharp nod.

Collins picked a Manila folder from the top of the pile and pushed the rest aside. He slid the report to Brooke as he spoke.

'The forensic pathologists confirmed what was suspected. This was homicide.'

Brooke felt her stomach swirl. Even though it's what she'd assumed, it still hurt to have Evan's murder confirmed. She began thumbing through the loose papers of the post-mortem report as Collins continued.

'Time of death estimated to have been between six and nine PM on Tuesday. Cause of death – fatal blow to the head. No evidence of a weapon used. Other injuries include multiple antemortem lesions across body – suggesting struggle. Fractured skull, broken ribs – antemortem again. All other broken bones have minimal haemorrhaging – suggesting these injuries are likely to have been sustained post-mortem. Bite marks on tongue – likely to have been self-inflicted. We're waiting on the toxicological test for drug use.'

Collins' words had become a murmur as Brooke reached the final page of text. Through the paper's translucency, she could make out the outline of a body. Only this time, it wasn't an annotated diagram. As she tentatively peeled back the page, a version of Evan stared back at her. His naked corpse was lying pruney and bloated on a steel surface. His time spent submerged at the waterfall's base had taken its toll. His skin was mostly ghost-white with patches of purple and an uneasy yellow. His limbs were waxy and broken.

Brooke pulled the photograph close to better see his face, which was almost unrecognisable. Bruised, swollen and cracked open on the left side. His eyes had a creamy gaze. Brooke tried to remember the spark they'd had when she had last seen him.

'I'm going travelling.' Evan kept his eyes on Brooke as he poured her a glass of red wine. 'Soon as the weather warms up in Europe, I'm jumping on a plane with nothing but my camera.'

Brooke beamed back and took a sip. 'You'll be working for National Geographic before you know it.'

He ran his fingers through his weighty side-fringe and stifled a smile. 'Hope so.'

'Ev, you can do whatever you want in this life. The world's yours.'

Evan couldn't hold his smile back any longer, so he allowed it to stretch across his face. He always loved it when Brooke was down. Somehow she seemed to just get him. Which was more than he could say about anyone in Taonga. Even his mum. 'Wait here. I've got something to show you.'

Evan darted to his bedroom and carefully pulled his new DSLR from its box. When he returned, Brooke was exactly where he'd left her at the kitchen bench, gazing through the window. 'Here, look. Mum gave me my Christmas present early.'

Brooke put her glass down and examined the camera carefully.

'It's a full-frame,' he said proudly. 'All the professionals use this model. All my favourite photographers.'

'It's beautiful, Ev. Can't wait to see what magic you come up with.'

'Hold on.' Evan took the camera back and switched it on. 'I'll take your picture.'

Brooke began fixing her hair. He knew she wasn't comfortable having her photograph taken, but he wanted her to see herself the way he did.

'Go on then,' she said with an awkward smile.

Evan placed his palms on Brooke's shoulders and continued to reposition her in the window light. 'Okay, now look out the window. Chin down. Don't smile.'

He crouched down to find the right angle, twisting the lens as he did.
Click.

Brooke couldn't look at the image of Evan's body any longer. She closed the file and returned it to the pile. 'Who would do something like this?'

'Whoever they were, they wanted it to look like an accident,' Collins said. 'Or suicide. But they did a shitty job. For starters, the body was found faceup.'

'You think he was pushed?' Brooke tried to swallow but her throat was too dry.

Collins blew softly on his coffee and took a small sip. 'More likely dropped. The post-mortem was also able to determine he was dead a few hours before that happened.'

Brooke bit her lip so hard it paled. 'Did it show anything else?'

'Just that he'd put up a pretty good fight, as you could probably see from the photo.' Collins' hands huddled around the polystyrene cup. The room didn't appear to have any heating. Or if it did, the peak of Taonga's winter was finding its way through. 'We're waiting for the results to come back to see if there's any DNA on his body. There's nothing on his clothing, so it's unlikely. Whoever did this at least knew how to cover their tracks.'

There was an inflated silence before Brooke spoke. 'Why am I here?'

Collins took another sip of his coffee and frowned. 'Few reasons. First, you're a detective. Two heads are better than one. You're also from this town, so you know how it works. How the people think.'

Brooke doubted that. 'It's been a long time since I lived here, Detective.'

'You know the Wileys. You knew Evan. I'm hoping you can tell me a bit more than Lana did. She barely said a word to me, which was understandable considering what I just had to tell her. It could take a day or so until she's ready to talk.'

Things had been a bit… different since you were last here… Lana's words played back in Brooke's head. She considered mentioning how Lana had said her relationship with Evan had become strained. Not right now. She'd at least wait until she'd gauged how much he already knew. The last thing she wanted was to get her friend into any sort of trouble when she was suffering enough.

'Just so I'm clear,' Brooke began, 'are you asking me to officially join you on the case?'

Collins polished off the dregs of his murky coffee. 'Well, we haven't got budget for a second detective at this point. But if you're interested in helping me out, sign-off from Auckland won't be an issue. How long are you down for?'

'A fortnight.'

'Perfect. So, what do you think?'

Brooke thought back to what Gary had said about needing to be there for her mum and sister. He was right. But he also said she needed to be there for Lana. What better way could she support her friend than trying to seek justice for her murdered son? She met Collins' gaze. 'Sure. I'd love to help.'

Collins broke out into a grin. 'Great. Leave it with me.'

Brooke looked back at the files. 'So, do we know who was

the last person to see him?'

'As of now, the last confirmed person is Lana. He told her he was visiting a friend. Course, he didn't say which friend.'

Brooke pursed her lips to the side.

'What's up?' Collins said.

'It's just… Well, I wasn't aware of Evan even having any friends. It was one of the reasons he wanted to leave town.'

'When Lana first reported Evan missing, she told the police he'd been hanging around with a couple of guys he used to go to school with.'

Brooke's forehead became furrowed. *Things had been a bit… different since you were last here…*

Collins leaned forward a touch. 'Did Lana speak to you about this?'

Brooke shook her head. 'We barely had time to talk. But it does come as a surprise to me. I'd always known Evan to be someone who kept himself to himself.'

'How would you describe your relationship with Lana?'

Brooke suddenly felt uncomfortable. Where was this heading? 'We've known each other since we were kids. We were inseparable growing up.'

'And since you left Taonga?' Collins began taking notes.

'Well, obviously things have changed. We've grown up, drifted apart a bit. But I'll always consider her my closest friend. Why are you asking this?'

Collins stopped writing and met Brooke's gaze. 'Just trying to get a full picture. You know how this works.'

Brooke fidgeted in her seat and nodded.

'Can you tell me a little bit about Lana's character?'

'Lana's normally the kindest, bubbliest person you'd meet. The way she's acting is out of character for her, but are you surprised?'

'Course not.' Collins scratched his cheek. 'And her relationship with Evan?'

Mine and Ev's relationship had become a bit… strained.

'It was good. It was always good. Lana had Evan young, so she was a young mum. They always seemed to get on.'

A gust of wind hit the window, carrying with it a drenching of rain. It was enough to steal Collins' attention. 'It was bone dry when I left Christchurch this morning. I've heard it never stops raining here.'

'That's where you live?' Brooke took the opportunity to swerve from the subject, even for a moment.

'I do, yeah. Born and raised. Once the post-mortem results came through, I was assigned to the case. Packed my bags as quickly as I could and checked into a motel on the way into town. They're down a senior detective here.'

Brooke peered out at the unrelenting rain. 'Things have gone downhill then. They at least had a detective living in Taonga when–' She clipped her sentence short.

'I heard about your brother,' Collins said delicately. 'I'm sorry.'

Brooke fluttered her hand as if to say it was okay. 'That's why I'm not completely surprised. About Evan being murdered. My brother's killer – he bullied him throughout school because of our family's…' She looked for a word to soften her privilege. *'Demographic.* I hoped – for the town's sake – that it was an accident this time. Even suicide. But like the press is already reporting, it looks like a similar scenario. A copycat crime.'

Collins wrote down a few more notes.

Brooke tried to make out the words but gave up. 'Those boys you mentioned – the ones Evan was hanging around with – have the police spoken with them yet?'

'Lana went over to each of their houses herself on Wednesday when Evan didn't come home or answer his phone. They said they didn't know where he was. Then a couple of constables checked in when he was officially declared missing. But the boys weren't much help from my understanding. I'm planning to go speak to them myself now, see if I can find out anything more. Do you wanna join?'

Brooke hesitated for a beat. What else was she going to do? Continue helping her mum sort out her wardrobe? 'Sure. Do you know who they are?'

Collins flicked back a page in his notebook. 'Their names are Bill Henderson and…' His index finger ran down the page. 'Mick.' He tapped the finger. 'Mick Saunders.'

Brooke's blood pulsed cold.

'You know them?'

There was a pause. 'Saunders.' She looked Collins dead on. 'He's the son of the man who killed my brother.'

Chapter Four

Collins weaved his roomy SUV through the wide country roads as they drove deeper into Taonga's suburban sprawl. Brooke didn't know this part of town well.

'You've never met Mick?' Collins said, driving with conviction along the wet road.

'No. Harry Saunders got his girlfriend pregnant just before he was arrested. By the time Mick was born, he'd already been put away.' Brooke kept her eyes ahead but her mind elsewhere.

'I understand he lives with his mum.' Collins stopped at an intersection and leaned against the strap of his seatbelt. Heavy rain obscured his view. 'Have you met her?'

'Tina Marshall,' Brooke said the name coldly. 'I remember sitting directly opposite her when she took the stand at Harry's trial. It was brutal.'

'You'll be all right if she's there, won't you?' Collins took his eyes from the road for a moment to meet Brooke's gaze.

'I'll be fine. But I'm not sure how *she'll* be.'

After a series of turns, Collins pulled up outside the front of a run-down house. Most of the once-white paint had peeled off, exposing the wood rot beneath. Its slanted roof had more than a few tiles missing. A yellow glow seeped through thread-bare curtains, which were pulled completely shut. Outside, a lone tire filled with rainwater hung from a beech tree. A ute was parked on a well-worn driveway, its metal exterior corroded by rain and sea spray.

'This is it,' Collins said flatly.

A flourish of fear swept through Brooke. The thought of seeing the son of Jack's killer lined her throat with bile. Could it have been he who'd killed Evan? Like father like son? She swallowed the bad taste.

'Did you know Evan's father?' Collins said out of nowhere.

Brooke avoided his focus. 'I knew who he was. But that's about it. Lana didn't know much more about him to be honest. It was a one-night stand. A mistake. She was only nineteen when she got pregnant. Her parents are devout Catholics, so you can imagine how that went down.'

'Ouch.'

'Yeah, ouch. We'd planned to leave Taonga together but obviously all that went down the drain. At least for her.' Brooke winced at the memory. 'Are you checking our stories match?' She realised she sounded defensive. She hadn't meant to.

'Let's work together,' Collins said. 'Not against each other.'

Brooke kept quiet and looked outside. The rain was finally easing. 'Do you think his dad might be a suspect?'

'Everything's on the table right now. We've tried to get in

touch with him, but we've been unable to track him down. Lana seems to think he moved overseas. I should hear back from the border on Monday to confirm.'

'Yeah, that's right. Australia. I think Evan always found that hard not having a father figure in his life. I saw my brother struggle with that too, but at least we had our stepdad.'

'I'm sorry. About your dad.'

'Don't be. He walked out. It was his loss.'

There was a heavy silence.

'C'mon, Palmer.' Collins gave a persuasive smile. 'We can't sit in here all day.'

The detectives lifted their jackets above their heads and climbed out the car with their backs hunched. As they approached the house across a yard that managed to be both under and overgrown, Brooke noticed the curtains twitch.

Seconds later, the front door swung open to reveal the thin frame of Tina Marshall. 'You have a nerve showin' up here.' Her words were lined with scorn as she hollered through the fly screen. Thick wrinkles around her mouth made her look much older than she was. The years hadn't been kind to her, Brooke thought.

Stepping forward, Brooke pulled her badge from beneath her coat. 'Detective Brooke Palmer.'

'I know who you are.' Tina placed a hand on her hip and looked Brooke up and down. 'You're the reason my fella's been banged up all these years.'

Brooke was surprised she still referred to Harry Saunders as her *fella*. She'd assumed she would have moved on in the time he'd been inside.

Collins stepped closer, pulling out his own badge. 'Look, we need to ask your son a few questions. Can we come in?'

'Not without a warrant.' Tina grimaced. Her yellow-blonde hair was scraped from her face with a blast of dark roots poking through. 'You're not goin' to blame that dead kid on my son, are you?' She looked to Brooke. 'You've already put my man away, and now you want to blame my boy, too?'

Mick Saunders appeared in the background. He looked different from how Brooke had imagined. She'd assumed he would look just like his father at his age. But he was thinner, a trait he'd obviously inherited from Tina, and tall enough to be described as lanky. His hair was shaved at the sides with an eruption of curls on top. But his eyes were pure Harry Saunders. Dull and grey. Their focus clung to Brooke's.

'We just need to ask you a couple of questions, mate.' Collins tucked his badge back inside his coat. 'It won't take long.'

'Okay,' Mick said simply.

Tina eased her glare. 'Fine. It better not.' She opened the fly screen with an uncomfortable creak.

Inside, a narrow hallway led to a small, clutter-filled living room. Tina sunk into a sludge-green armchair that seemed to engulf her; its springs wheezing beneath her force. She pulled a crumpled packet of cigarettes from the seat's side, sliding one out. 'I'd offer you one, but I'm guessin' you don't smoke.' She lit up and took a deep drag.

'No, thank you,' Brooke said.

'Good. Because I wouldn't have given you one anyway.' Tina started laughing at what Brooke presumed was meant to be a joke as she flicked ash into a glass tray perched on the armchair. 'Sit down.' She waved her hand at the murky-brown sofa opposite, which had a split running down the side like a wound. Yellow-stained foam bulged out. 'Where's he gone?' Tina looked around the room.

Mick reemerged with a lacquered dining chair, weaving it through what little space there was. He placed it on the floor, blocking a black entertainment unit thick with dust, and sat down. His sallow skin made him look ill. He would have been around the same age as Evan, but evidently wasn't as genetically blessed, with his narrow, withdrawn face and sunken eyes. His collarbone was visible through his faded Jimi Hendrix t-shirt and as he settled into the chair, his knees poked through the rips in his jeans.

'Where were you Tuesday night, Mick?' Collins asked directly, pulling out his notepad.

'I was here.' Mick didn't have to think about his answer.

Tina nodded. 'He was. That kid's mum already came 'round here. Then the cops came knockin' on the door and we told them the same thing. So why are you here?'

'All night?' Brooke probed.

'Yeah,' Mick said, eyes on the floor.

'I told you he had nuthin' to do with it.' Tina drew back on her cigarette. 'So you're wastin' your time.'

'You're not helping matters, Tina,' Brooke said sharply. 'Nor are you helping your son.'

Tina curled her top lip into a snarl. 'Excuse me? Don't you come 'round here tellin' me whether you think I'm helpin' my son or not. Like he said, he had nuthin' to do with it. So bugger off back to wherever you came from.'

There was tension in the air now.

'It's Brooke, right?' Mick said suddenly.

She nodded. 'That's right.'

He hesitated before speaking again. 'Do you really think my dad did it? Kill your brother, I mean.' Mick looked to his lap. 'He swears he didn't.'

Brooke's eyes pulsed with surprise. It wasn't just his appearance that set Mick apart from his father. There was something about his nature.

Tina had also been caught off guard. 'Course she thinks it's him. It's her fault he got arrested in the first place, dummy.'

'That's not exactly true,' Brooke said.

'Isn't it? The way I remember it goin' was you were questioned about the kids you didn't like at school, and you singled Harry out as the one you thought should take the blame.'

'That's not true!' Brooke couldn't hold herself back, although she knew there was some veracity in what Tina was saying.

'What happened then?' Mick said. His face laced with an ounce of naivety.

Brooke took a long breath. This was not a topic she wanted to rehash. She exhaled in surrender. 'Your dad conf–'

Tina hissed her dismissal before Brooke had a chance to finish her sentence.

Collins chimed in, with a shift in strategy. 'Evan was a friend of yours. Wasn't he, Mick?'

Mick shrugged. 'Yeah, he was all right.'

'So surely you want to help us figure out who did this to him?' Collins turned to face Tina. 'And surely you want to ensure the killer won't strike again? Target another boy Evan's age.'

Tina twisted her mouth. 'Don't you tell me what I want or think. You have no idea what we've been through. Him and I.' She pointed towards Mick. 'Poor kid havin' to grow up without a dad.' She shifted her eyes back to Brooke. 'And it's all *your* fault. You and your snobby family. You've ruined our lives.'

'That's enough,' Collins said.

'Mum.' Mick's face had grown pink. 'I can speak for myself.'

Tina sneered at her son. 'Well, it's your choice. If you wanna speak to these cops without a lawyer, don't come runnin' to me when you get banged up with your dad.'

'Nothing like that's going to happen if your son's telling the truth, Tina.' Brooke was growing impatient. 'And as a matter of fact, I do have an idea of what you've gone through. In case you've forgotten, my brother is dead.' She couldn't help herself. She faced Mick again. 'We just need to know anything you know about Evan Wiley. The last I'd heard, everyone he knew from school hated him. But now I find out that you were friends. New friends. Next thing, he turns up dead. So tell me, who had an issue with Evan, Mick? Was it Bill Henderson?'

Mick shook his head to dismiss the idea before it could settle.

'Do you know where Bill was the night of the murder?' Collins gave the room a cursory scan and turned his eyes back to Mick.

'No. You'll have to ask *him*.'

'We will,' Collins said. 'We're heading there next.'

'He's in Greymouth this weekend.' Mick rubbed his eyes.

'He works for his dad. They go up there a lot.'

Collins appeared frustrated. 'Do you know when he'll be back?'

'Tomorrow night, I guess. Or Monday morning.'

Collins noted down the specific with more friction than necessary.

Brooke took over. 'When did you last see Evan?'

Mick looked out the window, deep in thought. 'I can't remember exactly. We'd been hanging out less recently. He was getting ready to go overseas.'

'Okay, that's enough.' Tina shifted to the edge of her seat. 'You're not comin' back here again unless you have some actual evidence my son was involved. Now bugger off and leave us alone.'

Mick remained quiet. He stared blankly at the grubby carpet, his feet turned in.

'Okay, we'll leave you be,' Collins said. 'Thanks for your time, Mick.'

Brooke pulled a notepad and pen from her handbag and began to jot down her number. 'Give me a call if you think of anything we should know.' She tore the piece of paper off, passed it to Mick and turned to Tina. 'We'll show ourselves out.'

Tina hauled herself up from the armchair, her eyes fixed on Brooke. 'I'll show you out. Not gonna let you go snoopin' 'round when you're outta my sight.'

Brooke shot Mick one last look. 'Hopefully speak soon, Mick.'

He remained silent, his hands a tight ball in his lap – the

note safely inside.

'That won't be happenin'.' Tina stamped her cigarette out and blew a conclusive plume of smoke in Brooke's direction. 'Come on. You've overstayed your welcome. Had the moment you arrived, to be honest.' She ushered the detectives to the door.

A gust of glacial air blew in as Collins pulled it open. 'Thanks, Tina,' he said as though she'd been a gracious host.

The pair had made it halfway across the damp front lawn before Tina called out behind them. 'Oi, Detectives.'

Brooke turned back, bracing herself for one last threat. 'Yes?'

Tina lowered her voice to a whisper that was loud enough to reach them. Her tone had turned to one of concern. 'You don't really think my son had anythin' to do with this, do you?' She pulled her cardigan tighter, tucking her hands beneath her frail arms.

Brooke couldn't hide the surprise on her face. She wondered why the U-turn. Collins loomed in the background, equally lost for words.

'I can't lose someone else I love,' Tina went on. 'I can't.'

Brooke felt a twinge of pity for the woman standing in front of her, her face tarnished with anguish. After all, it had been her partner who had murdered Jack, not her. Maybe she really *did* believe he was innocent.

'It's very early in the investigation,' Brooke said. 'At this stage, we're trying to establish a timeline. If your son was with you on Tuesday night like you said he was, then he wouldn't have been the one to kill Evan. But that doesn't mean he doesn't know what happened, or even who did it. The sooner he speaks up, the better. For his own sake.'

Any signs of vulnerability Tina had shown were quickly dashed away. 'Good night. And like I said, don't bother me or my son again.'

She shut the door with an irrefutable thud.

Collins wound the car through the darkening streets. 'You all right?'

Brooke continued to stare out the side window as she spoke. 'Seeing him… it brought back a lot of memories.'

Collins offered a soft nod.

'His eyes,' Brooke continued. 'It was like looking at his dad when the jury read their verdict. He was staring at me. Mick had the exact same look in his eyes.' She paused. 'Maybe this was a bad idea.'

Collins turned to her, his face the vision of hope dashed. 'Look. I'll take you home. It's been a long day.'

He zigzagged his way through the quiet roads towards the coast. It was completely dark now, and the sky was illuminated with stars and a crescent moon. Brooke felt her eyelids grow heavy as the SUV traced the curvature of the road. Forcing her eyes open, she remembered the visit she'd yet to make since coming home. Not someone, but somewhere. A place that felt more relevant now than ever.

'Is it all right if you drop me off at the beach near my house? Take a left at the end of this road instead of straight ahead.'

Collins shot a glare from the corner of his eye. 'Are you sure? It's dark out.'

Brooke raised a single eyebrow and looked him dead on. He indicated left.

As the road that led to the beach came to an end, a wooden log lay below a modest sign that read *Little Taonga Bay*. Beyond it, a small stretch of dark sand glistened in the night's glow. To the right, a wooden staircase clung desperately to a rockface feathered with fern. At the top, Brooke's family home was a sub-minute walk. This was their favourite place to come as kids.

Brooke opened the car door. 'So it's Bill Henderson's place tomorrow?'

'I've got to head back to Christchurch tomorrow. But I'll be back Monday afternoon – so we can pay him a little visit then.' Collins' eyes glimmered hope. 'You're going to join?'

Brooke climbed out the car and turned back to him, one hand on the door, the other on her hip. 'I'm not giving up that easily.'

Collins exhaled a small laugh of relief. 'Catch you then.'

Brooke slammed the door of the SUV and watched it drive away before padding onto the beach. The grey sand felt soft beneath her boots as she made her way towards the crashing waves. The familiar mist that hung over the West Coast's wild coastline blurred the whitecaps as they rolled. The ocean beneath, black like ink. She settled onto the cold sand and wrapped herself tighter in her coat, buttoning it to the top. The icy sea breeze cut into her, causing a drip to form on the tip of her nose. She closed her eyes and inhaled an extended breath.

By the time she reopened her eyes, they were flushed with tears. Nineteen years felt like nineteen minutes. Like a fresh wound. An image of Jack's funeral flicked through her mind.

The long, black hearse. The deep-mahogany pews. The trudge of dark suits. The shrill of bagpipes. His narrow casket.

Brooke wiped her face with the sleeve of her coat. She looked ahead at the waves colliding into one another, forming foamy white crests as they broke. She remembered the day they'd scattered Jack's ashes like it was yesterday. Being here made her feel closer to him. Evan suddenly appeared in her mind. She imagined what it would have been like discovering his body at the foot of the falls. His youthful, eager face was rapidly replaced with the grim version from the post-mortem report.

Brooke's phone vibrated once in her jean pocket. A needed distraction. She slid it out and read the message to herself.

It's Mick. Can't talk when Mum's around. Wait to hear from me. There's more you need to know.

Chapter Five

Their hiking boots crunched the unthawed grass as they made their way from the car park to the track. It was the same trail they always took, usually on Sunday mornings and always on Christmas Day. Brooke and Hannah got a head start on a leisurely Barbara and Gary.

'How are you doing?' Hannah said, a deliberate note of concern in her voice.

'Getting there.' Brooke mustered a lacklustre smile. 'It's just hard to comprehend, isn't it?'

Hannah nodded. 'Sure is.' Her hair was different from the last time Brooke had seen her, now sitting just short of her shoulders. She'd lightened it, so it no longer mirrored Brooke's mousy shade. 'Mum mentioned you saw Lana yesterday. How was she?'

'Not good.' A fog of white air escaped Brooke's mouth as she spoke. 'Understandably.'

The pair picked up their pace as the track increased its pitch. A pale sun glistened over the hills in the distance.

Brooke bit her bottom lip, cracked from the cold. 'She mentioned things had been different since I was last down.'

A line appeared between Hannah's eyebrows as she furrowed them. 'Different how?'

'She said her relationship with Evan had become strained.' Brooke pulled the string of her windbreaker's hood to tighten it around the collar.

'That's weird.'

'I know. And there's more. I met the detective working on Evan's case yesterday. He told me Ev had been hanging around with a couple of kids from school. Including Harry Saunders' son.'

Hannah shivered and nodded. 'Yeah. He had.'

Brooke raised an eyebrow. 'You knew that?'

'Well, yeah. It's a pretty small town, in case you forgot. They'd been hanging out for a few months.'

Brooke swallowed her shock. 'Nobody mentioned. Doesn't that seem... odd?'

Hannah shrugged. 'I guess.'

'Lana must have known.'

Things had been a bit... different since you were last here...

'Are you girls trying to tell us something?' Gary's voice carried in the wind behind them. The two sisters hadn't realised how far ahead they'd got.

Brooke paused to catch her breath. 'I guess we should wait for the oldies.'

'We're catching up with them ourselves.' Hannah pulled

her left foot into a stretch. 'I can feel it in my thighs.'

Barbara and Gary trudged towards them, decked out in brand-new tramping gear with an exaggerated arm swing to match. Beyond them, a snow-capped mountain range underscored the sky. Mount Cook stood tall like the crown jewel of the Southern Alps. The familiar sight was deeply etched into Brooke's psyche and always brought with it a feeling of comfort. Until now.

'How are they these days?' Brooke said, her eyes back to Barbara and Gary marching up the hill.

'They're doing okay, I think. I'm so busy with Sean and the kids that I'm not around much. Mum still gets annoyed with Gary for working so much. But to be honest, money has to come from somewhere to maintain her lifestyle.'

'That's true.' Brooke laughed beneath her breath and turned back to the track ahead. 'Sometimes I used to wonder if their marriage would last. After Jack, I mean.'

It was easy for Brooke to forget at times what she and her younger sister had gone through at such an impressionable age. It's not that she didn't think about it, but when she arrived in Auckland, it was as if she'd started fresh. Although she appreciated Hannah had remained physically close to their mum, she found it hard to understand how she'd been able to set up her life in the town they'd lost their little brother. But Barbara had never had any intention to pack up and leave again. They'd already moved from her hometown in Christchurch and remaining in Taonga made her feel closer to Jack.

Hannah paused before she spoke. 'I think a life-changing event like that can make or break a couple. Gary was such a rock for Mum. For all of us. Give him credit where credit's due.'

'The credit card helped, too,' Brooke quipped. There was a fleeting silence and she continued. 'I went and spoke to Mick Saunders yesterday. With that detective.'

'You did?' Hannah looked cautious as she spoke. 'You don't think it was him who did it, do you?'

Brooke shrugged. 'Who knows. Maybe.'

'Be careful, Brooke. You're hardly going to be his favourite person.'

'He was different from how I imagined.'

'Different how?' Hannah pushed her fringe out the way of her eyes.

'I don't know. He seemed… nicer.' Brooke let that sit with her sister before she spoke again. 'But it could have all been an act.' She pulled her phone out and showed her the message.

Hannah read it twice and handed the phone back. 'I wonder what that's about.' She hesitated for a tick. 'Just promise me you'll be careful, okay? I don't want you to get yourself hurt.'

'I'll be fine, Han. You do realise this is what I do for a living, don't you?'

Hannah rolled her eyes and halfed a smile. 'You're relentless, you know that?'

The women shared a brief laugh and began the short-but-steep climb up the final hill of the hike. They brushed past the lush silver ferns, which had visibly seen more than enough rain this winter.

'So, what's next?' Hannah said through heavy breaths. 'What are your plans for the rest of the day?'

'I think I'll head to Lana's this afternoon. See if she's feeling any better. I'm hoping she'll also shed a bit more light on things.'

Soon, the sisters broke out from the tangle of scrub that gave way to a field of lush tussocks. An olive-green kea swooped overhead, its wings at full span, proudly displaying their vivid-orange underside. Barbara and Gary appeared from the covering, just in time for the final ascent to the lookout. As the family marched on, a morning sun hung low and faint in the sky. With each step, the breathtaking vista came more into view. Taonga sat snug in the lowlands, casting lengthy shadows on its surrounds. Beyond it, waves shimmered eagerly as the expanse of the Tasman made itself known.

Despite its postcard beauty, Brooke couldn't see past the ugliness of her hometown. How someone down there must have known what happened to Evan. No matter what it would take, she had to find out who.

*

Brooke followed Lana from the front door straight to her bedroom, bypassing the living space as it bathed in the mid-morning sun. The beach view was noiseless through the thick glass. 'How is it being back here?'

Lana kept her lips set in a firm line and darted her eyes around her house – a vast, timber-clad lodge that she'd lived in for the entirety of her motherhood. Her parents had built it just before Evan was born, on land that had been in the family for decades. Perhaps centuries. Their influence became public knowledge when consent was given to construct Taonga's only beachfront property – a move that enraged the locals.

'It makes me feel closer to him,' Lana said finally. Her words only a few decibels above silent, as if talking any louder would somehow make his death truer. 'I've been imagining he's still in his room.'

Brooke's eyes looked to the closed door at the end of the hallway. She imagined how everything would be in its original place, as Evan would've left it. Clothes piled on the floor, an un-made bed. Just how Jack's had remained in the days, weeks and months following.

The curtains were drawn as Lana climbed into the king-sized bed, her back against the linen-upholstered head-board. Her eyes bloodshot and staring nowhere. Beside her, a half-empty glass of water sat on the bedside table next to a box of tissues. Brooke perched atop the thick down duvet and began collecting strewn tissues, damp with tears, in her clenched palm.

'How did it go with Detective Collins?' Lana's question was devoid of any inflection. 'He seems nice.'

'Yeah, he seems to know what he's doing. Which is a good sign. I've agreed to give him a hand with the case while I'm down. Hope that's cool with you?'

'Of course it is. You're great at what you do, Brooke. The more chance of finding out who did this to Evan, the better.'

Brooke felt a dash of relief. She didn't want Lana to think she was overstepping any boundaries. After a fleeting moment of quiet, she shifted uncomfortably and began biting the corner of her thumbnail. 'He told me about who Evan had been hang-ing around with, Lan. Why didn't you tell me?'

Lana avoided Brooke's eyes and slid an inch down the

headboard. 'I haven't had a chance. I wasn't thinking straight yesterday.'

'Not just then. Before I arrived. How long have you known?'

Lana's eyes began to well up as they looked to Brooke. 'Please don't do this. I know you're trying to help, but I just need you as a friend right now.'

Brooke was overcome with guilt. 'I'm sorry.' She nestled closer to Lana, who placed her head on Brooke's shoulder to be soothed.

'If I'm honest, I didn't really want you to know.' Lana wiped her eyes with the back of her hand. 'I was ashamed. Ashamed he was hanging around with Harry Saunders' son.' Her sentence trailed off into a choke.

The two women were without words for a while as Lana cried into Brooke's jumper. She still found it hard to believe Evan would have wanted to associate with that crowd. 'You mentioned your relationship with him had become strained?'

A small crease appeared on Lana's forehead as she leaned back. She spoke more openly now. 'Yeah. He'd been acting off for a while. It didn't make sense, because he had so much to be excited about. He was so hyped about his trip to Europe. But a few months into the year something just... changed. His mood flipped all the time. He wasn't himself.'

Brooke pulled away a curl that had got stuck to Lana's tear-stained cheek. 'And you didn't suspect bullying? He'd gone through that before, right?' Brooke understood why Lana had wanted Evan to go to the local school. But considering their own experience at Taonga High, surely private would have been easier on him.

'No, it wasn't bullying. He'd finished school.' Lana shook away the thought. 'But I did find it weird when I heard the guys who had picked on him there were now his mates. At first, I thought maybe they'd just matured. But I quickly realised he'd got into the wrong crowd.'

There was a long pause until Brooke broke it. 'Drugs?'

Lana closed her eyes and nodded. 'Guess it should've been obvious. One day he came home and I could smell the booze and cigarettes on his breath. Then I smelled weed on his clothes.'

Brooke kept her face flat as she took it in.

'I eventually found out he was doing cocaine, too.' A lone tear skipped down Lana's cheek. 'I just didn't know who he was anymore.'

The room went quiet. Brooke thought back to Mick's message. *There's more you need to know.* She finally spoke again. 'That doesn't sound like Evan at all.'

Lana exhaled an exhausted sigh. A topic overthought. 'I guess that's what happens when you get into a bad crowd. We were lucky we had each other, right? Evan would have done anything to have made a friend. I just wish he'd been patient. Gone on that trip and realised there's a whole world out there.' Lana's red and wet eyes looked to Brooke. 'People would have loved him.'

Brooke nodded a faint smile. 'I know.' A life unlived flashed through her mind before being replaced with the image of the closed door at the end of the hallway. 'And you're sure there's nothing else? Nothing else I should know? I know this is hard, but with closure, it gets easier. And I want to give you that as soon as possible.'

Lana pulled the duvet up to cover her shoulders. 'That's all I know.'

Brooke scanned the room hopelessly. Why didn't she believe her?

Evan followed the path that led to the skate ramp. He knew that's where they'd be. It's where they always used to hang out after school into the late night, and that habit remained even now they had jobs.

Just as he'd predicted, Evan could make out the silhouettes of Mick and Bill as he got closer. Mick was on his board while Bill watched from the edge of the ramp. Flicking his fringe to the side, a street light created an amber haze over Evan, casting his shadow across the pavement. He pulled his backpack off and unzipped the front compartment to check it was still there. It was.

He took a few more steps before Bill spotted him. 'Look what we have here, eh?'

Mick ground his skateboard to a halt, flicking it to his hand with a clatter.

'What brings you to these parts?' Bill's short hair looked almost black in the darkness. So did his eyes. 'Wanna see how the other half live?'

Evan swallowed his fear and inhaled the autumn air deep. 'I've got something I think you guys might like.'

Intrigued, Bill and Mick strolled towards him.

'Well, go on then,' Bill said. 'What is it?'

Evan unzipped his bag and pulled out the plastic baggie filled with green.

A crooked smile formed across Mick's face. 'That better be what I think it is.'

Evan tossed the bag in their direction. Mick caught it. 'Shit, man. There must be at least a hundred bucks' worth in there.'

Evan's dimples appeared when he bestowed a smile. 'There's more where that came from. Much more.'

'Why?' Bill asked bluntly.

'Who cares?' Mick gave his friend a small shove. 'Long as he gets us more of it.'

'You should keep it out of sight,' Evan said. 'So you don't get caught.'

'Do you want some?' Bill said.

'You sure?' Evan raised an eyebrow.

'Sure, you scored it. Have you ever smoked before?'

Evan considered lying but shook his head instead.

Bill smirked mischievously. 'Come on, let's go under the ramp. No one will see us there.'

Evan hesitated for a few moments. His plan had worked – why back out now? Without giving it any more thought, he followed the two boys into the dark.

Chapter Six

Collins pulled a pack of cigarettes from his coat pocket and rolled down the window. 'You mind?'

Brooke shot him a quick look and turned her eyes back to the road. 'Didn't know you smoked.'

'I didn't.' Collins single-handedly slid a cigarette out while keeping the other on the wheel. He placed it between his lips. 'Well, I did. But I gave up. Looks like I've started up again.'

Brooke pressed the button to open her window, filling the car with brisk air. 'Be my guest.'

Collins flicked his lighter and lit up. He inhaled lovingly and blew a plume outside. 'Heard from Mick again?'

'Not yet.' Brooke glanced at her phone. 'If I don't hear from him by tonight, I'll give him a call.'

'His mother's quite the character, isn't she?' Collins took another drag, this time forgetting to blow it out the window.

'Sure is. I thought she might have moved on from Harry by

now.' Brooke took a breath of cold air from the window.

'Well, you know what they say absence does to the heart. She seems to think it's your fault he's locked up.' The ruts of Collins' brow deepened as he spoke. 'Why is that?'

Brooke thought about how to answer the question as she watched the streaks of vibrant green fern soar past. They were becoming denser as they drove inland, further away from town. 'When I testified at Harry's trial, I was honest about what he was like in school. How he treated us. He was the worst of the lot.'

Collins flicked the cigarette's ash from the car and took another drag.

'I found Mick's question strange,' Brooke went on. 'Whether I believe his dad really was guilty. And then Tina asks us whether we think her son is.'

Collins shook his head with a smirk. 'Paranoid family.' He sped up to overtake a car that was going at least twenty below the limit. 'Jeez, we'll never get to Henderson's at this rate.'

Brooke twisted her wrist and eyed her watch. 'Judging by Mick's message, he obviously wants to help us.'

Collins discarded the remainder of his cigarette out the window. 'I wonder what's in it for him.' His sat-nav urged him to take the next left.

'Who knows. Maybe he just doesn't want to turn out like his dad.'

'Maybe.' Collins slowed the car as they drove down the dirt track. A white, single-story house stood in the near distance. A wire mesh fence ringed the modest property. 'Sure we'll find out soon enough. This is it.'

Brooke noticed a man in the open garage, dressed in navy overalls with his head in a bonnet, seemingly unaware of the approaching SUV. 'Before we go in, there's something I need to mention. I saw Lana yesterday and managed to get a bit more out of her.'

Collins narrowed his eyes, pulling up the handbrake. 'Go on.'

'Sounds like the boys had got involved with drugs. Coke and weed. Not sure about the other two, but it's definitely out of character for Evan.'

'Interesting. Let's see if this Henderson kid can tell us more. Maybe you didn't know Evan quite as well as you thought.'

The idea made Brooke's heart beat double.

As they reached the house, the man in the overalls got his head out from under the hood and gave them a stare. His skin was tanned. His short scruffy hair, dark. Brooke assumed he was a similar age to Collins, making him a slightly older dad than Harry Saunders. He wiped the grease from his hands onto a rag, which he then threw over his shoulder as he walked towards them.

Collins slammed the car door, prompting a yet-to-be-seen dog to start barking. He pulled out his badge. 'Detective Tane Collins. Are you Bill Henderson's father?'

The man nodded his head and his eyes darted between the detectives. 'That's me, yeah.'

'We just need to ask your son a few questions,' Collins said. 'About his whereabouts on Tuesday.'

'Lana already came and asked me when Evan went missing. He was with me in Greymouth. The kid didn't leave my sight.

We told the same to those other cops.'

'It won't take long.' Brooke pulled out her badge. 'Detective Brooke Palmer.'

Bill's father eyed her up and down. 'I know you. You're working on this case then, are you?'

'She's supporting me,' Collins said. 'What's your name?'

'Craig Henderson. You better not be dragging my boy through the mud.'

As if on cue, a younger version of the man before them appeared from behind the house. 'Everything all right, Dad?' He even wore the same greasy overalls.

'Everything's fine,' Collins said. 'We just need to ask you a couple of questions, mate. Can we go inside?'

'We can talk out here,' Craig said assertively.

'Okay,' Brooke said, holding Bill's gaze. 'We've spoken to Mick, Bill. There are a few things we need to clarify with you.'

Bill was visibly discomforted by Brooke's loaded line. 'It's all right, Dad. I'll talk with them inside. You carry on.'

A deep groove briefly appeared between Craig's eyebrows. 'All right. Just tell them what we told the police. And don't be long. We've still got a lot to get through this arvo.' His tone had gone from concerned to curt.

Bill led the detectives into the living room, where they gave into a worn-out sofa. The room was relatively bare but for a mismatch of furniture and a handful of belongings. Textured wallpaper covered all four walls with two shades of intertwined white, each sheet noticeably misaligned with the next. In the corner, a games console blinked blue under a large TV. A Doberman skidded down the hallway, its claws long on the floorboards, making Brooke brace. It leapt up and began licking her face.

'Get down, Rambo.' Bill pulled the dog off by its neck.

'Tough name for such a sweet dog,' Brooke said, wiping her face with the sleeve of her coat. Rambo slumped beside her. There was a brief pause and she spoke again. 'We thought you might want to speak without your dad around. Mick didn't tell us about the drugs, but we found out.'

Bill looked up and made direct eye contact with Brooke for the first time. His stare cut right through her. 'Who told you then?'

'It doesn't matter.' Collins leaned in. 'How long had it been going on?'

Bill shrugged. 'Few months.'

Brooke took in Bill's features. He was clearly more handsome than Mick, and even though it was difficult to decipher his build through his overalls, he was also less scrawny. He had a strong jawline, like Evan, and striking green eyes, like his dad. 'Where did you get the drugs?'

Bill glanced at her again, this time his expression lined with surprise. 'From Evan.'

The detectives exchanged a look and Collins pulled out his notepad. 'From Evan?' He dictated his note but with an inflection that required a response.

Bill nodded, pushing Rambo away as he tried to clamber up. 'Yeah. He just showed up one day at the skate ramp in town with a baggie full of weed. Handed it to us without asking for a cent. It went from there.'

Collins noted as he spoke. 'Did he *ever* ask for money?'

He looked Bill in the eye, his pen hovering millimetres from the page.

Brooke didn't like where this was headed. Surely Evan couldn't have been a dealer.

'No.' Bill shook his head to Brooke's satisfaction.

Collins leaned back and scanned the room, as if looking for a reason why Evan would hand out freebies.

'Maybe…' Brooke checked she had the pair's attention. 'Maybe, he thought by buying you drugs it would change your opinion of him. From a bullied victim to your peer. To your friend.' Bill fidgeted in his seat as Brooke pressed on. 'From what I can remember, Evan didn't ever have mates in this town. In fact, he thought everyone at school hated him for what he had. Perhaps he thought if he couldn't beat them, join them.' Brooke looked Bill in the eye, her glare intentional. 'Join *you*.'

Bill dropped his focus to the floor, where Rambo had again given up and collapsed at his feet. 'I mean, I guess we just didn't give him a chance before. But once we got to know him, we realised Ev was cool.'

'He was once he started scoring you drugs,' Collins said with a snipe, adding his weight to Brooke's theory.

Keeping her eyes fixed on Bill's, Brooke continued. 'Where did he get the drugs from?'

'I dunno. Some dealer outta town. That's what he always said anyway. I never met him.'

'Convenient,' Collins said with a frown. 'Did he ever ask for anything in return?'

Bill cracked his knuckles. 'I already said no. He knew neither of us have any money.'

Brooke's eyes wandered around the room. A picture of Bill as a little boy sat undusted on the windowsill. He was a cute kid. His hair a few shades lighter than it was now. Behind it, a more recent photo of Craig with one arm slung around his doppel-ganger son. Their beams a lifetime away from the darkness that had overtaken Taonga again.

'I'm not talking about money,' Collins said. 'A favour. Did he ask you to do anything for him? After you'd become mates.'

Bill had become visibly uncomfortable. 'No.'

'When did you last see him?' Collins said.

Bill diverted his eyes back to the floor. 'A couple days before he went missing.'

'Where?'

'At the ramp. He seemed… agitated.'

Brooke leaned forward an inch. 'Agitated, how?'

'He said he owed the dealer money. For the drugs. I even tried to give him some money, but he said no. He had it sorted.'

Brooke swapped a look with Collins. Despite the wealth in their family, the Wileys were notorious for their frugality. 'Where do you think he'd been getting the money from? He didn't have a job or anything that I can remember.'

'He told us he was using the money from his travel savings. Didn't think much of it. He didn't seem too worried about go-ing on that trip anyway.'

That didn't make sense to Brooke. She'd seen the fire in his eyes when he discussed his overseas adventure.

'I doubt he would have been able to,' Collins said. 'Sounds like you guys blew all his cash on your habit.'

Brooke shot Collins a look and shifted her gaze back to Bill.

'Are you sure there's nothing else you can tell us about Evan's dealer? It's important we track him down. Especially if Evan had got himself in trouble with him.'

The room went silent. Brooke assumed Collins was on the same train of thought. She wondered whether Bill was, too.

'Nothing,' Bill said. 'I swear I know nothing about him. Not even his name.'

Craig appeared from the hallway. 'That's enough break time. We've got work to do.'

Bill flicked his eyes between the detectives. 'Any more questions?' His tone teetered on the edge of anxious.

Brooke straightened her spine and glanced at Collins. 'No, I think that's all for now. Right, Collins?'

Collins gave a quick nod. 'For now.'

Brooke offered a professional smile. 'Thanks for your cooperation, Bill.'

Instead of responding, Bill got up and paced outside. Rambo followed dotingly.

Craig replaced Bill's spot on the edge of the sofa and manoeuvred his eyes between the detectives. 'Listen, Bill's been through a lot lately. He doesn't need any more stress.'

Brooke stifled her response. *He'd* been through a lot?

'Believe me,' Craig continued, 'when I found the drugs in his room… that was a shock.'

Brooke sensed Collins' eyes on her but remained focused on Craig.

'I knew Bill could be stupid,' Craig went on, 'but I didn't think he'd be *that* stupid. He's too old for me to ground him, but I told him if I ever found out he was using again, I'd throw him out.'

The detectives kept silent.

'And look, of course it's awful what happened to Evan,' Craig said with a sympathetic twinge. 'It's tragic, and quite frankly terrifying, knowing there's someone out there who could do something like that to a boy the same age as my own. But let's not sugarcoat it. Evan was no angel either. Nor was he the perfect Catholic boy his family would like the world to believe. After all, *he's* the one who was supplying drugs to the boys. To *my* boy.'

Brooke held her tongue. Not only did Craig know about the drugs, but he knew Evan was the supplier. Why was Bill so keen on speaking in private?

'Look, Brooke,' Craig said. 'I know this is a stressful time in this town. Especially for your family, considering what you've been through in the past. But it's important to keep perspective. My son is not the person you're looking for. He's a fine young man. Sure, he's done some stupid things. Haven't we all? But he's not a killer.'

Brooke noticed a photograph of Craig with an attractive woman out the corner of her vision. She couldn't help but linger on it.

'That's my wife.' He paused and looked away. '*Was* my wife.'

'I'm sorry,' Brooke said softly.

'Thank you.' His eyes sunk. 'She had an aneurysm. When Bill was very small. It was tough. It's *still* tough.'

'Of course.' Brooke turned her gaze back to the photograph. Bill's mother's carefree smile a reminder of the fragility of life.

'That's why we moved here,' Craig said. 'I needed to get out of Greymouth. It's not far, I know, but we still need to be close enough to visit my mum who hasn't been well either.'

Brooke studied Craig's stare. He obviously worked hard, loved his wife and doted over his son. Had she been too quick to paint everyone in Taonga with the same brush? 'We should get going. We've taken up enough of your time.' She stood up and offered a genuine beam.

'Look, we're happy to help you both however we can,' Craig said warmly. 'But you're wasting your time here.' He led the detectives out the house and closed the front door behind him.

'Thanks again,' Collins said as he opened the gate with a well-worn squeak.

'Good luck.' Craig ducked into the garage and swerved around. 'I really hope you find out who did this soon.'

'So do we.' Brooke opened the front passenger door of the SUV. 'See ya.'

As Collins started the engine, Brooke caught Bill's stare from the back of the garage. Just for a moment, though, before he quickly disappeared into the shadows.

Chapter Seven

Swathes of unrelenting rain pummelled the road as Collins twisted his car through the morning traffic. Most of the commuters had already left for Greymouth, but there were enough late starters to keep the roads busy.

He stilled the SUV at a set of lights. 'So, what did Mick's message say exactly?'

'Just for us to meet him at the skate ramp before he starts work,' Brooke said. 'I got it pretty late last night.'

Collins yawned and tapped his fingers on the steering wheel. 'Funny that he picked there to meet. Maybe he'll offer us a joint?'

Brooke resisted a smile, watching as the traffic light glowed red.

'I'm guessing whatever Mick has to tell us is the real reason Bill wanted to speak to us without his dad around,' Collins said. 'Considering he already knew about the drugs.' He looked to

Brooke. 'Any thoughts on what it could be?'

'Heaps.' Brooke pointed towards the light as it flicked from amber to green.

'I guess we'll find out soon enough.' Collins followed Taonga's spine towards the skate park just south of town. 'So, do you want the bad news or the bad news?'

Brooke took a sip of coffee and looked to him. 'Ooh, choices, choices.'

'So, I managed to track down Evan's father.'

'Oh yeah?'

'Lives in the Gold Coast. He was able to prove that's where he was when Evan was killed. Not much help beyond that. Didn't want anything to do with the case.'

'What a great guy.' Brooke shook her head in astonishment. 'Lana definitely dodged a bullet there. What's the other bad news?' She drained her coffee and placed the empty cup in the holder.

'No further clues on the pathology front. The lab got back and there wasn't enough DNA to create a profile.'

'Shit,' Brooke said beneath her breath. 'Have you found anything on his phone? Social media?'

Collins shook his head. 'He wasn't all that active on social media from our investigations so far. His phone's missing, but the records didn't show anything of interest. Nor did his text messages. We've requested access to his WhatsApp, but I'm telling you now – it won't get granted.'

Brooke gave a knowing nod. 'Keep me posted.'

'Nothing came through from the blood work, by the way.' Collins slowed the car and veered into the left lane. 'They found no drugs or alcohol in his system.'

As they approached the skate park, Brooke could make out the slender silhouette of Mick. He was keeping dry beneath a nearby bus shelter. 'Interesting,' she said. 'Although, I guess it figures if he'd stopped being able to buy coke.'

'Yep. It writes off him being drugged, too.' Collins pulled up and flashed his headlights. 'Let's see if our pal here can shed some more light.'

Mick hesitated for a few beats, before walking up to the SUV and climbing into the backseat. Collins pulled a packet of cigarettes out and offered him one.

Brooke fired him a side-glance.

'What? He's old enough. Aren't you, mate?'

Mick nodded and slid a cigarette from the packet. 'Cheers.'

Collins rolled the windows down a fraction as they lit up.

'I don't know why I don't just start,' Brooke said with a note of sarcasm. 'I'm breathing enough of it in at the moment.' She turned her attention to Mick. 'Where do you work?'

'You know the carpenter's? On Tui Road?'

Brooke nodded. 'I do. It's been there a long time.'

Mick drew back the smoke and blew it out the crack in the window. 'I'm an apprentice there.'

'Good on you, mate,' Collins said. 'Good for you wanting to do something with your life.'

Mick tried to suppress a proud smile, but couldn't. 'Yeah, it's pretty fun.'

Brooke studied his grey eyes. 'We know about the drugs, Mick. That Evan supplied them to you and Bill in the months leading up to his death.'

Mick's grin melted to a frown. 'Yeah.'

'So is that what you texted me about? Or is there something else we need to know?' Brooke narrowed her eyes.

'Okay, well it was the drug stuff, yeah. And…'

'We're listening.' Collins gesticulated for Mick to continue.

Mick took another drag and shifted his eyes between the detectives. Brooke could see he was genuinely scared. 'Before I tell you what I know, can you guys promise that you'll keep me protected? From Bill, I mean.'

Brooke shot Collins a sharp stare and glanced back at Mick. 'From Bill? Why would you need protection from Bill?'

Mick drew a deep breath and remained quiet.

Collins, who had smoked his cigarette down as far as it could go, let the stump drift out the window with the wind. The side of his arm was drenched from the rain. 'You need to tell us anything that could help us, mate. There's a killer out there right now, and we need to find out who they are as quickly as possible to avoid any other kids your age winding up in a body bag.'

Mick swallowed hard. 'I know. That's why I'm doing this. I don't want to get the blame for something I didn't do either.' After one final puff, he threw the remainder of his cigarette out the window and closed it quick. 'Like my dad.'

Why did Brooke feel a twinge of guilt?

'Then clear your name,' Collins said as he pulled out his notepad. 'Tell us as much as you know.'

Mick shifted his focus outside and watched the rain – as if in a trance. 'We weren't nice to him. At first. When we were at school, we bullied him a bit. A lot. I know it wasn't right. Guess he had everything I didn't. Good looks. Nice family. Money. He was going somewhere.'

Brooke listened with intent. It was all too familiar. She leaned in closer. 'Go on.'

'That all changed a few months back when he started bringing us the drugs. I know that sounds bad. But that's just why we started hanging out with him. Once we did, we realised what a great guy he is.' Mick paused for a tick before correcting himself. 'Was.'

Brooke's heart stopped. She still wasn't used to Evan existing in past tense.

'We didn't have heaps in common,' Mick continued. 'But he was fun. Always up for a good time.'

That was the Evan Brooke remembered. Her heart kicked back into motion.

'At first, we just started smoking a bit of weed. Right there.' Mick pointed to the ramp. 'He'd come by most days. Sometimes we went to the falls.'

Brooke and Collins shared a stare. She looked back to Mick. 'Taonga Falls?'

He nodded. 'Occasionally, yeah. It's usually pretty quiet there, so it was a good place to get high. Sometimes we'd go over to my place. We'd smoke in my room, drink booze he brought.'

'Did your mum know?' Brooke said.

'Yeah, you saw what she's like. She didn't care. She knows I'm a bit of a stoner, but she also knew I didn't do anything harder. So when they started doing coke, I tapped out.'

'Did you try it?' Collins turned in his seat with a creak of the leather.

Brooke bit her tongue and shot him a cursory look, worried he was becoming restless. Jumping a few steps, perhaps.

Mick combed his fingers through his tight curls. 'Yeah. I guess just to see what all the fuss was about. But I didn't like it. So I just left Bill and Evan to it as they were really into it. I started hanging about with them less after that.'

Brooke tried to meet Mick's gaze, but he avoided it. His sallow eyes remained despondent.

'Where were they hanging out?' Collins said. 'Still here at the ramp and the falls?'

Mick nodded. 'I think so, yeah. They were hanging out at Bill's for a while, but he told me his dad found the coke in his room one day. He managed to get it out of him that Evan was supplying it and he banned him from seeing him. He went over to Evan's mum's and told her, too. Not that it worked because I saw them at the ramp again.'

'Do you think they were addicted?' Brooke said.

Mick shifted his bodyweight in the backseat and shrugged. He suddenly looked uncomfortable, Brooke decided. Restless.

'So, what next?' Collins tapped the steering wheel with an ounce of impatience.

Mick's body retracted. 'That day I saw them at the ramp. I was just on my own with my board. I must've been walking pretty quiet because they didn't hear me coming. I caught them under the ramp.'

'Still doing coke?' Brooke asked as if she knew the answer.

Mick touched his face nervously. 'Making out.'

There was a loud silence. Brooke realised she was holding

her breath.

'Kissing?' Collins' gaze was strong. 'They were… *dating*?'

Mick's shrug said it all. 'That's not what they told me. They pulled away from each other as soon as they saw me there. Bill said they were high from too much coke.'

'Did they look high to you?' Brooke delved.

Mick's chest lifted as he drew a deep breath. He unzipped his battered denim jacket and exhaled. 'I dunno. Not really. They just looked… shocked to see me.'

Brooke stared out at the rain that was beginning to subside. It didn't come as a huge surprise to her that Evan could have been gay. She'd never known him to have a girlfriend, nor had Lana ever spoken to her about him being into girls. But then, she'd never spoken about him being into guys either. Could she not have known? It was going to be a difficult conversation to navigate.

Brooke turned her attention back to Mick. 'When did this happen?'

'Can't remember exactly. Few weeks back. Maybe a month.'

'Was it the last time you saw Evan?' Collins said.

Mick's face dropped. He nodded.

Brooke leaned forward. 'What about Bill? Have you spoken with him since?'

Mick shook his head and fiddled with the zip of his jacket. 'No. I haven't seen him. I didn't have a problem with it. But I guess *he* did. He was always a bit… you know…'

There was a beat of silence before Collins broke it. 'Homophobic?'

'Yeah. I guess.'

Brooke chewed her bottom lip, processing the information. 'So that's why you want protection from Bill?' She slowly nodded as she spoke, looking in Mick's direction but not at him. 'You think he might have killed Evan. That he felt embarrassed about the whole thing and wanted him gone. He wanted the secret buried. With Evan.' Brooke stopped herself when she noticed the fear in Mick's eyes. He was now trembling.

Collins pushed back his hair. 'Bill hadn't mentioned any of this to us, but he did tell us Evan owed his drug dealer money. That he'd stopped being able to pay him. Do you know anything about that?'

Mick breathed heavy and slow in an attempt to recompose. 'No. But like I said, I'd stopped hanging around with them before he went missing.' He slid his phone from his jean pocket. 'Shit, I'm gonna be late. Can you give me a lift? I've told you everything I know now. I swear.'

Collins looked at Brooke and then back at Mick. 'Sure. Thanks, mate. You've done the right thing speaking to us.'

'I hope so. Are you gonna speak to him? Bill, I mean.'

Collins started the engine. 'We'll obviously need to talk to him, Mick. No matter how you look at this, he's now a suspect.' He twisted the car onto the road.

'Well, you won't be able to until he's back in town tomorrow,' Mick said. 'He's working up in Greymouth with his dad again today.'

'Does anyone else know about this?' Brooke said.

'I dunno if Evan told anyone. But I haven't. And I doubt Bill would have. Which is why he'll know it came from me.'

'Bill will have bigger things to worry about, mate,' Collins said, merging onto Tui Road.

'The main thing is you've told us everything you know,' Brooke said. 'Which you have, haven't you?'

Mick nodded. 'Yeah. That's everything.'

Collins stopped the car outside the carpenter's. 'Thanks again, mate. Stay out of trouble, won't you?'

'I will.' Mick got out the car, slammed the door and made his way inside without looking back.

After a few moments of quiet, Collins turned to face Brooke. 'Well... what do you think?'

She traced her finger along the condensation on her window. 'I don't know. There's so much to take in. If Mick's telling us the truth, which I can't see why he wouldn't be, it seems a bit of a stretch that Bill would have wanted to kill Evan over something like that. Especially after meeting him and his dad.'

Collins rubbed his eyes and started the car. 'Stranger things have happened. The world's changing, but towns like this... they're not always as progressive.'

'Tell me something I don't know.' Brooke looked at the storefront. 'Poor kid. I see why he's scared. If Bill killed Ev to squash a secret, what's to stop him doing the same to Mick? In Bill's mind, he's the only other person who knows what happened.'

Collins scratched his chin, deep in thought. 'At least one of those boys knows what happened to Evan. I can feel it.' He turned to Brooke. 'Where to next?'

She thought for a blink. 'Can you drop me at Lana's? I want to find out how much she knew about all this. If anything.'

'Okay, great. Let's go.' Collins began gliding the SUV in the direction of Lana's home.

'I think I should do this alone. She might feel a bit more at ease.'

'Good thinking. I'll head back to the station and type everything up. I'll also get my team searching for any potential dealers that service the area.' Collins stopped the vehicle at a red light just in time and pulled out his phone. 'I'll message Bill now, telling him to be at the station first thing tomorrow for another chat. Feel free to join.'

Brooke gazed at the slate-grey sky and pictured his green eyes. She imagined all the things they could be hiding. 'Wouldn't miss it.'

The sound of Taonga Falls crashed in the back of her mind.

Chapter Eight

'Brooke.' Amanda's outstretched arms spanned the width of the doorway. Her bell sleeves dangled eagerly like welcoming white wings. She'd clearly been crying, but her makeup remained perfectly intact.

'Hey.' Brooke hugged her back. She would have known Amanda was at Lana's had she called first, but she hadn't wanted to risk her friend telling her she wanted to be alone. 'How're you holding up?' Brooke released the embrace as she spoke.

Amanda slumped her shoulders and dropped her eyes. 'It's been… a tough few days. As I'm sure you can imagine.'

'Of course.' Brooke ran a sympathetic palm down Amanda's arm.

'Come in, come in. Would you like a coffee? Tea?'

'Thank you. Coffee would be great.' Brooke stepped into the house, which was notably warmer than her last visit.

'It's on its way. Frank? Could you make one?'

Frank, who had been sitting on the sofa poring through the New Zealand Herald, hopped up. 'Hello, Brooke. Of course, milk and sugar?'

'Just black's fine. No sugar. Thanks, Frank.'

'How's your mother?' Amanda rubbed Brooke's shoulder.

'She's distracting herself by sorting through clothes for your charity event.' Brooke felt guilty as soon as the words left her mouth.

Amanda closed her eyes and slow-slapped her forehead. 'Oh dear. I'd completely forgotten about it.'

Brooke waved her hand dismissively. 'Don't worry. You know what Mum's like. It's just keeping her busy. She wouldn't expect you to have thought about it.'

Amanda smiled weak. 'She's such a trooper. Just like you. Lana will be pleased to see you. She's barely left her room. Let me go get her.'

'I totally understand if she'd rather be alone.'

'Oh, I'm sure she will be thrilled to see you. Sit down, I'll go get her.'

Amanda disappeared into the hallway's shadow. Brooke perched on one of the two saddle-brown leather sofas that flanked a wood burner. It let off a soothing heat as it hung impressively from the pitched ceiling, narrowly missing its interconnecting beams. She took a moment to bask in its warmth before her eyes were drawn to the bookshelf towering behind the opposing sofa. It displayed a mix of books, picture frames and the odd trinket. A photo of Evan as a baby with a brilliant burst of blonde hair and doughy eyes stood out. Brooke remembered him like that as if it were yesterday. In the next picture, he was proudly clutching a medal, unashamed of his gappy grin. The Olympic-sized swimming pool he was standing in front of dwarfed him. He must have only been nine or ten. The medal sat beside its photo in all its golden glory.

Lana had encouraged Evan to pursue swimming given his natural talent, but it was during his teens he'd found his true calling – which another photo on the below shelf authenticated. He was probably fifteen. His boyish good looks making way for the handsome man he was to become, if only for less than a year. He held a camera up to one eye, as if he were taking a picture of the person taking the picture. There was something comforting about the photo for Brooke. His determination. His ambition. His talent.

What went wrong?

'Here we are.' Mick pulled his keys from his backpack and turned to face Evan. 'Don't worry about my mum. She's a bit weird when she's had a drink.'

'A bit?' Bill smirked.

'Fuck you.' Mick unlocked the door and pushed it open.

Evan took in his surroundings as he entered the house. He wasn't sure what he'd expected, but he knew it would be a different world to the one he'd grown up in. He didn't care. None of that mattered. He'd grown up in luxury, but he'd been alone. Finally, he had friends, and it was the best feeling in the world. He'd give up all the money his family had to keep that feeling going.

Tina debated getting up when the boys walked in but changed her mind. Instead, she pulled out a packet of cigarettes. 'Well, look what we have here.' She slid out a smoke and lit up. 'The three fuckin' musketeers.'

'This is Ev, Mum,' Mick said.

Tina took a long drag and blew the plume over her shoulder. She studied Evan's face. 'I recognise you. You're the Wiley kid.'

Evan gave a small nod. He'd assumed she would know who he was. After he'd told his mum about his new mates, she'd made her concerns known. Warning how it could hurt Brooke. That was the last thing he wanted to do. She was like family to him. But Mick wasn't his murderous father. And Evan wasn't going to sacrifice one of the only friendships he'd ever had for something that happened twenty years ago.

Tina took back another puff and gave a wry smile. 'Does your mum know you're here?'

Evan shrugged. 'She wouldn't mind.'

'Ev's cool, Mum,' Mick said, attempting to ease the tension.

'I'm sure.' She kept a firm stare. 'Well, don't be rude, Mick. Offer your guests a drink. Fix me one while you're at it.'

Evan and Bill followed Mick into the dimly lit kitchen. After he'd opened the fridge and pulled out a bottle of cheap lemonade, Mick retrieved a half-empty litre of equally cheap vodka.

'Have you lived here long?' Evan said, gliding his eyes along the canary yellow walls and wooden cabinet doors, one of which was missing completely.

'My whole life.' Mick lined up four glasses, no two the same. He poured a splash of vodka followed by the lemonade. 'Mum moved in here when Dad was put away.'

It was the first time Evan had heard Mick reference his dad's arrest. He decided not to probe further.

Mick handed the boys their drinks and Bill snatched the vodka to top up his own with an extra shot. Mick carried his, plus the additional for his mum. 'Here you go.' He passed Tina her afternoon fix.

'That's my boy. Wanna smoke?'

'We've got some, thanks. We've got some weed too if you want any?'

Tina raised a thin, pencilled-on eyebrow. 'Have you now?' She shifted her eyes to Evan. 'Are you havin' some?'

'Ev bought it for us,' Mick said.

A twisted grin broke across Tina's face. 'Did he now?' She held her gaze a tad too long.

'Do you want any or not?' Mick asked impatiently.

Tina stamped the remnants of her cigarette. 'Course not. I'm a responsible adult.' She threw back a large gulp of vodka lemonade. 'And I'm watchin' my health.'

'Hey.' Lana entered the room in her dressing gown.

Brooke dragged her eyes from the photograph and fixed them on her friend. Much like the last time she'd visited, Lana's hair was pulled back into a loose bun and she wore no make-up. This time the dark rings framing her eyes were even more prominent – her cheekbones more angular.

'Hey.' Brooke reached out to hug her. 'I'm sorry I haven't been in touch. I wanted to give you time.'

'I know, it's fine. Thank you. I wouldn't have been great company anyway. I can't even think straight right now.'

Brooke took Lana's hand. 'You should take all the time you need.'

A short-lived silence was ended by the hiss of the coffee machine.

'Do you have any thoughts on who could have done this?' Lana said suddenly.

The question caught Brooke off guard, but the fact her

friend had approached the subject first offered a shred of relief. 'Well, I wanted to speak with you about that actually.'

Amanda appeared clutching a mug in each hand. 'Would anyone care for something to eat? Perhaps a spot of brunch?'

'I'm okay, thanks,' Brooke said, carefully taking one of the mugs. 'I ate this morning.'

'I'm fine,' Lana echoed.

Amanda crumpled her features in concern. 'You must start eating. You're fading away.'

'I said I'm fine.'

Amanda turned to face Brooke. 'Lana mentioned you're helping Detective Collins with the case. I'm so glad. That's why I gave him your number. I hope you didn't mind.'

'Of course not. I'm happy to help, however I can.'

Amanda's face dropped. 'I take it he took you through the post-mortem?'

Brooke nodded. 'He did.'

Amanda recoiled at the confirmation. 'Terrible. Just… terrible.'

'I know.' Brooke blew gently on her coffee. 'It's unthinkable.'

'I hope he hurries up and finds the bastard who did this.'

It was unlike Amanda to swear, Brooke thought. But if there was ever a time to start, it was now.

'Now they have what they need,' Amanda continued, 'we're able to have Evan back. You know, from where he's being kept in Christchurch. It looks like the funeral will be this Thursday. Please let the family know.'

'I will.'

'Anyway, I'll let you girls catch up. I'm going to make some eggs à la Française. Do let me know if either of you change your mind.' She fixed her eyes firmly on Lana and made her way back to the kitchen.

Brooke waited until Amanda was out of earshot before she started speaking again. 'Collins and I met with Bill Henderson yesterday afternoon. And Mick Saunders this morning.'

Lana looked intently into Brooke's eyes. 'How did it go?'

Brooke paused for a heartbeat, readying herself for what was next. 'Lan, did Evan ever mention anything to you about being in a relationship?'

'No.'

Brooke cleared her throat. 'Okay, how about being... *gay?*'

A look of unease overcame Lana's face. 'What?' Her voice was tight now.

Brooke ducked to try and regain her focus. 'If you don't want to talk about this right now, I understand. But this could be linked to the reason Ev was killed.' A tiny pause. 'Basically, Mick mentioned he caught Ev and Bill kissing. About a month ago.'

Lana scraped her hair back with her fingertips and tightened her ponytail. 'Shall we go for a walk? I could do with getting some air.'

'Uh... sure.'

'I'll just go change.' Lana disappeared into her room, her coffee left untouched.

Brooke pulled out her phone. She didn't notice Amanda had reappeared over her shoulder.

'Is everything okay? Where's Lana?'

Brooke slipped her phone back into her jean pocket. 'Just

getting dressed. We're going for a walk.'

A broad smile broke across Amanda's face. 'That's wonderful. It'll do her a world of good. I knew your being here would help. You guys have always been like sisters.'

Lana reappeared in black activewear. She was pulling a long, woollen coat over the top. 'You ready?'

Brooke drained the last of her coffee. 'Now I am.'

Sitting cross-legged on his bed, Mick opened his laptop with a plasticky snap. 'What do you wanna listen to? Ev, your choice as you bought the stuff.'

'Yeah, what are you into?' Bill had taken a seat in a black inflatable chair, printed flames emerging from its edges. He looked genuinely interested.

Evan was sitting on the carpet that would have once been beige. Now it was approaching brown. 'Mainly rock. I'm really into The Lost Wolves right now.'

Mick gave an approving nod. 'Nice. Let's play them.' After a few moments, he blasted a track through the tinny speakers of his laptop.

Evan fished the baggie of weed and rolling paper from the front of his backpack and passed it to Mick. 'Here. You're better at rolling than me.'

Mick swallowed some vodka and grinned. 'Works for me.'

Bill kept his eyes on Evan. 'Does your mum ever talk about it? What happened to Mick's dad, I mean.'

There was a thick silence. Mick kept his eyes fixed on Evan as he rolled the joint. 'It's all right, mate. We don't have to talk about it.'

Evan thought hard. The last time they'd spoken about it was when he had told his mum he'd started mixing with Mick, but before that, he couldn't remember. The story of Jack Palmer's murder had always been off limits. There were photographs of him dotted around Brooke's house, which he had been inquisitive about as a child, but he'd quickly discovered it wasn't a topic to be discussed. The mere mention of his name made everyone emotional. 'Not really,' he said finally. 'I don't really know much about what happened to be honest.'

Mick and Bill exchanged a glare.

'So… you haven't listened to the podcast?' Bill said.

Evan shook his head. 'Nope.' Of course he remembered it. How could he not? The podcast had been huge news in Taonga, and across the world, when it came out a few years back. But his mum had told him to stay well away from it. She'd said it brought up too much pain for her, Brooke and their whole families. He'd respected her wishes.

Mick tightened the joint and admired his work. He opened the window, lit up and drew back. 'It was hard to listen to. Hard to have everyone talking about it at school.'

Evan remembered that now. He'd had enough of his own problems during that time, so when the podcast came out, it actually took the attention off him for a while and onto Mick. 'That sucks.'

Mick gave a shrug and passed the joint to Bill. 'Doesn't matter. It's not your fault. It's my old man's fault.'

Evan watched Bill draw back the joint and then faced Mick again. 'Do you ever see him?'

Mick took another mouthful of his drink. 'Now and again. Me and Mum go up to Christchurch sometimes where he's locked up. He tells us both he didn't do it. Mum believes him.'

Bill passed Evan the joint.

'Trouble is, he doesn't do himself any favours in there,' Mick continued. 'He gets in fights and all sorts. No chance of an early release for good behaviour.'

Evan took a deep drag and thought about how difficult it must have been for Mick. Sure, his own dad hadn't been present in his life, but at least he wasn't a murderer. How could Mick carry that burden? It explained a lot about his behaviour towards him at school. As Evan let the smoke go, he realised now that he forgave him. He forgave them both.

He also realised it was time to listen to the podcast.

Chapter Nine

The grass in the park was still wet from the rain, so the pair kept to the gravel path that snaked its periphery. Brooke submerged her chin in her coat's collar as she sidestepped a puddle. 'I take it you didn't want to speak with your mum around?'

'You know what my parents are like.' Lana looked to Brooke briefly. 'Their beliefs. It's all a bit much for them to handle.'

'So you did know?'

A beat of a pause. 'Evan had mentioned to me about a year ago that he thought he might be into guys. They say a mother always knows, but I'd never got that impression from him. Then one day I could just tell he had something on his mind. So I guided the conversation in that direction and he told me.'

'What did he say?'

'He seemed a bit uncomfortable. Said how he hated himself for even having those thoughts.' Lana's eyes were glazed with tears by the time they looked back to Brooke. 'He told me he was worried he would go to Hell.'

Brooke flinched and remained quiet for a few moments. 'I didn't even realise Evan was religious.'

'Neither did I, to be honest. You know me, Brooke. I never pushed him into believing anything. I don't even know what *I* believe anymore. But Mum and Dad... he listened to them.'

'He was always close to your mum, wasn't he?'

'Worshipped her. He went through that phase in his mid-teens where he wasn't so close to her. Or me. Then up until a few months back, he'd gotten close to us again. He even started coming to church with us on Sundays like he used to. But everything suddenly changed. When he started hanging out with those boys.'

Brooke narrowed her eyes. 'Do you think it's likely he was involved with Bill Henderson?'

Lana looked to the sky and kept her pace slow. 'I honestly have no idea. After he talked about his confusion, he never brought it up again. I figured maybe he realised he wasn't gay after all. We both know what this town is like. It was bad when we were kids, and it's still bad now. Things might have changed in the outside world, but Taonga's stuck in another era.'

Brooke nodded her agreement. She always felt like she was travelling back in time when she returned to her hometown. And if Evan's murder had proven anything to her, it was that history has a way of repeating itself. 'So you never mentioned it to your parents? What he told you?'

Lana shook her head, her hands wrist-deep in her coat pockets. 'I thought it would be easier if I didn't. I should give them more credit, but I just didn't think they would take it well.'

As lovely as Amanda and Frank were, their deep-rooted Catholic beliefs often jarred with Brooke. She thought back to the many a time Frank would quip when a male TV presenter would come across more effeminate than he could stomach. Amanda wasn't as vocal with her views, but she often shared the sentiment.

'I understand.' Brooke felt a drop of rain on her cheek. 'They'll need to find out at some stage though, Lan.'

'Will they?' Lana's tone was arched.

'Well, Mick told us Bill was homophobic. If it's true that he and Ev were involved, that makes him a suspect. Collins and I will need to explore this.'

Lana agreed with her eyes as a tear formed. 'I see what you mean. You're right. I'll speak to them tonight.'

'Good idea.' Another drop.

'I'm sorry I didn't mention this before, Brooke.' Lana pulled a tissue from her pocket and dabbed each eye. 'I guess it didn't feel right, as he'd confided in me.'

'Don't be silly. I understand. It wasn't your secret to tell.' Brooke drew in a breath of fresh air. She needed it. 'But it's important you tell us everything you know now. As I said before, if you hold anything back, it could slow us down finding out who did this. Even if you don't think it's important or relevant – we need to know.'

Lana opened her mouth to say something but stopped as soon as she noticed the reporter approaching them. Brooke had seen her too now. It was the blonde journalist who had tried to interview her when she'd first arrived at Lana's family home. A man walked alongside carrying a camera he was swiftly setting up.

'Excuse me, ladies,' the reporter said. 'Can I just get a few minutes of your time?'

'Oh, God.' Lana concealed her face in her hands. 'I don't need this.'

'I'll handle it,' Brooke said. 'You go back to the car.'

Lana retraced the path with a nervous jog. As she did, the skies opened.

'Ms Wiley!' The reporter called out. 'Ms Wiley, it will only take a few minutes.'

'She's not ready,' Brooke said bluntly. 'Please leave her alone.'

'Ms Palmer.' The woman's face was camera-ready and the vision of determination. 'How are you holding up? This must be so difficult, bringing everything back up about your brother, Jack.' If her question inserted the dagger, the lipstick grin that followed twisted it.

Brooke clenched her fists so tight her knuckles began to pale. Instinct urged her to reach out and grab the woman by her peroxided hair, but she knew what would hurt her more: 'No comment.'

The reporter's face dropped. Her tone changed to its off-camera equivalent. 'Look, if you change your mind, give me a call.' She proffered her card.

Brooke gave it a glance without even absorbing her name. 'I wouldn't hold your breath.' She paced back to her car and the skies opened up.

'Are you okay?' Brooke asked Lana as she climbed into the

driver's seat. In the distance, the cameraman was scrambling to protect his equipment from the rain as the reporter made a phone call.

'I thought I was ready. But I'm not.' Defeat smothered Lana's voice to the point where it was almost inaudible.

'They'll back off sooner or later. They always do.' Brooke started the engine and reversed. 'Come on. Let's get you home.'

Evan stared at his screen. The word ENVY *was written in blood-red capitals against a background of dark green clouds. How had he resisted listening to it for this long? Would he be betraying his mum if he did? Or Brooke? Now that he considered Mick a friend, he felt like he at least needed a clear picture of what happened. It had been shielded from him long enough.*

'What are you reading?' Lana said from the opposite sofa.

Evan locked his phone. 'Nothing. Just Instagram.'

It had been a couple of days since Evan had visited Mick's house and he'd avoided speaking with his mum about anything they had talked about. But the yearning to bring up Jack's murder was strong.

'Are you all right?' Lana found her son's eyes. 'You seem a bit... distant.'

'I'm fine.' He didn't sound convincing.

Lana tilted her head. 'Come on.'

Evan gave her a long look. 'Why don't we ever talk about Jack Palmer?'

There was a brief but loaded silence. Lana took her time with her response. 'What happened to Brooke's brother was a tragedy. It was a painful period in all of our lives that we don't enjoy reliving.'

'I get that.' Evan hesitated. 'But it doesn't take away the fact it happened. And shouldn't we want to honour him by keeping his memory alive?'

Lana slumped with defeat. 'Of course. It's just… it was such a horrible time. For all of us.' Tears had emerged.

Evan wanted to press further, but he also hated seeing his mum upset.

Lana straightened her spine. 'This is because of Mick Saunders, isn't it? Have you been speaking to him about it?'

Evan avoided her eyes. 'A bit.'

'I knew it. Ev, you know how I feel about you hanging around with him. It would break Brooke's heart.'

Evan kept quiet. The thought of hurting Brooke pained him, but he didn't want to feel guilt-tripped into losing one of the only friendships he'd ever had. And if he lost Mick as a friend, he assumed he'd lose Bill, too. He just wasn't prepared to do that. He latched back onto his mother's gaze. 'Have you ever listened to the podcast?'

Her eyes turned dull. 'A bit, yes. But it was too difficult to get through. Why… have you?'

He shook his head the smallest fraction. 'No. Been thinking about it though.'

Lana's expression changed. It was less tight. 'Well, maybe you should. Maybe it's the right time.'

Evan hadn't expected that. 'Really?'

'You're an adult, Evan. If you want to listen to the podcast, that's your choice.' She paused for a moment and sighed. 'Maybe it will make you realise why I'm concerned about you hanging around with the son of Harry Saunders.'

Evan opened his mouth to respond. Instead, he smiled.

Lana gave her son a concerned stare. 'Don't lose focus on what's important, Ev. You've always been so driven. Don't get too caught up in things that happened a long time ago. You've got your own life to live.'

Evan's smile faded and he took to his feet. He'd heard all he needed to *hear. He had the approval he'd craved.*

Brooke manoeuvred the sedan as close to the house as possible while minding Lana's and her parents' cars, which were parked in the driveway with little consideration for a third. Seeing the lodge glow and its chimney smoke brought Brooke back to a happier time. When she would surprise Lana with an impromptu weekend visit, and they would stay up and share a bottle of wine or two. When they would talk about, and then toast, the survival of their youth.

A wave of rain brought her back to the current. 'I'm glad they're staying with you at the moment.' Brooke unbuckled her seatbelt.

'Yeah. They've been great. They've offered for me to stay with them, but I want to be at home now. Closer to him.'

Brooke formed a weak smile. 'Of course.' She thought of Evan's closed bedroom door at the end of the hallway. 'Hey, Lan… I take it the police have searched Ev's room?'

Lana paused for a moment, studying her friend's gaze. 'Of course. Why? You want to take a look, don't you?'

Brooke hesitated before she spoke. 'I obviously wouldn't want you to feel uncomfortable. And I'd totally get it if you wouldn't want me to.' She couldn't read Lana's expression.

'I guess a pair of fresh eyes wouldn't hurt. But don't move anything around. I want to keep it as he had it.'

'Of course. You know I understand that. Will your parents mind?'

Lana shook her head and opened the car door. 'They'll be happy you're trying to help.'

The women made a dash for the house.

'You were quick.' Amanda emerged from the back room. 'How did you go?'

'Fine,' Lana said. 'We almost covered the entire park before we were pestered by a reporter.'

Amanda rolled her eyes as she took Lana's coat. 'They really are relentless. Well, I'm glad you got a little fresh air. Would either of you like anything to eat or drink?'

'We're fine, Mum. Brooke's just going to take a quick look in Evan's room. See if the police missed anything.'

Amanda's face tightened with apprehension, but she nodded her approval. 'That's a good idea. Thank you.'

Brooke offered a small smile and followed Lana towards the bedroom.

'I'm not ready to go in there,' Lana said. She stared vacuously at the door. 'But you take as long as you need.'

Brooke tipped her head. 'I understand. And thank you.'

As soon as Lana was out of sight, Brooke inhaled deeply and opened the bedroom door.

Evan tapped his phone, lighting up the darkness. Twelve past two. He couldn't sleep. He'd tried for hours to no avail. Despite being given his mother's blessing to listen to the podcast, something had held him back. Did he fear what he'd discover? Did he worry he wouldn't be able to look at Mick the same way again? No. That shouldn't have mattered. He needed to remind himself to separate Mick from his father. He was his own person.

Using his phone's screen as a torch, Evan located his AirPods and fixed them in his ears. He then found the podcast, took a long breath and pressed play. It was now or never, he thought, as an advertisement for alcohol preceded the introduction.

Ambient music swelled alongside the sound of a quickening heartbeat that eventually flatlined. A man's voice with an Australian accent began to speak.

'This podcast deals with distressing incidents. If at any point you need support, contact your local crisis centre. Details in the show notes or on our website.'

The man's tone shifted as he began telling the story. It became cold. Matter-of-fact. But with an intention to grip the listener in with every word. Mission accomplished.

'It was on a rainy autumn evening, in the remote coastal town of Taonga in New Zealand's South Island, that fifteen-year-old Jack Palmer was first noticed to be missing. The affluent family were sitting down to have dinner when it became clear he wasn't just late home from school. At first, they'd thought nothing of it. He often stayed back, partly due to his devotion to his studies, partly to avoid the bullies who would give him a hard time on his way home. But it was his oldest sister, Brooke, who ultimately phoned the school and had it confirmed he'd left on time. Soon after, he was declared missing, and a search began across the small town. Five long days later, his family's worst nightmare became reality when the bloodied corpse found by a dog walker was confirmed to be Jack. The boy who had everything suddenly had nothing. And the hunt for his killer had just begun.' The man's voice was replaced with a flourish of music.

Evan spent the next hours listening to all three episodes as the podcaster deep dived into the captivating case. He detailed the state of Jack's body when it was found, depicting the post-mortem with chilling effect. He examined his family's affluent lifestyle and how it contrasted that of the town's cash-strapped population.

Heart-pounding motives were theorised as the podcast honed in on multiple suspects, before whittling them down to a boy called Glen Harris and, ultimately, his best mate: Harry Saunders. A tiny piece of evidence exposed him as Jack's killer. An unsettling confession was read aloud as sinister music danced to its death in the distance.

Evan lay there, his eyes wide and too dry to blink. A stream of daylight poked through the blinds, but his thoughts had never been darker. If only Jack had been around long enough to see things get better, the way they were getting better for him. He searched the internet for a picture of Harry Saunders and was met with multiple versions of the same image. A mugshot of a man dressed in fluorescent orange overalls stared back at him. Tight curls. A bloated face. A menacing scowl. And those eyes. Grey. Vacant. Piercing.

Returning Harry Saunders' hard stare, Evan could only see Mick in the convicted killer's eyes.

Chapter Ten

Evan's bedroom managed to look both familiar and un-known at the same time. Brooke had only stepped inside one or two times before, giving it little attention. Now, it could have been the room of any teenage boy. The walls were painted a muted navy, a more mature take on the bright blue she remembered. Posters were tacked up in an artful cluster, championing a selection of bands and festivals. Below them, an acoustic guitar leaned nonchalantly against the wall, scratching it with its tuning pegs to reveal that bright blue beneath. To its right, a pile of records was stacked knee-high.

Brooke's eyes panned to the bed. It was unmade, the pillow still dimpled from where his head had been. Her mind flashed back to the photo of his head crushed and swollen, but she blinked vigorously before the image had a chance to settle.

Opposite the bed, a television hung angled on the wall, at least three sizes too big for the room. A tangle of cables led to a games console on a desk, where, noticeably absent was his computer. Brooke made a mental note to ask Collins if they'd found anything on the presumably seized machine.

Leaning on the desk was a corkboard pinned thick with glossy postcards, photographic prints and inspirational quotes. *It is more important to click with people than to click the shutter* one read, typed atop a photo of Marilyn Monroe and crediting Alfred Eisenstaedt. There must have been a dozen portraits printed small, some celebrities she recognised, others not. But one photo, in particular, caught Brooke's eye. A silhouetted figure looking to the distance. It was a powerful, dramatic shot. It wasn't until she got closer that she realised it was the photo Evan had taken of her at Christmas. A tear ran down her cheek as she felt a sense of honour.

The memory of Evan proudly showing her his new camera flooded back into her thoughts. Of how excited he'd been to see the world. She had always admired Evan's determination. She'd resonated with how she'd felt at his age. Despite all the kids who hated him, he'd had his eyes fixed on the prize. Taonga didn't deserve him. Just like it hadn't deserved her.

Smoothing her lower lid with an extended index finger, Brooke continued to scan the room. Next, her attention was drawn to his bedside table. It housed the usual suspects. A lamp. A phone charger. A box of tissues. But it was the small black book that gave Brooke pause. Its embossed cross glistened gold in the light of the window. *He told me he was worried he would go to Hell.* Brooke suddenly felt a pang of guilt as she thought back to Lana's words. She wished she could have been there for him when he was feeling alienated. Would things have turned out differently?

Brooke took a big breath and continued to canvas the room. She sifted through a chest of drawers. Nothing. Checked the wardrobe. Nothing. She looked under the bed, opened up books and trawled through notepads to no avail.

She looked back to the guitar and thought to check inside. Returning to where it was placed, she crouched down and picked it up, giving it a rattle. Nothing. Now she knew she was clutching at straws. Collins would have thought of everything already.

Turning around, Brooke glanced back at a mound of photography work that was neatly stacked in the corner of the room. Folders, photographs and books. Next to it was the box his new DSLR had come in, lovingly kept. She looked around for the camera, before remembering Lana mentioned it was missing with his backpack. Brooke picked up the top folder. Arty, black and white photographs of abandoned buildings were accompanied by typed-up descriptions revealing their meaning.

A glossy book on the photographer Annie Leibovitz lay wedged beneath. Brooke slid it out and began flicking through. As she did, a few loose prints fell facedown onto the kauri floorboards. She leaned down to pick them up and sat on the bed.

The first was a black and white photo of Evan, looking particularly serious. He stared directly at the camera, his bare torso on show. He looked older and leaner than he'd been at Christmas; the outline of his ribcage visible. The second photograph was also black and white and showed a different male torso. It was slightly more well-built than Evan's, but with the same smooth skin of youth. The subject was cropped at the neck, but an identifiable scar sat above his waistline. The two photos were clearly taken in the same session.

She glanced at the final photograph, which was the only one in colour. It was another of Evan, this time fully clothed and laughing, stood next to a man she didn't recognise. He must have been in his mid-forties. He had long, greyish-black hair and creases that ran across his face, emphasised by his wide smile. He wore a black sweater and a professional camera around his neck. A good-looking man with what looked like Latin Europe heritage and, judging by his neatly groomed stubble, he took good care of himself.

'Brooke,' Lana said through the door. 'Mum's about to make some more coffee. Would you like any?'

'No, thanks,' Brooke said, rising. 'I should get going.' She opened the door, the photographs still in her hand.

'What are those?' Lana stared blankly. 'I said not to move anything.' The disappointment in her voice thickened the air.

'Do you recognise this man?' Brooke passed her the third photo.

Lana studied it momentarily. 'That's Mr Pérez. Santiago. Evan's photography teacher. Where did you find this?'

'It was tucked away in a book. Along with these.' Brooke passed Lana the other photographs.

As she stared at the photo of Evan, the colour drained from Lana's face to match its monochrome. Her eyes clenched shut in a failed attempt to stop the tears.

'Oh, Lan. I'm so sorry.' Brooke wrapped her arms around her friend. The photographs pressed between them.

'Do you think it could have been him?' Lana's voice cracked between each word as she pulled away from Brooke's embrace. 'His teacher?'

'I don't know. I don't think I would have thought much of these photos had they not been hidden.'

'Do you think the boy with the scar is Bill Henderson?'

'That was my first thought. I'm going to find out. Would you mind if I keep hold of these?'

'Of course not.' Lana passed her back the photos. 'Mr Pérez always seemed such a good guy. He was determined to see Evan achieve his dreams. Evan used to stay late at school, working in the darkroom.' Her last words hung in the air between them as she realised what she'd said.

Dark images plagued Brooke's mind. A moodboard made up of the photos in her hand and those in the post-mortem report, her imagination filling the gaps in terrifying detail. *Fatal blow to the head. No evidence of a weapon used.* She hoped her friend wasn't thinking the same.

Brooke forced herself to break the silence. 'Get some rest. Leave this with Collins and me. We won't stop until we find out who did this.'

'I know. Thank you. I love you.'

'I love you, too.' Brooke hugged Lana again, this time a little tighter. 'I better go.'

'Keep me posted.'

'I will. Promise.'

The falling water was deafening as the three young men climbed carefully over the rocks. One wrong foot and they could have slipped and fallen, get-

ting swept away by the forceful current of the river. Mick was first to reach the muddy bank, landing on his knees with his hands preventing him from getting a mouthful of wet dirt. Bill was next, less clumsy in his descent. Last came Evan, doing his best, as ever, to keep up with his peers.

'You're nearly there,' Bill said with encouragement. 'Here, reach out. I'll pull you up.'

Evan extended his outstretched hand for Bill to clasp. It felt strangely warm, despite the autumn chill. He tightened his grip and helped Evan make the transition from the final rock to the river's edge.

'There you are,' Bill said with a note of triumph. 'We made it.' He looked up at the waterfall. 'She's roarin' hard today, eh?'

The three boys gazed at the thunderous water for a few moments until Mick finally spoke. 'C'mon, you hippies. I'd appreciate this way more with a joint in my hand.'

Evan was doing his best to push the thought of the podcast out of his mind. He hadn't told them he'd listened to it. Every last second. Mick seemed like a decent guy. It wasn't his fault that his dad had turned out the way he had. Sure, it troubled him that he still visited him. But it was his dad, after all. And who knows, perhaps there was a part of him that wondered whether his dad was innocent. But after hearing the podcast, there was no doubt in Evan's mind.

The boys entered the bush and walked beneath the towering rimus, their flaky bark an even deeper red from the morning's rainfall. Evan brushed his hand along the wet ferns as he walked, readying himself to announce his latest surprise. Soon, they reached the isolated opening they'd grown to favour as their hangout spot. Although trickier to get to, it didn't feel as risky as the ramp in town, which the odd constable had started to swing by as of late.

'Here we are,' Mick announced, dumping his backpack on the moist earth. 'This is where you tell me you forgot the weed, Ev.'

Evan pulled out a pack of cigarettes. 'Don't worry, I've got it.' He lit up and took a drag. 'Got something else with me too I thought you might want to try.'

A look of intrigue broke over Bill's face. His lips curled into a mischievous grin. 'What is it?'

Keeping the cigarette pursed between his lips, Evan opened his backpack and pulled out a picnic blanket.

'Jesus, Ev,' Mick said. 'Have you baked a cake or something?' He and Bill began to snigger.

'Fuck you,' Evan said with a smile. He shook the blanket with one hand while holding his cigarette in the other. 'You're welcome to get a wet arse.'

Mick and Bill took the blanket and spread it across the ground before lowering themselves down and huddling together. 'Nah,' Bill said. 'Good call, mate.'

Evan crouched down and offered them both a cigarette, to which they hastily accepted. He passed them his lighter, took another toke of his own and unzipped the front of his backpack. 'Hold on.' He retrieved a plastic baggie filled with white powder.

Bill's eyes grew large. 'Fuck, Ev! What's that?'

'Coke. Just a gram.'

Mick angled his eyes towards Bill. 'That's serious shit.'

'We don't need to do it if you don't want to.' Evan stamped his cigarette out on the ground. 'Just thought you might wanna try it.'

Bill swiped the packet and eyed it close. He wedged his unlit cigarette behind his ear. 'Course we want it. Cheers, mate.' He opened the baggie, licked his pinky finger and placed it in the powder. 'Have you tried it?'

'Nah, not yet. Hopefully it's good stuff.'

Bill dabbed the cocaine on his tongue. His features tightened, suggesting bitterness. 'It tastes good.'

Mick lit his cigarette and inhaled deep, before exhaling a cloud of smoke. 'I've never tried it. Have you guys?'

'I have,' Bill said with a touch of self-satisfaction. Evan wasn't sure he was being totally honest.

'I haven't.' Evan opened the main compartment of his bag and withdrew a small mirror. He caught a glimpse of his reflection and barely recognised himself.

Mick gave him a glare and wrinkled his nose. 'Think I might just stick to the weed. Thanks, anyway.'

Bill poured the cocaine onto the glass and wriggled the sides of the mirror. 'Shut up, Mick. You're having some of this.' He whipped his wallet from his jacket pocket and pulled out a bank card. 'Got a note, Ev?'

Evan opened his wallet and slid out a twenty-dollar note. 'Don't do it if you don't want, Mick. No pressure.'

Bill separated some of the powder into three equal sections and carefully formed them into slim stripes. 'He's doing it. It'll be more fun if we all do.'

Mick rolled his eyes and flicked some residual ash from his cigarette. 'Fine. But just one line.'

Bill twisted the note tight and snorted one of the white stripes. He leaned his head back and called into the sky. 'Fuck!'

After a few moments, he passed the note to Mick, who swiftly vacuumed it up. He took a huge drag of his cigarette, almost finishing it in one toke.

Evan took the note and retightened it. An image of his mum entered his mind. He shook it away. It had taken him far too long to be accepted. There was no going back now.

Leaning south, he sucked the powder up his nose in a rapid sniff. Tilting back with his eyes clenched, he felt the world start to spin. When he reopened them, he caught Bill's gaze. Just for a fleeting moment, though, before Bill looked away and retrieved the cigarette from behind his ear.

'Who's got that light?'

Brooke strode at pace through the station to the back office where Collins had been set up. The beige vertical blinds were corded shut. She clutched the photographs in one hand and with the other reached to open the door. Before she committed, she heard his voice. It was raised with the staccato of someone whose point wasn't being understood. She withdrew her hand from the handle, but before she had a chance to consider eavesdropping, a constable chimed in.

'Everything all right?' He didn't look up from his computer screen as he spoke from one of three desks in the open area – his tone markedly different from the one emanating the thin walls of Collins' office.

Before Brooke had a chance to respond, Collins had hung up with an audible thud and the door opened.

'Palmer.' He was standing in the doorway, his face still red but his tone jovial to compensate. 'Missing me already?'

'Um. Yeah.' She decided to cut to the chase. 'Lana let me take a look in Evan's room and look what I found.' She passed Collins the photos. 'They were hidden in a book, the three of them together.'

He studied them one by one, his face returning to its usual tone as he did. 'Interesting.' He sat back down at the desk, his eyes pinned to the colour photo. 'Know who this guy is?'

'Name's Santiago Pérez. He was Evan's photography teacher when he was at school. It looks like it was taken recently as that was exactly how Ev looked when I was down at Christmas. The other two are even more recent than that.'

Collins spread the three photos out on his desk and tapped his finger on the headless torso. 'Bill?'

'We suspect so. Me and Lana, I mean.'

Collins' finger tapped again, this time on Santiago's Cheshire Cat grin. 'This guy must have meant something to Evan.' He turned his attention to Brooke. 'I guess we should pay Mr Pérez a visit.'

Brooke flinched and a twinge of guilt followed. The support from her teachers had been something of a salvation at school when the other kids had been awful. They'd encouraged her to tune out the bullies and focus her energy on succeeding. Had Mr Pérez played the same role in Evan's life? A part of her hoped so.

Collins prised open his laptop and typed in Taonga High School. 'Let me see if he's working today.' He copied the number to his phone and held it to his ear. 'Hello. Detective Tane Collins here from Canterbury District Police. Can you tell me if Santiago Pérez is working today?' A short pause. 'Okay, thanks.' He hung up and ran his fingers through his hair. 'Bingo.'

Chapter Eleven

Brooke was awash with dread as she turned the car onto Park Street. That long-forgotten feeling of going back to school after the summer break had returned, and it was just as nauseating as it ever was. Apart from during the occasional recurring dream, she hadn't returned to Taonga High since graduating.

As soon as she caught sight of the main building, it occurred to her that nothing had changed. The same faded pink brick walls, unintentionally brutalist in their assembly. The same galvanised wire fence, punctuated with rust patches and perished vines. The same expressions of anguish on the faces of students who wished they were anywhere but there, weighed down by their oversized backpacks unabashedly embroidered with Taonga High's motto: *Committed to lifelong learning.* Not saying much for the growing percentage who end up in a body bag, Brooke thought.

'You all right?' Collins said.

Brooke realised she'd been silent the whole journey. Mentally preparing herself for the unpreparable. 'I'm fine. I just never thought I'd be coming back here. It's hard enough coming back to Taonga. But returning to the school that caused my family and me so much…' Brooke finished the sentence with an over-emphasised inhale, her anxiety evident in its quiver.

'You don't have to come in with me.' Collins peered through the windscreen.

'No, it's okay. I want to. I want to speak to him.'

Collins nodded his support. 'Just remember, you're here as Detective Palmer now.'

Brooke straightened her back and felt her confidence reinstall. 'You're right.'

They parked up and made their way to the entrance, brushing past young students as they scrambled on their lunch break. Their elders loitered in the distance, cigarettes and alcohol undoubtedly hidden among their schoolbooks. As the detectives stepped into the building, it quickly occurred to Brooke that while the school's exterior remained untouched, inside was a different story. The reception had been renovated, and the hallways had been given an uplifting lick of paint. Māori artwork lined the walls, while a large photograph of the current principal hung above a slew of awards. His choice of tie intended to bring out the medium-brown of his eyes, which looked confidently just north of the camera's lens.

'Can I help you?' The receptionist examined the pair over the top of her glasses.

'Detective Tane Collins.' He pulled his badge from the

inside of his coat pocket. 'We're here to speak with Santiago Pérez.'

The woman pushed her auburn fringe to the side and picked up a phone. 'Oh yes, I spoke to you when you called.' She dialled a number and paused a few moments. 'Santiago, the cops are here to speak to you,' she said with a spring in her voice. 'Will do, thanks.' She slapped down the phone. 'I'll take you through.'

Collins gave a tight nod.

Brooke's eyes darted to familiar-but-forgotten details as she followed Collins and the receptionist down the hallway. The cherry-red fire alarm buttons. The textured ceiling tiles. The heavily frosted window of the staff room door. It was as if both nothing and everything had changed. She focused on the faces of oncoming students as they whispered to one another, no doubt excited about the investigation. They should have been scared. Their own lives were in danger until the perpetrator was caught. She wondered how many of their parents she'd have known. How many of them had taunted her, ridiculed her, made her feel alone. It wasn't the time to revisit those painful memories. She was here for one reason. To seek justice for Evan.

The receptionist led them from the building into a smaller wing, which hadn't been there when Brooke was at school. Long overdue funding had obviously permitted the addition of an art and photography block.

'Here's his class,' the receptionist said, motioning to the door with a slow flick of the hand. 'I'll leave you guys to it.'

Collins nodded his gratitude and led the way into the room,

where Santiago Pérez was already standing at his desk. He looked just the same as he had in the photograph, except his hair was now tied back in a ponytail.

'Hello,' Santiago said to Collins in a thick Spanish accent, before shifting his gaze to Brooke.

She pulled out her badge. 'Detective Brooke Palmer. We just need to ask you some questions about Evan Wiley. We won't take too much of your time.'

'Sure. No problem. Take a seat.' He gestured towards the two chairs he'd already positioned in front of his desk, which was precisely as Brooke had expected it to look. A clutter of photographs, hardback books, a couple of cameras and reels of negatives.

As Collins whipped out his own badge and introduced himself, Brooke scanned the room. She instantly noticed an image of Evan blown up on the wall next to a line of other student photographs. It was different from the picture she'd found in his room. He had his t-shirt on, for a start.

'Evan Wiley was in your photography class last year, correct?' Collins retrieved his notepad from his satchel.

Santiago gave a quick nod, tears appearing in his eyes instantly. 'That's correct. It's just terrible, what's happened. Myself and the rest of the school are heartbroken.'

'He was liked then?' Brooke said. 'By everyone in school, I mean?'

Santiago fixed his glassy eyes on Brooke's. They were a dark shade of brown, not far off black. Brooke couldn't decipher what was behind them.

'Not everyone,' he said. 'Of course there were people

jealous of what he had. But he started to make friends towards—'

'Towards the end?' Collins finished.

'Yes.' Santiago wiped his eyes.

Collins pulled a folder out from his bag and spread the photographs across the desk in front of Santiago. 'Can you tell us a bit about these photos?'

Santiago sat up straight and looked in swift sequence from Collins to Brooke and then to the photographs. He lifted the one that featured him and studied it closely. 'This was taken by a student. Evan had asked for a picture together, on the last day of term if I recall correctly.'

'We found it buried in a book in his bedroom,' Collins said. 'With these.' He pointed towards the other prints.

Santiago picked both photos up. 'I've never seen these before.'

'Do you know what they could be for?'

He shook his head. 'I assume they were working on something. Maybe testing their cameras… or doing something creative.'

'So, they're not for a school project?' Collins said.

Santiago took one final look. He stroked his stubble a few times. 'No. Not for my class. Besides, that looks like a more recent photo of Evan to me.'

Collins threw Brooke a glance. He then turned his focus back to Santiago. 'So you've seen Evan recently? Since the last day of term?'

Santiago remained quiet for a breath or two, clearly digesting the question. 'Is it a crime to catch up with an ex-student?'

'No, of course not,' Brooke said calmly. 'But we'd like to

understand the relationship you had with Evan if it went beyond a student-teacher one.'

Santiago's shoulders shot back. 'I don't like where this is going.'

'Just answer the question, Mr Pérez,' Collins pressed, pulling out his notebook.

Brooke couldn't tell if Santiago's face had turned pale or whether it was just the artificial light of the classroom.

'Okay. Well, yes, I saw Evan a few times after he'd finished school. He was a very talented young man with big ambitions. I saw a lot of potential in him. He looked to me as a mentor. I saw a bit of myself in him. When I was younger and had big dreams.' He glanced at the photograph of Evan on the wall and then outside the window. His eyes had welled up again. 'I was guiding him.'

'Do you think that was appropriate?' Collins said.

'Why not? I'm a teacher. I want the best for all my students.' Santiago shifted in his seat. 'It could be another one of them found at the bottom of those falls soon if you keep wasting your time on me.'

'No need to get defensive, Mr Pérez,' Brooke said. 'We're just having a chat, but we can take this down to the station if you'd prefer?'

Santiago's glare cut into her.

'So, where were you last Tuesday night?' Brooke pressed. 'Taonga Falls?'

Santiago shook his head with both defeat and disbelief. 'I was at home. Where I usually am if I'm not here. I haven't been to those falls since I moved here.'

Collins jotted a note before continuing. 'Do you live alone?'

A pulse of silence. 'Yes.'

'So no one can confirm you were at home Tuesday night?' Brooke knew the answer but wanted Santiago to get the point.

'No, but I was. I'm sure I can figure out a way to prove it. You've put me on the spot.' Santiago thought hard for a couple of moments to no avail.

'Can you tell us about the last time you saw Evan?' Collins said. 'When was it? How was his mood?'

'It was a couple of weeks ago. He was a bit apprehensive, about his trip I guess, which was coming up. Understandable for a small-town boy.'

'Did anything unusual happen?' Collins said.

Santiago looked to the ceiling. 'Not unusual, but he did ask a favour of me.'

Brooke leaned in an inch as Santiago returned his attention to the pair.

'He asked if I could buy him a new lens for his trip. A camera lens. I asked which one he needed, as I knew he had a few, but he never said. Asked me to forget about it.'

Brooke briefly met Collins' eyes and they both went to speak. Collins beat her to it. 'Did he ask for you to buy him a lens, or did he ask for you to give him money to buy a lens?'

Brooke thought back to Bill Henderson's words. *He said he owed the dealer money.*

Confusion came across Santiago's face. 'What's the difference?'

'Did he ask for a lens, or did he ask for money?' Brooke reiterated as simply as she could. 'Cash?'

'I can't remember his exact words.'

'Didn't you find it weird he would ask you to buy him a lens?' Collins tapped his pen impatiently against the desk. 'And not, say, his mother?'

'I assumed he came to me because I could use my education discount. I didn't give it too much thought, to be honest. Maybe his mum said no.'

'Evan had become involved with drugs,' Collins said matter-of-factly. 'Did you know anything about this?'

Santiago's eyes narrowed. 'No. Not at all.'

'We have reason to believe Evan owed a dealer money,' Brooke said. 'Perhaps that's why he came to you. Not for a lens, but for cash to pay back the dealer. The lens just being an excuse.'

Santiago relaxed into his chair. 'Well, there you go then. Have you spoken to this dealer yet?'

'Not yet,' Collins said. 'We're trying to track him down.'

Santiago placed his elbows on his desk, his hands aclasp. 'Well, I'm no detective, but–'

'Mr Pérez,' Collins interrupted. 'You do your job and leave us to do ours, okay?'

Santiago's tongue gave a small tut.

Brooke glanced at the photographs and back at Santiago. 'Were you aware at all that Evan might have been struggling with his… identity?'

Santiago stroked his bristles. There was a brief pause that bordered uncomfortable. 'You mean his sexuality?'

'Yes.'

He gave a small nod. 'Evan confided in me once, yes. A few

months back, he came to see me here. He said I was the only openly gay person he knew. I guess he looked up to me in that way, too. Came to me for advice.'

Collins glanced at Brooke and then Santiago. 'Is that all he came to you for?'

Santiago's eyes grew wide. 'What are you insinuating, Detective?'

'Well, come on. You're an educated man. You can see how this looks, can't you? Evan was clearly fond of you. He kept a bloody photograph of the pair of you together tucked away in his bedroom. I remember having a crush on one of my teachers.'

'The thought never even crossed my mind.' Santiago's tone had sharpened.

Brooke was concerned Collins might have gone in too strong. She didn't want them to lose their momentum. 'Did he ever talk to you about Bill Henderson?'

Santiago thought for a moment. 'No. Why?'

'He didn't say anything about being involved with him in any way?' Brooke took some balm from her pocket and began coating her coarse lips.

'No. He did tell me he had feelings for a guy, but he didn't say who. I don't tend to get involved in my students' love lives. But I do know Evan had been hanging around with Bill a lot in recent months.' Santiago diverted his eyes back to the picture of the bare torso with the scar. He held it up. 'Do you know if this is him? Did it not cross your mind that Bill Henderson could be your guy? He used to pick on Evan before they became friends.'

'We're still in the early stages of our investigation,' Collins said. 'We're not writing anyone off right now.' He gave him a firm stare.

'Okay. Well, if you're not going to arrest me, can you please let me get on? I have a lesson to teach shortly and I need to squeeze in a cigarette break. God knows I need one now.' He opened his drawer and pulled out a packet of smokes.

'Still on the Fortunas, I see,' Collins said as he bagged his notebook and pen. 'How long did you say you've been here?'

'I didn't.' Santiago gave a satisfied smile.

Collins paused as his eyes glared from beneath his furrowed brow.

'About five years,' Santiago said, giving in. 'I lived in Christchurch for the first three before relocating here for work. I love it.'

'Even the rain?' Collins looked at Brooke one last time and took the photographs back.

'That part not so much. I do miss the Spanish sun.'

'Thank you for your time, Mr Pérez,' Collins said definitively. 'Can I take your number?'

Santiago read it aloud.

'Thanks.' Collins passed him his card. 'Let us know if you think of anything else. We'll be in touch.'

Santiago shot him a final look. 'Will do.'

Santiago had just finished packing his bag when Evan appeared in the doorway. 'Evan! What a nice surprise. Come on in, how are you?'

Evan sat on the table closest to Santiago's desk. 'I'm good, thanks. Getting excited about my trip in a few months.'

'Oh yes. You're still going to Europe?'

'Sure am. Can't wait.'

'And you're still going to Spain?' He smoothed his hand over his thick hair, which was held tight in its pony.

'Of course. I've got your list. Can't wait to check it all out.'

Santiago beamed. 'You will love it. You're going to take so many amazing photos. I can't wait to see them. You'll have to show them to me as soon as you get back, okay?'

'I promise.'

A small silence.

'So what brings you back here? You want me to teach you some Spanish?' Santiago laughed off his question.

'There was something I actually wanted to talk to you about. If that's okay?'

Santiago glanced at his watch. 'Sure. As long as it doesn't take too long. I should already have left by now.'

'It won't.' Evan flicked his fringe to the side. 'It's just... uh, it's kind of awkward. It's a little personal.'

Santiago kept his frown light. 'Personal? Personal how?'

'Um, I hope you don't mind me asking, but when did you know you were gay?'

Santiago's expression changed from confused to knowing. He looked out the window. 'Pretty young. Maybe thirteen, fourteen.'

'And did you tell people straight away?'

'No, not straight away. I had to come to terms with it myself first. I tried a few things out in my mid-teens. Kissed a girl, kissed a boy. I knew then what I was into.'

Evan dropped his eyes to the floor. 'I see.'

Santiago turned his head to the side. 'If you need to speak to someone, I can see if the school counsellor is around. I know you're not technically a *student here anymore, but I'm sure she'll be happy to have a chat with you.'*

'That's okay. My mum's actually a psychologist – I don't think that's what I need. I just thought… given the fact you've been through it yourself…'

'Oh no, of course. I'm happy for you to speak with me. I just wish I had more time.'

Evan's eyes were fixed on the floor. His posture defeated.

'So, you're having a bit of confusion around your sexuality?' Santiago dropped his bag to his desk and folded his arms.

Evan shrugged. 'Yeah, I guess. There's this guy… I think I like him. I know I like him.'

'Well, have you considered talking to him about it? Telling him how you feel?'

Evan looked back at the floor. 'Not yet. I'm worried he won't feel the same.'

Santiago's phone buzzed in his pocket. 'Sorry, I have to take this.'

Evan held up his hand. 'No worries, I should get going anyway. Thanks, Mr Pérez.'

'Please, Santi.' He gave a wink and a thumbs up as he pulled his phone from his jean pocket. 'Hey. Sorry.' Santiago spoke down the line. 'I got held up at work. I should be home in half an hour.'

Evan turned back to give Santiago a final look before he left the classroom. They shared a momentary smile.

Brooke tapped the steering wheel, deep in thought. 'Well, what do you think? Do you believe him?'

Collins gazed out the window. 'He was quick to point the blame to the dealer, and then to Henderson. Seemed a bit desperate. What do you think?'

'I think he was being honest with us. The whole lens story matched up to the fact Evan needed money. But whether he told us everything… I'm not so sure.'

Collins' phone chimed in his pocket. He pulled it out and read the message. 'Henderson. He'll be at the station at nine AM tomorrow.'

'Perfect. I'll drop you back at the station, but I better get home. Get some rest before then and see how the family's doing.'

'That's not a bad idea.' Collins slid his phone back in his pocket. 'I'm actually heading back to Christchurch tomorrow arvo. I'll be back Thursday.'

Brooke stopped the car at a red light. 'No worries. That reminds me, Evan's funeral is Thursday.'

'That's quick.'

'Catholic, remember?'

Collins gave a small nod. 'Of course. I hope it goes as well as it can. It'll be a tough day.'

Brooke stared at the road ahead, waiting for the light to change to amber. 'It certainly will.'

Chapter Twelve

The fatigue in Collins' eyes was visible through the glass of his office as Brooke strolled towards it. Two takeaway coffees sat snug in a cardboard tray in her left hand, a lip balm mark the only thing differentiating hers from his.

'I come bearing gifts.' She pushed the already-ajar door open with a hunched back.

'There is a god.' Collins pushed his palms into a prayer, his eyes mesmerised by the steam. 'Thanks, Palmer. Been up most the night.'

'Tell me about it.' She checked each lid in the light and passed him the unsipped cup. 'Flat white okay? I know you drink black in the office, but–'

'Flat white's perfect. Thanks.' Collins opened the lid of his drink and pulled a sachet of sugar out from his drawer. 'I know, bad habit.' He watched Brooke eye him pouring the white granules into his drink. 'I'm trying to give up smoking again, so

I'm swapping one vice for another.'

'I'm not judging you,' she lied. 'Mine's biting my nails.'

Collins widened his eyes with feigned shock. 'Did you know there are more germs under our n–'

'Yes, I know. Now come on. Any news? I take it Bill's not here yet.'

Collins blew a dent into the coffee's foam and took a sip. 'Not yet. But there is some news actually. We were contacted by a man this morning who owns a dairy on the northern edge of town. He spotted Evan on his CCTV footage. The day he went missing.'

Now it was Brooke's eyes that had grown wide. 'Serious? That's huge.'

'It is. We'll head over there after we're done with Henderson to take a look.' He sipped his coffee, leaving an off-white stain on his upper lip, which he quickly licked away. 'Sound good?'

'Sounds perfect.'

A constable entered the room. 'Detectives, the Henderson boy's here.'

'Great,' Collins said. 'Take him to the interview room. We're on our way.'

Collins slammed the photograph of the torso on the table. 'Look familiar?'

Bill leaned forward and squinted his eyes, his arms folded. He retracted to his original position and kept his face blank. 'No.'

'Show us.' Collins' tone remained firm.

'Show you what?'

'What was it, appendicitis? We can check your medical records if you prefer.' The tip of Collins' index finger was bent backwards by the pressure he used to point at the scar in the picture.

Bill rolled his eyes. 'Fine, yeah. It's me. So what?' He paused for a tick. 'It was for Evan's portfolio. It didn't mean anything. This is dumb.'

'You know what else is dumb?' Collins said before taking the last of his flat white with an audible gulp. 'Lying to the police.' He leaned into Bill, close enough for him to smell the coffee on his breath. 'Now, tell us the truth about your relationship with Evan Wiley.'

Bill wrinkled his brow. 'What do you mean?'

'Bill,' Brooke said with a sigh, who until this point had remained quiet, sitting neatly in her chair. 'We know you and Evan were more than just friends. So, come on. Start telling us the truth.' She replaced her hands to her lap.

Bill's gaze plunged to the floor. 'I'm not a f–' He stopped himself from finishing the word.

Collins leaned back and tilted his head left. 'A what? A friend?' Collins exaggerated the F. 'No, you're not being a good friend to Evan if you don't start trying to help us. And if you were going to say something else, you might want to reconsider because you're not going to get very far in life with that homophobic attitude.'

Bill went to speak, but nothing materialised.

'Look, Bill,' Brooke said. 'We're just trying to build a picture of Evan's life in the months and weeks before he was killed.' She pushed the photo closer to him. 'And by the looks of things, he was very fond of you. Please, if you have any respect for Evan, now's your chance to show it. Don't you at least owe him that?'

Bill took a long breath and lifted his head to Brooke. The whites of his eyes had become pink and tears lined his lower lids, thick lashes the only thing holding them back. She could see he was on the brink of telling them what happened. She sympathetically pinched her eyes and offered a nod, gentle enough to give him the reassurance he needed without upsetting the room's calm. His irises pulsed green, ready to reveal the truth.

'I liked him.' A tear hit his cheek. 'I liked him a lot.' His nostrils flared as he breathed.

Brooke crossed her arms and gave Collins a wide-eyed glance. They shared a silent moment of triumph, bracing for Bill's side of the story.

As he got closer, it occurred to Evan that Mick wasn't there. He could make out Bill's silhouetted profile beneath the ramp, his relaxed stance framed by a criss-cross of supporting poles. A shadow of cigarette smoke dissipated in the early evening glow.

'Hey,' Evan said as his eyes panned the otherwise empty skatepark. 'Where's Mick?'

Bill released his lean and gave a quick shrug. 'He didn't wanna come.' He took a drag of his cigarette. 'I told him you've got some more coke. He said it's not for him.'

Evan felt a pang of guilt as he dropped his backpack from his shoulders, catching it with his wrists. 'We don't have to do it. I don't want him to feel left out.'

Bill barked a laugh and flicked his stump to the ground. 'We're not fifteen-year-old schoolgirls, Ev. He can do what he wants. Besides, all the more for us, eh?' His devilish grin was back.

Evan smirked. 'True.' He couldn't deny to himself that he didn't mind Mick's absence. Not only would this make his mum happier, but it also meant he had Bill to himself.

'Come on then, what you waiting for? Let's rack up.'

Evan unzipped his bag and pulled out the picnic blanket they'd become accustomed to lying on, and spread it on the damp concrete. They took a corner each as Evan reached in to retrieve the mirror and a small plastic bag filled with cocaine.

'Who do you get this shit from anyway?' Bill sat cross-legged as he eyeballed the baggie.

'Some guy out of town. I found him through Insta.' Evan chopped up two lines.

'How much is it?'

Evan pulled a note from his wallet. 'Doesn't matter.'

'Must be nice not to worry.' Bill watched Evan roll up the note. 'About money, I mean. Growing up with a rich family.'

Evan met his gaze. 'Well, to be honest, I'm burning through my travel fund. I should really slow down. Or get a job.' He snorted his line and passed the note to Bill.

'Maybe you could work with me. Sure my dad could do with an extra pair of hands.' He inhaled the powder.

'Yeah?' Evan ran his fingers through his thick hair. 'That could be cool.'

'For sure. Lemme ask him.'

'Thanks.'

Bill flicked his hand. 'Forget it. Least I could do. All the shit you've *supplied me and Mick.'*

Evan pulled out his cigarettes and offered one to Bill.

'All good, mate. I've got my own. Snuck some of Dad's.'

Evan lit up and angled his face to the side. 'Can I ask you something personal?'

Bill paused a moment. 'Uh, sure.'

Evan sucked his cigarette. 'Have you ever been with a girl?'

Another pause, but shorter this time. 'What?'

'You know, slept with one.' Evan could feel the cocaine kicking in.

'I know what you meant.' Bill pulled his packet of cigarettes from his pocket. 'Course I have. Why, haven't you?'

Evan wondered if Bill was telling the truth. He opened his mouth to speak, but nothing came out.

'You haven't, eh?'

Evan drew a puff. 'Maybe.'

Bill slid a cigarette out and gestured for Evan to pass the lighter. 'Don't worry, mate. Your secret's safe with me.'

Evan passed the lighter and kept quiet as Bill slid the cigarette between his lips. He imagined what they would feel like. How his tongue would taste.

'Were you in a relationship with him?' Brooke said.

Bill shook his head and leaned forward, his eyes still bleary. 'No. It was nothing like that.' He rested his forearms on the table and began fussing with his fingers. 'We were just… messing around. It was all the drugs we were taking.'

Collins cleared his throat with a rasp that echoed the room and thumped his chest in preparation to speak. Bill looked up from his hands.

'See, I'm not sure you're being entirely honest with us.' Collins didn't blink as he spoke. His eyes fixed to Bill's. 'You said you liked Evan. A lot. I mean, you tear up at the thought of him. But you've also made it clear that you're…' Collins looked around the room for the word. 'Uncomfortable… with the fact you're gay. So you had to solve the problem. And in this case, that meant killing Evan Wiley.'

'I didn't do it!' Bill shot up and pushed his chair back. It fell with a clash of plastic and metal. 'I didn't kill Evan. And I'm not gay!' He went to kick the upturned chair.

'Sit down, mate,' Collins said. 'You're not helping yourself when you flip out like that.'

Bill breathed heavily through his nose and obeyed Collins' orders, picking up the chair and sitting back at the table. His face remained incensed as he looked to the space between Collins and Brooke. The white fluorescent lights flickered, their reflection visible in his dilated pupils.

Brooke swallowed her final drop of coffee and threw the cup into the bin. 'You say gay like it's a dirty word. Why is that? You do know what year it is, don't you? You do realise gay people are accepted in New Zealand? That they can get married and have the same rights as straight people?'

Bill stared at the table. 'I guess.' He looked back to Brooke. 'Why do you care so much anyway?'

'What do you mean?'

'About defending gays.'

'It's called being a decent human being, Bill. Why do you care so much about whether we think you're gay or not?'

Bill picked up the photograph of his torso and turned it

over, as if disgusted by his own physique. 'I dunno.' He looked
Brooke in the eye, his chest still heaving. 'I guess I'm scared.
About what my dad would think. He hates fa–' He clipped him-
self short again. 'He hates gays.'

A silence sliced the room.

'Have you spoken to him about any of this?' Brooke said.

'No. He'd have kicked me out by now if he found out about
me and Ev. He'd already banned us from seeing each other because he found out we were doing drugs.'

'We know,' Collins said. 'He found it in your room, correct?'

Bill's expression grew tight. 'Mick's such a little snitch.'

'That's enough,' Collins said. 'Mick has been very helpful.
It would be good if you could be, too.'

Bill searched their eyes. 'What about if *he* did it? Mick, I
mean. Did you think about that?'

Brooke shot Collins a glare and looked back at Bill. 'And
why would he have wanted to do that?'

Bill clicked his neck. 'I dunno. Maybe he was jealous. Of
mine and Evan's friendship. He hadn't been hanging out with
us so much and we used to be best mates. Maybe he wanted
him gone. Get back to how it used to be.'

Collins folded his arms. 'Seems a stretch, mate.'

The room went quiet again.

'I didn't do it,' Bill finally muttered beneath his breath.

Collins fidgeted in his seat and gave Brooke a look. She
could tell he was becoming impatient. Irritated.

'Just because you keep telling yourself that, it doesn't make
it true,' Collins said. 'Just like you keep telling yourself you're
not gay. Lying to yourself, to us, is only going to make it worse.

You know full well Mick didn't do it. You were the one in love with Evan and it scared you, didn't it? It scared you so much that you wanted him gone.'

'That's not true,' Bill said defiantly. 'I didn't love him.'

'You wanted him gone, so you killed him. Plenty of people in this town are jealous of the Wileys, so you knew you stood a chance of getting away with it.'

'That's not true!' Bill slammed his fist on the table.

'Quite the temper you've got there, eh?' Collins said with a dash of satisfaction.

Bill sighed. 'Look. I did what you guys told me. I came in. I answered your questions. Now, when can I leave? I don't technically need to be here, do I? Unless you're arresting me. In which case I'll need to hire a lawyer. That's what my dad told me.'

Collins held a deep breath a moment before letting it go. 'Fine. Get outta here.'

Bill didn't need to be told twice.

'But we've got our eyes on you.' Collins tracked Bill with an accusatory glare as he paced to the door.

'Then you'll never find out who really did this.' The door slammed as he let it go.

Chapter Thirteen

Only when the detectives left the station did the skies crack open. They made the short dash across the car park as rain pummelled its blackened concrete.

'What time do you need to be in Christchurch?' Brooke held her coat overhead as Collins paced to the driver's side, thumbing his key to unlock the SUV with a double-beep.

'Long as I set off within the next hour, it should be fine.'

They climbed in and slammed the doors in unison. Brooke blew warm air into her cupped hands and rubbed them together. She shot Collins a look and held it, attempting to decipher his mood. She could write-off how tough he'd been on Bill as a tactic. But the heated phone call he'd had in his office? It didn't take a detective to work out something was going on.

He caught her glare. 'What is it?'

She paused for a tick. 'Is everything all right?'

Collins kept quiet. He started the engine and cranked up

the heating.

'Sorry, I don't mean to pry.' Brooke hoped she came off sincere.

'No, no – it's fine. I mean, it's not really.' Collins rolled the car onto the road. 'My ex-wife's trying to get custody of our daughter. We're going through the courts at the moment.'

'Oh. I'm sorry.' Brooke dropped her eyes. 'That must be tough. I had no idea you have a daughter.'

'It's okay.' He hesitated. 'Feels like I don't sometimes these days.'

Brooke used his expression as a gauge to see how far she could push the topic. 'So, your ex-wife wants full custody?'

Collins watched the road. 'She wants to move them back to Auckland, where she's from. But I'm fighting for her to stay. At least until she finishes school.'

'How old is she?' Brooke held her hands against the vents of the dashboard as warm air filtered out.

'She's eleven.'

'They grow up fast, don't they? I mean, I know from Lana and my sister.'

'You don't have any of your own?' Collins gave her a glance out the corner of his eye.

'No.' Brooke knew what was coming next.

'Did you – I mean – do you want them?' A soft silence. 'Sorry. Now it's me who's prying.'

'I did. Kind of.' She gazed outside where the cloud cover made it look like night. 'But I can't, unfortunately. It wasn't meant to be for me.'

'I'm sorry to hear that.' Another pause. 'But there are

different options these days, right?'

Brooke unscrewed a plastic bottle and took a sip of water, her face warm from the tender subject. 'There is, yeah. But I'm just not sure kids are for me. Not sure I'm wired that way.'

Collins smirked as he stopped for a red light. 'Not sure any of us are.'

Brooke dipped her head. 'And after seeing what Lana's going through, and what my mum went through, I think I'd be too afraid.' She shivered despite the hot air. 'I'm not sure I'm strong enough.'

Collins paused to choose his words. 'You underestimate yourself, Palmer.'

Brooke went to say something in response, but decided to change the subject instead. 'So, you haven't seen this footage yet?'

Collins inched the car forward in anticipation of the lights changing. 'No, not yet. The dairy's just up on the corner here.'

'Oh, I know the one.'

'Looks like young Evan must have been heading out of town.'

The detectives parked outside the store and sprinted inside to avoid a drenching. A middle-aged man with lank black hair and a sleeve of greened tattoos sat hunched over the counter listening to the radio.

'—residents have been told to remain on high alert while homicide detectives continue to investigate the murder of eighteen-year-old Evan Wiley, who was found dead almost a week ago at—' The man switched it off.

'Detective Tane Collins. Are you Nick?'

'Yes.' He eyed Collins' badge then averted his gaze to Brooke.

She pulled out hers. 'Detective Palmer.'

Nick's dark-rimmed eyes widened. 'Palmer?'

Brooke watched as he processed the situation in his head.

'You're Brooke, the sister.' He pointed in triumph. 'Sorry, I've listened to the podcast about your brother. So, you're investiga–'

'Can you show us the CCTV footage now?' Collins interrupted, tucking his badge away. 'We haven't got a lot of time.'

Nick nodded. 'Come through. I'll close the store for a few minutes.' He strode to the front door and flipped the open sign. 'Come out back.'

He led the detectives into a small stock room that smelled like a combination of lollies and stale cardboard. He switched on a small black computer screen and a live view of the empty store fuzzed to life. He minimised it and navigated to a video that was saved to the desktop. 'Sorry, the quality isn't great.' He double-clicked.

Brooke locked her eyes on the screen intently. The dull recording showed a slim teenager walk into the store wearing jeans and a grey hoodie. The hood was pulled over his head, and the angle of the camera meant not much of his face could be seen. But everything about the boy was Evan. His posture. His walk. His distinctive blonde fringe. He held the straps of his backpack as he stalked through the small store. Was he nervous? Brooke couldn't tell. In the corner of the screen, Nick could be seen behind the till. Slumped in a chair with a magazine curled open in his hand.

'Great customer service there,' Collins quipped, keeping his eyes on the monitor.

'It's called product research,' Nick said with a sniff as his on-screen self flicked to the next page.

In the video, Evan picked up a packet of chips, spending no time to decide. He then walked towards the fridge, stopping two metres short. He reached into his jean pocket and pulled out his phone. He looked at the lit-up display which appeared to tremble in the grainy footage.

'Is he shaking?' Brooke said, her face close to the screen.

'Could be the phone strobing with the camera,' Nick suggested.

Evan stuffed the phone back in his pocket and opened the fridge, pulling out a bottle of water. He let the fridge door close itself as he paced back to where Nick was sitting. Evan placed the items down and said something to Nick, who pulled something out from behind the counter and passed it to him.

'What was that?' Collins said.

'A lighter.'

Evan handed over a note, took the change and his items and disappeared from the screen.

Brooke looked at the time stamp. *17:44.* Hard to believe he only had an hour or so left to live, she thought.

'That's all I've got,' Nick said, stopping the video with a click. 'I'm sure it's him.'

'Oh, that's him all right.' Brooke kept her eyes fixed on the screen, which now displayed an empty store.

Collins scratched his chin and looked through the open stockroom door. 'Come with me.' He paced through the store and back out the entrance. The rain was still steady, but Collins took little notice.

Brooke followed him across the car park to a bus stop. A stained map of Taonga's small bus network wilted behind a scratched acrylic panel.

'Evan didn't drive here,' Collins said. 'His car was left parked at home. He was out of petrol.' He pointed to a bus stop on the map labelled *Beach View Drive*. He traced his finger along the grey line to a red dot. *You are here*. 'If you stay on that bus, you end up in town. But if you change here…' Collins pointed to the only other route that serviced the red dot and followed its line north. It ended with an arrow and two words: *To Greymouth*.

'He was heading to Greymouth.' Brooke looked down the road the bus would have taken before turning back to Collins.

'And you know who was in Greymouth on the day of Evan's murder?'

Brooke cast her mind back to Craig Henderson, standing in his greasy overalls. *He was with me in Greymouth*. 'Bill.'

Collins nodded with a satisfied smile. 'I think we've got enough on this kid to get a search warrant. See if we can find something concrete in the house.'

Craig still stood in Brooke's mind, wiping his hands on that blackened rag. *The kid didn't leave my sight*. He was defensive, sure, but there was something about the Hendersons that Brooke trusted. Was Collins leading them down the wrong road?

'Didn't Bill's dad say he didn't leave his sight?' Brooke questioned Collins, her eyes holding his with a squint.

'Oh wow, you're right.' The sarcasm in his tone bordered patronising. 'A dad would never lie for his son.'

'Okay, okay.' Brooke paced back across the car park alongside Collins. 'So, when do you reckon we'll search their house?'

'With my contacts, we'll be turning the place upside down tomorrow.'

The day of the funeral. Brooke cringed at the thought.

From inside the dairy, Nick approached the door with a USB drive between his index finger and thumb. 'As requested, a copy of the video.'

'Thanks,' Collins said as the drive dropped to his upturned palm.

'Sorry I can't be any more help,' Nick said.

'No, this is great. Thanks.' Collins turned to Brooke. 'Right, I better get on the road.'

As the detectives stepped outside, Collins flipped the sign on the door: *Come in, we're open.* 'Shall I drop you home?' He unlocked the car.

'Yeah. Thanks. I better find out whether I packed something black for tomorrow. Otherwise I'll be wearing one of my mum's Dress for Success dresses.'

'Dress for what?'

'Never mind.'

'Hey.' Evan pulled the hood of his hoodie down. 'Has your dad left?'

'Yep.' Bill was standing at the door wearing a plain white t-shirt and his favourite denim jeans. 'Left about an hour ago. Come in.'

Bill agreed to stay home and look after his dog while his dad visited his grandmother in Greymouth. When Evan received the text to come over, he had to restrain himself from replying too quickly.

As he walked into the house, Evan eyed up its dated interior. Secondhand furniture sat atop scuffed floorboards. Mildew speckled the ceiling's corners. Much like Mick's place, it was another world to the one he'd grown up in, but he didn't feel sorry for Bill. Nor did he feel superior. Both growing up with just one parent, he wondered who had even lived the happier life.

'Want something to drink?' Bill said. 'Maybe a beer?'

'Sure, thanks.'

A large Doberman scurried through to the living room, his growl fast transforming to a whimper once he realised Evan was a welcome guest.

He gave him a heavy pat. 'Nice dog.'

Bill reappeared carrying two bottles of beer he'd already cracked open. Froth had spilled a little down the sides. 'Yeah, Rambo's all right. Can be a bit of a pain. Here, cheers.'

They clinked the bottles.

'Cheers.'

Bill took a swig and slumped on the sofa. 'Hey, I asked Dad about you coming to work with us.'

Evan took the seat beside him, tucking his backpack to the side. 'Oh yeah? What did he say?'

'He said it should be fine. Money's a bit tight at the moment, so not sure he'd be able to pay out right now, but we're hoping things will pick up soon. Usually does as we get closer to winter; heaps of cars end up needing repairs. If not, I'm sure I could split my earnings with you or something.'

Evan was taken aback. 'I wouldn't expect you to do that.'

Bill took another sip. 'We'll figure something out. How are things going with your money?'

Evan sipped his beer and scanned the floor. 'Not good. I'm getting low on my travel fund.' He looked back at Bill. 'But it should be fine. I'll just ask Mum for some more. She's pretty good like that.'

'Oh yeah?' Bill pushed Rambo off the sofa.

'Yeah. I'll just tell her I need some more stuff for my camera. She won't care. Long as she doesn't find out what it's really going on.'

Bill grinned. 'Speaking of – did you bring anything?'

Evan returned the mischievous smile. 'Sure did. Want some now?'

'We can wait 'til later.' Bill took another gulp of his beer. 'We've got all night, remember?'

Evan leaned back and beamed. He couldn't lie to himself about how happy that made him feel. 'I brought my laptop. Got heaps of films we can watch, too.'

'Awesome. So, you must be getting excited about your trip?' Bill said out of nowhere.

Evan shrugged and swigged his beer. 'I guess. I mean, I was. Not so much now.'

Bill cocked his head to the side. 'Why not?'

Evan shrugged. 'I dunno. It's weird. A while back, when I was planning this trip, there was nothing I wanted more than to get the hell out of Taonga and as far away as possible. I don't feel like that so much now. Something's changed.'

Bill drained the last of his beer in one. 'What?'

Evan paused for a moment, realising he was being too vocal. He decided it was time to change the subject. 'Hey, can I take a picture of Rambo? With my proper camera, I mean.'

Bill laughed. 'Sure. He's not exactly a model dog though.'

Evan whipped his camera from his bag and began adjusting the settings. 'Beauty's in the eye of the beholder, my friend.' He dropped to his knees and started clicking the camera. Slumped on the floorboards, Rambo looked away with disinterest. 'I'm trying to build up my portfolio anyway. Get a bit of variety.'

'Oh yeah? Want a picture of me?'

Evan felt a flourish of butterflies. 'Really?'

Bill shrugged. 'Sure.'

Evan thought for a few moments, finishing his beer, then spoke without thinking. 'Okay. Take off your shirt.'

'What?'

'For the picture. Take off your shirt. Unless you want that beer stain in the photo.'

'Are you queer or something?' Bill's tone had changed.

'What? No. Sorry, don't worry. Forget it.'

Bill looked at him hard for a few moments. 'Nah, it's cool really. I'm just playing. You're the artist, not me. I'm just a dumb mechanic, eh?' He pulled off his t-shirt, revealing a toned physique. His smooth skin interrupted only by a neat, pink scar on his stomach. 'Keep my face out of it though. I don't want anyone getting the wrong idea.'

'Okay, sure.' Evan bit his bottom lip as he looked Bill up and down. 'You're not dumb. It takes skill to be a mechanic. Not sure I'd be any good.'

Bill beamed. 'You'll pick it up, don't worry.' A tiny pause. 'What d'you want me to do?'

'Here, stand up. Keep your back straight.' Evan knelt down and angled his camera so that the light reflected off Bill's scar. There was something beautiful about it. He took a shot, reviewed it on the camera's screen and readjusted the settings.

'All good?' Bill said.

'Perfect, thanks.' Evan clicked the camera once more.

'Okay, that's enough. Your turn.'

Evan's face creased with confusion. 'What do you mean?'

'Take your hoodie off. I'm gonna take your photo now.'

Evan froze for a moment, unsure whether to follow the order.

'Come on then,' Bill said. 'We haven't got all day.'

Evan handed him the camera and pulled off his hoodie.

'And your shirt,' Bill said. 'Not fair if you get to keep yours on.'

Evan removed his t-shirt and dropped it to the sofa.

Bill studied his torso for a long moment before taking a full profile shot. 'There we are. Your first self-portrait.'

Evan smiled, deciding not to correct his misunderstanding of the term.

Bill placed the camera on the sofa and paced slowly over to Evan. 'Sorry.'

'For what?'

'For calling you queer.'

Evan's eyes fixed firmly with Bill's. 'That's all right. I don't care.'

Bill stepped closer, so their exposed chests were inches apart. 'So, are you? Into guys, I mean.'

Evan kept still, his heart pounding in his chest. He wanted to lie, tell him no. But somehow he couldn't bring himself to. 'I guess.'

Bill leaned in further still, so their faces were adjacent. 'That's cool.'

Evan wasn't sure who kissed who first.

Chapter Fourteen

'Parasites.' Gary shook his head as he rolled the Range Rover around the corner.

A news van that had been parked outside Lana's family home was now situated opposite the church. Close enough to get a good view, but far enough to demonstrate their supposed respect for the family. The familiar blonde reporter and her camera-shouldering sidekick lurked close to where guests had begun funnelling inside. Her desire to get good vision evidently skewed her moral compass. A couple of other journalists showed a slither more consideration by staying further back.

'As if today won't be hard enough,' Gary continued as he managed to claim one of the few parking spots outside the church. Black cars were pulling up, oversized and overpriced. The first defining characteristic of any Wiley event.

Brooke turned her focus to her mother, who rode shotgun. After insisting she'd needed to buy something to wear, Brooke had found the simple Versace dress her mum now donned among an array of black styles in her walk-in. She knew how her mum's mind worked. When she was upset, she spent. This time, Brooke hadn't allowed her to indulge in her habit. Barbara's eyes were hidden by her thick-rimmed sunglasses, but Brooke could tell by her clenched jaw she was barely holding it together. Brooke knew exactly what was running through her mum's mind. The same thing was going through her own.

Gary switched off the engine and shifted around to face his wife. His black suit was a different cut to his usual business options. He squeezed Barbara's hand and gave Brooke a look. 'It's going to be okay.'

Brooke managed a fragile smile. It wasn't the first time Gary had been the backbone of the family, and it wasn't lost on her.

It was a dry day, with a brilliant blue sky, but the cold cut directly into the marrow of Brooke's bones as she climbed out the Range Rover. She gave a cursory glance at her reflection in the tinted window. Her hair hung just the way it always did, but her cheeks looked a touch more angular. Her dress wasn't as stylish as her mother's, but it did the job. Hopefully it wasn't something she'd need to wear again for a very long time.

Brooke kept her head down as they strode quickly past the reporters, but the eager blonde couldn't resist her chances.

'Ms Palmer, how are you feeling on this sad day?' The journalist was also dressed in black, as if she'd been invited to the service.

Gary turned his head to face her with a craggy brow. 'How do you think we're feeling?'

Barbara tugged on his lapel. She didn't want them to twist

his words into clickbait for the gullible.

As they approached the church, Brooke noticed it wore a crown of construction. Barbara had given her the heads up that a huge refurbishment project was in its final stages. She'd rolled her eyes at the thought of it being so close to completion on the important day. Not that it mattered to anyone now, as Brooke led the way up the grey stone stairs. She drew a vast breath as they approached the open doors. Amanda was greeting the guests one by one as they entered the building, managing to maintain her hospitable manner. Her bright personality contrasted the dank, flyer-filled vestibule in which she stood. She wore a wide-brimmed hat, large sunglasses and a demure black dress. She almost looked like a different woman when she wasn't wearing white.

'Brooke.' A cashmere shawl hung from Amanda's outstretched arms. Her usual cross necklace had been upgraded to a dramatic crucifix, its silver Jesus dug into Brooke's chest as she squeezed her tight. After a long moment, she released and lowered her sunglasses a fraction, offering direct eye contact. 'Lana's at the front with Frank. She needs you.'

Brooke gave an aware nod and continued through the church. Amanda greeted Barbara and Gary with a sob she'd obviously been suppressing. Brooke wondered whether Lana had found the right moment to inform her parents about Evan's sexuality and how it might be connected to the case. This morning wasn't the time to ask.

It might have been a bright winter's day outside, but inside, the church was as dark as a womb. What little natural light that entered the nave was heavily tinted by the saints stained on the building's few arched windows. Brooke clocked Lana standing beside a dark-suited Frank, both humouring their guests with a brave face as they offered their condolences. Behind the father and daughter and beneath a spectacular floral display, the priest readied himself for the service. His pulpit stood uncomfortably more modern than its surroundings, his eulogy for Evan taking up less than half a printed sheet of A4.

Brooke strode towards Lana, her anguish intensifying with every step. Her friend's wild curls were tamed in a small bun, and her formal black dress marked the first time Brooke had seen her in anything but sweats or activewear since she'd arrived. By the time Lana met her gaze, both women crumbled. They held each other firmly, their bodies stuttering from the tears.

Once everyone had taken their seats, it dawned on Brooke just how small the extended Wiley family was. They were dwarfed by the modest church despite sitting in their entirety. She wondered how many family members on Amanda's side had made the long flight over from England. Someone who had was Deborah, Amanda's sister, who she'd always been close to. No doubt she would have been Amanda's pillar of strength on the other end of many tearful phone calls when the time zone permitted. Brooke beamed at her sheepishly across the church to which she returned a meek smile, dabbing her already-drenched eyes with a white handkerchief.

'It all feels a bit hypocritical, doesn't it?' Lana whispered, her brave face back.

'What do you mean?' Brooke kept her eyes on the crowd.

'Just how everyone shows up when you lose someone.

Would've been nice if some of them had made the effort when Ev was alive.'

Brooke knew what Lana meant, but she didn't want to fan the flames. Instead, she kept quiet.

'Did you see the press outside?' Lana said.

Brooke inhaled hard. 'I did. They're more relentless than ever.'

'It's just wrong. I'm going to take legal action, once things calm down.'

Brooke squeezed her friend's hand. 'They'll back off soon. They'll move on to something else.'

'I hope so. Although… I suppose if they do, people will lose interest. There will be less push to find out who did this.'

Brooke remembered feeling the same conflict when they were searching for Jack's killer. How they would have done anything to prevent the case from turning cold. She gave Lana's hand another gentle squeeze. 'Don't worry. We'll find out.'

The heavy mid-brown doors creaked as they opened after having not long been closed. A self-conscious Mick slipped through, wearing a creased black shirt that was two sizes too big and his signature ripped jeans. He caught Brooke's eye but didn't return her half-smile. Nevertheless, she was glad he came. He took a seat on the back row, mirroring Bill's position who sat alone in a far corner. Brooke wondered whether they were speaking, in light of everything that had transpired.

Bill's eyes had been downcast since he'd arrived, leaving Brooke unable to read into their gaze. Unable to decipher any meaning behind them. The house search would be happening now if the message Brooke had received from Collins earlier this morning was anything to go by. Did Bill even know a team of police officers were trawling through his belongings as he sat there, staring at the floor? If he did, it said something about his character that he'd still decided to come to the funeral. What that was exactly, Brooke wasn't sure.

Bill rubbed the powder from his nostril and inched closer to Evan. It was the third weekend in a row that his dad had been away in Greymouth, and Evan knew what was coming. As Bill pulled the condom from his back pocket, Evan's mouth went to ask. But he couldn't. As much as he needed to know, now wasn't the time to put a label on their relationship.

Evan leaned back as his hips allowed Bill to unbuckle and release his jeans. Something about his solid touch made him feel safe. And excited. He could see Bill was, too.

Soon, any concerns that Evan had about the status of their relationship were gone. He was ready to be fully his.

And he'd never felt more alive.

A forlorn Santiago sat a few rows in front of Bill. He wore an expensive-looking suit with a purple handkerchief folded neatly in his jacket pocket, adding a dash of creative flair. Beside him, was the man Brooke recognised to be Taonga High's reigning principal. He looked exactly as he did in his school portrait, down to the brown tie. The only difference was a few additional frown lines. Unsurprising, really. With Evan's killer still on the loose, the last thing he needed was one of his current pupils winding up in a body bag.

Amanda paced down the aisle, offering a small wave to selected guests.

'Shall we sit down?' Lana asked rhetorically, eager to get the service going.

As they took their seat, Brooke panned the half-empty room one last time. No one else Evan's age was there, aside from the odd cousin Brooke recognised from past Christmases, including the one just gone. Taonga's sole catholic church was as eerie as she remembered. The small fortune they'd spent on fresh flowers did little to lessen the dread deep in her stomach. As she slid closer to her friend, the wooden pews were just as creaky as the last time she'd sat on them. Which, as she wrapped an arm around Lana, she realised was Jack's funeral.

Her brother's service resurfaced in her mind. Although there had been more guests, mostly because of Brooke's bigger family, it was definitely more understated. Things had been different then. There had been media interest, but only domestic at the time. The New Zealand press thankfully avoided the funeral. It wasn't until the court case began that they transformed into ravenous vultures.

As the priest lifted his head from the few pages he shuffled, it occurred to Brooke that he was the same man who had conducted Jack's service. Father Arnold Peters. Her family had started going to church quite often upon moving to Taonga, mostly after Barbara and Amanda became friends. Brooke had seen Father Peters many times in those days. She noted how his hair had now grown thin and white, while his skin was pallid. Everything about his appearance spoke of the toll years of conducting funerals had taken.

'We are gathered here today,' he spoke with a dry mouth, 'to celebrate the joyful life of Evan Wiley.'

Tragic. Short. Secretive. Brooke could think of many words Father Peters could have used to describe Evan's life. Joyful definitely wasn't one of them.

Until now, Brooke had resisted fully taking in the sight of Evan's casket, which the family would have had open if it hadn't been for the condition of his body. She'd given it a couple of brief glances from the corner of her eye, but had withheld for as long as possible. Finally surrendering her gaze to the mahogany shell that contained his corpse, her welling eyes traced its elegant design. Draped with a pall and embellished with a bunch of white roses, a large wooden cross and the Bible, Brooke visualised Evan's teenage body enclosed within. What clothing would Lana have picked for him to wear? The mortuary makeup artist would have done their best to return Evan's beaten and broken face to the handsome picture positioned neatly in front of the casket, but it would have been no easy task. It was the same photograph the media had used in all their reports. Possibly the most recent professionally taken picture his family had. The photo was blown up large enough for everyone to see just how young Evan really was before his life was brutally cut short.

The priest proceeded to read out his summary of Evan's life, from excelling in school to building his photography portfolio. Brooke cradled Lana as her whole body jutted. Despite her best efforts to remain strong, nothing could have prepared her for how she'd feel when the service began. Brooke knew that all too well.

Lana turned to whisper in Brooke's ear. 'I don't know how I'm going to make it through my speech.'

Brooke clasped her hand. 'You will. You'll find a way.'

'Will you come up there with me?' Her voice was small.

Brooke looked at her friend's tear-swollen face. 'Of course.'

When the priest finished his eulogy, Brooke assisted Lana up to the altar, her arm draped across her back. From this angle, the floral arrangement looked like a waterfall of flowers with Evan's casket at its base. In any other context, it would have been beautiful.

Looking out at the humbly sized audience, Brooke spotted her mum and Gary. Next to them, was Hannah, Sean and the boys, who were being startlingly well-behaved.

Lana's eyes flitted around the room as she cleared her throat and wiped her eyes with a crumpled tissue. 'I really don't know what to say. I had never imagined having to do something like this. I tried to plan a speech, to honour my incredible, talented, beautiful son, but all I kept thinking was... no parent should have to bury their −' She broke off.

Brooke reached out to hold Lana's hand. She gave it a gentle squeeze. 'You okay? Do you want to stop?'

Lana shook her head and recomposed. 'But... this is the reality. And in time, it's a reality I will have to face. Right now, though, we remember Evan.' She looked to his casket before quickly turning away. 'That beautiful little boy who never stopped smiling. That determined young man who would have no doubt gone on to do amazing things. I−' She bit the words short again. 'I promise, Evan − my perfect son − that I will not give up until justice has been served.' She clutched Brooke's hand. '*We* won't stop.'

Brooke's attention shot to Bill as he shifted in his seat. His usually green eyes were bloodshot red. His face wet from tears. Was she looking at the guilt of a murderer, on the edge of being caught? Or the tears of a boy who accidentally killed his friend? A misstep, perhaps, that his dad helped cover. Or was she looking at the grief of a young man mourning the loss of his lover? A relationship cut tragically short.

Reading a situation was usually a strong suit of Brooke's, but there was something about the enigmatic look in Bill's eye that left her none the wiser. She pictured the police searching through his drawers, flicking through his notebooks. All it took was one shred of evidence to tie him to Evan's death. One simple find could answer the question mark hanging over Bill's head. With Jack's investigation, it had been the note left on the inside cover of a schoolbook that was the nail in the coffin for Harry Saunders. Three simple words that ended up blowing his cover, inciting his confession in court. *Watch your back.* The threat had been signed off by *Hazza*, his moniker of choice.

Once Lana and Brooke returned to their seats, Father Peters read a passage from the Old Testament, followed by Amanda reading a passage from the New. She remained stoic and composed. No matter the situation, she would keep her lips pursed and back straight. Brooke thought of the many times she and Lana had returned home from school, upset by their bullies. She'd stay sharp and say: 'It's important you come across these life challenges. You mustn't hide from them, just because you're privileged. Life is a journey that God has mapped out for you.'

Amanda returned to her spot next to Lana. Father Peters then sprinkled the casket with holy water and incensed it. After a farewell hymn was sung, the guests followed the casket outside into the bitter air. As she walked alongside Lana, their arms hooked, Brooke found herself wondering about Evan's relationship with religion again. How Lana had told her he'd been concerned he would go to Hell. The thought made her shiver even more than the winter chill.

Father Peters led the group towards a frosty graveside, and Brooke's eyes wandered down the deep hole. The bleak finality of the open grave made her stomach drop. The priest read a verse of scripture and spoke some further prayers, before the tearful gathering recited the Lord's Prayer. Father Peters delivered a final blessing, and the rite ended with a hymn as Evan's casket was lowered into the ground. Although Brooke knew the words, she couldn't sing. She couldn't even think. She just stood, frozen, with one question permeating her brain.

Who would do this to him?

Chapter Fifteen

Amanda poured a generous glug of vodka into two tumblers. Her wide sunglasses remained perched on her narrow nose, despite being inside. 'Soda water?' The arch of a raised eyebrow was just visible as she dropped in a couple of ice cubes.

'Please,' Brooke said as she watched the late-morning sun refract through the cut crystal in a dizzying display of rainbow-coloured light. She placed a palm on Lana's knee, who looked exhausted from a long morning of emotion and forced interaction. Her eyes were still red from crying, but her skin had a touch more colour. Brooke recognised that feeling of relief to have made it through the funeral.

Barbara topped up one of the tumblers with fizz and handed it to Brooke.

'I'll take mine neat,' Lana said unspurred, her voice thick.

Amanda shot Brooke a look of surprise, barely visible

through the black lenses. It would be Lana's first drink since Evan was found. 'Oh, of course.' Amanda pulled another glass from the lower shelf of the gold drinks trolley. It rattled slightly as she balanced a few fingers on its handle. 'Coming right up.' Another heavy pour spilled into the tumbler.

Lana reached for the drink, her arm quivering under its weight. Brooke swallowed her reaction to her friend's thinness, which was much more noticeable now it wasn't hidden beneath a slouchy knit.

Amanda lifted her drink. 'To Evan.'

The glasses gave a solid chime as they clashed. 'To Evan,' the women echoed.

Amanda removed her sunglasses, blinking to readjust her vision to the room which was now filled with the hum of small talk. She canvassed the room. 'I'd better do the rounds.' Clutching her heavy tumbler like a shield – a waxy lipstick mark smudged on its rim in deep red – Amanda slipped into the crowd of family and friends, ushering Frank to prepare their drinks.

Brooke took a sip of hers, its potency burning her throat. She'd needed that.

'I guess this is it then,' Lana said, looking at no one in particular. She swallowed a large mouthful of pure vodka.

Brooke shifted in an unsuccessful attempt to regain eye contact. 'What do you mean?'

Lana's mouth was tight as her eyes skipped from one guest to the next. 'Everyone will drink and eat up, toast my son, then go home and carry on with their lives.' She took another mouthful. 'But not me. I won't be able to just carry on.'

Brooke leaned in and rubbed Lana's arm. 'I know. Of course everyone is heartbroken, but no one will carry this the way you will. But I'll be here for you. Every step of the way. You know that, don't you?'

Lana finished her drink with an effortless gulp and looked at her with mournful eyes. 'I know. It's just hard, you being so far away. Of course you know I'm happy for you. That things have gone so well for you up there. But I still miss you. I miss this.' She put down the glass with a hollow clink before placing her hand atop Brooke's.

An air of guilt blanketed Brooke. Lana had always been incredibly supportive of her decision to move to Auckland, but deep down, she knew their friendship had never been quite the same since. Why would it have? Life had changed. They'd become adults, Lana a mother and Brooke a detective. A career that took over every waking minute. Their once-strong sisterhood had slowly become distant. Daily phone calls became weekly, now they'd be lucky to catch up every other month. That was until now. Funny how death brings people together, Brooke thought.

'I miss this, too,' Brooke said. 'But we will always have it, okay? No matter where we both are in the world. And right now, I'm here. And I'm determined to get to the bottom of who did this to Ev.' She locked onto Lana's eyes. 'In fact, I promise you now, I won't go back to Auckland until I figure it out.' She regretted her words as soon as she'd spoken them. It must have been the vodka talking.

Lana's face gave way to a feeble smile. 'You don't need to make that promise. But I know I have your support. And it means everything to me.' She stood up to unscrew the vodka. 'Another?'

Brooke looked down at her glass which remained mostly full. 'Sure. Why not?' She took a large swig.

Lana had already poured her own and handed Brooke the bottle. 'How's the investigation going anyway? Detective Collins seems pretty on to it.'

'Yeah, he's good. A quick thinker.' Brooke avoided Lana's question. It wasn't the time to get into it.

Lana took a sip, still standing by the trolley. 'That's good I suppose. I need to catch up with him actually. Get an update.'

'That's a good idea.' Brooke noticed Amanda was now speaking to Father Peters. It was no surprise he'd joined them for the wake. He'd long been close to the Wileys. A thought occurred to her. 'Lan, you know that thing you told me about Evan… about him worrying he might go to Hell?'

'Yeah?'

'I was wondering, do you think he ever spoke with Father Peters? Maybe he confided in him.'

Lana looked over at the priest. 'Not to my knowledge.'

Brooke held her gaze on Father Peters for a few more beats, making a mental note to pay him a visit soon. She turned her eyes back to Amanda and paused, unsure whether to ask Lana her next question. The vodka prompted her along. 'Did you manage to speak to your parents about Evan? About his sexuality?'

Lana searched her friend's eyes, which had finally reconnected with hers. 'I did, yeah. It wasn't easy. It would've been challenging even before – you know – we lost him. But something about telling them without him being here… it just felt wrong. Like, it wasn't my secret to tell.'

Brooke gave a reassuring nod. 'I'm sure Evan would be very comfortable with you talking with them about it.'

Lana sipped her drink. 'They took it surprisingly well actually. They were very accepting.'

Brooke watched Lana's upper lip stiffen as she distanced her focus. 'That's good to hear. Perhaps they're more progressive than we give them credit for.'

Lana gave her a look that said she wasn't so sure. 'Not much they could say about it now anyway. I think they're more concerned with how this could be related to his murder.'

There was a chilling silence. Brooke wasn't sure whether to say anything more on the subject. She decided to follow her friend's lead.

'Course, that's not completely clear to us either, is it?' Lana waited for an answer.

Brooke shook her head. 'No. Sadly not. But hopefully we'll know more very soon.'

'I'm surprised those boys came this morning. Neither of them said a word to me. They probably wouldn't have known what to say.'

Brooke gave a small nod. She wasn't sure what to say herself right now.

'And his teacher,' Lana continued. 'Santiago. You went and spoke to him the other day, didn't you? How did that go?'

Another sip. 'We did, yes. I'm still unsure what I think about him.'

Lana stood in silence for a few moments, deep in thought.

After a final swallow of her vodka, she straightened her stance. 'Hey, I better mingle a little bit. There's a lot of people I haven't even said hi to yet.'

Brooke offered a gentle nod. 'You go. I'll go see Mum.'

As Lana disappeared into a small cluster of Wileys, Brooke looked around the room. She only realised she was biting her nails when she caught the gaze of Lana's Auntie Deborah. She was sitting with her mum and Gary.

'Brooke!' Deborah's hair was a neat chignon of dull blonde and grey, remnants of her youth fading. Her eyes were shadowed in thick plum with the rest of her face smoother than it should have been. Even though she was younger than Amanda, she was already doing all that she could to resist the reality of ageing.

Brooke planted a kiss on each of her cheeks, which were stained with mascara. She pointed to an empty seat to her right. 'May I?'

'Please do,' Deborah said, patting the chair with a big smile. 'I would say it's reserved for my husband, but we'd both know I'd be lying, wouldn't we?' Deborah had been divorced from Lana's uncle for about five years now, which was possibly the last time Brooke had seen her. He'd been having an affair with a woman at least twenty years younger. Not that Deborah had overly minded. The passion had faded from their marriage long before, so if anything, it was the perfect excuse to move on. She was the one with the money, so she made sure he walked away without a penny. 'And how are you coping?'

Brooke looked down at her drink. 'It's rough. Not as rough as it's been for all of you, though.'

Deborah wiped the black tears from her cheeks. 'It's awful for us all. But it means everything to Lana that you're here.' Her lamenting eyes searched for her niece. 'I don't know how she's coping. Amanda's tried to get her to see someone, but I think you just need to give it time. Lana would know better than anyone how grief works.'

Brooke traced her eyes across the room to see if she could see her friend, but she couldn't. She was certain that no psychology degree or years of listening to people talk about lost loved ones could have prepared her for the pain of losing her son like this. 'She's a strong woman.'

Deborah took a swig of her red wine, the hand that cupped the glass noticeably older than her face. 'Of course she is. She takes after her mother.' She gave a quick wink. 'And auntie.' She took another sip. 'Course, in some ways it's hardly surprising that something like this happened.' Her voice became a whisper. 'Considering how he'd turned out.'

Brooke's eyebrows furrowed as she checked her blind spots to ensure no one was listening. Her mum and Gary were speaking with someone she didn't recognise. She turned back to Deborah. 'What do you mean?' She feigned naivety, assuming she was talking about Evan's sexuality. Lana had been right when she'd said her mum had taken the news well if she'd already gossiped about it with her equally-as-conservative sister.

'Well, Evan had been acting strange for months. That's what Amanda said. None of them knew what had gotten into him.'

'I've heard he was acting a bit... out of character.' Brooke took no chance to posthumously out Evan to his great aunt, just in case she was talking about something else.

Deborah nodded and reached across to grab a muffin off the coffee table. 'He'd been hanging around with the town riff-raff.' She recoiled at the thought. 'I'm sure you've heard all about that already. He spent his savings. Racked up credit card debt. It's no wonder Lana cut off his allowance in the end.' She took a bite of the muffin and washed it down with another glug of wine.

Brooke shifted her eyes across the room again. Perhaps Amanda *hadn't* been accepting enough of her grandson's secret to pass the news on to her sister. 'I didn't know that. Do you know how long ago that happened?'

'Oh dear, me and my big mouth.' Deborah picked at the muffin. Crumbs spilled onto her lap as she tucked into another mouthful. 'I really shouldn't be gossiping. It must be the jet lag. Either that or I've had too much wine already. It's gone straight to my head. I don't drink very much these days.'

Brooke knew that was a lie. 'No, it's good. I appreciate you telling me what you know.'

Deborah's eyes narrowed into slits. 'My money's on one of those boys. The ones that were at the service. I'm not sure which, but it makes the most sense. Maybe even both. I take it you heard about their… habit?' Her voice was a whisper again.

Brooke replied with her eyes and kept quiet.

'I don't think Lana was aware that was where the money was going at first,' Deborah went on. 'But once she found out, she wasn't going to let him continue wasting it.'

'You can't blame her,' Brooke said beneath her breath. She could tell a part of Deborah was getting a thrill from this exchange.

'Not at all. See, people might look at us from the outside, and think we don't need to worry.' She brushed the crumbs from her lap. 'But if we weren't careful, we wouldn't have what we have.' Her wink wasn't so quick this time.

Brooke nodded but had stopped listening. All she could think about was the CCTV footage from the dairy. It replayed in her mind as if it was stuck on repeat. How Evan had seemed in such a hurry. Almost… desperate.

'It's no wonder they got into that huge fight,' Deborah said. 'Poor girl, the last time she would have seen him.'

Brooke had tuned back in now. 'Wait. What did you just say?'

Deborah's eyes flexed. 'Okay, now I know I've said too much.' She swallowed the last of her muffin and took a sip from her glass. A few crumbs were now swimming in the wine. 'You should probably talk to Lana about all this. When the time's right, of course.'

Brooke nodded, her eyes fixed on a picture of Evan hanging on the wall. His innocent eyes hiding so much. Secrets that were yet to be uncovered. 'Believe me, I will.'

In the photo's reflection, she saw Lana finishing off another drink. How could she not have told her? Something as big as that. An argument between her and Evan on the day he was killed. Brooke suddenly felt completely alone. Somehow surrounded by strangers in her best friend's family home.

With her eyes still fixed on the picture of Evan, Brooke heard a short vibration muffled by the black leather clutch she'd borrowed from Amanda. She unclipped the metallic monogram and slid out her phone. A message from Collins. *Hope the service went well. We searched the Henderson house. Found Evan's laptop. Call me when you're ready.*

Brooke's heart sank to her gut.

Chapter Sixteen

The wake had dwindled to just a few remaining guests. Deborah, who was staying at the Wileys', had called it a night and made her way upstairs. Her heels were discarded on the first step, mitigating the risk of a drunken tumble. Barbara and Gary had left an hour or so ago, while Brooke had decided to stay to support Lana and help Amanda clear up. As she collected side plates and empty flutes, Brooke couldn't stop thinking about the message. *We searched the Henderson house.* A vision of Bill in the back pew. *Found Evan's laptop.* His face swollen and drained of tears.

'Thanks for today,' Amanda said, giving Brooke's arm a small squeeze. 'Lana couldn't have done it without you. None of us could.'

Brooke summoned a tired smile. 'I'm just glad it's over. Well… you know what I mean.'

Amanda curled Brooke's hair behind her ear. 'I do. You

must ensure you get enough rest, too. I know you're helping Detective Collins with the case – which we all greatly appreciate – but don't forget to take care of yourself. This will be opening up so many old wounds.'

Brooke thought to mention Collins' message, but withheld. She didn't want to generate false hope. The day had been long enough. Besides, what they'd found couldn't have been enough to warrant an arrest. If it had, Collins would have said. She glanced outside at the now pitch-black sky. 'I better get going.'

Amanda gave a nod and inspected the room. 'Yes. I don't know where Lana is. Probably gone to lie down.'

'I'm not surprised. I'll catch up with her tomorrow if she's up to it. Give her a kiss goodnight from me, won't you?'

Amanda reached out for a final embrace. 'Of course. Let me call you a taxi.'

Stepping out into the cold air, Brooke took her phone from her clutch and called Collins. She gazed at the stars. She'd forgotten how much more visible they were than in Auckland on a clear evening like this. Just as he answered, the taxi pulled up.

'Palmer. How'd it go?'

'Yeah, it was a nice service. One sec, I'm just jumping in a taxi.' She climbed into the back seat, holding her phone to her chest to tell the driver her address before continuing. 'Hey. Very sad, of course. But beautiful. It was the send-off he deserved.'

'I'm sure it would've been.'

Brooke thought about Lana, and the secrets she'd still kept. The allowance. The argument. She broke a short silence. 'There were a couple of developments.'

'Always the way,' Collins said. 'At the wake. Drinks start

flowing, relatives start gossiping.'

'Bingo,' Brooke said, borrowing Collins' word. She clocked the driver's eyes in the rear-view mirror. Now wasn't the time to elaborate.

'Fancy going for a drink to debrief?' Collins read Brooke's mind. 'I can tell you about the search.'

'Sounds good. Where do you want to go?'

'You're the local. Don't you have any favourite haunts?'

Brooke glanced at the driver, who had sensed the change of plans and slowed down. 'To be honest, I don't think I've ever even set foot in a Taonga pub.'

'Well, I've got one I go to. Meet me at the Taonga Arms.'

Brooke laughed. That place was an institution. 'Of course. See you there in five.'

Evan clicked the Wi-Fi icon as he perched on the edge of the bed. 'What's your internet password?'

Bill didn't respond. Instead, he leaned back with his hands clasped behind his head.

'That's okay,' Evan said. 'I can hotspot.'

'Put that down.' Bill clicked his tongue. 'Get over here.'

Evan paused before he found his words. 'Don't you wanna watch a movie?'

'Not really. I'd rather watch you.'

Evan couldn't help but smile as he shut his laptop. 'Isn't your dad here?'

'I think he's down the pub.'

Evan looked to the door. 'Shall I check?'

'Nah, we can be quiet.' Bill's eyes scanned Evan, his lids heavy and

lower lip bitten.

It wasn't that Evan didn't want to. He couldn't get enough of being close to Bill like that. But when would they get close in other ways?

When would it be Bill's turn to let Evan in?

Brooke tipped the driver for messing him around and climbed out of the taxi. She fixed her eyes on Taonga's oldest pub, its stony exterior nodding to the gold rush era. She pushed the heavy door open and felt the warmth wrap around her like a glove. It didn't take long to spot Collins. He'd picked the prime position of a stool at the bar, swilling the last half of a beer.

Brooke smiled as she ambled towards him. 'Where's my drink then?'

Collins gave her a scan up and down. 'I'm a detective, not a mind reader.' He took a large swig. 'You look nice.'

The barman made his way to the pair, mopping the counter as he did. 'What can I get for you?' His eyes switched between them.

'I'll have another, Terry.' Collins drained his dregs before turning to Brooke. 'And what would you like?'

'Pinot noir, thank you.' Brooke looked around at the pub's punters, anticipating a few familiar faces from school. She recognised a handful.

Terry passed Brooke her wine. 'There you go. Come from the funeral?'

She gave a small nod and took a sip. The effects of the vodka had started to wear off, so she welcomed the top-up. 'It's been a tough day.'

Terry shook his head. 'I bet. Just awful.' He fixed his eyes on

Collins. 'Hope you catch the bastard soon.' He shifted his gaze back to Brooke. 'This one's on the house.'

'Thank you,' she said with a smile.

'Thanks,' Collins repeated.

Terry gave him a friendly glare. 'Not yours, mate.' He turned away to serve another punter.

'So, you've really never been in here before?' Collins lifted his brow.

Brooke took another sip. 'Nope. Why would I? When I said Lana and I were hated in this town, I meant it.'

'Bah, you were kids.' He waved his hand dismissively. 'I thought maybe you'd have come since. On one of your trips home perhaps.'

Brooke eyed her surroundings in more detail as she made herself comfortable on the stool beside him. The scarlet wallpaper was intricately patterned, with reproduction paintings displayed in cheap gold frames. The ceiling was stained a sticky yellow, exacerbated by warm sconces dotted around the room. She looked from one punter to the next, now spending time to take them in. Her gaze fixed on the man she'd heard found Evan's body. Brooke remembered him from when she was a young girl. He'd practically lived in the pub, from what her mum had told her. Unhappy marriage. After the mine closed down, he and many other men just about moved into the Taonga Arms. He gave her a polite nod and shifted his eyes away.

Collins sipped his fresh beer. 'You must've been so happy to get to Auckland. Leave all this behind.'

Brooke nodded, taking a slightly bigger mouthful of wine. 'I was. But it's funny how quickly you get caught up in the rat race. Grass is always greener, I guess.'

Collins took another sip. 'Sure is.'

There was a beat of silence. Brooke shifted around and levelled her eyes to his. 'So… the search?'

'Right, yes. As you know, we searched the place when Bill was at the funeral. Craig was there, didn't take his eyes off us as we went through every room in the house. We spotted the laptop straight away, which matched the description of Evan's. It was in plain sight, on a chest of drawers. I had the officers search for the other items. The camera, the backpack, his phone. But after two and a half hours we'd still found nothing.'

Brooke looked in his eyes. She saw vanquish.

'By the time we'd wrapped up,' Collins went on, 'Bill came walking through the door.'

'What did he say when you asked him about the laptop?'

'Claims Evan lent it to him to watch movies on. I gave him some grief about why he'd kept it. Said he should have told us about it, but he just said he wasn't thinking. Says he's had it for ages, so he didn't think it was a big deal. He didn't seem to realise how bad it looked.'

Brooke thought back to Bill's red, wet eyes in the church. 'Or he was past caring. He was pretty cut up at the funeral.'

Collins nodded. 'I've sent the laptop to forensics to see if it'd been used by Evan recently, otherwise it sounds like the kid's telling the truth.' Collins took a swig, knocking his glass down in defeat. 'About the laptop at least.' He wasn't giving up all hope.

Brooke couldn't decide if it was just the case bothering him. 'How are things going with your daughter?'

Collins chewed his bottom lip lightly. 'Nothing new. I'll be going back up there on Sunday. Spend a bit more time with her before the hearing on Monday. We should get the verdict then, all going well.'

Brooke managed a small smile. 'I'll have my fingers crossed for you.'

Collins threw back a large glug of beer. 'Thanks. Think I'll need it.'

Brooke tucked her hair behind her ears and took a sip of wine. 'So, you live alone in Christchurch?' She hoped her question wasn't intrusive.

'Yep. Haven't met anyone since the divorce. Haven't really wanted to either. I always seem to mess it up.'

Brooke wasn't sure how to respond to that, so she kept quiet.

'What about you? Anyone special waiting for you in Auckland?'

A roar erupted from the corner of the room. Someone had either won or lost big on the pokies. It was hard to tell.

'Nah, it's just me right now. Has been for a while, to be honest. I was in a relationship for a long time. He was a guy from Tauranga. Suffered badly from depression. I think the fact that I couldn't have kids didn't help things.' Brooke's eyes grew foggy.

'I'm sorry to hear that.' Collins' mouth formed a thin line.

Brooke had surprised herself by being so open. She was certain now it was the combination of vodka and wine. 'It's okay. Sorry, I don't know why I'm telling you all this.'

'I asked, didn't I?' Collins passed a napkin from the bar. 'But we can change the subject if you like.'

Brooke gently wiped each eye. 'No, it's okay. I mean, I

always felt bad I couldn't give him the one thing he seemed to really want. But I always knew we wouldn't stay together. I don't think I ever loved him.'

'Yeah, it's a weird thing, right? You think you're in love at the time, then you look back in retrospect—' Collins cut himself off.

'Exactly. I've always had a hard time letting men into my life. I think it's ever since my dad walked out on us.' Now Brooke knew she'd been too vocal. Collins went to say something, but she abruptly changed the subject. 'I just realised I haven't even told you what I found out at the wake.' She took back another dash of wine.

Collins paused for a beat, as if switching gears in his head. 'You're right. Go on.'

Brooke gave a cursory pan to ensure no one was listening. Terry was on the opposite side of the bar now. 'Well, it was Lana's aunt I got talking to. She told me how Evan was racking up debt and maxing his credit card when he got into the drugs. Nothing new there. But what she also said was that Lana cut off his funds and they got into a big fight the last time she saw him.'

Collins paused, soaking up her words. 'She didn't tell me about a fight.'

'Me neither.' Brooke felt a fraction of guilt for passing this information onto Collins when she hadn't even discussed it with Lana. But at this point, she wasn't sure she could even trust her friend to tell the truth, which was troubling. Was there something she was trying to cover up for Evan?

'We need to know everything,' Collins said flatly. 'Every last little detail.'

Brooke swallowed hard. 'I know. I'll talk to her. I didn't want to today, it wasn't the right time. But I will. Next possible opportunity. I'm sure there's an explanation for her holding that back.'

Collins kept quiet for a pulse and nodded. 'Okay. I'll let you handle that one when I'm back in Christchurch.'

The chatter throughout the pub, which had been growing louder, suddenly went silent. It was clear someone had walked in.

Brooke spun on her barstool for her eyes to be met by Tina Marshall. Her worn face was scrunched into a vexed expression.

'You stupid bitch.' Tina spat as she spoke.

'Enough of that,' Collins said. 'We're just here to have a quiet drink, minding our own business.'

'Mindin' your own business is the last thing either of you do.' Her steely tone was saturated with malice.

Brooke pivoted around to look at Terry but realised he was still talking with a punter on the other side of the bar, none the wiser to Tina's arrival.

'I know you met with my son again,' Tina continued. 'I knew somethin' was up with him that night. I got it outta him.'

'He came to us,' Brooke said with a cool tone. 'He was very helpful, which is more than we can say for yourself.' She couldn't help herself, but regretted the words as soon as she parted with them.

'How dare you?' Tina stalked forward and pointed her finger. 'Showin' up back in this town, determined to ruin my life. First, you accuse my man of somethin' he never did, now you're accusin' my son.'

Collins stood up as if to defend Brooke from being knocked to the floor. 'That's enough, Tina. You seem to be forgetting you're speaking with two cops.'

'Oh, big deal. And *some* cops you are, sittin' in here gettin' pissed when you should be out there figurin' out who did this.' Her mouth formed a crooked scowl.

A couple of onlookers sniggered from a nearby table.

'Hey, what's all this?' Terry's voice. Brooke sighed relief that he'd finally registered the disruption.

'Nuthin',' Tina said shrilly. 'Just surprised you let these two in here. Especially *her*.' She pointed her finger again. Her crimson nail paint was chipped on the index finger.

'None of that, Tina,' Terry said. 'I don't want any trouble. So you can either get yourself a drink or get out.'

Tina narrowed her eyes and glared at Brooke. 'I don't want to have a drink anywhere near *her*.'

Brooke bit her tongue.

'Okay, that's enough,' Terry said. 'Tina, off you go. If you're not willing to act like an adult, you're not welcome in here.'

Tina's face became flushed. 'Stupid bitch! Why don't you just fuck off back to where you came from?' She launched forward with her fists clenched.

Collins grabbed Tina's arm and twisted it behind her back. 'Do you really want to attack a cop? Want me to arrest you right now?'

'Get off!' Tina twisted her torso with abrupt force, attempting to escape Collins' grip.

'Out!' Terry pointed towards the door.

'All right, all right. I'm goin'.'

Collins released her from his armlock.

As Tina left the pub, she turned back a final time and shot Brooke a loaded glare. 'Stay away from my son.'

Once she was out of sight, Collins revolved to face Brooke. 'You okay?'

'Yeah, I'm fine.' She downed the last drop of her wine. 'Now do you see why I don't come in Taonga pubs?'

Chapter Seventeen

Brooke wasn't sure whether it was the dream that woke her or the wet wind buffeting the window. A visual of the fight was fresh. The last time Lana had seen Evan. Raised voices. Flared nostrils. Venomous words exchanged. The dream had been frighteningly lifelike, but lying awake, the realism was slipping away with every second that passed. It wasn't the Evan she'd known.

Mine and Ev's relationship had become a bit… strained.

Brooke reached for her phone on the bedside table, quickly dimming the screen so as to not blind her in the dark. Six-twenty. Not as early as she'd feared. A message from Lana sat just under the time. It had been sent an hour ago. Turned out she wasn't the only one having trouble sleeping. *Thanks for yesterday. I couldn't have done it without you.*

Brooke tapped a fast reply. *Of course. I'm here for you always.*

She noticed Lana instantly typing back. A new message

came through. *The rain's meant to stop in the next half hour. I want to go to the falls. I think I'm ready. Will you come?*

Brooke knew this was coming. She'd had a similar urge to visit the bridge where Jack was found soon after his funeral. It had felt like the natural next step, and a necessary one to getting some form of closure. Not that anything close to closure was in sight for Lana yet. Not until Evan's killer was found. *Of course. See you soon x*

The rain had already started to ease by the time Brooke entered the kitchen.

'Morning,' Barbara said, peering over the glasses she wore when she didn't have her contacts in. Dressed in a plush pink dressing gown, she leisurely stirred a saucepan over the stove.

'Morning.' Brooke took the stool beside Gary, who was at the breakfast bar browsing the New Zealand Herald. She peered over his shoulder. 'Anything new?'

Gary's reading glasses were resting on his nose until he pushed them back into place. 'There's a small piece on the funeral. Other than that, it just says the investigation's ongoing.'

Barbara shot her daughter a worried glance as she scooped the porridge into three bowls. 'You need to take it easy, Brooke.' She divided a punnet of blueberries. 'Yesterday was a big day for us all. You must be exhausted.'

Brooke shook her head, but the dark rings around her eyes said otherwise.

Gary snapped the paper shut and placed it out of sight. 'Your mother's right, Brooke. This can't be doing you any good.' He took the bowl Barbara passed him. 'You're meant to be on a break. Not working.'

Brooke blew gently on her spoon. 'I'm not here on a break. I'm here to find out who did this.'

'You're here to support your friend,' Barbara said, now turning her attention to the cafetière.

'That too.'

'Thanks, babe,' Gary said as Barbara passed him a coffee. He shifted his focus back to Brooke. 'When are you due to head back to Auckland? They must be missing you at work.'

Brooke folded her features. She hadn't wanted to think about her impending departure. 'A week Monday. But if we haven't figured this out before then, I'm going to request unpaid leave.'

Barbara's face became rigid. 'Are you sure you want to do that? Of course I'd love for you to stay here as long as possible. I'm just wondering if getting back to your routine might be what you need.'

Brooke placed her spoon down and glared at her mother. She felt like a teenager again. Except this time, she actually wanted to be at home. 'I can't imagine going back before figuring this out. Besides, I promised Lana I wouldn't leave until I do.'

Gary and Barbara shared a look of concern. They sipped their coffees in unison.

'I'm fine, guys,' Brooke said in response to her mum and stepdad's not-so-subtle expressions. 'You don't need to worry about me. I'm a grown woman.'

Gary stepped in. 'We can't help but worry, Brooke. This is an incredibly difficult time for us all. Especially for you, Hannah and your mother. But we feel like you're taking on more than you should. Why don't you leave it to the detective assigned to the case and get back to the life you love in Auckland?'

Brooke kept quiet. Her life in Auckland felt further away than ever.

'We understand they're letting you help with the case,' Barbara began, 'but you don't want to do anything to rock the boat.'

'My God, stop being so dramatic,' Brooke said, rising. She'd heard enough.

'Where are you going?' Barbara said. 'You haven't finished your brekkie.'

'I'm not hungry anymore.' Brooke scraped the porridge in the bin and rinsed the bowl in the sink. Now she definitely felt like a teenager. 'I'm heading out. I'll speak to you both later.'

'Where?' Barbara called out.

Brooke paused at the doorway. 'To be there for Lana. Just like you said.' Her expression grew tight. 'I'm not the one you should be worrying about, guys. It's all the kids in this town who are in danger from this bastard striking again.'

She disappeared into the hallway before either her mum or Gary had a chance to reply.

Lana's distant silhouette cut against the pale grey of the sky. She was kicking the ground with her hands pocketed, her hair free for the first time since. Brooke wondered in which direction she'd go emotionally when faced with the site. Brooke's first visit to where Jack was found gave a brief but comforting sense of closeness. Before the heart-pounding anger kicked in. She drew a long breath as she neared, promising herself to remain strong.

'Hey.' She reached out her arms.

'Hey.' Lana returned her embrace with little force.

Brooke could feel a thick sweater beneath her friend's waterproof jacket as she hugged her. She eventually pulled away and looked deep into her eyes. 'How're you doing today?'

'I'm okay,' Lana said in a small voice. 'Nervous.'

Brooke gave a brief nod. 'It'll be okay.'

The two women followed the track wordlessly for a few minutes through the bush. Before long, they could hear the familiar crash of Taonga Falls. What used to be a soothing and majestic sound now filled both women with dread.

Soon, they broke out from the ferns and the waterfall was exposed in full force. A thick white mist sheathed the heavy flow of water battering the rocks. Brooke eyed the foot of the falls and the rocks that surrounded them, trying to identify where Evan's body would have been found.

'What are you thinking about?' Lana said.

'Nothing,' Brooke lied, breathing in the fresh mist. 'It's calming, isn't it?' She hoped her words would somehow direct Lana's emotional response.

'Yeah. If you didn't know, you'd never be able to tell what happened here.'

Brooke nodded her response but remained silent. She didn't want to bring up the fight, but she knew she had to. She just needed to wait for the right moment.

The two women paced along the side of the falls. Brooke with her arm around Lana, consoling her as the tears fell. It was hard to believe not even twenty-four hours ago they'd watched Evan's casket be lowered into the ground. Each of them throwing a thud of dirt as it lay shadowy in its grave. Evan's final resting place. This was the strong Lana that Brooke knew and admired.

After a while, they took a seat on a patch of grass close enough to feel a light spray. There was a long silence except for the pummel of the chute.

'Will this ever get any easier?' Lana placed her fingertips beneath her eyes and smeared away her tears.

Brooke paused, trying to find the right words. The old, psychologist Lana would have known how to answer her own question. But the Lana sitting before her needed reassurance. 'Yes and no. Finding out who's behind this will be an important step to moving forward. You need to remember we're still in the thick of it. It's hard to move on with unanswered questions. But once you have some sense of closure, there will be moments of joy. Happiness. But…' Brooke paused. '…they will always be mixed with other emotions.'

The wind howled, and the falls answered with their roar. Lana's expression was a blend of understanding and confusion. 'Like what?' She had a timid voice.

Brooke gazed at the water. Her dry lips blistered and sore. 'Well, it might be different for you. And I hope it is. But for me, I always feel a sense of guilt when I'm happy. When I laugh. When I forget. Guilt that Jack isn't here to experience that happiness for himself.' A brief pause. 'But mostly I just feel sad. Sad for all he's missed.'

Another silence. So deep this time you could drown in it. Brooke twisted to face Lana, whose tears were silently streaming her cheeks. 'I'm sorry. I shouldn't have said all that.'

'No, I'm glad you did.' She wiped her face with her sleeve. 'I asked. And I'd rather you be honest with me. Best friends don't lie, right?'

The opportunity had presented itself. 'Lana… there's something I need to ask you.'

Lana paused for a beat. 'What is it?'

Brooke took a big breath. 'Yesterday at the wake, I got talking to your aunt.'

'Auntie Deborah?'

Brooke's nod was quick. 'She told me you and Evan had a fight the last time you saw each other.'

The quiet cut like the cold. Lana looked uneasy now. 'Yeah. That's right.'

'Why didn't you tell me?'

Fresh tears lubricated Lana's eyes. 'I don't know, Brooke. I've been trying to block it out.' Her voice was just above a croak. 'Mum's the only person I've told, so she obviously couldn't keep it to herself.' She took a few moments to recompose. 'I guess by saying it out loud makes it feel real. I'll never forgive myself for that fight. It's been playing over and over in my mind ever since he went missing. My first thought when they–' She cut off. 'When they found him… was… you know.'

'That he'd taken his life.'

'Yeah. That's honestly what I thought.'

A blink of breath. 'What was the fight about?'

Lana dropped her eyes. 'Well, it all stemmed from me cutting off his funds. I just had to do something about his spending, Brooke. It had gotten out of hand. I always gave him an allowance, which really I should've weaned him off earlier…

especially when he turned eighteen. He just assured me he was saving for his trip. I should have waited and given it to him in a lump sum once I knew everything was planned.'

Brooke waited to see whether Lana had finished her story. She hadn't.

'That morning, before he left, it was like he was picking a fight. He started bringing up the fact I'd cut his money off again. Said he was serious about taking the trip, but he needed some more cash. I just couldn't…' She gave way to her tears. 'I just couldn't trust him.'

Brooke placed her hand on Lana's arm and gave it a brief rub. 'You can't blame yourself for this. It's not your fault. I just wish you'd told me. Or Detective Collins. It's important for the investigation.' Brooke's tone had grown terse and her face flushed. 'It's not the first time, either. You didn't tell me about him being gay or—'

'Brooke!' Lana cut her off. 'We just buried my son yesterday, and now you're attacking me? This is the first time I've visited the place his dead body was found. I asked you to come here to support me, not interrogate me.'

Realising she'd overstepped the mark, Brooke recoiled. 'I'm sorry. I don't mean to attack you.'

'I know you're a cop, but that doesn't give you the right to grill *me*.' Lana slumped forward. 'And we don't know for certain he was gay.'

The sound of laughter in the distance was carried by the wind.

Brooke bit her lip. Was Lana in denial about Evan's sexuality? Why did it matter so much to her? Had her parents' strict

Catholic beliefs rubbed off on her? Perhaps she'd just been in Taonga for too long.

'Look, I'm sorry.' Lana's voice had softened. 'I know I shouldn't have kept that from you. It was stupid of me. I'll tell Collins today.'

'He already knows.'

Lana nodded. 'Okay. I'm sorry. Of course I want you guys to know everything.'

'So… *is* that everything?'

Lana sunk deeper into her jacket, pulling over her hood as a few raindrops began again to fall. 'It is, yeah. I promise.'

Brooke looked back at the falls. She followed their gush to a large flat rock at the base. That must have been the spot. It matched the photographs she'd seen in Collins' files. She stared at it as she spoke. 'I wonder where he was going. After you had the fight, I mean.'

'I wish I knew. You should have seen him that day. When I told him I wouldn't be giving him more money, he got angry.' Lana levelled her eyes to Brooke, emphasising the last word. She continued, quieter, 'He frightened me.'

Brooke tried to imagine Evan like that, but couldn't. His boyish charm. His contagious laughter. There was nothing frightening about him. At least, there hadn't been. 'I guess that's what happens when you get hooked on something. You lose yourself.'

'Yeah. What I can't work out though is whether he was hooked on the drugs or to the attention he was getting from his new friends.'

Brooke chewed her lip. 'Probably a bit of both.'

Two boys appeared from the mouth of the trail. They couldn't have been much older than fifteen. Running side by side and watching the sky, Brooke realised they were piloting a drone. The futuristic object starkly juxtaposed its natural surroundings. 'Surprised their parents are letting them out on their own right now.'

'It's hard to stop boys being boys,' Lana muttered beneath her breath. A strange look suddenly overcame her face.

'What is it?' Brooke met her friend's gaze.

'Okay, don't shout at me. But I just remembered something else.'

Brooke's expression remained steely. 'Go on.'

'Something he said to me… when we were having that fight. I told him that if he wanted to get the money to take his trip, he'd have to get a job. He then said something like, I've found a way to get what I need.'

Brooke narrowed her eyes and processed the information. Could he have taken a job with the drug dealer, in lieu of paying him back?

'I didn't think much of it,' Lana continued. 'I was so riled up at the time, just talking about it now reminded me. He'd mentioned before something about working with Bill Henderson, but I'm not sure if that's what he meant.'

Brooke's blood dropped a few degrees. She'd forgotten to tell her about the finding. 'Lan, Collins searched Bill's house during the funeral. He had Evan's laptop.'

'What?' Lana's eyes grew wide. 'Collins didn't tell me?'

'I told him I'd speak to you today. But we can't jump to any conclusions yet. That's all they found. It sounds like it could be innocent. It's with the forensics now.'

Lana stared at the falls. Her smile was small, but there. 'It's like finding a piece of him.'

Brooke kept her eyes on her. She knew that feeling. Wanting something, anything to hold on to. For her, it had been Jack's favourite graphic tee. Overworn and threadbare. She'd been surprised her mum had parted with it, but she'd been fair and made sure both daughters got something. She kept it tucked away with a small collection of treasured items in her Auckland apartment.

Lana found Brooke's eyes again. 'If it was Bill, why would he have done this? I don't get it.'

Brooke lowered her gaze and gave a genuine shrug. 'He admitted to liking Evan. But maybe he just didn't like how it made him feel.'

Lana folded her arms and shivered. 'People can be evil.'

The two women exchanged a knowing look as the raindrops grew in frequency. The kids with the drone had now disappeared completely out of sight.

'Shall we make a move?' Lana said with a conclusive note.

'Sure.' Brooke helped her friend to her feet.

The women made their way through the scrub with their arms locked. The pale winter sun had broken through the clouds and painted a golden glow amidst the trees. Weaving their way back to the car park, Lana stopped at a fork in the path.

Brooke gave her a concerned stare. 'You want to go, don't you?'

'I just want to see where it happened. Where he was dropped.'

There was a strange silence. Brooke finally nodded her approval.

The ascent to the top was steep, but the view from the waterfall's crest was always worth it. The pair stared out at the sweeping vistas of the distant ocean. Swirls of mist hovered over the vast fern forest. She doubted Lana could still see the beauty in it.

'How does it feel being here?' Brooke eventually said.

Lana panned their surrounds. 'Not as bad as I thought it would. It's strange. It makes me feel closer to him somehow.'

'It's not strange at all. I totally understand.'

Silence, but for the clicking caw of a tui as it circled the trees.

After a while, Lana pulled her eyes away from the river's tip. 'I think I'm ready to get going,' she said with a sigh.

'Come on then. Let's take the shortcut.'

'There's a shortcut?'

Brooke laughed at Lana's lack of local knowledge as she led her through the clearing in the bush.

They had barely taken a few steps before Brooke spotted it. She crouched to get a closer look, reaching out to pick it up.

'Gross, don't touch that,' Lana said.

Brooke ignored her, narrowing her eyes to read the grey text wrapped around the crumpled cigarette in her hand. *Fortuna.*

'Bingo.'

Chapter Eighteen

Brooke hadn't seen the elderly couple when she forced through the station door. The flannel-clad pair flinched out the way, giving Brooke an up and down.

'I'm so sorry.' Her words came out clipped and breathy.

'Are you okay?' The man repositioned his glasses. 'You can go ahead of us if you like? I'm sure it's more important.'

The woman fired the man a sharp glare. 'And reporting our inconsiderate neighbours isn't?'

'Sorry,' Brooke repeated. She turned to face the woman and beamed politely. 'I hope your neighbours get what's coming to them.'

By the time she reached Collins' office, Brooke's heart was beating double.

Collins pulled his eyes from the paperwork on his desk. 'You all right, Palmer?'

Without saying a word, she reached into her bag and fished

out a tightly bound tissue. She unravelled it with the flair of a magician, dropping the damp cigarette on the desk with a dash of victory.

Collins fixed his eyes on the cigarette, which was flattened, a split running along its side. He then turned them to Brooke. 'Where did you find this?'

'The falls. With Lana. Took the shortcut back to the car. Cops must have missed it.' Her sentences were blunt as she caught her breath.

Collins shook his head with disbelief.

'Unless it's found its way there since,' Brooke offered.

Collins stared at the wrinkled cigarette closely. 'It looks like it's been there a while. The rain we've been having hasn't been kind to it.' He referred to a page in his notebook before continuing. 'But it certainly hasn't been there two years. That's how long Mr Pérez claims it's been since he was last at the falls.' Collins looked to Brooke with a domed eyebrow. 'Surely no one else in this town smokes these.'

'My thoughts exactly.'

He pulled an elastic glove on with a satisfying snap and picked up what was left of the cigarette. 'I'll get it sent off, see if we can pull a print. One sec.'

Brooke tapped the Facebook app on her phone and began typing *Santiago Pérez* into the search bar. She hadn't even reached his surname when his profile appeared at the top of the page. She recognised his smile instantly. Not from their brief encounter, which had been solemn at best, but from the photograph of him standing with Evan, their motionless beams encapsulated for eternity. She visited his profile but gave a groan when she realised she could only see limited information.

Collins reappeared with a bounce in his step. 'All sorted. I've asked for the results to be fast-tracked, so we should have them back within twenty-four hours.'

Brooke proffered her phone. 'Pérez is clearly on top of his privacy settings. Figures, being a teacher.'

'Tried his Insta?'

'Listen to you.' Brooke mock-dropped her jaw and opened the app.

'I'm not that much of a dinosaur,' Collins said in jest and retook his seat. 'Just don't ask me about TicTac or whatever it's called.'

A second or two passed as Brooke absorbed her findings. 'His profile's private on here, too. But looks like he's got an account for his photography which is public.' She scrolled through the first few pictures. On the most recent, she noticed a comment that had been left beneath. *Beautiful babe. This is one of my faves.*

She tapped the profile. A clean-shaven man with a tan and toned physique smiled teeth. She figured he must have been in his early thirties.

'We could go pay him another visit,' Collins said. 'See if our finding spooks him into talking. But let's get a little more on him first, to be sure. He'll be on the database from his visa application, so if the cigarette is his, we'll get a match.'

'Here.' Brooke passed Collins her phone. 'This guy commented on one of his latest photos. Name's Keane Harding. There's heaps of pictures of them together on his feed.'

Collins studied the photos. 'You reckon they're dating?'

'I assume so. Here, pass it back. I'll send him a message. See if he's able to have a chat with us.' Brooke tapped out a direct message and sent it off.

'Good thinking.' Collins relaxed into his chair.

'This morning was tough with Lana,' Brooke said as she returned her phone to her pocket. 'Although I think it did her good.'

'Did you mention anything about what her aunt told you?'

Brooke gave a little nod. 'Yeah. I get it, she felt guilty about the fight and didn't want to accept that it happened. Especially after she first thought that Evan had killed himself.'

'I see.'

'She did mention something else, though. During the argument, Evan told her he'd found a way to get what he needs. Referring to money.'

Collins frowned, absorbing the information. 'And this would've been after he'd asked Santiago. You reckon he'd found a job?'

Brooke gave a short nod. 'That's what I figured. Evan had mentioned he might be able to get some work with Bill and his dad, on the cars.'

Collins stroked his stubble. 'They didn't mention anything.' A pause. He picked up a pen and made a note. 'More likely it's connected to the dealer, no? Perhaps he'd made a deal to wipe off his debt.'

Brooke bit her lip. 'I thought the same.'

'Okay. It's good we have this information. But Lana needs to start being more open with us. You reckon that's really all she knows now?'

'I do this time. I knew there was more before, I know Lana well enough. This time felt different.' Brooke's phone vibrated. She reached it out. A reply from Keane Harding on Instagram. 'Wow, that was quick.'

'What did he say?'

Brooke read the message aloud. 'Hey, Brooke. Yeah, I dated Santi. We just broke up. I'm living in Christchurch now. I can meet you on my lunch break? There's quite a lot I could tell you about this guy.'

The detectives exchanged a firm glance.

'Come on,' Collins said, checking his watch. 'Let's get on the road.'

'So, your next appointment is Thursday,' Lana said. 'I'll see you then.'

Evan waited until he heard the click of the phone hanging up before he entered her office. 'Mum, can we have a quick chat?'

'Of course.' Lana slid a folder into a filing cabinet. 'What's up?' Her eyes searched for contact.

He took the seat opposite her desk. 'Nothing. It's just… you know my trip's getting closer.' He panned the room without motive, fixing on the fiddle-leaf fig tree in the corner. Its oversized leaves were motionless against the white wall. 'There's a few extra bits of equipment I'm going to need. For my camera.'

Lana observed her son's eyes cautiously. 'You want me to increase your credit limit again, don't you?'

Evan took a moment before he spoke. 'Just a little. This equipment will really make a difference to the photos I take.'

Lana rolled her head back and clasped the back of her neck. 'Evan, I've already given you a considerable amount for your trip. So has your grandmother. Have you even booked your flights yet? Or your accommodation?'

'I'll be doing that soon.'

'With what money? We helped you build up a travel fund that was meant to help you with your flights and accommodation. You told us you were going to get a job and save up for your spending money and any extra equipment you need. What happened to that idea?'

Evan shifted his eyes to the floor. 'I've tried finding a job. There's nothing in this town.'

'There are plenty of jobs going. I saw one just yesterday in the new Countdown.' Lana shut her laptop with a slap.

Evan's eye roll was obvious.

'What, you think it's beneath you?' Lana was growing visibly frustrated.

'No, of course not. Bill said I might be able to start working with him and his dad anyway.'

'On the cars?'

'Yeah.'

Lana furrowed her eyebrows. 'Do you think that's something you would enjoy?'

Evan gave a moody shrug. 'I dunno. More than sitting on a stupid checkout.'

'Evan! I didn't bring you up to be like that.'

'Like what?'

'Entitled. Ungrateful.' She softened her tone slightly and placed her hand on his. 'Look, Ev. We're very blessed to have what we have. But you can't take anything for granted. We still need to work hard. That's what I did. Even though I had you at a young age, which is the greatest thing to ever happen to me, I still worked hard to get where I am now. I stayed up *all hours studying—'*

'Studying your psychology degree, I know. This isn't the first time you've told me.'

Lana's eyes grew slender. Evan could tell he'd touched a nerve. Pushed too far. 'What's got into you? I feel like I don't know who you are right now.'

'Forget it. I should never have asked.' Evan stood up. 'I'll speak to Grandma instead.'

Lana took to her feet. 'No you will not. She's given you enough, as have I. This is because of those boys you're hanging around with, isn't it? They've influenced you. Spending all your money, no doubt. You must think I'm stupid.'

'Leave me alone.' Evan marched to his room, the door slamming in his wake. He buried his face into his pillow. He knew his mum was right. That he should be making his own money and taking responsibility for his actions. But was it his friends that were the bad influence? Or he who had a bad influence on them?

Evan's phone shivered in his pocket, interrupting his thoughts. It was Bill. He instantly felt better.

'Hey.'

'Hey.'

Evan could tell straight away something was up. He could hear it in his voice. 'Are you okay? What's wrong?'

There was a pause. Evan was sure he heard Bill sniff.

'It's Dad. He found the stuff in my room.'

'What stuff?' Evan's heart sank.

'You know what stuff.'

'What? How? Why was he in there?'

'I don't know. Said he was looking for something. Some tool I'd

borrowed. He's fucking furious, Ev.'

'Shit. I'm sorry.'

'He's on his way to your place now. He's gonna tell your mum.'

'What? Serious?'

'Serious.'

Evan's skin felt hot. Prickly. 'Fuck, she's gonna kill me. She's already pissed with me.'

'It's over, Ev. We're not gonna be able to hang out anymore.'

A lump formed in Evan's throat. 'What?'

'Dad's banned me from seeing you. You should just go on your trip to Europe. It's what you wanted to do anyway.'

Evan's stomach churned. Europe was the last thing on his mind. All he wanted was Bill. His touch. 'They can't stop us from hanging out. We're adults.'

'I know. But he told me he'd throw me out if we do.'

Evan couldn't believe what he was hearing. His life had changed so much for the better since Bill showed up. He didn't want that feeling to end. He couldn't let it.

'I'm sorry, Ev. I better go.'

Searching for the words, Evan felt the tears beginning to well. Before he had a chance to say goodbye, he realised Bill had hung up.

The doorbell rang.

Collins coasted the sleepy road that snaked out of Taonga onto State Highway 73. A heavy blanket of clouds upholstered the sky.

Brooke tapped her phone to look at the time. 'You think we'll make it to Christchurch by lunch?'

'Easy.' Collins eyed the dashboard, its clock blinking *10:16*.

'Long as the road stays as clear as this. And we don't get stuck behind a logger.' He pulled a pack of cigarettes from his coat pocket and dropped his window.

Brooke shot the pack a stare. 'Thought you gave up.'

'I did. The sugar cravings got too much.' He withdrew a cigarette and placed it between his lips. 'It's either get fat or kill myself slowly.' He flicked his lighter, drew back and blew out a thick curl of smoke. 'I decided on the latter.'

Brooke watched the words *Thanks for visiting Taonga* flash by. 'That sign always makes me happy,' she said through her grin.

Collins kept quiet for a few moments, smoking. 'How old were you when you moved here?'

Brooke had to think about it. 'About eight. We moved from Christchurch actually.'

'Oh yeah?' Collins arched an eyebrow. 'I didn't know you're from my neck of the woods.'

'Yep. I never wanted to leave. I liked my school there, had plenty of friends. My family didn't have that much money, so they had nothing to be jealous of, I guess. My dad left with some British lady he'd been having an affair with. They moved to the UK. Not even sure if he's still there. I haven't seen or heard from him since. I guess Mum got the last laugh. She met Gary and he's kept her more than comfortable since.'

Collins paused for a beat or two. 'Have you ever wanted to try and track your dad down?'

Brooke pulled out a piece of chewing gum and slipped it between her lips. 'No.'

A long silence.

'Your brother, Jack,' Collins began, 'he must have been

really young when you moved here.'

'He would've been four.' Brooke traced the horizon with her eyes, chewing. The timbre of her voice had changed. 'Sad, right? Taonga is all he ever knew.'

Collins kept his eyes on the road. The cigarette smouldered between his fingers as he clasped the wheel. 'This is obviously a difficult time for you, Palmer. I don't take that for granted.'

Brooke swivelled her gaze from the approaching mountain range to Collins. 'It's been tough. But in some ways strangely healing, you know?'

His nod lasted less than a second. She wondered if he really did understand.

'The similarities to this case are disturbing in many ways,' Brooke said plainly. 'Jack was also found by a passerby.'

Collins swallowed, clearly unsure what to say.

'Under a bridge, on the north side of town. It was somewhere they'd already searched, so he'd been put there later.' She removed her gum and enclosed it in a tissue before stuffing it into her pocket.

'I'm sorry.'

Brooke pawed the air between them. She assumed he knew the story from the podcast anyway. 'An old woman found him. Walking her dog, just like most people when they find a body, right? Poor woman. It must have been frightening. He was lying facedown with multiple stab wounds in his back.'

The silence cut like a knife. Collins allowed the remnants of his cigarette to be carried out the window by a strong gush of alpine air.

Brooke stared at the road as it banked ahead, as if she was

hypnotised. 'I'll never forget the sound Mum made the day the cops broke the news.' She didn't blink. 'A deep howl right into my stepdad's chest. There was something primal about it. Guttural.' She paused for a heartbeat. 'It was the sound of a mother being told her child was gone forever.' Her last words grew fainter until they were nothing but a shaky whisper.

Collins chose his next sentence cautiously and spoke it slow. 'No parent should have to bury their child.'

'They shouldn't. Which is why we have to find out who did this. We owe it to Lana. We owe it to Evan.'

Collins wiped an eye, but Brooke couldn't tell if it was a tear or the brisk wind.

'Yes we do,' he said, clearing his throat. 'Let's hope this Harding guy can shed some light.' He floored the pedal with conviction.

'Evan! Let me in right now!'

Evan unlocked his bedroom door and Lana swung it open. She stared at her son, her chest heaving with fury. 'That was Mr Henderson here just now.'

'I know. Mum, I'm so—'

'I don't want to hear it.' Lana held her hand up, an index finger pointed. 'I just about let you off for the weed. Now you've overstepped the line. You've made a fool out of me and this family.' Her eyes were filled with tears and the skin between her freckles red. 'I am so disappointed in you.'

Evan's eyes sank. 'I'm sorry, Mum.'

Lana's stance eased an inch. 'Why did you do this, Ev? To be liked? You're enough as you are. It's their loss if they don't get you.' There was desperation in her voice.

'We're gonna stop.'

Her eyes grew wide. 'Of course you're going to stop. I'm cutting off all your funds. No more credit card, no more travel allowance. And no more Bill. You're on your own now.'

'Mum!'

'I don't want to hear it! You're a grown man now, Evan. It's time you start acting like one.' She slammed the door with such force it rebounded ajar.

Evan collapsed, tears rolling down his face and his palms pressed hard against his crown.

What was he going to do now?

Chapter Nineteen

As soon as they swapped the cold air for the warmth of the busy cafe, Brooke caught sight of Keane Harding. Despite the bustle inside, his mauve shirt drew focus against the sea of uncompetitive grey and navy business suits. She recognised his slicked-back quiff from Instagram as he sat alone, scrolling his phone.

'Hey there,' a young waitress said. She gazed at them both wholeheartedly from beneath a dense curtain of tawny bangs. 'Have you got a reservation?'

'We're with the guy over there.' Brooke gestured towards Keane.

The waitress grabbed two menus, her beam over-enthusiastic. 'Oh, perfect. Come this way.'

The detectives followed the twenty-something through the trendy eatery. An array of fauna hung from the rafters of the industrial ceiling as communal wooden benches striped the cafe's concrete floor.

'You know this place?' Brooke asked Collins as they weaved.

'I've passed it before. My local's a bit more basic. And looking at the prices on the menu over there, cheaper, too. Do you know it?'

'Nope. Christchurch seems to change each time I visit. This place wouldn't look out of place in Auckland.'

The afternoon sun poured through the converted warehouse's oversized windows, making the copper cutlery glisten as it fanned out of upcycled tin cans. Keane clicked his phone locked, placing it facedown on the table as he saw the detectives approach.

'Here you are,' the waitress said. 'Coffees?'

'Please,' Collins said. 'Long black for me.'

'I'll have a flat white,' Brooke said with a polite smile. 'Thanks.'

'Mr Harding?' Collins said.

'So formal! Call me Keane.' He stood up and flashed a charming beam, extending his hand for Collins to shake.

'Detective Tane Collins.' He revealed his badge. 'This here's Detective Brooke Palmer.'

She displayed her badge. 'I'm the one who reached out to you on Instagram. I hope you didn't mind.'

His grin remained as he shook her hand. 'Not at all. I'm happy to help.'

Brooke decided not to hang around. 'So, you were romantically involved with Santiago Pérez?'

'Steady on, Sergeant. I'm not one to kiss and tell.' Keane looked around for a laugh.

Collins' face was straight. 'Well, we don't need a kiss, but we're gonna need you to start telling. Detective Palmer told you this was about a homicide, didn't she?'

Keane dropped his head and looked at his latte, its fern sipped to distortion. 'Yes, she did. It's heartbreaking. That poor family.' His spritely tone had turned cool.

There was an uncomfortable silence that hung on longer than anyone would have liked.

'What happened between you and Santiago, Keane?' Brooke finally said.

Keane gave her his eyes. They were a hypnotic hazel. He leaned back with his clasped hands behind his head. 'Long, long ago in a faraway land… Well, actually, not that long ago. And not far either. Santi and I met three years back in a gay club down the street.' Keane was now upright, his elbows on the table. 'He was living here too, then. He'd moved over from Barcelona on a working-holiday visa and ended up sticking around when he found work. But when an even better opportunity came along in Taonga, we ended up moving down there after about a year. I should've seen that as a red flag really. It's where I'm from.'

Brooke arched her back. 'You're from Taonga?'

Keane took a sip and gave a short nod. 'Sure am – for my sins. So I know all about you, Ms Podcast Superstar. Surprised me when I saw you slip into my DMs.'

Brooke avoided his eyes for a moment, swallowing her discomfort. The thought of being made a celebrity from a podcast focusing on her brother's murder was nothing short of horrifying. She fixed her focus on him again. 'What went wrong?'

The waitress reappeared clutching two cups. 'Can I get you guys anything to eat?' She placed the coffees down. A touch of the flat white's foam spilled onto the table in the process.

'We're fine.' Collins glanced at Keane. 'Ate on the way.'

'Eggs Benny for me,' he said with a wink. 'Thanks.'

Brooke waited for the waitress to disappear before she spoke again. 'Did you ever meet Evan Wiley?'

He paused for a moment, taking in her gaze. 'He came over a couple of times. To our house. Well, Santiago's house now.'

Brooke gave him a firm stare. 'He came to your house?'

Keane drained the remnants of his latte. 'Yep. Weird, right? I thought so, too.'

Collins shifted in his seat and leaned forward. 'What happened during the occasions he visited your house?'

A crash across the room drew everyone's attention. A different waitress took to the floor to begin picking up the smashed plates. 'I'm so sorry,' she nervously assured. 'It's my first day.'

Collins dragged his eyes back to the table. 'What happened when Evan Wiley visited your house, Keane?'

Keane pushed his fingers through his quiff, ensuring it was still in place. 'He came over for dinner first. Santi had told me he was going through some stuff. Trying to figure himself out. He said he thought we should be there for him. But, to be honest with you, I didn't like it.'

Brooke lowered her voice. 'You were threatened?'

Keane thought for a moment. 'I wouldn't say *threatened*. Come on, look at me.' He ran his fingers through his quiff and flashed the grin again. 'But yeah, he was a good-looking guy. And I know Santi has a thing for younger men. I mean, he's got a good ten years on me.'

Brooke shot Collins another stare, this time loaded. She re-eyed Keane. 'So, you never saw anything happen between them?'

'No. But I feel like I didn't have to – if you know what I mean?'

'Had Santiago done anything like that before?' Collins asked with quickening tempo. 'Was he ever unfaithful?'

Keane averted his eyes to the table. 'We had a fairly… open relationship to begin with. It became more exclusive when we moved to Taonga. I thought we were serious. But it didn't work out. I couldn't trust him.'

'Because of Evan?' Brooke probed.

'That was the straw that broke the camel's back, to be honest. We'd been fighting a lot in the months before Evan visited. I had essentially given up my career to move to Taonga, but Santi just seemed to spend all his time at that school. He'd often get home too late for dinner because he'd be working in the darkroom. He held after-school classes. I know when Evan was in school, Santi spent a lot of time mentoring him. I picked up on it even then.'

'Picked up on what?' Collins' tone implied he was growing restless.

Keane hesitated for a beat, searching for the words. 'The possibility that he might have been involved with Evan. Intimately.'

There was another pulse of quiet, aside from the eager chatter of young professionals competing for airtime. Brooke side-glanced Collins and pulled out a folder. She presented Keane with the photograph of the pair she'd found in Evan's room.

Keane studied the photo for just short of a minute before passing it back. 'Way too close and personal. Don't you think?'

'One Eggs Benny.' The waitress placed the meal in front of him.

'Great, thanks.' Keane cracked the pepper mill.

Brooke drew a deep breath and leaned forward. 'Keane, do you think Santiago had it in him to hurt someone?' Her voice was almost a whisper now.

Keane slid the knife through the egg, sending a streak of gold oozing across his plate. 'Santi's a very manipulative man. With me, what you see is what you get. But when *he* sets his mind on something, he'll do whatever it takes to get it. That's what he was like with me. Our move to Taonga. His career even. I wouldn't be surprised if Evan was a shiny new toy he set his eyes on.' He took a bite. 'But maybe something went wrong.' His eyes darted between them.

'Went wrong how?' Collins raised an eyebrow.

'I don't know. You're the detectives, not me.' Keane took a sip of water. 'Maybe Evan said no.'

Evan glanced at his bloodshot eyes through the camera on his phone. He'd been up most the night crying, but it hadn't got him anywhere. He wanted nothing more than to be in Bill's arms right now. Lying there, talking shit. Pretending to be asleep when Bill drifts off so he can listen to his breath. Feeling his chest moving up and down. But it wasn't going to happen. That was over now. Perhaps Bill had been right, Evan thought as he strode through the hallway that led to Santiago's classroom. Maybe he should just go to Europe. What was there for him in Taonga now? He hoped Santiago could relight that flame within him. The fire he'd managed to spark when he first enrolled in his photography class.

He could see Santiago at his desk through the glass of the door as he approached it. He checked his watch. Eight-thirty. His students would be arriving soon, so he couldn't be long. In some ways he envied them. Despite how much he'd hated school, he missed his photography lessons. He missed the way they'd helped him to escape his troubles. Maybe he'd consider going to university after his gap year. He'd always hoped he'd just fall into an opportunity that would fulfil him, but perhaps he should have listened to his mum. Maybe he really did need to put the work in.

'Evan, hi!' Santiago stood up and looked at him with bright eyes. 'How are you doing?'

'Hey.' Evan's voice said it all.

'What's wrong?' Santiago looked Evan up and down. 'Here, take a seat. My class will be here soon, but we can talk for a minute or two.'

Evan slumped into the chair with a sigh.

'What is it, Evan? Is everything all right at home?'

'Kinda. Mum and I had a fight.'

Santiago paused for a beat. 'I'm sorry to hear that.'

'And that guy I like. It's over.' Evan's eyes skipped past him. He felt them well up.

Santiago went to say something but held back.

'I feel so alone.' Evan covered his face with both hands and slumped to the table in defeat. The tears were coming. 'I don't know what to do.' He knew his voice was barely audible through his sobs. With his head still buried, he felt Santiago's hand on his shoulder.

'You're not alone, Evan.'

Evan slowly lifted his head and wiped his eyes with the back of his hand.

Santiago pulled a tissue from a box on his desk and passed it to him. 'What are you doing Friday night?'

Evan blew his nose. 'Nothing.' He spoke with the tissue to his face. 'Why?'

'Why don't you come over to my place for dinner?' Santiago tilted his head to the side. 'You can meet my partner, Keane. He'll be happy for you to join us.'

Evan looked at him through reddened eyes. 'Are you sure?'

'Of course I'm sure. It'll be nice. I can imagine it must be difficult coming to terms with yourself in a town like this. Things were different when I came out. The world was a bit less accepting back then, but at least I was living in a big city like Barcelona. It'll be nice for you to spend time with a couple of guys who've been through what you're going through and have come out the other side.'

Evan grinned. 'That would be nice. Is Keane into photography?'

'Not really. I think he gets a bit sick of me talking about it, to be honest. But you'll like him. He's a good guy. Easy to get along with. Do you have any dietary requirements?'

'I don't think so?'

Santiago laughed. 'Okay. Well, if you think of anything, let me know. Sound good?'

'Sounds great.'

'Perfect. I'll text you my address and when to come over.' He twisted his wrist to check the time. 'Sorry to rush this chat, but my class starts soon.'

'No worries. I'll get going. Thanks, Santi.' Evan reached out for a hug.

Santiago paused for an instant, before giving Evan a small pat on the back. 'See you Friday.'

'See ya.'

Keane placed the knife and fork on his empty plate. 'So is Santi your only suspect?'

Collins folded his arms and kept his face stern. 'The investigation is very much ongoing. But we'd greatly appreciate any information you can provide us with that you think might be relevant.'

Brooke finished the final foamy sip of her flat white and paused for a few moments as she considered her impending question. 'Was Santiago ever violent with you, Keane?'

Keane fiddled with the button of his sleeve cuff. His whole demeanour had changed. Less assured. 'Oh, no. No.'

Brooke and Collins swapped an unconvinced look.

Collins unlocked his arms. 'Was he ever heavy with his fists?'

'No.' Keane's eyes were busy. 'But don't get me wrong, he did have a bit of a temper.'

Collins looked to Brooke then back to Keane. 'We might need you to come down to the station to make a more formal statement soon. Once we've gathered a bit more evidence.'

Keane's nod was automatic. 'Like I said, I'm happy to help however I can. What's happened to this young man is a tragedy. It makes me sick to think someone I spent the last few years of my life with could've had anything to do with it. But if he did, he needs to be stopped before he acts out again.' Keane checked his watch. 'Right, I better get going. I'm already late for a meeting. Good job I'm fashionable,' he quipped with a wink before handing Brooke a thick business card. 'For when you want to next speak. You're lucky, these just arrived today. I've only started working at this place.'

Brooke gave the card a glance. *Digital Garden* was printed in pearlescent text, beneath it: *Digital Marketing in the Garden City*. 'Thanks. I'll message you my number in case you think of anything else.' She shot him a small smile and turned the card over to read his title. *Senior Account Manager*. Didn't mean much to her.

Collins lit a cigarette as he leaned against his SUV, the dim sun gleaming on its bonnet. 'Well he's a cocky bastard, isn't he?'

Brooke smoothed balm across her grin. 'Remind you of anyone, Detective?'

Collins drew back again and released a cloud of smoke. 'Watch it.'

A gust of air glided by, biting Brooke's exposed hands. She dug them deep into her pockets and gave a small shiver. 'He definitely doesn't lack charisma. But something about him came off a little…'

Collins angled his gaze in her direction. 'Pretentious?'

'Rehearsed.'

Collins smirked. 'Probably his line of work. Gotta be able to play the game.' He flicked a build-up of ash. 'Besides. He's obviously a bit bitter. Masks it well with his one-liners. Something I also know a thing or two about.'

Another blast of air, this time stronger, blew Brooke's hair into her face. She defiantly pushed it away and read Collins' eyes. It was easy to forget what he was going through himself right now. 'That's true. I'm probably overthinking it. And let's face it, Santiago was the one who said nothing about Evan going over to his house.' The hair was back. This time she didn't bother pushing it away. 'Question is, did it innocently slip his mind because he thought nothing of it? Or is there more he doesn't want us to know?'

Collins stamped his cigarette on the cracked concrete and gestured towards the road. 'Either way, we're going to find out. We'll question him on the record when his prints come back on the cigarette.' He opened his car door and hopped in.

Brooke hesitated for a few more lingering moments, consumed by her own thoughts, before following suit.

Soon, there was only silence. Just the muted purr of the engine and the occasional passing car as they followed the long road back to Taonga.

Chapter Twenty

Brooke could hear her breath starting to synchronise with her sister's as their sneakers pounded the ashy beach, its sand taking a cast of each step. The sky, which had been clear and crisp all morning, was now shrouded with a patchwork of monochrome. A familiar mist spilled from the sea, cold but welcomed by Brooke, who was growing warmer with every stride.

'It makes me feel sick,' Hannah said between rapid breaths. 'To think one of Evan's teachers could've done this.'

'We don't know for sure yet.' Brooke stopped running and curved her body forward with her hands on her thighs. She could taste the salty air with each inhale.

Hannah side-swiped her fringe. It was two weeks too long. 'Who else do you suspect?'

Brooke scanned the foggy horizon. The jetty reached into the mist like an outstretched arm. Beyond it, waves whipped against each other as if at war. 'Well, there's whoever Evan's drug dealer was. He owed him money, which alone gave him motive. And we have reason to believe he could have started working for him.'

Hannah wiped the bead of sweat that had formed on the tip of her nose. 'Evan? A drug dealer?'

'Possibly. Maybe they'd reached some sort of arrangement, to get him off Ev's back. But maybe it didn't turn out the way he'd planned.' A transient pause and Brooke spoke again. 'Who knows. We'll need to find the dealer first. As you can imagine, he's not the easiest guy to track down.'

There was another beat of quiet until Hannah summoned her next question. 'What about Bill Henderson?'

Brooke twisted her pursed lips to the side, followed by a slow nod. 'We have something of a motive for Bill. It sounds like he was afraid of what he felt for Evan. But, that's it. We found Ev's laptop in his house, which sounds a bit suss, but we think it might be innocent. They were hanging out, after all.'

Hannah turned to face her sister. 'I would never have guessed something was going on between them. If Bill can keep *that* hidden, then who knows what else?'

The sound of thrashing waves filled the ensuing silence.

'What does your gut tell you?' Hannah finally said.

'That's the thing,' Brooke said with a shrug. 'It's not telling me anything right now.'

Hannah hooked an arm around her sister. 'You'll work it out. You always do.'

'I'm not sure this time, Han. And I'm going to have to head home soon. I told Lan I wouldn't go back without finding out who did this, but I'm starting to wish I hadn't made that promise. I wish I hadn't promised myself.'

'Come on,' Hannah said as she began jogging on the spot. 'Let's not think about that yet. We should at least finish the length of the beach before we call it a morning.'

The women resumed their run and a seagull cawed overhead.

'How are the kids?' Brooke tightened her ponytail which had come loose.

'They're good. Trying to shield all this from them as much as possible, you know?'

'I bet. They're too young to understand.'

'Exactly. Just because we had to grow up fast, I don't want it to be the same for my boys.'

Being the eldest of the two, Brooke had always felt she needed to be the most responsible. When Jack died, Barbara had understandably taken a back seat, meaning Brooke took on an even greater responsibility to nurture her little sister. This made it all the more difficult for Brooke to leave Hannah behind when she made the move to Auckland.

Despite Brooke having gone through all the phases of growing up first – teenage rebellion, dating, starting a career – it all changed when Hannah got married and had kids. Milestones Brooke hadn't yet experienced, and maybe never would. She'd watched Hannah become the responsible sister, as well as an incredible mother. Brooke was deeply proud. She knew Jack would have been, too.

'It must be hard to keep it from them, though,' Brooke said. 'It's the talk of the town.'

'It really is. It's on the news constantly. All because of that stupid podcast.'

The sisters stopped running again as they reached the far end of the beach. In the distance, trees lined the hilltop and swayed in the wind, which was growing stronger as the morning matured. In the moving clouds, Brooke attempted to picture an older Jack. She tried to imagine what he would have looked like now. But all she could see was his youthful smile. His bright young eyes.

Hannah glanced at Brooke, noticing the tears. 'You okay?'

'I just miss him so much, Han.'

Hannah threw her arms around her sister and held her tight. 'I know. I miss him, too.'

The sisters seldom discussed Jack. It was as if they had secretly made a pact of silence once the case was over. But under current circumstances, it was hard not to bring up their late little brother who never got a chance. The only thing that gave a sense of comfort was knowing his killer was locked behind bars.

Brooke squinted at the sky, wanting nothing more than the same for Lana. That feeling of taking the deep breath, knowing justice was served. The clouds formed the shape of Santiago's Cheshire Cat grin. 'I was so certain it was one of the kids in this town. That killed Evan, I mean. Just like what happened with Jack. But the thought that it could've been someone he trusted...'

Hannah went to speak, but instead just shook her head.

There was an inflated pause. Santiago's smile broke off into what looked like a question mark on its side.

'Come on,' Hannah said with a clap. 'Let's go get coffee. We've earned it.'

The women began walking in the direction of the car without saying a word.

Evan clocked Santiago's car in the driveway as he approached the house. For a moment, he hesitated. Should he even be here? Had his former teacher purely invited him out of pity? He shook his doubts away. He knew Santiago saw something in him. A talent. A spark. He was also more than just a mentor to him. Tonight, he had been invited over as a friend.

He rang the doorbell. Thirty seconds or so passed before Santiago appeared. Much like at school, he wore a plain t-shirt and jeans. But his hair was free of its pony, swept back over his shoulder. 'Hey. Come in.'

Evan followed Santiago through the hallway of the modern house. It was painted bright white and decorated minimally, the occasional black and white photograph hanging on the wall. 'Your place is really nice.'

'Thanks. We'd like to do more with it, but we're actually renting at the moment. I have an investment property back in Spain that I'm planning to sell soon. Hopefully I'll be able to buy this place.'

Evan's eyes fixed with Keane's as he entered the living room. 'Hey, I'm Evan.' He held out his hand.

Keane glanced at it and gave it a soft shake. 'Keane.'

Santiago averted his eyes between his partner and ex-student. 'I'll pour some wine. Red okay, Evan?'

'Red's great, thanks.'

'Please, have a seat. Keane is eager to learn all about you.' Santiago left the room.

Evan took one end of the sofa and Keane sprawled the other.

'It's great to meet you,' Evan said.

Keane twisted slightly and spoke quick beneath his breath. 'I don't know what your intention is, but Santiago is mine.'

Evan's eyes widened, his mouth now slack. 'What?'

'You heard what I said.'

There was a chilling silence and Santiago reappeared carrying two glasses of red. 'It's an Aussie Shiraz. Hope you'll like it.'

Evan kept his eyes on Keane as they accepted the drinks. Was he really threatened by him? Why? Evan knew his intentions were pure. He suddenly felt unwelcome. Should he just get up and go?

Santiago disappeared again momentarily to fetch his own glass. He was gone long enough for Keane to shoot Evan another dagger. His frown switched to a smile when his boyfriend reappeared. 'I was just telling Evan about how we met.'

'Oh yeah?' Santiago knocked his wine glass against Keane's and then Evan's. 'Cheers.'

As the chime of his glass rang out, Evan felt his heart stop with it.

'Yeah,' Keane said. 'It was one of those moments, wasn't it? When you know, you know.'

Santiago took the seat beside his partner. 'It's crazy to think that's almost three years ago. And who would have thought you would wind up living back in Taonga?' He turned to Evan. 'Keane grew up here.'

Evan tried to nod but wasn't sure if he actually did.

'So he knows a thing or two about the struggles you're going through,' Santiago continued. 'I mean, we both do, but Keane even more so considering he grew up in this... interesting town.'

'Yes, it can be very challenging,' Keane said with a grin, which Evan saw right through. 'But you'll get through it. It gets better.'

Santiago sipped his wine and stood up. 'Right, you two take a seat at the table. I just need to heat up our dinner and then I'll bring it over. We're having paella, Ev. It's my mother's recipe, you'll love it.'

'Sounds great,' Evan said in a voice so small it was barely audible.

Keane led Evan through to the dining table, which had already been set. Jazz music played from a mock-vintage record player. At the table, Keane pushed his fingers through his quiff and turned to face Evan. His hazel eyes appeared almost black in the dim lights. 'So, what's your intention?' He spoke low beneath the saxophone.

'Nothing like that. I'm just here as Santiago's friend. I've been going through a lot lately as he's obviously told you. He's been there for me.'

'Bullshit.' Keane spoke the word with a hiss. 'Do I look stupid? I was eighteen once, too. Young, dumb and full of—'

'It's nothing like that!' Evan clenched his fists and felt the tears surfacing. He did everything he could to resist them from falling.

'Look, Santi and I have had some problems lately. The last thing we need is some pretty boy showing up and driving even more of a wedge between us.'

Evan opened his mouth to respond, but Santiago had reemerged, this time carrying a large steaming pot.

'Smells delicious, babe,' Keane said. 'My favourite.' Mussel shells clashed with the steel spoon as he mounded a serving onto his plate.

Santiago beamed at Evan, who returned a semi-smile. All he could think about doing was finishing his dinner and getting home. He knew now he had no place in Taonga.

No place and no one.

Brooke and Hannah waded through the reeds that led to where the car was parked.

'Thanks for this morning, Han. It felt like old times.'

Hannah rubbed her sister's arm. 'It was great. We should sneak a few more runs in before you leave.'

'For sure.'

The two women climbed into Hannah's car, and Brooke fished her phone from the front compartment. Two missed calls from Collins and a voice message. She ignored the message and called him straight back. 'Hey, what's up?'

'Palmer, are you busy?' The usual nonchalance in his voice gave way to urgency.

'I was just going to get a coffee.' She eyed Hannah. 'What is it?'

'Come down to the station now. We've got the dealer.'

Brooke's blood beat cold. 'On my way.'

'I take it that coffee's out the window,' Hannah said once Brooke pocketed her phone.

'Sorry. Can you take me to the station?'

Hannah started the engine and shifted into reverse. 'What's happened?'

'They've found the drug dealer.'

A tick of quiet and Hannah reversed. Once she was on the road, she responded. 'You reckon he's the guy?'

'I don't know. Maybe. If not, hopefully he'll know something.'

Santiago walked Evan to the door. A fresh gust of air blew inside when he pulled it open. 'Thanks for coming tonight, Evan. I hope you had fun.'

Evan stood outside, peering behind Santiago to check Keane wasn't there. He wasn't. 'I did. Thanks for having me.'

A look of concern overcame Santiago. He shot a brief glance over his shoulder. 'Listen. I'm sorry if Keane seemed a bit... cold. He's been having a bit of a tough time recently himself.' He spoke so quietly Evan had to lean in to hear him.

'That's okay. I don't want to make him feel uncomfortable. I'm not trying to get in between anything.'

Santiago's eyes flicked wide. 'What? Of course not. Don't be silly. I'm sorry if you were made to feel unwelcome in any way.'

Evan shrugged. 'It's all right. Thanks again for dinner. Goodnight.' He gave a quick nod and got into his car.

Evan had only been driving for a few minutes before he decided to pull over to the side of the road. He slid out his phone and scrolled down his contact list. His thumb hovered tentatively above Bill's name as the screen underlit his face. No. Not yet. He continued to scroll down until he reached his dealer's number and tapped without a second thought. He caught a glimpse of his reflection in the windscreen and pulled the phone to his ear. The features of his face cut against the dark country road outside, hollow sockets for eyes.

'Hello?' Warren said.

'Hey. I was wondering if you could do me a favour?'

Chapter Twenty-one

By the time Brooke arrived, the heavy clouds had unleashed their rain, lashing the station. She paced briskly to Collins' office, her ponytail loose and ruffled from changing out of her activewear in the car.

'Where is he?' Brooke spoke without taking a breath, releasing her hair and giving it a shake.

Collins pulled out a document. 'He's in the interview room waiting for us. We'll go through in a sec. I just wanted to show you something else.' He handed her the buff-hued folder.

Brooke opened it. It was the results from the cigarette she'd found. Two smudges were printed in black ink. *No match*.

'Un-*fortuna*-tely, the prints they got from the cigarette weren't good enough.'

Brooke met Collins' eyes, ignoring his failed pun. 'But it must be Santiago's, right?'

'It's probable. Difficult to prove without prints. So the best thing we can do is ask him and hope he trips up. We'll pay him a little visit later.' Collins rose to his feet. 'Let's see what this guy can tell us first. Name's Warren Silvers.'

Brooke tailed Collins through the station. 'How'd you find him?'

Collins stopped and swerved to meet her eyes. 'My team in Christchurch tracked him down in Greymouth, where he lives.'

Brooke's eyebrows lifted. That must've been why Evan was heading there.

'I know. I thought the same,' Collins said, as if reading her mind. 'He confirmed he used to sell to Evan, and he'd seen on the news he was murdered. But he's insisting he had nothing to do with it. Oh, and he has a lawyer with him.'

'Does he have an alibi?'

'Apparently so. Some woman he was supposedly with that night.'

Warren Silvers was sitting in silence when the detectives entered the interview room. He had a thin frame and clear skin aside from the odd blotch of red. His hair was shaved. To his left was a lawyer, her black hair bunned at the nape – her navy suit a touch oversized.

'Hello, Mr Silvers,' Collins said with a firm note as he took his seat. 'And this is?'

'Miranda Liu.' The woman's smile gave nothing away.

Collins returned his attention to Warren. 'Can you confirm that my team has read you your rights and you understand that this interview is recorded?'

Warren kept quiet. His lips thinned to almost nothing.

'I'm Detective Inspector Collins and this is Detective

Sergeant Palmer. We hear you used to supply Evan Wiley drugs?'

Warren raised his lip, so it almost looked like a snarl. His shadowy eyes gazed at the detectives for a blink. He averted them to Miranda, seeking her approval.

She gave a mechanical nod. 'You can answer the question.'

'Yeah. I have nuthin' to do with what happened though. I've already said everythin' I know.'

Collins gestured to the camera. 'Well, consider that a dress rehearsal. Now's your time to shine, so please, start from the beginning.'

Warren rolled his eyes and leaned back in his chair. 'Evan first reached out to me a few months back on Instagram. I was surprised, 'cause I don't get much business in Taonga. Barely any. But he got in touch and asked if I could score him some weed.'

'Which you did.' Collins ran his hands through his hair. His forehead displayed three thick creases.

'Yeah. And that was it for a while. Him buyin' weed, I mean. Every few days I'd get another call or message asking for more. He was sharin' it with his mates.'

'That's right,' Brooke said. 'And then he turned to the hard stuff?'

Warren scratched his bristled chin and his lawyer gave him a nod. 'Yeah. He said the weed wasn't workin' so much for them anymore. He wanted to score a bigger high.'

'So you came to their rescue.' Collins' sarcasm couldn't be disguised.

Warren shot him a glare. 'I was told I'm not bein'

interrogated about my—'

'My client was informed that any *historical* activity was irrelevant to the case and wouldn't be questioned,' Miranda said sternly. 'He is happy to cooperate regarding his interaction with Evan Wiley.'

Collins waved his hand for him to continue. 'Go on.'

'Then a few weeks back he called me up, askin' if he could score some coke. But he asked if I could do him a favour. Let him have it without givin' me the money up front, and he said he'd pay me back in a week.'

Brooke arched her back and side-glanced Collins. 'And he didn't?'

'Nope. The kid died on me before he had a chance to pay me back.'

An uncomfortable quiet invaded the room.

Collins folded his arms. 'When did you last see Evan?'

Warren tilted his head to the side and scrunched his features into a grimace. 'I went and saw him. To chase him up about the money.'

Brooke leaned forward. 'Do you know when that was exactly?'

Warren shook his head. 'Nah. Couple weeks back.'

'What happened when you saw him?' Collins unfolded his arms.

'He told me he needed more time. That he'd pay me next time. I let him off.'

'Did you though?' The question came from Collins' mouth with such conviction it was as if it had been caught in his throat for some time.

'Yes! I didn't fuckin' kill him.'

Miranda gave Warren a firm look and cleared her throat.

'Look, you understand how this thing looks, don't you?' Brooke said, softening the tension.

Warren paused for a beat and shrugged. 'I guess. But it's got nuthin' to do with me, I swear. I already proved I was outta town the night of the murder.'

'That doesn't mean anything,' Collins said. 'We have CCTV footage of Evan heading out Taonga in the direction of Greymouth. He could've been going to meet you.'

Warren shook his head. 'That's bullshit. I was with my girl. She can vouch for me.'

Brooke leaned in again, her outstretched hands pressed on the table. 'We have reason to believe Evan had just secured himself an income. Did you offer him a job with you?'

Warren's narrow jaw fell agape. 'What? No way. No one works for me. I work–' He cut himself off for a moment before continuing. 'I used to work alone.' He gave Miranda a not-so-discreet wink.

Brooke and Collins exchanged a frustrated glance. Collins gave him another look. 'Well, maybe you gave someone else a job. I'm sure you know plenty of people who'd do anything for some cash. Or cocaine.'

Warren sighed his frustration. 'You think I put a hit out on the kid? This is a fuckin' setup.'

Brooke wondered if there could be any truth in that. 'So that was the last contact you had with Evan? The day you went and chased him up for the money he owed you?'

'Yeah. Oh, hang on. No.' He pulled out his phone and

flicked through some old WhatsApp messages. Miranda became unsettled in her chair. 'I got this message from him. He wanted to prove to me he'd be gettin' me the money.' He handed Brooke his phone.

It was a close up of a watch secured to what she assumed was Evan's wrist. It had an elegant, cream face and leather strap. It looked expensive.

'I looked it up,' Warren went on. 'Worth more than enough to pay me back.'

Brooke checked the date the image was sent. 'Hang on, this was the day he went missing. The day he was killed.' She passed the phone to Collins.

Warren folded his arms and leaned back in his chair. 'Exactly, why would he send me a message if I was with him?' He turned to Miranda with a sneer. 'I don't know why I bothered bringin' you here.'

Brooke shared a knowing glance with the lawyer at her client's false sense of security. Before she had a chance to say something, she noticed Collins.

As he stared at the photo, his eyes opened to capacity. His face drained of any colour.

'You okay?' Brooke said.

Trembling, Collins spoke. 'Can you send this to my phone? And then I think we're done here. Thanks, Warren.'

Warren swapped a brief look with Miranda. She didn't seem convinced, but he ultimately made up his own mind.

'Perfect, thanks.' Collins pocketed his phone and pivoted to Brooke. 'Come with me. Now.'

Brooke gave Warren and his lawyer a final fleeting glance

– who both looked equally as confused as her – and followed Collins out the room.

The camera remained recording.

Evan huddled beneath the ramp as raindrops spotted the pavement. Would Warren even show? And if he did, would he go through with the favour? He knew he was reaching, but it was the only thing he could think of. If he could just get hold of some more coke, maybe Bill would agree to see him again. Maybe then he'd want him back.

He pulled out his packet of smokes. He was getting low. He'd even have to start being sparing with those. How had he let it get to this? Cupping his hand over the cigarette's tip, he lit up and drew back with his eyes closed. As he exhaled, he thought of Bill. Why had he been so irresponsible? He'd asked to keep some of the coke with him, in case he got desperate. Evan knew it was a bad idea. He knew Bill was becoming too reliant on it. Was he addicted? He wasn't sure. It wasn't a trait he'd noticed in himself. Sure, he enjoyed the rush. But it was Bill's company he was really after. His smile. His touch.

When Evan opened his eyes, they'd glassed over. He thought about how he and Bill may never be the same, whatever they'd been. It had been something they hadn't defined. Hadn't discussed. But it didn't matter. What mattered was that it felt good. That it felt right. For the first time in his life, he'd felt like he'd belonged. Like he'd been accepted. Like he'd mattered. He wondered if Bill had felt the same.

Taking another drag, Evan felt his lungs warm while the rest of his body shivered. He released a puff of smoke and thought of his mum. How he'd let her down. She'd done everything for him, everything she could to make up for the father he'd never had. He thought of his grandparents, his grandmother in particular. He knew his mum wouldn't have told her what he'd done, but it didn't take away the feeling that he'd let her down, too.

He drew back a final time and let the stump skip to the ground, where he stamped it out. Visiting Santiago had been the final straw. His intentions had been pure, but Keane had made his feelings clear. And maybe he was right. Maybe it was wrong for him to have been there. Before their current issues, they'd obviously had a happy and loving relationship. Why would he want to do anything to come between that? It's what he longed for himself deep down. Bill found his way back into his mind. This time, slightly older. He imagined them both living together in a modest house, just like Santiago and Keane's. He imagined Bill getting home from work to a dinner he'd prepared. He even imagined their pet dog, jumping up in excitement, Bill patting its head as he leaned over to kiss Evan.

The fantasy was interrupted by the arrival of Warren.

'Oh, hey,' Evan said. 'I wasn't sure if you'd actually show. Thanks for coming.'

Warren spoke through a grimace. 'You're lucky I did. I normally wouldn't make the journey down like this. But you've been a loyal customer.'

Evan straightened his back. 'I know. I'm sorry. I appreciate you doing this for me.'

'It's a one-off.' Warren looked over his shoulder and pulled out a couple of plastic baggies filled with white powder from his backpack. 'You've got a week to pay me back.'

Evan took the baggie and nodded. 'No worries. I'll get it to you.'

Warren gave him a small nod. 'Yeah, you will.' He disappeared as quickly as he came.

Evan crouched down and stuffed the coke into his backpack. A crack of lightning signalled the start of a storm. Soon, the rain crashed down upon the ramp above him. He pulled out his phone and found Bill's number. Was he doing the right thing? Of course not. It was the drugs that had been the catalyst to the end. Why would Bill suddenly decide to go behind his dad's back to see him? The only shred of hope Evan had was that Bill's obsession with the white stuff would lead him back to him. That it would make him want him again.

Evan tapped Bill's number and held his breath.

As they approached the dairy, Collins still hadn't said a word. Brooke racked her brain as to why they'd be going there, but the car didn't slow down. Instead, Collins drove as if automated. The car glided past the bus stop and joined State Highway 6. They were Greymouth-bound. Brooke tried to think what the watch had to do with this. Did Collins have a suspicion where it could have been bought? Or did he notice something else on Warren's phone that she hadn't spotted? Before she had a chance to ask, Collins was indicating to leave the highway.

Brooke had passed it many times over the years. After all, it had been around longer than her. Situated just off the highway, just outside of Taonga, was the Lucky Star Motel. It hadn't appeared to have changed since she was a kid. It had the same neon vacancy sign and, sitting directly outside, the same bus stop.

Collins kept mute as he parked outside one of the rooms. The single-level cluster of buildings was painted thick burgundy, with patches of timber exposed and rotting. Thin windows were slick with condensation, beclouding the floral print of the curtains within.

'Is this where you're staying?' Brooke said.

'Yep.'

'I could have recommended somewhere nicer,' she said in

an attempt to lighten his mood.

'It's cheap,' he sniped as he climbed out the car. 'But I have a horrible feeling it's about to become a whole lot cheaper.'

Collins was still shaking as he fumbled for his key and opened the door. Once inside, he switched on the dim light and pulled out his phone. Within seconds, he'd found the picture of Evan's watch and presented it to Brooke.

Her heart plunged. 'He was here. The night he was murdered. Evan was here.'

Chapter Twenty-two

The winter chill had found its way through the motel room's wooden walls. Collins sunk into the bed and pushed his hands through his hair. His face had greyed, its only colour given by the cast of daylight, filtered by the vivid beige of the net curtains. 'I just need to gather my thoughts.'

Brooke tipped a nod. 'Of course.'

She couldn't help but stare at the bed. She thought back to what Evan had said to Lana. *I've found a way to get what I need.* Maybe that wasn't with Bill, or the drug dealer. Had Evan turned to selling his body? Brooke's breath became heavy. She wanted nothing more than her mind not to go there, but she couldn't shake it off. 'Evan's post-mortem. Were there any signs that he'd had sex that night?' A visual of Evan being held down against his will forced its way into her head. 'Or that he'd been... raped?' It hurt to even ask.

Collins shook his head, keeping his eyes on the faded carpet.

'Not likely.' He spoke slower than usual. 'None of the usual in-flammation or micro-tears you'd expect to see. No seminal flu-id.' Collins picked up his eyes. 'That's not why he was here.'

'Unless he was killed before it got to that.'

He shook his head. 'That would be a first.'

Brooke felt an ounce of relief. She tapped to wake Collins' phone, which had dimmed again, and looked at the photo. She hadn't initially noticed the tiny pink English roses in the back-ground, despite them sitting atop an insipid yellow hue. But now they bloomed behind Evan's watched wrist. It was the ex-act pattern that lined all four walls of Collins' motel room, and in the flesh, they appeared to twitch and grow. She suddenly felt like the walls were closing in on her. 'So...' Brooke swallowed. 'Do all the rooms have this wallpaper?'

Collins rolled to the corner of the bed, his skin had gone from grey to almost green. 'I bloody hope so.'

Brooke thought back to Evan's demeanour in the dairy. How he'd seemed agitated. Desperate. 'Come on then, let's go find out. And see if they have any CCTV while we're at it.'

Collins released a long breath through pursed lips. 'Good idea.' He stood up with a jolt.

The detectives walked across the near-empty car park with-out speaking another word.

In the dimly lit reception, an elderly woman peered over her glasses with close-set eyes. Behind her, a grid of hooked keys sat below a trio of plastic clocks labelled London, New York and Taonga. Her silver hair was cut short and manageable. 'Can I help you?'

'June,' Collins said with a familiar note. 'Is Martin around?'

'Yes, why?' Her tone was prickly.

'We just need to ask him a few questions. There have been a few developments with the case.'

She swerved her gaze to Brooke and her cloudy eyes looked right through her. 'What case?'

A man of similar age appeared from the back room. Also wearing glasses, his white hair frail, much like his skin. His khaki cardigan frayed at the edges. 'It's okay, June. I'm happy to speak to Detective Collins.'

Collins gave a cordial nod. 'Thanks, Martin.'

Martin held out his outstretched hand to shake Brooke's. 'It's nice to meet you in person, Ms Palmer.'

Brooke obliged. His hand felt cold and his knuckles swollen with age. 'It's nice to meet you, too. We appreciate your help.'

Martin invited the pair into the back room with a beckoning palm. June kept her lips tight as they walked by, still staring somewhere Brooke couldn't quite pinpoint.

The back room of the motel was just as Brooke had imagined. Littered with paperwork, short of natural light and coated in thick layers of dust. The wallpaper was different from that in Collins' room, but looked even older. Faded and stained with murky marks.

'Please, sit down.' Martin dragged two uncomfortable-looking chairs from the front of the desk. 'How can I help?'

Collins sat down slow. 'We have reason to believe Evan Wiley may have been here.' He unpocketed and unlocked his phone. 'He took this photo the night he was murdered.'

Martin examined the image closely. He glared back at Collins and returned the phone. 'Okay. It's possible he stopped by.

I spend most of my time out here with my head buried in paperwork. You see, we're up to our ears in bills and I'm not the best accountant.' He gazed in the direction of the front desk and lowered his voice to a purr. 'June used to handle all of this, before the dementia set in.'

Collins exchanged a glance with Brooke. He turned back to Martin. 'Can we check the logbook, please?'

'Sure. Give me a moment.' Martin disappeared momentarily before reappearing, carrying a thick black file. 'So not Tuesday just gone, but the one before. Correct?' He licked the tip of his index finger, its nail brittle and brown.

Collins gave a quick nod. 'That's correct.'

Martin flicked through the logbook until he found the correct page. He pushed his glasses up and leaned in close. 'Hmm. No mention of a Mr Wiley.'

Collins pinched the bristles on his chin. 'He could've just entered a room where someone else was staying.' He reached over to take the logbook. 'Do you mind?'

'Sure.' Martin didn't sound it.

Collins scanned the page and exhaled. 'Nobody I recognise.' He passed the logbook to Brooke.

After a cursory scan, Brooke confirmed the same with a head shake. 'Nope. No one familiar.' She chewed her lip, trying to catch Martin's eyes. 'Do you have CCTV footage we can look through?'

'We have a camera outside reception, but that stopped working last year I'm afraid.' Martin looked up in thought. 'Or was it the year before that?'

Brooke flicked her focus around the room, trying to contain

her frustration.

'We're going to have to search the place, Martin,' Collins said firmly. 'Every room.'

Martin removed his glasses to rub his eyes and gave a little nod. 'I understand.'

'I'll call the station now to get the paperwork. Thanks for your cooperation.' Collins stood. 'We'll try to cause the least disruption we can.'

'Thank you.' Martin took to his feet slow, his knees cracking in the process. 'As you know, business has been bad enough for us lately.'

The detectives each gave June a polite nod on their way out as Collins called the station and requested a warrant.

'What now?' Brooke said.

'We should have it in the next hour or so.' He found another number in his contacts and held the phone to his ear. 'Let's use this time to go pay another of our friends a little visit, shall we?' A brief pause. 'Mr Pérez? It's Detective Collins. Are you free for a quick chat?'

It was nearly two-thirty by the time Bill finally showed up. Evan had got close to calling him but decided to wait. He didn't want to appear any needier than he already felt.

'Sorry,' Bill said as he swooped beneath the ramp. 'I had to get a bit of work done before heading out, and it took longer than I thought.'

The sight of Bill gave Evan a shot of adrenaline. It had only been a couple of weeks, but he'd grown concerned he'd never see him again. 'That's okay. I'm glad you came.'

Bill sat beside Evan awkwardly and said nothing.

Tension hung heavy in the air now. Evan considered whether to hug him or not. He assumed Bill was wondering the same. Ultimately, they both decided against it.

Bill narrowed his eyes. 'How you doing?'

Evan wasn't sure whether to lie. 'It's been... rough.'

Bill took a big breath. 'Me too.'

It went quiet. A seagull squawked in the distance.

'So, do you want some coke?' Evan said.

Bill paused for a few moments, as if choosing his words carefully. 'You know that's not the only reason I wanted to hang out with you, don't you?'

Evan looked up and found his gaze.

'That first time you found me and Mick here,' Bill went on, 'when you offered us the weed. Why did you do that? Just to get us to hang out with you?'

Evan shrugged. 'I guess.'

'You could've just come and talked to us.'

Evan raised an eyebrow. 'And you really would've wanted to hang out? After how you guys were with me at school?'

Bill kept his eyes to the ground. 'I know we were arseholes. If I could go back and change that I would.'

It suddenly occurred to Evan that Bill's bullying might not have been driven entirely by jealousy. Had he been attracted to him back then? Evan recaught Bill's focus. 'So, it really wasn't just about the drugs?'

Bill thought about this for a moment. 'I mean, at first it was. But I didn't expect this... thing that happened between us. I've had some doubts before. About what I'm into. But it all just kinda... made sense with you.' He bit his lip and then shrugged. 'You can't help how you feel.'

Evan suppressed a smile. It made him happy that Bill was finally opening up. 'I feel the same.'

'But it could never work.' Bill's face flattened. 'With us, I mean.'

It felt like a blow to Evan's stomach, leaving him winded. He finally managed a single-word response: 'Why?'

His back growing hunched, Bill kept his eyes south. 'My dad would hate me if I was gay.'

Evan flinched. Hate was a strong word. He thought back to when he first spoke to his mum about his confusion. Sure, she hadn't jumped for joy. Her own conservative upbringing had evidently taken its toll. But he knew she'd love and accept him no matter what. Ultimately, he believed his grandparents would, too. It pained him to think Bill's dad wouldn't feel the same.

'You don't have to tell him,' Evan eventually said.

'What sort of life would that be?' Bill's face had reddened. Tears varnished his eyes.

'Better than a life of lying to yourself.'

'We're not even allowed to see each other. I shouldn't even be here now.' Bill returned his eyes to the ground, lips trembling. 'I just need to... change this part of myself somehow. Then it'll all be okay.'

There was another silence, this time deafening. Evan wondered if this was the moment he should be telling Bill he was in love with him. After all, that was how he felt. Wasn't it? Either way, he decided to hold back. He wasn't sure he'd be able to get the words out anyway.

Out of nowhere, Bill leaned over. Their faces less than an inch apart for a long, warm breath. His eyes dropped to Evan's lips before he closed the gap and kissed them. Bill's lips were as supple as ever, but rough where he'd grown a shadow. Evan closed his eyes, and all his despair began to lift. Drift away. This was exactly where he was meant to be and who he was meant to be with.

Evan had no idea how much time had passed when he first heard the steps. Bill must have heard them too, as he pulled away fast. The boys twisted around to be met with someone standing there.

Mick.

'Uh, sorry,' he said, awkwardly avoiding their eyes.

'This isn't what you think.' Bill moved away from Evan, his face turning so red it looked like it might explode. 'We've just got through three grams and now we're fucking high. I think we thought we were chicks.'

'It's all good, man,' Mick said. 'I don't care. I just came for a skate and thought I'd check to see if you guys were around.'

Bill stood up so quick he almost fell forward. 'I gotta get going anyway. We've nearly run out of coke. Ev's still got some if you want any. See ya.' He slipped away into the afternoon fog.

Evan remained frozen, unsure what to say.

Mick's stare was unapologetic. 'You all right?'

'Yeah. I'm fine.'

'I'll see you around then, yeah?'

'Yeah. See ya.'

Mick disappeared, obviously changing his mind about skating.

Moments turned into seconds. Seconds became minutes until Evan was able to gather his thoughts. That was it then. Bill had made himself clear. They could never be. It's not that Bill didn't feel anything for Evan, at least he knew that now. But what they had would have to remain a secret. A teenage experiment that Bill would occasionally reminisce over when he kissed his wife. A hidden part of himself that he would try the rest of his life to ignore. It would eat away at him until he snaps, or dies — whichever comes first. That wasn't the life Evan would lead — a life in the shadows. But what would life be without the one person that had ever really meant something to him? Was it even worth living?

Evan pulled the mirror and cocaine from his backpack. He didn't want to feel anything right now. He didn't want to get caught in his own head again. He poured the entire contents of the baggie across the glass. The white powder completely enshrouded his reflection as he leaned close and breathed in.

Chapter Twenty-three

'This is the place?' Brooke peered at the unassuming house through the windscreen. It was one of Taonga's newer builds that made up the handful of nondescript suburbs that had sprung up in recent years. This particular area had been nothing but pastures a decade ago, bulldozed in favour of unaffordable-affordable housing.

Collins killed the engine. 'It's the address he gave me. Unless he's sent us to the other side of town and made a run for it.'

Brooke could have almost laughed if the thought of Santiago leading Evan to the motel didn't occupy her mind. Beating him to death before disposing of his body over the waterfall, sliding out a cigarette to calm his nerves and accidentally dropping one in the pitch-dark bush. She quivered as she unbuckled her seatbelt.

Within seconds of Collins ringing the doorbell, Santiago emerged. His hair, which was tied back in a ponytail the same way it had been when they first met him, appeared to have more greys than Brooke remembered. He steered his glance at them both systematically. 'Come in. Would you like anything to drink?'

'No, thanks,' Collins said stonily and followed Santiago through the stark-white hallway. 'Thanks for meeting us with such short notice.'

'Of course. Please, sit down.' Santiago directed his hand towards the sofa. 'How can I help?'

Brooke sunk into the plush fabric, moving a large velvet cushion out the way as she did. Her eyes swept the room. No photographs of loved ones. Just striking abstract photography. It figured, she supposed.

'We spoke to your ex, Santiago,' Collins said. 'Mr Harding.'

There was a pulse of quiet. 'You were snooping on me?'

Brooke leaned in a pinch. 'Mr Pérez, you have to understand our suspicion. You were unable to verify where you were the night of Evan's murder.'

'I told you where I was. I was here.' He'd grown noticeably flustered.

'According to you,' Collins chimed in. 'You have no alibi.'

Santiago breathed heavy and recomposed himself. 'Go on then. What did Keane have to say? I can tell you a few things about him, too.'

Collins observed Brooke from his peripheral vision. 'He told us Evan came here a couple of times.'

Santiago eyed them both carefully. 'That's right. He came once for dinner, and then once more uninvited. He just turned up.'

'You didn't mention this before.' Brooke's voice remained calm and monotonous.

'I made sure to answer your every question. It's not my fault you didn't think to ask.' He turned to Collins. 'Besides, you told me to leave you to do your job. So I did.'

'Watch it,' Collins said.

Brooke clasped her hands on her lap. 'When you said you'd met with Evan, I assumed you meant you'd been at school, maybe even the park or the beach. Helping him with his photography. Not at your home. It's a bit more intimate, don't you think?'

Santiago honed in on her. 'Just what are you insinuating, Detective?'

Collins crouched forward. 'As we speak, we're waiting on a warrant to search the Lucky Star Motel.'

Brooke didn't blink. She didn't want to miss a second of Santiago's reaction to the revelation.

'Do you think that's where it happened?' Santiago's voice sounded dry now.

'We have reason to believe Evan may have been there on the evening of his murder, yes,' Collins said with a touch of resolve. 'Have you been?'

Santiago's face remained deadpan. As did his tone. 'Yes, I have. I stayed there when I had my interview with the school. But I mean, that was a long time ago.'

Collins shifted back a touch. 'That answer sounds familiar. Isn't that what you said about Taonga Falls?' He reclined fully and pivoted to Brooke. 'Tell Mr Pérez here what you found at the falls, Palmer.'

Brooke anchored her eyes on Santiago's. 'A cigarette. Which isn't unusual, but it was the brand that caught my eye. Fortuna.'

Santiago maintained her stare. Deep in thought until suddenly, his eyes amplified. 'I did give Evan a packet of cigarettes. The last time I saw him. When he visited me asking me to buy him the lens.'

Brooke side-glimpsed Collins for a beat, who hid his disappointment well. 'And you're only mentioning this now?'

'My apologies. That obviously slipped my mind. I was caught off guard that day.'

Brooke thought hard for a moment, unable to think up a scenario of how the cigarette got there. She hoped Collins had a better idea. But judging by his disinterest in pushing Santiago on this, he must have believed his story.

Santiago broke the long silence. 'Look, I can see now where I made some serious errors in judgement when it came to Evan. Did I take him under my wing? Yes. Did I see him as a younger version of myself? I suppose. I saw Evan like a younger brother, even a son. I felt for him. I knew he was missing a father or even a sibling. He'd had no friends in Taonga until Bill and Mick came along, and their intentions were questionable at best. The whole town knows that. Should I have had him over for dinner? Probably not. But there was nothing dark or sinister about my invitation.'

'Keane might disagree with you,' Collins said with a pinch of provoke.

Santiago shuffled on the adjacent sofa. 'Well, of course he would.' He paused for a tick. 'Look, I loved Keane. A lot. I still do. But it was too difficult being together. His jealousy got in the way. He hated me having a friendship with Evan.'

'Can you blame him?' Brooke arched an eyebrow. 'He was a good-looking young man. I'm sure you could see that.'

Santiago observed her eyes cautiously. 'Yes, I could see that. But that doesn't mean I looked at him in that way.' He leaned in. 'Just because I'm gay, it doesn't mean that I want to sleep with every man in front of me.'

Brooke's mouth almost fell slack.

'Well, that's what you're suggesting,' Santiago pressed. 'Isn't it?'

Her face grew a pinkish tint. 'That's not what I meant.'

Santiago smoothed his pony. 'Besides, I was committed to Keane.'

Collins intervened: 'We heard you weren't very committed at the start of your relationship.'

Santiago wrinkled his brow. 'What do you mean?'

'Mr Harding told us you were in an open relationship to begin with.'

'He's delusional.' Santiago gave into an eye roll and his Mediterranean complexion started to redden. 'Since the start of our relationship, Keane was certain I was cheating on him, which was never the case. I suppose he didn't mention that he was cheating on *me* towards the end? That he walked out on me and moved straight in with another man?'

The room went still. 'He didn't mention that,' Brooke said plainly.

Santiago eased his defence. 'I didn't think he would have. See, I think Keane's paranoia about my commitment to him was just an excuse in the end. A reason to leave me for another man. Either that, or he really did think I was doing something I wasn't — driving himself to have an affair.' Santiago paused for a pulse and stared out the window. 'Either way, I think us not being together anymore is for the best. It's healthier for us both.'

Brooke noticed Santiago had become tearful. He was convincing if nothing else, she thought. He was different from Keane in that respect. 'Do you think Keane had it in him to be violent?'

Santiago rubbed his eyes and firmly held Brooke's gaze. 'Honestly, I didn't. But now I'm not so sure. I'm not sure what he's capable of.' There was an uneasy silence that Santiago eventually interrupted. 'Look, I know Keane very well. At least, I thought I did. In my opinion, much of his behaviour is a result of him growing up gay here in Taonga. He would often tell me what it was like. Something I know Evan could attest to, despite how times have changed. That's why I hoped they would have got on. I'd hoped Keane could have helped him somehow. Shown him how things get better.'

'So things did get better for Keane?' Brooke prompted.

'Of course they did. A lot better. You met him, didn't you? That confident front you see, that wasn't always him. Keane has overcome a lot. And he's a hard worker, I'll also give him that. An overachiever, even. And he deserves everything he's worked for. I think he found it hard being back in Taonga because his lifestyle changed. He could no longer afford the expensive suits and watches.'

Brooke's breath stopped, and Collins noticed. The photo of the watch ticked to life in her mind.

Santiago continued, 'I'm sure he's much happier, and richer, now he's back in the city. Sorry, I'm going on too much. I haven't really spoken to anyone about this, and now it's all coming out.'

'No, it's helpful.' Brooke's heart was still thumping and the watch still ticking. 'We appreciate it. Did you ever lend Keane your cigarettes?'

'Oh, God no. He doesn't smoke. Hates it.'

There was another short silence before it was broken by Collins' phone ringing. 'It's the station.' He held it to his ear. 'Hello? Great, thanks. We're on our way.' He hung up and averted his stare to Brooke. 'The warrant's been granted.'

Brooke turned her eyes from Santiago to Collins. 'Great.'

'Thank you for your time, Mr Pérez,' Collins said, rising. 'You've got my details. As I said last time, you think of anything else, please call.'

He gave a short nod. 'I will. I really will.'

Brooke and Collins left the house fast and jumped into the SUV.

'Were you thinking what I was thinking?' Brooke said.

Collins waited for a car to pass and reversed out the driveway. 'That Keane's our guy? Motivated by jealousy and revenge? Took one of Santiago's cigarettes to frame him?'

'Bingo.' Brooke thought back to their meeting with Keane in Christchurch. How something about his demeanour hadn't added up. How he'd wanted to paint Santiago in such a bad light.

'Let's get this motel searched first.' Collins drove just a fraction over the limit. 'Then we can figure out our next move.'

The wind whistled across the waves as Evan paced the beach. He'd sobered up now, but his head ached from the bottle of vodka he'd started drinking not long after he woke. The last week had been a haze. Each day had trickled into the next, and he'd spent more time intoxicated than not. While Bill's words had hurt, it was the way he'd discarded him when Mick caught them that had broken his heart in two. Although he understood Bill's resistance, he thought maybe he would have reached out by now. Apologised and asked to meet again. But nothing. No call or message had come. So Evan drifted through Taonga like the fog.

The beach had been empty until Evan spotted a figure appear on the horizon. It took him a few minutes to work out who it was. How had he found him? Evan had been ignoring his calls and messages, the same way Bill was ignoring his. But there were only so many places to hide in Taonga. And now there was nowhere left to run.

Evan paced towards Warren until he was close enough to hear him. 'I'm sorry. I—'

'You said a week.' Warren's tone was searing. 'I don't give freebies. That stuff was worth about a thousand bucks. That might not be a lot of money to someone like you, but it is to me.'

Evan swallowed his fright. 'I know. I'll get it to you. I promise.'

Warren came close enough to Evan that he could smell his breath. He had the vexed expression of a tyrant. 'You better. Or else.' He punctuated his sentence with a shove.

There was a thud as Evan fell on the sand. The shock made his head spin. Staring at the steely sky, Warren loomed above him, his mouth twisted. He coughed up some phlegm and released it. The web of spit hit Evan's face. Warren gave him a kick, just to drive the point home, before he walked away.

Evan shut his eyes, as if it would shut out the world. His lips turned dry and his face a meek white. Lying on the sand, listening to the waves beat the shoreline, he wondered if Warren's threat was just words. And if it wasn't, would it really be all that bad?

Chapter Twenty-four

Collins laid the document flat on the reception desk with a satisfying slam. 'The warrant.'

June ran a finger across the printout and her overcast eyes met Brooke's. 'What's this for?' The grooves lining her gaunt face seemed even deeper now. Either she'd completely forgotten, or maybe more likely, Martin was keeping his wife in the dark.

Collins gave Brooke a brief look, loaded with a mix of impatience and pity. 'We need to search the motel, June. In relation to the murder of Evan Wiley.'

Before June had a chance to respond, Martin emerged from the back room, his face tight and withdrawn. He struggled to make any eye contact beyond a fleeting moment. He studied the warrant carefully. 'Don't worry, June. You just stay here and ensure any guests are looked after.' He managed Collins' focus. 'Let me just get the keys.' Within seconds, he reappeared with a clipboard and a large ring, a couple dozen keys dangling from it. They gave a metallic rattle with his every movement.

'We'll start by surveying each room,' Collins said with a note of authority. 'And if we see any signs, we'll go from there.'

As they cut across the car park through the cold, Martin turned to face them both. 'Please remember there are people staying here. This will be very disruptive for them.'

Brooke once again noted the shortage of parked cars and wondered just how many guests the motel had right now. Other than a slight pick up thanks to the podcast, Taonga's tourist trail had been far from booming for years. Even less so during the winter months. Sure, the odd backpacker passed through town year-round, no doubt attracted to the Lucky Star's competitive prices. But beyond that, she struggled to picture the clientele – aside from a homicide detective on the Canterbury District Police budget.

'Of course,' Collins said. 'But I'm sure they'll be understanding. We're investigating a murder, after all.'

Martin ignored his comment and glanced at his clipboard as they approached the first set of rooms. 'Okay, let's get started.' He knocked the door gently.

Brooke noticed there was no car parked in front. 'Is someone staying in here?'

Martin shook his head. 'Not according to my list. But as I mentioned, June gets a bit muddled. I'll probably give each room a little knock, just in case.'

Brooke gave Collins a small smirk. This wasn't going to be quick.

'No answer.' Martin unlocked the door and stepped inside

slowly. 'Hello?' He called out to be sure the room was empty. 'Okay, you can come in.'

The room had a similar decor to Collins' and the same musky smell. It was an amalgamation of mildew, dust and something Brooke couldn't quite pinpoint. The detectives each slipped on a pair of thin latex gloves.

'Are those really necessary?' Martin said, taking a touch of offence.

'You can never be too careful,' Collins said with a wink.

Martin didn't reply, but instead strode over to the bathroom and gave it a little knock. 'Hello?' He held his ear to the door. 'Anybody in there?' He looked at Collins and smiled. 'You can never be too careful.'

The detectives looked over the bed first. And then beneath it. Brooke kept her eyes out for any signs of struggle. She leaned in to get a closer look at a series of indents on the familiar floral wallpaper behind the wooden headboard. Multiple marks, but no scratches. As Collins checked the kitchenette, Brooke canvassed the faded carpet, looking for a stain. She noticed a patch that was a shade paler. She smoothed her hand over the pile and inspected it closely. The dust particles that sprung from between its tufts proved it hadn't been a recent clean up.

Next, they scoured the bathroom, which Martin had hesitantly opened. Brooke looked under the sink, in the shower. Nothing. She got to her knees, hoping to spot even the tiniest strand of blonde hair. Nothing. Just a whole heap of dust where the room could do with a thorough clean. She stood up straight and brushed herself off. The only crime that had taken place in this room was installing the avocado-green suite, she decided.

Collins shifted his attention to Martin. 'Okay. Next room, please.'

Martin tapped the neighbouring door with his knuckle. This room had a vehicle parked out front. A classic camper-van that looked like it had done a fair few kilometres across the West Coast's wild terrain. The door opened a dash to reveal a thin-framed man somewhere in his twenties. It was hard to tell which end, thanks to his bushy beard and skin that had seen a touch too much sun.

'Hello,' Martin said in his professional tone. 'Sorry to bother you. We just need to give your room a quick inspection.'

The man pushed back a loose dreadlock, which had sprung astray. His bloodshot eyes grew a fraction wider. 'Is this about that dead kid?'

Collins drew his badge from his coat pocket. 'It won't take long, mate.'

Brooke picked up the scent of weed on the man's striped Baja hoodie as they brushed past him. Inside, a woman leaned forward on the bed, her muddy-blonde hair also twisted into dreads. The smell of marijuana lingered in the air, slightly disguising the stagnant smell the previous room had held.

'Are they allowed to smoke in here?' Collins asked Martin through the side of his mouth.

Martin dropped his gaze to the floor. 'Not really. But I must admit, June and I have been turning a blind eye as of late. As I mentioned before, times are tough.' He reached under the kitchenette's sink and pulled out a canister. 'Besides, nothing a bit of freshener can't solve.' He gave it a spray and smiled.

Frangipani. That was the mystery ingredient Brooke

couldn't pinpoint. The dreadlocked woman overplayed a wave in front of her face and gave a fake cough.

'Why are you searching here?' The male guest buried his hands in the pockets of his hoodie. 'Thought the boy died at that waterfall.'

'It's an ongoing investigation,' Brooke said coldly.

The two backpackers looked to one another.

'We went down there yesterday,' the woman said. 'To the falls. That's the reason we came through this town. Wouldn't have otherwise.'

Brooke tried to swallow but her throat had turned too dry. While her brother's case had put Taonga on the map, Evan's murder had secured it. What fan of crime fiction wouldn't want to take a trip through the mysterious town that had now seen two of New Zealand's most horrific homicides? But this wasn't fiction. It was reality. *Her* reality. She caught Martin's beady stare from the edge of her eye. Somewhere deep down, was he relishing in the touristic intrigue? It would no doubt be good for business. Hell, if it turned out something happened in his motel, perhaps he could turn the place into some kind of grotesque attraction. *Martin's Murder Motel*. It definitely had a ring to it. Pay extra to stay in the room it took place. Brooke flinched at how bleak her thoughts had become and did her best to repress them from growing any darker.

After finishing examining the room to no avail, Brooke gave each of the backpackers a loaded glare on her way out the door. 'Do me a favour. Go visit Mount Cook next. This town's still grieving.'

*

'Only a few rooms left.' Martin leaned against the door of a vacant room they'd finished checking and pulled out a packet of cigarettes. 'You guys don't mind if I take a short break, do you?'

Both Brooke and Collins gave their blessing with a head shake.

Martin flipped open the pack and presented it between the detectives. 'Smoke?'

'No. Thanks.' Brooke kept her arms folded.

Collins shook his head. 'Oh, go on then. Could do with one actually.'

Martin locked eyes with Brooke as he handed Collins his lighter. 'You don't really think something could have happened here, do you?' His tightened features hinted at genuine fear.

A shard of guilt engulfed Brooke. This place must have been all he had, she thought. It had been there for as long as she could remember. She assumed he'd been there just as long.

'We're not ruling anything out,' Collins answered for her.

Martin drew back on his cigarette. 'I know it's not much to look at. These days it's all about a *luxury* experience. That was never meant to be the idea of this motel. It was supposed to be somewhere warm and inviting. Somewhere to kick your shoes off and feel at home. Somewhere anyone can afford.'

Brooke traced her eyes along the verandah. She imagined Evan's body being dragged along it to a car boot in the dead of night. She searched for a streak of blood. A piece of his hoodie caught on a nail snag. Any sort of sign. But she saw nothing. Martin's mumbling speech had faded into the background. It sounded like marketing spiel. Something he came up with back when the motel first opened. Maybe that's what it once was, but now it was anything but a home. She realised it wasn't just the motel she was thinking about.

Her eyes found their way back to Martin. 'So it's just you and June that run this place?'

He gave a tiny nod as his hair wisped in the brisk breeze. 'Sure is. Kids have never been interested. I always thought this would be something they could have carried on. A legacy, you know? Both of them up and left as soon as they could. Not enough for them here in Taonga.' He met her gaze with what Brooke couldn't make out was a tear or just the cold. 'I suppose you can relate to that, Ms Palmer?'

The reminder that everyone in town knew her story un-eased Brooke. Why couldn't she just be anonymous? Like she was in Auckland. She decided to divert back to his story. 'Where are they now?'

Martin took another drag. 'Both in Melbourne. The boy went first and his sister followed soon after. We barely see them these days. Too much hassle making the trip with their own families. Last time we were all together was about six Christ-mases ago. Only time we get to see the grandkids these days is through a screen.' He squinted at Brooke through his specta-cles, which had become misty. He removed his glasses momen-tarily and wiped a lonely tear.

Brooke turned away. The guilt was back, stronger this time. Not only for what could be in store for Martin and his family, but for the years she'd also spent not returning home as much as she could. Except, she assumed she'd had more to run from than Martin's kids. Sure, the motel didn't seem much. Not in comparison to what Gary had brought into her own family's life. But nothing could have made up for losing Jack. She shook her head as if to dispel the thought. She had to remain focused. What mattered was bringing justice to Evan.

'Come on.' Collins stamped his unfinished cigarette on the deck. 'Let's wrap this up.'

Martin closed his eyes and took one final puff before sending the butt over the verandah. 'Roger that.'

As soon as Martin opened the first door of the last set of rooms, Brooke's breath got caught in her throat. She looked Collins in the eye who shared her uneasy stare. She then turned to Martin. In his small, watery eyes, all she could see was dread.

Martin blinked three times and stepped into the room, attempting to ignore its overwhelming scent. 'Come on then, what are you waiting for?' He almost choked on his words.

Once inside, Brooke was certain. The smell was undeniably different from every other room. The muskiness was there, the faded frangipani, but it was coupled with a clinical bite that stung her throat. The amount of bleach that would have been used to justify the room's smell made her heart pound. The fumes seeped into her nostrils and didn't leave.

Brooke pictured the room lit up in luminol blue. Beneath its worryingly pristine facade, circular smears of cleaned-up blood spatter would glow bright on the walls. Evan's smudged handprints grasping for help in his final moments. Had he still been wearing the watch when he suffered the final, fatal blow to the head? Its hands forever frozen in time at that fateful moment.

Brooke's heart ticked back to life as it dawned on her that this could have been the last place he saw alive. The thought made her dizzy. Or was it the bleach? The intricate pattern of the wallpaper didn't help. She left the room just as the taste of bile rose to her mouth. There was no stopping it. She leaned over the verandah and vomited. After a minute or so, she spat the remnants and wiped her mouth. As she did, she heard Collins on the phone.

'Constable. Send a couple of guys down to the Lucky Star Motel. Right away. We're gonna need a room sectioned off until the forensics show up.'

Chapter Twenty-five

'I'll go get June.' Any remaining colour had now drained entirely from Martin's complexion. He looked down to where Brooke had thrown up. 'And the hose.'

'We'll all come back to reception,' Collins said with a pinch of an order. 'I don't want anyone else to come near this room.'

Martin gave a gentle nod. 'Understood.' He locked the door and led the way. 'It was probably just the cleaners.' The Lucky Star really was everything to him, but it was clear he was clutching at straws.

'They only cleaned this room?' Brooke managed sarcasm despite herself.

Martin looked her up and down. 'Perhaps someone vomited in there.'

Brooke swallowed as the trio paced across the car park to reception. The bell above the door gave an optimistic chime when they stepped inside.

June greeted them with a wide beam. 'How are you all?' It was the most cheerful Brooke had seen her. She wondered if she even remembered what they'd been doing.

'They'd like to see the logbook again,' Martin said. 'They want to check who was staying in room nineteen.'

'Of course.' June licked the tip of her index and began flicking through the pages. 'Give me a moment.'

'I'll go get our guest a glass of water,' Martin said to his wife who was looking increasingly confused. 'She had a bit of a stomach upset.' He skipped to the back room.

'Oh, you poor thing. What am I looking for again?' June squinted to Brooke.

'Tuesday last week. Who checked in to room nineteen?'

'Oh, I don't know what I'd do without you.'

Brooke wondered if she'd mistaken her for someone more familiar.

When she found the page, June fished her glasses from the chest pocket of her blouse and stared at the words close. 'Here we are. M Rivers. Mr M Rivers.'

'That's who was staying in the room that night?' Brooke said.

June nodded. 'It appears so.'

Martin reappeared with the water and handed the glass to Brooke. She swilled her mouth and reluctantly swallowed. 'Thanks, Martin.' She washed it down with a fresh mouthful.

Martin fingered the name. 'Hmm.'

'Do you remember him?' Collins ridged his brow.

As Martin shook his head, which was pinkening back to life, June squinted to the ceiling.

'I don't,' she said. 'Which is unlike me. I remember most of our guests.'

Brooke glanced at Collins for a beat before shifting her gaze back at June. 'So he's not a regular?'

Martin's head shake intensified. 'Definitely not. I've never seen that name before.'

The room shared a long silence.

'I'm sorry,' June said, her cool tone finally giving away to a tremble. Tears welled in her eyes. 'We're not much help, are we? And something awful might have happened here. Right in front of my eyes.'

Brooke was surprised she now seemed aware of what they were discussing. It comes in waves, she remembered from her grandmother's mental decline. She pressed a palm on June's shoulder, giving it a small rub. 'It's okay, June. You're helping as much as you can. And we still don't know for sure that it happened here.'

June drew a steep breath, pulled a handkerchief from her pant pocket and wiped her eyes. 'This will be the end of us, if it's true. The end of our motel.'

There was a brief pause. Brooke opened her mouth to speak again, but refrained. There was nothing left to say.

As they veered away from the motel, Brooke gave the rear-view mirror a glance. The dreadlocked couple stood among a small cluster of fellow guests. Two coffee-clutching constables guard-ed the room in question. 'I wonder who'll get here first,' Brooke said. 'The forensics or the press.'

Collins met the road. 'My money's on the press. Forensics

will be at least a couple hours. They'll be on their way from Christchurch.'

Brooke shuddered at the thought of the developments hitting the headlines before Lana found out. 'I better give Lana a heads up.'

'Good idea.' Collins kept his stare ahead. 'Hey, I've gotta head back to Christchurch tomorrow. The ruling for my custody battle is Monday morning. I want to spend a bit of time with my daughter before then.'

Brooke gave a small nod. 'Of course.'

'You should spend a bit of time with your family, too. While you're here, I mean. I'm sure they could do with seeing you right now.'

Brooke stared out the window and thought back to what Martin had said about his kids. 'Yeah, you're probably right. We don't want to burn out either. Even though I feel like we're getting close.'

Collins remained quiet for a pulse. 'A day won't hurt. I'll be back by Monday afternoon and we can keep going. We should hear back from the forensics by then, too.'

'Sounds good. Would you mind dropping me home?'

Collins broke a smile. 'Not at all.'

*

Brooke traced the inky outline of the ocean and scraped the surplus from her plate. She caught her mother's reflection in the window.

'How are you going?' Barbara's question was loaded with concern. 'You barely said a word over dinner.'

Brooke slid the plate into the dishwasher. 'I'm just tired. And I didn't want to go on about the case. It brings it all up, doesn't it?' She'd given a brief overview of where she and Collins had got to with the investigation, but spared her mum and Gary the details.

Barbara retrieved a half-empty bottle of Sauvignon Blanc. The gold of its label shimmered in the fridge light. 'There's only enough for you and me.' She winked and closed the door with a hip thrust. 'Sounds like Gary's already secured his place on the sofa anyway. That's what happens when you don't help clean.'

The sound of the evening headlines blasted from the living room.

Barbara generously filled two wine glasses as even as she could. 'I just don't want you to get too sucked into all this. You're obviously great at what you do, and I'm sure this detective is very grateful to have your support. But you can't forget you're grieving, too.' She proffered a glass. 'Here.'

Brooke gave a pinched smile. 'Thanks. You're right. I think I've been moving so fast I've forgotten to take care of myself.' She sipped. 'What about you?'

Barbara took a seat at the dining table. 'What about me?'

'How are you coping?' Brooke sat beside her mother. 'You're also grieving.'

Barbara twisted her glass by the stem and took a sip. 'I'm just trying to take it a day at a time. I saw Amanda yesterday. She seemed pleased with how the funeral went. It was a lovely send-off, don't you think?'

Brooke took another sip. This time bigger. 'You're allowed to say you're struggling, Mum. That it brings it all back.'

Barbara's eyes hooked her daughter's, and she paused for a blink. 'Of course it brings it all back. There's never a day that goes by I don't think about him. Even before all this.' Her eyes had grown wet.

Brooke clutched her mum's hand. 'I miss him so much.'

Barbara wiped a tear and gave her throat an abrupt clear. 'I know. So do I.'

A stillness overcame the room. It was strangely comforting.

Brooke shifted her gaze to a photograph of her, Jack and Hannah that was framed on the wall. It must have been taken about a year before his murder. 'I think about what he would have been like now. All grown up.'

Barbara's laugh was so small it could have easily been mistaken for a sniff. 'I know. I think about what he would have done with his life. He was very logical. A problem solver. I know he would have gone far.'

Brooke wiped a tear and gave the ghost of a smile. 'I know. He was much brainier than me and Hannah. He just wasn't sure what he wanted to do with his life.'

'That would have changed,' Barbara said with a feigned grin. 'He was still so young.'

Brooke's face folded. 'Too young.' There was another pause. This one wasn't so comfortable.

From the television in the living room, Brooke could just about make out the voice of the blonde reporter. '...recent development in the case...' Her words were too fast and the volume too low. '…the Lucky Star Motel…'

Brooke tuned out the white noise of the news and turned back to her mother, who was staring at the family photo. 'I'll never forget that evening. When we realised he'd gone missing.'

Barbara clutched her wine as if it were her son's hand. 'I know. He'd been staying late at school so often around then. You all did at his age. It just didn't cross my mind that he wouldn't be home by dinner.' A fresh tear slid down her cheek. 'That was the last time I felt complete. When I was cooking dinner that night, blissfully unaware.'

Brooke clasped her mum's hand and gave it a firm squeeze. The news reporter's voice had now been replaced with that of the backpacker, his mumble managing to be both recognisable and inaudible.

'Anyway,' Barbara said, wiping her face and composing herself. 'We were lucky to catch that–' She inhaled. '*Boy* so quickly. I pray the same for the Wileys.'

Suddenly, Brooke was back in the courtroom. Harry Saunders sitting at the stand, his menacing eyes peering at her through narrow slits. She'd held their contact for a moment too long, before dropping them in defeat. Hearing the word guilty should have set her free, but somehow it hadn't. It still hadn't.

'It sounds like you're making progress anyway,' Barbara went on. 'Once you've found who did it, hopefully you'll get a confession out of them in the courtroom. Like we did with *him*.' Satisfaction glazed Barbara's eyes. 'Can you imagine if the trial had gone on any longer? I don't think I could've taken it.'

Brooke stared at her wine as if mesmerised, the confession echoing in her ears. *I did it. I killed him.* Brooke wasn't sure if it was Harry's voice in her head, or that of the podcaster.

'How was Lana yesterday? You went to the falls, didn't you?' Barbara took back more wine, this time a gulp.

'She was surprisingly strong. I think it was just something she needed to do. Do you remember I was the same wanting to visit the bridge? Straight after Jack's funeral.'

Barbara downed the last drop of her wine, as if it would make the memory disappear. 'Come on. Let's go spend some time with Gary. See if we can take control of the remote. What are your plans for tomorrow?'

Brooke followed her mum's lead and drained her wine. 'I'm seeing Lana in the morning. We're going to take a walk along the beach.'

Barbara smiled as she stood, her knee giving a crack in the process. 'That's good. She needs you right now.' She gave Brooke's shoulder a tap. 'And not just on the case.'

'I know.' Brooke rubbed her face in a bid to energise, but it just left her feeling even more tired. 'I'm doing my best to do both.'

Brooke started to follow her mum towards the living room when her eyes were drawn to something. It was an article on the Greymouth Star, which lay atop a pile of newspapers on the kitchen counter, ready to be recycled. *Construction nearing completion on $15m renovation to Taonga Church and accompanying Clergy House.* She knew there was something she'd been meaning to do since the funeral. Visit Father Peters. She'd go first thing tomorrow before Sunday Mass. Even if he had nothing more to offer than prayers, she'd take what she could get right now.

Overhead, through the dining room skylight, the wind

whistled.

Evan waited until he heard his mum leave the house before he dialled Bill's number. He'd spent all morning wrestling with the decision to make the call, but he couldn't hold back any longer. He crouched on his bedroom floor with his back to the wall and listened to the phone ring. No answer. He hung up.

He should have known calling Bill would be a waste of time. He'd made it clear he didn't want things to go any further between them. But right now, Evan didn't even care about the prospect of having a relationship with him. He just needed a friend. He needed someone.

A few minutes passed and a message from Bill came through. Evan thumbed his phone heavily to read it: Don't call me. I'm working with Dad. He'd kill me if he found out you were trying to speak to me.

Evan felt a surge of sadness. He considered not replying, but decided he didn't have much to lose. Sorry. Just need a friend right now. I'm in trouble.

Evan saw Bill had seen the message straight away and was typing.

What's happened? You okay?

Evan responded quick: I'm fine. For now.

Bill had seen the message but wasn't typing a response. Evan let out a sigh and instantly regretted reaching out. A moment or two later, Bill started typing.

Dad's in Greymouth again this weekend. I'll meet you at the falls Sat morning. 10am. You can tell me what's going on then.

A smile overtook Evan's face. Even if only for a moment, he felt joy.

See you then.

Evan was about to get up when another message came through. This time from Warren. It was a GIF of an hourglass with the sand pouring through until the top of the glass was empty.

For a few seconds, he forgot to breathe.

Chapter Twenty-six

The sun hadn't yet risen when Brooke arrived at the church. The sky was only just teasing its early purple from behind the distant alps. It had just gone six and Mass started at seven. She wasn't even sure if Father Peters would be around, but she decided it was worth a shot. She tightened her red woollen scarf and kept her gloved hands deep in her coat pockets as she ascended the stone stairs. Exhaling a cloud of white air into the morning's darkness, she thought back to Evan's funeral. So much had happened in such a small period of time, yet she still didn't feel much closer to having any answers. The thought made her shiver.

Brooke was relieved as the heavy doors pushed open. She drifted through the cold building until she could spot Father Peters setting up at the pulpit, the same way he'd been at the funeral. She noted the shock in his eyes when they locked with hers.

'Brooke Palmer. What a pleasant surprise.'

She stretched out her arms for a fleeting embrace once she reached the stand. His body felt less frail than she'd expected. 'Hello, Father. How have you been?'

He paused, his stare tender. 'It's been a tough time for us all. No one more than the Wileys.' He closed his eyes for a tick. 'I keep them in my prayers.'

'I know. It's incomprehensible.' Brooke's eyes grew glassy as she gazed at the stained Mary holding baby Jesus in the window.

'And how are you holding up?' Father Peters tilted his head to the side a fraction. 'I've been keeping you and your family in my prayers, too.'

Brooke looked to the stone beneath her feet. His familiar tone managed to solicit both comfort and pain, taking her back to a time when her family would come to church often. To a time when Jack was alive.

Father Peters placed his hand on Brooke's shoulder, his long fingers outstretched. 'It's okay. God is with you. Always.'

Brooke straightened her back and gave her eyes a quick dab. She wasn't here to fall apart. Nor was she here to decide whether or not she still held any spiritual beliefs of her own. 'I'm doing okay. Thank you.'

Even in the dim light, she could see Father Peters wasn't convinced. 'It was nice to see your mother at Evan's funeral. I haven't seen her in so long. Years, probably.'

Brooke kept quiet. Why did she feel a sudden twinge of guilt?

Father Peters thought carefully for a long moment before he spoke again. 'I know it was very difficult for your family. After what you all went through. Your mother and Gary stopped coming after God decided He wanted Jack to join Him in heaven a little early.'

That was one way of putting it, Brooke thought.

'He was such a lovely boy.' Father Peters looked somewhere beyond her.

Brooke rediscovered his eyes. 'Father, I'm actually here to talk to you about Evan. If you wouldn't mind?'

His stare turned stern. 'Evan? What about him?'

'Shall we sit down?'

'Please.' He gestured towards the front pew.

The wooden bench groaned as they gave it their weight.

'So, what is it you'd like to know?' Father Peters looked at her with intent.

'Lana was telling me about how Evan's behaviour shifted in the months leading up to his death.'

Father Peters remained quiet, taking in her words.

'She also mentioned how Evan had been exploring aspects of himself that left him concerned for his soul. In the afterlife.'

There was a sharp pause until Father Peters filled it. 'I see.'

'I was wondering if Evan came to speak to you at all during that time?'

He gave her a flat look. 'Yes. He did.'

Brooke shuffled in her seat. Her instinct had been right.

'I assume it's been a long time since you've practised Catholicism, Brooke. But I have no doubt you remember, or are aware of, the Seal of the Confessional?'

'Of course. But I haven't come to you this morning as a detective, Father. I've come here as an old friend.'

Father Peters lowered his glance and narrowed his eyes. 'You put me in a truly difficult position.'

'Maybe it'd be easier if I just told you what I already know. I know that Evan had questioned his sexuality and that he had been exploring this.'

Another silence. Father Peters avoided her gaze.

'I also know that Evan had been purchasing drugs from a Greymouth dealer that he'd been sharing with his friends,' Brooke went on. 'I know that he owed this dealer money and that he'd spent all of his savings.' She was trying to see in Father Peters' eyes whether any of this information was coming as a surprise. She figured it was. 'We're at a critical point in the case, Father. Anything you tell us will be confidential but could help us in the search to find out who did this to Evan.'

Father Peters finally found her focus again, the downturn in his mouth exaggerated by its surrounding folds. 'I'm not sure how much help I would be. It sounds like you know more than myself.'

Brooke shifted to face him fully. 'So he'd been confiding in you?'

'Yes. Evan had been coming to see me for quite a long time. I too saw a shift in his behaviour. How he'd been unhappy at school, and, as you say, questioned his desires. But it was in the months and weeks leading up to his murder that he really… began his fall from grace.' His mouth shot shut.

Brooke observed the priest closely. 'That must have been very difficult for you. Knowing what you knew and not being able to go to Lana. Or Amanda and Frank.'

Father Peters' lips remained pressed for a touch longer. 'I

am not here to judge. It is only God who can judge our souls.'

Brooke bit a nail in frustration. 'As we sit here, forensics are examining a room at the Lucky Star Motel, just out of town. You've probably seen it on the news already. We think that might've been where Evan was murdered.'

A bolt of silence. Father Peters lowered his head and gave it a heavy shake.

'Father, did Evan ever speak about…' Brooke licked her dry lips. 'Did he ever discuss that he might be thinking of selling his body?'

Father Peters' eyes were off to the distance again, as if in search of something.

Long light cut through the church, dappling the stone floor in a kaleidoscope of vivid colours. Evan walked slowly towards the oak confessional, pulling in a deep breath with each stride. Inside, he waited a few claustrophobic minutes before Father Peters took the bench on the opposite side of the booth. 'Hello, Father. I'm not here to repent.' Evan swallowed. 'I just want to talk.'

'Of course.' Father Peters' voice hummed comfortably through the divide. 'How are you?'

Evan closed his eyes and took in the familiar, musky smell. 'Not great, Father. I've got myself in a bit of trouble since we last spoke.'

'Whatever it is can be repented.'

There was a pause while Evan decided what to reveal. 'I owe someone money, but I can't pay.'

'The wicked borrows and does not repay. But the righteous shows mercy and gives. Have you thought about asking this person to show you mercy?'

Evan fumbled his fingers anxiously. 'He won't. He's not religious.' A short pause. 'I can't ask my mum or grandparents. I need to find another way.' He caught Father Peters' stare through the lattice just as his eyes flicked away. 'There is someone… someone who I can go to. But–' Evan cut himself off. Sharing his concerns would only sabotage the opportunity.

'My boy, there is no shame in asking for help in your time of need. It says in the Bible that we are to give those who ask, and to not turn away from those who want to borrow.'

Evan felt tears welling. How had he gotten himself into this mess? 'Thank you, Father.'

'Remember, son, we all fall down from time to time on this journey here on Earth. It's how we pick ourselves back up again. That's how we will be assessed in the afterlife.'

After wiping his eyes with the sleeves of his grey hoodie, Evan straightened his back and cleared his throat. 'I hope so.'

'Remember this final passage. Let no debt remain outstanding except the continuing debt to love one another. After all, love is God and God is love.'

Evan stood up and left the confessional. If there really was a God, he needed Him right now. And it would take more than love to save him.

'Father?' Brooke found Father Peters' gaze.

'Sorry.' His eyes were hard, but his smile soft. 'It's been such a distressing time. My mind gets hazy.'

'I understand. Can you recall anything?'

'Evan came to me about the debt you speak of.' Father Peters checked his empty church before continuing. 'He told me there was somebody who he could go to. I assumed to ask for money. I told him there was no shame in asking for help. I assured him that we all fall from time to time. But what you're saying could be a possibility, yes.' His eyes dropped. 'If I had known it was this serious, I would have spoken to Lana.'

Brooke remained quiet. Could this *somebody* be Santiago? Was his whole story about the lens a lie? Some kind of preemptive excuse? Or was there someone else? She released a breath and gave Father Peters a long look. She couldn't help but feel uncomfortable about how much he'd known but not acted on. She eyed her watch. 'Speaking of Lana. I better get going. I'm meeting her.'

Father Peters gave a slow nod, punctuating it with his smile. 'Send her my love and prayers.'

Just as Brooke went to stand up, he held out his hand to stop her. 'Brooke, I know how difficult this must be for you. Not just because Evan was part of your family and Lana your best friend. But because of what you went through yourself.'

Brooke averted his gaze. She didn't want to have that conversation.

'And I know the hurt you must carry. I can see it in your eyes. Holding any resentment and anger is only going to hold you back. But if you can find it in your heart, you must search for a way to forgive. It's the only way you will be able to move forward. As it is written in the Bible, love your enemies, do good to them, and lend to them without expecting to get anything back.'

She bit her lip. If he was in any way insinuating she should forgive Harry Saunders for what he did, she didn't want to hear it. Brooke stood. The back pews had begun to populate and, in the growing crowd, she spotted the forlorn faces of Amanda and Frank.

'Goodbye, Father.' Brooke gave him a brief hug and ambled towards the Wileys.

Amanda reached out for an embrace. 'Brooke.' That waft of perfume. 'What a pleasant surprise seeing you here. Will your mum be joining, too?'

'I'm actually not here for Mass. I came to speak to Father Peters.'

Amanda glanced ahead at the priest, before honing back in on Brooke. 'Oh?'

Frank, who had remained quiet until now, shot her a brief look she couldn't quite read.

'Yes, I've been meaning to come and see him since the funeral,' Brooke said. 'I wanted to tell him what a wonderful job he did.'

The confusion drained from Amanda's face, giving way to a beam. 'How lovely of you. Yes, it really was a lovely service.' She turned her attention to the floor. 'Devastating, but lovely.' Her stare met Brooke's once more. 'You should join us. For Mass.'

'I'm actually off to meet Lana now. At the beach.'

'Oh, how lovely. It will be good for her to see you. Some days she just doesn't even want to get out of bed.'

Brooke felt a pang of pain. 'I better get going. I'd hate for her to be waiting for me.'

Amanda swerved to the aisle's side and gestured for Brooke to go. Frank gave a small smile, but Brooke couldn't seem to find much warmth in it.

It was still dark when Brooke descended the stone stairs. The lavender glow gave little light, but enough to see his face as he brushed past. They exchanged an awkward nod, and he disappeared inside. Brooke hadn't known Santiago was practising. Nothing about their prior encounters had suggested as such. Perhaps it was something he'd taken up since Evan's death.

Was it a guilty conscience?

Chapter Twenty-seven

'Sorry I'm late,' Lana said as she approached Brooke. 'It's been a rough morning.' The sun, which had not long appeared, was weak, but she wore oversized sunglasses Brooke assumed were to conceal puffy eyes.

'Don't apologise.' Brooke dusted the cold sand off and took to her feet. She gave Lana a small but tight hug.

'Thanks for giving me a heads up about the motel. It's all over the news. My phone hasn't stopped ringing.'

Brooke shook her head. 'The media doesn't make it any easier.'

'Yeah. Well, like I said before, I guess in some ways it's a good thing. The minute they move on, so will everyone else. And the investigation will be forgotten.'

'It won't be forgotten. Promise.'

Lana tightened her coat and shuddered. 'It's freezing. Shall we walk?'

'Please.'

The women paced the sand in silence for a couple of minutes, watching the waves lap the shoreline. Brooke thought about telling Lana about her pit stop at the church, but decided against it for now.

'What do you think he was doing there?' Lana said suddenly. 'At the motel.'

Brooke fussed with her scarf and kept her eyes low. Lana hadn't stayed on the call long last night. The development had been too upsetting. She must have had time to absorb it a little. 'I don't know. Hopefully we'll know more soon.'

There was an uncomfortable pause. Brooke wondered whether Lana had connected Evan's comments about making money to the location he was potentially murdered. Her friend's innocent nature made it highly possible she hadn't.

'Have there been any other developments?' Lana's hair blew into her mouth. She pulled it away. 'What happened with the cigarette?'

Brooke stared at the swirls of haze lining the ocean. 'Collins and I went to Christchurch to have a chat with Santiago's ex while we were waiting for the fingerprint results, which came back without prints. He gave us some insights into Evan and Santiago's relationship. How Evan had gone over to their house. But when we got talking to Santiago, he said something that turned our attention back to the ex.'

The hair was back. 'I'd take that with a pinch of salt. We all know how exes can be.'

'Well, what he said wasn't intentional. He said something about Keane buying expensive watches. Remember what I told you last night? About the watch in the dealer's picture? It's a loose link, I know.'

Lana had already stopped walking and was searching for Brooke's focus. 'Hold on. Did you just say... *Keane?*'

'Yeah. Harding.' Brooke knew that look. 'You know him, don't you?'

'I treated him.' Lana's words came out clipped, beneath shallow breaths.

Brooke bit her lip and thought about how Santiago had painted him as a jealous ex. He clearly had bigger issues. 'Did you know he was Santiago's partner?'

Lana's expression confirmed she didn't.

'How long did you treat him?' Brooke pressed.

'Not long at all. He hired me a couple of months ago because he was having trouble with his relationship. I tried to convince him to bring his boyfriend along, that I offer couples' therapy, but he told me his partner didn't even know he was coming to me.'

'What did he say about him?'

Lana took a quick breath before opening her mouth to allow a fog of white air to protrude from her lips. 'His partner? He talked about him a lot. Said how he was worried he was having affairs. At first, I thought it sounded like he had good reason to be concerned. But after a while, I realised it was projection. He was insecure about his own fidelity.'

The squawk of a gull overhead cut through the unnerving silence. Brooke opened her mouth but then pulled it back shut to form a narrow line. She leaned against the wind.

Lana removed her sunglasses. Dark rings framed her

widened, bloodshot eyes that spoke of a sudden realisation.

'What is it?' There was a concerned note in Brooke's voice.

'What if Keane hired me as his psychologist knowing I was Evan's mother? Maybe he wanted to get closer to him... to plan something.' Lana's last few words curled.

'I think you would've picked up on that at the time. You're great at what you do.'

Lana nodded unsurely.

'It's good you're telling me this, though. Collins and I will follow it up as a lead. But we can't dismiss other possibilities.'

Defeat came over Lana's face. Brooke knew that feeling.

'I'm still finding it difficult to completely trust Santiago,' Brooke continued. 'Did you know that Evan had gone to his house a couple of times?'

'No. I didn't.' Lana stared out to the sea as she spoke. 'Looks like there was a lot I didn't know about my son.' She didn't wipe away the tear that shed.

There was another silence, in which even the seagull partook.

Moments later, Lana was trudging towards the ocean. Brooke kept still at first, watching her from afar, until she realised she wasn't stopping at the shoreline. Lana's steps sunk into the shallows, fully clothed and in her boots. Brooke dropped her coat and scarf to the sand and ran into the water. 'Lana, wait!' But her words were swallowed by the wind.

Lana paused before falling back into Brooke's arms. The force of her collapse pulled the pair into the seafoam. The first breaker was freezing when it lapped their embrace. But with each wave, Brooke could see a layer of Lana's guilt wash away.

She held her tight.

'I miss him so much.' Lana's words were split into hysterical sobs as she was cradled.

Brooke tightened her embrace, as if to stop her friend from drifting away into the blue abyss. 'I know.' She swayed with the motion of the sea, pulling a deep breath when a large wave drew away. It crashed back with thunderous force. Lana let out a piercing scream, muffled only by Brooke's body and the water's fall. Seconds stretched into a lifetime.

Evan thought about turning his car around one last time before he finally gave in. He knew what he was doing was wrong. But he didn't know who else to turn to. He didn't know where else to run.

Once parked, he focused on steadying his breath. He needed to appear as normal as possible. He glanced at the house, checking the lights were on. They were. With a final exhale, he climbed out of the car and drifted towards the door.

'Evan, hi.' The shock was evident on Santiago's face. 'Are you okay?'

Evan realised his attempt to appear like nothing was wrong had failed. 'I'm fine. I was just in the area and I thought I'd pop by. Don't worry if you're busy.'

Santiago hesitated for a moment, clearly wrestling with his own thoughts. 'No, not at all. We've just finished dinner. We're about to watch a film. You can join us if you like?'

Evan's lips curved into a smile. 'Sounds great.' He followed Santiago into the warmth of the house.

Keane got up from the sofa when they entered the living room. His eyes said it all when they met with Evan's. 'What's he doing here?'

'Evan was just in the area,' Santiago said. 'He thought he'd swing by.

I said we're about to watch a film. Have you found one yet?'

Keane's ears turned red. 'How cosy. Why don't I leave you both to it?' He skimmed Evan as he stormed past.

'Keane!' Santiago reached out his hand.

But it was too late. The slam of the front door echoed down the hallway and with it came Evan's sense of unease. 'I'm sorry. I should go.'

'No, it's okay, Evan. Sit down. Let's have a quick talk.'

Evan perched on the edge of the sofa. He couldn't hide his discomfort.

Santiago took a seat in the armchair beside him. 'What's wrong? Has something happened?'

Tears glazed Evan's eyes. He couldn't hold them back any longer.

'Is this about that guy?' Santiago went on. 'The one you like?'

Evan sniffed and wiped his eyes but said nothing.

'Evan, you have to tell me what's wrong for me to be able to help you.'

There was an extended silence until Evan finally replied. 'I– I need to borrow some money.'

Santiago tilted his head to the side and narrowed his eyes. 'Some money?'

'Yeah. Like… a thousand.'

A sense of foreboding clasped the air. Santiago opened his mouth to respond, but Evan beat him to it. 'It's for a new lens. For my trip.'

Santiago released his breath. 'Oh, I see. Of course. Which lens do you want?'

Evan tried not to swallow. 'Actually, forget it. I'm sorry. I don't know why I asked. Look, I should go.'

Santiago fixed a firm stare. 'Listen, Evan… if you're in any sort of trouble–'

'I'm not. I promise. Hey, I don't suppose you have a cigarette, do you? I've run out and could do with one.'

Santiago said nothing for a beat, as if he was scrambling for the words. 'Wait there.' He disappeared momentarily and reappeared with a packet of Fortunas. 'I shouldn't be encouraging you really. But take these.'

Evan glanced at the red and white packet. 'Really? The whole pack?'

Santiago shrugged. 'Keane hates it anyway. That's one less pack he'll be pleased I'm not smoking.'

Evan smiled and stuffed them in his jacket pocket. 'Cheers.'

'You're welcome. Let me know about that lens.'

'It's fine. I should go. I didn't mean to get in between you and Keane. I'm sorry.'

'That's okay. I think I mentioned this to you before, but Keane's been going through a bit recently. He's had a few… problems.'

Evan flicked his fringe to the side. 'What kind of problems?'

Santiago glanced at his phone. 'Nothing he can't work out. I should call him. Make sure he's all right.'

Evan gave a short nod. 'Good idea. Thanks again. See ya.'

'See you.'

Evan considered reaching out for a hug, but decided against it. He felt guilty enough for driving a wedge between Santiago and Keane tonight. It seemed like everywhere he went, problems followed. Was he the cause?

Driving home, Evan unwrapped the pack of cigarettes and placed one between his lips. As he lit up, he imagined touching down in Barcelona. Armed with nothing but his camera and the list of Santiago's recommendations. His breath felt heavy at the thought of how he'd sabotaged his own dreams. What for? A few cheap thrills and a stupid infatuation? His thoughts were quickly replaced with the memory of Bill's warm embrace.

He couldn't pretend to himself that he regretted a thing.

'I didn't realise how good screaming makes you feel,' Lana said through chattering teeth.

'It's underrated. Maybe you can start recommending it to your clients.' Just as she gave Lana a grin, Brooke's phone started to vibrate in her coat, which lay crumpled on the sand beside her. She fished it from the deep pocket. Collins. 'I better take this.'

'Of course.'

'Hey.' Brooke stood up and stepped away from Lana. 'How's it going?'

'Palmer. I got a message from Santiago.'

'Go on?' Brooke traced the horizon with her eyes. The faint outline of a cargo ship had appeared.

'He had a thought. Keane Harding's mother still lives in Taonga. He suggested we pay her a visit. Said she knows him better than anyone.'

'Good idea. Especially considering what I just found out.'

'What?'

'I'm with Lana right now. She told me Keane was one of her patients.'

A small pause before Collins spoke again. 'Serious?'

'Dead.' She looked back to Lana, who was almost smiling to the sea. 'What's her address? I'll pop 'round this afternoon.'

'Fifty-five Canary Drive. Name's Margaret.'

'Thanks. I'll let you know how I get on.'

'Please.'

Brooke swept her drenched hair from her face. 'Oh and Collins…'

'Yeah?'

'Good luck tomorrow.'

'Thanks. Gonna need it.' He hung up.

Brooke stalked back towards Lana. 'That was Collins.'

'What did he say?' Her face met Brooke's before her eyes did.

'He gave me Keane's mum's address. I'm going to pay her a visit.'

Lana managed a delicate smile. 'Sounds promising.'

'Come on, let's get you home. Before we completely freeze over.'

Brooke helped Lana to her feet and back towards her house. The women padded, arm-in-arm, leaving nothing behind but a frenzied zigzag of footprints and an ocean full of tears.

Chapter Twenty-eight

Through the mist, Brooke could make out a light was on inside Margaret Harding's house. It had only just gone noon, but the morning's clarity had been replaced with thick clouds, like an oil spill in the sky. Once parked, Brooke waited a few minutes, watching the windscreen wipers sweep hypnotically from side to side. Taking a big breath, she finally switched them off. If Margaret was going to turn her away, it was out of Brooke's control. It was worth a shot.

She'd only just pushed through the white picket fence when the front door swung open. An overweight woman who looked somewhere in the latter end of her fifties stood with her arms crossed. 'Can I help you?'

Doing her best to keep her umbrella up, Brooke presented her badge. 'Detective Brooke Palmer. Are you Margaret Harding?'

Her crow's feet deepened. 'Yes, why?'

Brooke slipped her badge back inside her coat. 'I was hoping I could have a quick talk with you about your son.'

Margaret's mouth fell agape and her eyes began to swell. 'What's happened? Is he all right?'

'He's fine. It's in relation to the murder of Evan Wiley.' A short silence followed, except for the sound of the rain beating the fabric of Brooke's umbrella.

Margaret unfolded her arms. 'Come inside. You'll catch a chill out there.'

'Thanks.' Brooke felt the warmth of the house enclose her as she followed Margaret into the hallway. She collapsed her umbrella and placed it in a holder.

'Here, let me take your coat. Tea?'

Brooke decided a cup would go down well. 'Great, thanks.'

Margaret hung up Brooke's dripping coat and led her through the house. The classic Kiwi villa's interior looked fresh for its years. The panelled walls were painted soft hues, complementing the sepia of the photographs that hung. They worked together to make it feel like a loving home. Among black and whites of relatives from another era and Kodak moments of potential grandchildren, was a framed printout of a grinning teenage Keane.

Margaret guided her into the kitchen. 'Here, take a seat.' She waved her hand at the small breakfast table and filled the kettle. 'English brekkie okay?'

'Perfect, thanks.' Brooke scanned the kitchen. It was the perfect balance of cluttered and clean. 'Do you live alone?'

'I do. Milk and sugar?' She began boiling the kettle on the stove.

'Just milk, thanks.'

Margaret went to run her hands through hair that wasn't there. Judging by the photos on display, it was freshly cropped and coloured. A deep cocoa instead of the pictured grey. 'Keane's father and I went our separate ways a long time ago. I've had trouble finding the right man since. Probably where Keane gets it from.' She half-smirked and fetched the milk.

Brooke returned the grin. She liked Margaret already.

'You're Barbara's daughter, aren't you?' Margaret pulled two mugs from the cupboard and dropped in the bags.

'That's right. You know her?'

'No. I've seen her around town a couple of times. I remember what happened to your brother. I'm very sorry.'

'Thanks. It's been a rough couple of weeks. Brought up a lot of buried pain.'

'I bet. It's just awful what happened to the Wiley boy.'

The kettle started to hiss. Once Margaret had poured the tea and taken the chair beside Brooke, she met her eyes properly for the first time. They were the same hazel shade she'd passed down to her son. 'Now, tell me how I can help.'

'What can you tell me about your son's relationship with Santiago Pérez?'

Margaret poured milk into her mug. 'I'll let you do your own. I always make it too milky.'

Brooke trickled a dash but kept quiet, her mouth tight.

'I liked Santiago a lot,' Margaret said eventually. 'At first I wasn't sure, knowing he was a bit older than Keane. But considering some of the guys Keane has involved himself with over the years, I figured an older man with a proper career would be good for him.' She blew her tea and took a sip. 'I also liked that they decided to move to Taonga. It was nice to have him close again.'

Brooke tested the tea with her tongue. It was a minute too hot. 'How old was he when he left?'

'Eighteen. Soon as he could. What's this about? You don't think Keane had anything to do with the murder, do you?' A sharp line appeared across Margaret's forehead as she folded her brow.

'I haven't come to that conclusion, no,' Brooke white-lied, hoping Margaret couldn't hear the watch ticking in her mind.

'Then why are you here?' Margaret's tone had shifted slightly. Less soft.

Tick. Tick. 'Ms Harding—'

'Margaret is fine.'

Tick. Brooke pushed the watch from her thoughts. 'Margaret, your son seems like a great guy. And I'm sure he had nothing to do with this. I appreciate you taking the time to talk to me.'

Margaret didn't take her eyes from her tea.

'Were you aware that your son was seeing a therapist while living back here?'

Clutching her steaming mug, Margaret honed her gaze. 'I wasn't. But I know he's had... I know he's battled demons in the past. But that doesn't make him a killer.'

'I'm not saying that—'

'What *are* you saying, Detective?' Margaret's words had an edge to them now. A note of scorn. Brooke wondered if she'd been too quick to warm to her.

'Evan had been struggling with his identity,' Brooke said carefully. 'He was coming to terms with the fact he might be gay and he'd gone to Santiago, who used to be his photography teacher, for some advice.'

Margaret listened close. 'Go on.'

'Santiago told us that Evan had visited their house a couple of times in the weeks leading up to his death. And Keane had become jealous.'

'Can you blame him?' Another sip. 'Sounds highly inappropriate if you ask me.'

'I agree. And believe me, we're very much treating Santiago as a suspect. We're just trying to get as clear a picture as we can. We need to understand the full story.'

Margaret's face loosened a dash. Her eyes fell back to her tea. 'Look, Keane does have some… issues. His dad walked out on us for another woman. He was badly bullied at school.'

It all felt too familiar to Brooke. She wondered how he'd have coped with losing a sibling on top of that. She subsided her thoughts and kept listening.

'Obviously it was hard for him to come out in a town like Taonga. Evan might have had an easier time, now things are changing, but it was still challenging for Keane.'

'I think Evan had his fair share of struggle.' Brooke took a drop of tea. 'How old was Keane when he came out?'

Margaret looked at the ceiling for a beat, thinking. 'Sixteen. Maybe seventeen. But I always knew. A mother always does.'

Brooke thought of Lana. Not always.

'But despite his issues,' Margaret went on, 'he's never been aggressive or violent. He doesn't have it in him to *kill*.' She accentuated her final word.

Brooke hesitated. 'Santiago told us Keane used to question him about cheating. Do you know anything about that?'

Margaret gave a minor shrug. 'He spoke of his concerns about their relationship from time to time. He's very insecure for such a handsome man. It's all up here, right?' She tapped her index finger on her left temple.

Brooke agreed with her eyes and kept quiet for a moment or two. 'Did you know Keane was actually cheating on Santiago in the end?'

Margaret took back the last of her tea. 'I know Keane hadn't been happy with Santi for a while. He met Dee and they just clicked. Obviously, I don't approve of cheating. Especially considering it happened to me. Keane knows my feelings about that. But, I want him to be happy. And he assures me he is.'

Brooke used her teeth to pull a flake of dry skin from her bottom lip. 'Have you met this Dee?'

'Deepak. No. Not yet. Only on FaceTime. I'm planning to visit them next weekend. So I can give you my verdict then.' She gave a swift wink. The warmness had returned. 'Hang on, I have his number actually. Maybe you should give him a call? I'm sure he'll be able to confirm Keane was with him the night of Evan's murder. That'll make this easier for you.' She scrolled through her phone. 'Here you go.'

'Thanks.' Brooke repaid her with a smile and saved the number into her phone. 'I hope things work out for them both.'

Margaret rubbed her eyes to signal exhaustion. 'So do I.'

'I'll get going,' Brooke said, rising. 'Thanks for the tea. And your help.'

'No problem. Let me fetch your coat.' Margaret went ahead into the hallway.

Brooke followed behind. This time, she noticed a door was slightly ajar, with a pile of cardboard boxes in the centre of the room. Folded neatly on top was a grey hoodie. The sight made her blood pulse cold. She was thinking of the grainy CCTV footage of Evan in the dairy.

'Here you go.' Margaret passed her still-damp coat. 'Looks like the rain has eased. It's been dreadful lately, hasn't it?'

Brooke pulled it on and retrieved her umbrella. 'It sure has. Bring on spring.' She couldn't contain her eyes wandering back to the boxes in the bedroom.

Margaret gave her a suspicious stare. 'What is it?'

'What's in there?'

A short pause. 'Just some of Keane's things. He moved it in here before heading to Christchurch. He hasn't had a chance to pick it all up yet. Why?'

Brooke kept her eyes focused on the hoodie. 'No reason.'

Margaret's lips thinned to nearly nothing. 'I think you should leave now, Detective.'

Brooke gave a tiny nod and trudged back to her car, avoiding an enormous puddle on the way. Inside, she buckled her seatbelt and stared at Deepak's number for a long minute before deciding to give him a call. Just when she expected it to kick into an answering machine, someone picked up.

'Hello?'

'Hello, Deepak?'

'Who is this?' His voice suggested a similar age to Keane.

'My name's Detective Brooke Palmer. I was just wondering

if I could ask you a couple of questions about your partner, Keane Harding?'

A beat of wordlessness until he spoke again. 'Is he all right?'

'He's fine. I was hoping you'd actually be able to clarify whether you were with Keane on a particular night?'

'Why? Is he in trouble?'

'It's in relation to the murder of Evan Wiley in Taonga. At this stage, we're just trying to rule out suspects.'

There was a lengthy silence.

'So can you confirm whether you were with him on the night that happened?'

'I can try.'

Brooke told him the date and there was a longer silence, this time not even the sound of Deepak's breath. 'Are you still there?'

Nothing.

'Hello?' Brooke checked her phone to make sure she hadn't been cut off. She hadn't.

'Hi, sorry. I was just checking my messages. Wanted to be sure. I wasn't with Keane that night. He told me he was down in Taonga with his mum.'

This time it was Brooke's turn to be silent. She glanced through the windscreen at the front window of Margaret's house. She noticed the blinds had been pulled shut.

'Is there anything else?' Deepak said. 'I haven't really known Keane that long to be honest. Not sure how helpful I can be.'

'Believe me, you've been helpful.'

Evan closed his eyes, and listened to the water's roar. The rain had been persistent the last few days, and the forecast said they were in for more, so the falls were crashing even harder than usual. He pulled the hood of his windbreaker over his head and imagined how it would feel for the current to pull him off the waterfall's crest. Would the world go into slow motion as his body catapulted down the chute? He imagined how it would sound as his body hit the rocks at the base. And when he landed, would his eyes be open or shut?

'Are you meditating?'

Evan opened his eyes. Bill had on his favourite jumper. The one with blue and white stripes. His hair was shorter and he looked withdrawn. Like he hadn't been eating properly.

'I guess. Kinda.'

Bill slumped beside Evan and twisted his body to face him. 'How've you been?'

Evan buried his hands into his denim and shrugged. 'Not great. You?'

Tilting his head to the ground, Bill fiddled with the lace of his sneaker. 'Same. Pretty shit, actually.'

Evan pulled out the Fortunas. 'Want one?'

Bill glanced at the pack. 'Where'd you get those?'

Evan pulled out a cigarette and placed it between his lips. 'From a friend.'

Bill shrugged and took one. 'Thanks.'

The two young men lit up and stared at the crashing falls, smoking.

'Seen much of Mick?' Evan said after a while.

A wisp of smoke curled intricately from Bill's lips. 'Nah, not since that day he caught us. Have you?'

Evan ran his tongue across the ridges of his teeth. 'Nope.'

There was a surge of silence.

'What's wrong?' Bill discarded the butt of his smoke into the water.

'Are you in trouble?'

Evan took one last drag and let his cigarette be carried by the wind. 'My dealer. The one I get the drugs from. He's after me.'

Bill squinted his eyes. 'What do you mean he's after you?'

'I owe him money. For those last couple of grams I bought.' Evan's eyes grew tearful from the cold. 'I'm skint, Bill. Totally out of cash.'

A flash of turquoise splashed the water. Within moments, the kingfisher was airborne again.

'How much do you need?' Bill said. 'I'm sure I can get it to you somehow.'

A gust of wind blew Evan's hood off. He pulled it back over his head. 'It's fine. I'll sort it out.'

Bill blinked impatiently. 'Why won't you let me help you, Ev? I'm sure I owe you enough. The number of times you've supplied stuff for me and—'

'I said I'll sort it out.' Evan's tone was firm.

The two young men sat silently in a moment that rippled with tension.

'Why did you want to meet then?' Bill straightened his spine. 'If you don't want my help, I mean. You said you were in trouble and you needed a friend.'

Evan's gaze hit the ground. 'I do need a friend.' A brief pause. 'I need you.'

Bill's expression turned despondent. He kept his lips pinched.

Evan searched his mind for the words to say next. But nothing came.

'You know I can't see you, Ev. That last time we met… it was a mistake.'

A snake of sorrow coiled Evan's heart. 'Did you come here to say goodbye?'

Bill's wordlessness, along with the chorus of falling water, was the response Evan didn't want to hear.

'I'm sorry, Evan. I just can't be who you need me to be.' After another couple of swollen seconds, Bill stood up and left, vanishing step by step into the thick mist.

Evan remained frozen, his back against the bank. Once again, his mind turned to the fantasy of plummeting down the falls. Being swept over the brink and making his final descent.

Chapter Twenty-nine

'How can I help?' The receptionist kept her eyes fixed on the computer screen.

Brooke leaned on the desk. 'I'm here to see Keane Harding.'

The woman, who was somewhere in her mid-twenties, met Brooke's glance with heavily made-up eyes. 'Is he expecting you?' Her braids swayed as she spoke.

He wasn't, unless Deepak had given him a heads up. Brooke had made the drive to Christchurch as soon as she'd gotten off the phone. She had to. Knowing that Keane had lied to his boyfriend about his whereabouts on the night of Evan's murder was too unnerving. She didn't want to give him the opportunity to organise a new alibi. 'Tell him it's Detective Palmer.' Brooke flashed the receptionist her badge.

The lady's lips peaked in the corner. 'Of course. I'll go get him now.' She rolled her chair back and stood in one motion.

As she slipped through the glass divide, Brooke skimmed her

eyes across the contemporary offices of Digital Garden. Young professionals brushed past one another in varying directions, some smart and others jeaned. A man frantically tapped out code on his laptop while another casually thumbed his phone. The lift pinged and a woman entered the reception, speaking into her phone with rapid jargon while clutching a reusable coffee cup. She didn't offer Brooke a smile as she scanned her ID, unlocking the glass door with a click. Brooke wondered if she'd assumed she was here for an interview.

Brooke tried to imagine how different her life would have been if she *had* pursued a different career. Even Jack would have probably laughed at the idea of her being a detective, despite his murder being the catalyst. She'd never really known what she'd wanted to do when she was at school, while Lana had always had her heart set on psychology. When she'd first moved to Auckland, Brooke had taken on a few office roles, but nothing had lit her spark. After many long phone calls with Lana, and with Jack's murder still fresh in her mind, her friend convinced her to undertake the sixteen weeks of training at the Royal New Zealand Police College in Porirua. She'd never looked back.

The receptionist reappeared. 'Keane's on his way.'

Brooke flexed a smile. 'Thanks.' She glanced at her phone. Nothing from Collins. He still didn't know she was in Christchurch this morning. She hadn't wanted to bother him. She hoped more than anything he'd leave the hearing with good news. He was a decent guy, even if a little broken. But who isn't? The question played out in Brooke's mind as Keane came into view. His tightened expression a combination of apprehension and disdain.

'Keane. Hi.' Brooke considered offering a hand but changed her mind.

'What are you doing here?' He methodically searched her eyes. His tone was far less chipper than it had been on their first encounter.

Brooke's face grew stern. 'I need to talk to you. Can we go somewhere more private?'

Keane shot a glance over his shoulder. The receptionist, who was now back at her desk, averted her eyes to her screen and began typing with a faux flourish.

He pressed the lift's button, which opened without delay. 'Sure. Let's go out. Take a walk along the river.'

The punter wore Edwardian attire as he effortlessly pushed the pole into the riverbed, propelling the group of amused tourists along the Avon. The shallow boat sent ripples through the otherwise calm waters, twisting the reflection of bare trees and marble sky.

'What's happened?' Keane's quiff quivered in the cold wind.

Brooke kept her hands deep in her coat pockets, pacing the bank. 'We spoke to Santiago. About our conversation.'

'I thought you might have.' Keane seemed irked.

Brooke held her nerve and kept her eyes on the wooden walkway under her boots. 'He told us that you were jealous of Evan.'

Keane shook his head and rolled his eyes.

'I also know that you were seeing a psychologist,' she went on.

'Isn't that confidential?'

Brooke kept coy. 'So it's true?'

'Yeah, it's true. So what?' He gave her a glare. 'I've got nothing to hide.'

Brooke watched a fog of cold air drift from her lips. 'Were you aware that the psychologist you saw was Evan's mother?' She couldn't tell if Keane was shocked, or caught out. 'Santiago also called you a liar.' She paused, waiting for a reaction. She didn't have to wait long.

Keane twitched with agitation. His cool composure had melted away like a cube of ice in the sun. 'Of course he's going to say that. He's a suspect for murder, isn't he?'

A man on a bike shot between them.

'Watch it!' Keane called out.

Brooke observed his body language with reserve. She waited a few moments before forming her next set of sentences. 'Santiago also told us that he never cheated on you. He said it was all in your head and that it was actually you cheating on him towards the end of the relationship.'

Keane froze and spun around to stare at Brooke directly. 'What is this? Are you accusing me of something?'

Brooke pulled her hands from her pockets and gave a thick shrug. 'I'm just trying to get the facts. When I'm hearing slightly different versions of the truth, it's hard for me not to feel like someone's... withholding.'

Keane resumed his slow pace, this time avoiding Brooke's gaze while maintaining a rut in his brow. 'I did meet someone else, yes. It wasn't long ago. At first, I thought it was just going to be a friendship. Someone to talk to, which was something I felt I couldn't do with Santi as time went on. This guy, he makes me happy. He reminded me I deserve better. That I'm worth more. So I left.'

Brooke paused for a beat, wondering how to approach her next move. She decided there was no easy route. 'Your partner. His name's Deepak, right?'

Keane stopped again. His eyes had expanded to the point of almost breaching their sockets. 'You *have* been checking up on me. What is this?'

Brooke leaned in close and spoke beneath her breath. 'I had a chat with Deepak, Keane. He told me you were with your mother on the night of Evan Wiley's murder. I also spoke to your mum, who thought you were with Deepak. Can't you see how this looks?' Her voice had sped up now, her tone terse.

Keane stilled for a tick or two, holding back his words. 'So that's why she was trying to call. Come on, let's sit down.' He pointed towards a nearby bench. 'If you have to know every-thing about my personal life, I might as well just tell you.'

Brooke examined Keane as they took a seat. His guard was dropping.

He blew warm air on his hands and rubbed them together. 'Okay, look. I did start seeing Evan's mum. But it had nothing to do with him. She's the only reputable psychologist in Taon-ga, and I needed help. I won't bore you with my life story but living in a town like that, being someone like me, that shit kinda fucks you up. It takes its toll. It took its toll on me, anyway.' He glanced at an elderly couple passing by who must have heard him swear. The woman shook her head and the man overacted his disapproval with a scornful frown. Keane directed a sarcas-tic simper to them both and continued.

'When Santi showed up, it's like everything changed. For the first time in my life, I felt like I belonged. I was madly in love. And no matter what he tells you, no matter how he twists the truth, I *did* worry about his intentions. I was really insecure from the day we met and he knew that. I was putty in his hands.'

Brooke observed Keane's mannerisms closely. She couldn't read him. 'Did he do anything to prevent you from trusting him?'

Keane gave a nonchalant shrug. 'It was just little things. Subtle looks he'd give to guys. Sure, some of it was probably in my head. My own issues. But there was something about Santi that stopped me being able to fully trust him.' There was a brief silence as Keane watched the river. 'Anyway, when he started talking about Evan not long back, about how he'd come in and see him before class, that really got to me. I know he'd taken a fondness to him when he was his student. As I mentioned to you before, I knew they'd often spend time after school in the darkroom, which I didn't like. He assured me there were other students there, too, but it was always Evan's name I'd hear. Santi's face would light up when he talked about him.' Keane squinted at the faint sun poking through the gloom.

Brooke inhaled deep. 'So you met someone else?'

Keane's gaze hit the ground. 'It's not like I went out looking for someone. Dee just kinda… came to me. I have a good friend here in Christchurch that I met when I used to live here. I'd been confiding in her about Santi. She was never completely sure about him either. She introduced me to Dee. It all happened pretty quickly. He hooked me up with this job.' He motioned in the direction of his office. 'I should get back.'

Brooke gave a frustrated fidget. It was time to get to the point. 'So, where were you the night of Evan's murder, Keane?'

His eyes found hers. They spoke of embarrassment. 'I think the last three years with Santi, living with this constant fear and anxiety, it's messed me up a bit. It's pushed me to do things I normally wouldn't do.' He shifted his focus back to the river. 'And it's still very early days with Dee, so I shouldn't be too hard on myself.'

'Cut to the chase.'

'I was with another guy.' Keane pulled his phone from his pocket. 'I know, I'm an arsehole. Hang on, I'll call him. Prove it to you.' He flicked through his contacts until he found the desired number.

With each ring of the phone, Brooke felt her lead slip away. It felt like she was playing a game of snakes and ladders.

'Hello?' A man's voice on loudspeaker.

'Greg, hi. Sorry, this is completely random, but I just need you to confirm to a detective that you and I were together the week before last. The Tuesday.'

A pause. 'O-kay?' There was a fleeting silence and Greg spoke again. 'Yep, you were here at my place that night. What's this about? Am I in trouble?'

Keane met Brooke's defeated eyes. 'You're fine, don't worry. Sorry to bother you, mate. Thanks.' He hung up. 'Now are you happy?'

'Ecstatic.' Brooke's stare was intense. 'It looks to me that Santiago should've been the one to have been paranoid.'

Keane scrunched up his features like a petulant child. 'Well, you don't know Santi like I do. If I were you, Detective, I'd be spending my time on him. Has he confirmed where he was the night of the murder?'

Brooke avoided his eyes and kept mute.

'He hasn't, has he? So he has no alibi?' Keane's jaw fell slack and he shook his head. 'Man, I can't believe it. He could really have done this.'

'But why?' Brooke's tone had tightened. 'What motive would he have had?'

Keane locked her stare. 'Like I said before, maybe something went wrong. Maybe he didn't mean to kill him. I honestly don't know. Either way, I don't want to be dragged into this. So unless you can prove my involvement with this, which you won't, it's probably best to stop wasting my time. I've been more than enough help.' He stood up and gave an affirming nod. 'Goodbye.'

As Brooke watched Keane disappear out of sight, she pictured a game piece sliding down the snake, past the hoodie, past the watch and all the way back to the beginning of the board. She released an oversized sigh and directed her gaze back to the water. Its stillness was so far removed from the crashing current of the river that ran through her hometown. Of the ruthless pull and deadly drop of Taonga Falls. She inhaled the cool air and fought with her mind, doing her best to resist imagining Evan's murder. Somehow, the vision always found its way back inside her head.

The horrific visualisation was replaced by Father Peters' words playing back in her mind. *...if you can find it in your heart, you must search for a way to forgive. It's the only way you will be able to move forward.* She knew where she needed to go next. Maybe not for forgiveness, but for her own healing. It wouldn't be easy, but she had to follow her instinct.

It was finally time to visit Harry Saunders.

Chapter Thirty

A lone magpie cut through the concrete-grey sky that framed the bleak compound. The structures of Christchurch Men's Prison sat low in the landscape, as if ducking out of sight. Brooke stepped from her car to the cold and stared blankly through the fence. The brick buildings were painted pale, their barred windows repeating endlessly. It was just as depressing as she remembered.

Moving slow through the car park, her eyes focused on the barbed wire that ran like a menacing Slinky. She followed its loops to the muddy beige reception tower, which stood marginally more decorative than its fenced-in sisters. In the distance, pines swayed mockingly in the breeze, their surrounding grass unbearably green. The whole thing gave her an eerie sense of nostalgia.

As she walked, Brooke thought back to the day Gary had slowly driven the family past the prison following Harry

Saunders' sentence. It had been his attempt to make them feel safer. And despite Barbara's concerns, it had worked. Though not apparent at first, Brooke remembered how that night had been the first she'd slept through. It had been the same for Hannah.

Stalking towards the entrance of the building, Gary's words still hung in the air: 'He'll rot in there for what he's done.' Brooke swallowed. Was she really going to do this? She thought about turning back, but it was too late. She had reached the reception and her feet weren't slowing.

An overweight guard with a shaved head and creased features flicked his hand dismissively from behind a reinforced screen. 'It's not visiting hour yet.'

Brooke revealed her badge. 'I'm here to see an inmate. It won't take long.'

The guard's face crumpled. He clicked a hidden computer. 'Name?'

'Harry Saunders.'

The man wedged a black phone between his shoulder and ear and kept his mumble intentionally inaudible. He gave a short laugh and hung up, returning to Brooke with a flat face. 'Keep it brief, Detective. Saunders will be on ground maintenance soon.'

Following a different but equally impolite guard through a series of locked corridors to the visiting room, Brooke cast her mind back to the last time she'd seen Harry in the flesh. His empty eyes and sinister snarl. The collective gasp that echoed through the courtroom when the verdict was delivered. She'd been haunted by him ever since. He'd visited her nightmares.

Found his way into her daydreams. Even the most joyful memories of Jack would be tainted by the arrival of Harry's icy glare. His haunting gaze.

The guard slapped the back of a chair and gave Brooke a grunt before withdrawing to a corner. She took the seat and raised her hands, realising they were trembling. Why was she doing this to herself? Wasn't she going through enough right now? As if she needed any more reason to dig up demons from the past. But for some reason, she just needed to see his face. Even if she didn't manage to say anything, that would be enough.

A few torturous minutes passed until the door before her unbolted and swung wide. Brooke's eyes gripped on his instantly and, just as she'd feared, they had that same cold stare. Only now, each eye was ringed with age.

Harry slumped on the opposite side of the white metal table, handcuffed and scruffy. His worn skin nodded to a tough life. He'd bulked up with both fat and muscle, but otherwise looked the same as the day he'd been sentenced for Jack's murder. Brooke took in his grey eyes fully, disturbed by how much of Mick she could see in them.

The pair sat without words, locked in an intense stare. Harry eventually broke the silence. 'Why are you here?' His voice was slow and drawn out. The faux tone of a teenager impersonating a man replaced with the genuine depth of age, all the coarser from years of smoking.

Brooke took her time with her response, straightening her back and strengthening her stance to remind both him and her who was in control. 'I was in the area. Felt like it was something

I needed to do.' She leaned in a dash. 'Just wanted to see if you were still alive, really.'

The snarl from Brooke's memory was back, exposing a flash of his stained-yellow teeth. 'Tina told me you've been pesterin' our son.'

Brooke wriggled in her seat. Stay in control, she told herself. 'We met with him a couple of times, yes.'

'Who's we?'

'It doesn't matter. Obviously you're well aware of what happened to Evan Wiley.'

Harry's features became even more folded as his face tightened. 'I know nuthin' about what happened to him.'

'I'm not saying you do. I'm just telling you why we spoke with Mick. He—'

'He had nuthin' to do with it either. Just like I had nuthin' to do with what happened to your brother.'

Brooke wasn't ready to go there. Even hearing him speak those last two words made her tense up. 'If you'd let me finish what I was saying, you'd know we aren't blaming Mick for anything.'

Harry kept quiet, his eyes not letting go of hers.

'He'd been hanging around with Evan in the months leading up to his death,' Brooke went on. 'We spoke to him hoping he could help us. Which he did.'

There was a brief silence. Harry was watching her close, as if trying to read her body language. After another sequence of uncomfortable and stretched-out seconds, his posture changed. He leaned back and loosened his features. 'How did he seem?'

Brooke chewed her lip. 'How did who seem?'

'Mick.'

The question caught her off guard. 'He seems very well. He comes to see you, doesn't he?'

'Not for a while.' The disappointment was clear in Harry's wince.

Brooke took a sharp breath. 'He's a good kid. It probably did him good having you in here.' She couldn't help herself. It was what he deserved, she decided.

Harry's face crimsoned as he leaned forward, his voice a weighty whisper. 'You bitch.'

'Watch your tongue.' Brooke surprised herself with her valour.

A pause followed, filling the empty room with thick air. After time, Harry spoke again. 'Why are you really here?'

Brooke looked at him hard, unsure of what to say. She finally settled on: 'You don't deserve much, but I thought I should at least give you the opportunity to apologise.'

Harry remained quiet, allowing the air to thin. 'I didn't kill your brother.'

Something about the way he spoke startled Brooke. His breathy words were fatigued. Defeatist. 'And why would I believe that?' She couldn't help but ask the question. She knew she should just go. Why was she even giving him the time of day?

Harry leaned back and lowered his eyes. 'I don't expect you to. You've already made up your mind.'

Brooke could have laughed. 'It's got nothing to do with making up my mind. The evidence was there.'

'What evidence?' Harry spat as he spoke.

'Watch. Your. Back.' Brooke enunciated each word of the note he wrote, her face spittle-distance from his. 'You openly bullied my brother for years. You and that sidekick of yours.' Brooke couldn't remember the name of Harry's school-yard wingman, nor did she want to. 'Oh, and did you forget that you confessed? Under oath.'

Harry sunk lower into his chair, causing the plastic to creak.

'You can't just decide because you're bored of being locked up that you didn't do it all of a sudden.' Brooke shook her head in disbelief. This wasn't a good idea. This was the opposite of forgiveness.

The guard loomed in, his frown strong. 'That's enough for today, Detective. Saunders has got a lot to do.'

'Five minutes.' Brooke held out an outstretched finger for each set of sixty seconds.

The guard gave a brief scowl. 'Fine. Five minutes max.'

She turned her eyes back to Harry. 'If you didn't do it, why did you confess?'

'He told me to.' Harry's voice was small. Boyish.

Brooke raised an unconvinced eyebrow. 'Who told you to?' Was he suddenly trying to scapegoat that school friend?

'The lawyer.'

'*Your* lawyer?'

'That's what I just said, wasn't it?'

'And what reason did he give?'

Harry shrugged. 'Said I wouldn't get as long a sentence.' It was his turn to almost laugh as he looked around the visiting room.

Brooke released her held breath. 'Well, maybe that would

have been true had you behaved in here.'

After a minute or two of tense silence, the guard returned. 'Okay, that's enough. Come on, Saunders. Say goodbye to your friend here.'

Harry gave her a loaded glare as he was strong-armed out the door. Its heavy metal slam rang in his wake.

Brooke closed her eyes and attempted to slow her pulse. Her hands were still shaking.

With each quickening step back to the car, Brooke tried to forget what had just occurred. How could she even think about forgiving a man who wouldn't even acknowledge what he'd done? The pain he'd caused. Even after nineteen years behind bars, he still couldn't look her in the eye and be honest. Didn't he owe her that much? She shook her head in an attempt to dispel his final stare. Those hollow eyes somehow full of resentment, when they should have been full of remorse. She felt her pulse pump harder and realised she needed to distract her thoughts.

Collins. Surely his hearing would be over by now. Perhaps they could meet for coffee before heading back to Taonga. What would he think about her encounter with Harry? Part of her didn't want to tell him. She didn't expect him to understand. Two steps short of her car, she slid her phone from her coat pocket and gave him a call. As the phone rang, Harry's eyes came back into focus. She couldn't not tell him.

'Palmer. I've been try… call you.' His tone was urgent and the call choppy.

'Oh, really?' The prison walls must have blocked the signal. 'I'm in Christchurch. Where are you?'

'You are? Shit, I'm already halfway... Taonga. What... do-ing there?'

Brooke pressed her opposite ear shut. 'I'll explain later. What's happened?'

A static pause.

'Hello?' Brooke checked her phone. The call was still active.

'Sorry, just... the alps.'

'I can barely hear you. What is it?'

'...forensics have confirmed... blood in the...'

She only caught a few broken words, but it was enough to piece together what he was saying. All of a sudden, her meeting with Harry Saunders didn't matter anymore. His evil eyes had been replaced with the brutal vision of Evan's murder. This time, it wasn't going anywhere.

'I'm on my way.'

Chapter Thirty-one

The quick air howled as Brooke locked her car and dashed to avoid the shower's inaugural drops. Collins was stood outside the station, smoking. His weary face spoke volumes. Brooke braced herself.

'Palmer. You're just in time.' His unfinished cigarette hissed when it hit the ground.

'In time for what?' She tailed him inside.

'I've brought in the motel owners for questioning.' Collins rubbed his eyes. 'They're in the interview room now.'

Brooke sharpened her focus. Her stomach twisted tight. 'You think they could be involved?'

They entered the office and Collins scrambled his increasingly cluttered desk in search of something. 'I'm not sure.' He found it. 'But I'm sure they know something. I'm hoping we might be able to jog June's memory about who stayed in the room that night.' He wagged the folder in front of Brooke, his eyebrows raised.

When the detectives entered the interview room, they were met with Martin and June embracing each other, their glistening cheeks almost touching.

'Martin. June. Thank you both for coming in.' Collins took a seat and began to set up the recording device.

Brooke kept her eyes fixed on the couple as she sank into her seat. June's gaze met hers through the shine of a tear.

'Hello, Detectives,' Martin said quietly. 'Of course. As I said before, we'll help in any way we can.' He removed his glasses and wiped his eyes. 'We're just in shock right now. It's hard to believe something like this could have taken place in our motel.'

Brooke met Martin's stare. 'Is it still open?'

He gave a tiny nod. 'The kids have finally made that trip back. It's lovely to see them, but a shame it's under such awful circumstances. They're going to help out with the motel for a few days while June and I come to terms with what's happened.'

'I don't think we'll ever come to terms with it.' June's voice cracked through her tears.

'Now, what was the name you had in your logbook again?' Collins said. 'Do you have it here with you?'

June unzipped a well-worn handbag and retrieved the logbook. 'I thought you might ask to see it.' As she flipped through the pages, Brooke noted how she must have been riding a good wave. 'Mr M Rivers.'

Collins stared at the page for a long minute. He looked up and met June's cloudy eyes. 'And you said this man has never stayed with you before?'

Martin shook his head. 'I went back through our records to

double-check. You're welcome to do the same.'

Collins looked back at the page. 'Says he checked in that evening and checked out the next morning. Paid in cash.'

Martin wiped his steamed glasses with his shirt. 'As you can see, cash isn't unusual among our guests.'

'And you said you have cleaners who look after the rooms?' Brooke said.

'I used to do them myself,' June chimed in. 'But it all got too much.'

'And they didn't mention the fact that one of the rooms had a strong smell of bleach?' Collins couldn't hide the bewilderment from his voice.

Martin looked to June, who shook her head with some confidence.

'Okay.' Collins opened his folder and spread photographs across the table. 'These are our lead suspects right now. We're hoping one of you might remember seeing one of these men check into the motel.'

June and Martin studied each photograph slowly. Bill Henderson. Santiago Pérez. Keane Harding. Even Warren Silvers.

Martin was the first to speak. 'I don't recall any of these men staying with us.'

June pointed to the photo of Santiago. 'I remember him,' she said with satisfaction in her nod.

It was true, Brooke thought, Santiago had stayed at the motel. But that was years ago.

June then picked up another photo and studied it for an uneasy minute. 'This one looks familiar.' It was Bill Henderson.

Brooke felt Collins' eyes on her, but she kept hers on June.

Martin leaned in. 'She might recognise them from around town. She gets confused.' He turned to his wife. 'It's okay, June.'

June's eyes welled again.

'Are you okay?' Brooke said.

June removed her glasses and pulled a handkerchief from her pocket. 'Sorry. I get frustrated with myself.' She dabbed her tears. 'I never used to miss a beat. Not a single detail. I fear because of my mind's weakness I let this happen right under my nose.' She broke down and clung to her husband.

'Okay,' Collins said. 'Let's leave this here. You're both clearly in need of some rest. If you think of anything else, anything at all, please don't hesitate to get in touch.'

Martin gave a conclusive nod. 'Of course.' He broke into a slight smile. 'We know where you live.'

Back in his office, Collins took a seat and stared at his desk. 'So why were you in Christchurch?'

Brooke stood up from leaning against the wall and straightened her back. 'I spoke with Keane's mum and partner. They both thought Keane was with the other on the night of the murder.'

Collins cocked his head to the side. 'Really?'

Brooke paced over to the desk and took a seat. 'Yep. So I went and spoke to Keane in person. Course, he had a reason for it. Sounds like he'd been playing around town since breaking up with Santigo. He called some guy to prove he was with him that night.' There was a silence. Brooke glanced at Collins. 'How did the hearing go?'

His eyes dropped to the floor. She wondered if he was about to break down.

'Come on,' she said finally. 'Let's go to the pub.'

Collins looked up with ample eyes. 'You sure?'

'I think we could both do with one.'

Collins managed a half-smile. 'You're not wrong there.'

'What can I get you?' Collins leaned against the bar.

'This one's on me.' Brooke pulled her wallet from her coat pocket. 'Two pints of Detective Collins' usual, please.'

Terry drew back on the pump allowing golden liquid to swell in the glass, thick foam forming across its top.

'Thanks,' Collins said. 'Just what the doctor ordered.'

The detectives nestled into a booth just as an eruption of cheers roared from the corner of the pub. The All Blacks had won.

'We picked the worst time to come to a pub.' Brooke sipped her beer.

'At least they didn't lose.' Collins took a large swig. 'Wish I could say the same.'

Brooke studied his gaze. 'So, what happened?'

Collins kept his lips pressed. His eyes grew glassy as he kept them on his drink. 'I knew it was coming. I suppose I was in denial. Nothing could've prepared me for how much it would hurt when it actually happened.' He wiped a single tear.

Brooke didn't know where to look. 'I'm sorry. I can't imagine how this feels.'

Collins shook his head and wrinkled his nose. 'You've been through worse. I need to keep it in perspective.'

She held her tongue for a blink. 'This is a different kind of pain.'

The detectives sat without words for what felt like longer than it was.

'Why did you lose?' Brooke finally said as she watched a pair of punters shuffle to the bar.

Collins stared into his pint glass as if reading tea leaves. 'She made it out that I put my job before being a dad.'

Brooke held his gaze and bit her bottom lip. A lick of blood seeped from a crack.

'She knows that's not true,' he went on. 'I don't even know who she is anymore. Definitely not the person I married.'

A breath of silence as Brooke thought what to say. 'Who was the person you married?'

Collins inhaled deep and stared out the window behind them. Rain drubbed its glass as if attempting to respond. He exhaled. 'You know, it's hard to even remember. We were both different back then. Wanted the same things.'

'Your daughter's eleven, right?'

'Yep. Her name's Aroha by the way. Not sure if I've ever mentioned.'

'No.' Brooke smiled. 'Beautiful. *Love* in Māori, right?'

A twitch of the lip. 'Yep. It was my mum's name. Rachel suggested it, actually.'

'Nice idea.'

'Yeah, she had a lot of nice ideas back then. I met her soon after I finished my police training. She was so carefree. Complete opposite of me at the time.'

'At the time?' Brooke's teeth breached her grin.

'Do you want to hear this or not?'

'Go on.' She sipped her beer, its cold soothed her lip.

Collins scratched his cheek and tilted to look back outside, the rain reflecting on his skin. 'She's a few years younger than me. She'd just finished art school and was planning to take a gap year to see the world. She didn't expect to meet me and get all tied down, I guess.'

Brooke found herself strangely identifying with Rachel. Except in her case, it hadn't been a man holding her back from seeing the world. It had been her career. 'So she never went away?'

'Not in the way she'd planned. But we did travel together. We explored Asia, America. We had a month in Europe. We actually got engaged in Paris.'

'How romantic.'

Collins barked a laugh. 'She said it was cliché. It was my idea, but she said no at first. Didn't believe in it and all the rest. It wasn't until she got knocked up that she finally agreed to make it official.'

'Religious?'

'Her parents are. She did it for them really.'

The detectives watched two men skid into the booth next door, fresh beers in hand.

'Anyway, to cut a long story short, it just didn't work. Once we got married and had Aroha, it was a downward spiral. My work took up more and more time. She went from one failed project to another until she finally met her current boyfriend, who happens to be a successful businessman. Part of the corporate machine, which goes against all her principles. But at least I don't need to worry about Aroha being looked after if you get what I mean?'

Brooke slumped her posture. 'And I suppose it didn't hurt when it came to the case.'

Collins gave an affirming shrug. 'Exactly. You and I know how this stuff works. It's all gone the way she planned. She's the caring mother with the wealthy boyfriend while I'm the guy who picks apart dead bodies for a living.'

Brooke stared at the small puddle of water that was growing on the windowsill. The bubbled wallpaper below suggested it wasn't the first leak. 'I'm sorry.'

Collins finished his beer. 'Okay, that's it. I'm gonna need another one after all this. Same again?'

Brooke improved her posture. 'It's all right, you go ahead.'

He didn't need any more convincing.

Once Collins had disappeared to the bar, Brooke leaned against the faded fabric of her seat and shut her eyes. She tried to untangle her web of thoughts. She kept coming back to what Evan had said to Lana. He'd found a way to get what he needed. What had he meant by that? Either he'd agreed to offer his body in exchange for money and something had gone wrong, or someone had lured him to the motel intending to kill him. As she wrestled with her mind, Brooke thought she heard her name mentioned in the booth behind. Typical Taonga. According to her mum, it had taken years for the town to stop gossiping about Jack's death – despite the case being long closed. But as the slurred murmur progressed, Brooke couldn't help but listen in.

'You seen him 'round?' The man's voice was gravelly.

'Nah,' another man said. 'Reckon he's layin' pretty low. They reckon his kid's involved. What I heard.'

'What… Bill?'

A cheer from the crowd watching the highlights.

'Reckon it's 'cause… y'know?'

'Maybe.'

A bloated pause.

'Don't know what I'd do if my kid turned out like that.'

A pint glass slammed the table. 'Sure you don't want another?' Collins said. 'Last chance before my wallet goes away.'

Brooke shot him a stern glance. She placed an index finger vertically on her lips and pointed to his seat with her other hand. Collins did as he was told.

The cheering had begun again, this time making the conversation completely inaudible. Brooke leaned over and lowered her voice to a whisper. 'The guys sat in the booth behind me. They were just talking about the case.'

Collins rolled his eyes. 'Getting tips from gossipy locals now, are we?'

'Listen.' Brooke's eyes were serious. 'Sounds like Craig knew about Bill and Evan all along.'

Collins' eyes widened. Brooke knew he was thinking the exact same thing as her.

All this time, could they have been suspecting the wrong Henderson?

Evan had only made it halfway through the park when he realised he was being followed. Either that or he was being paranoid. He picked up his pace and kept his hands buried in the pockets of his hoodie. Just a few more metres and he'd be where the street lights spilled onto the park's edge. Out of its pitch-black centre.

Striding fast, Evan resisted the urge to turn and look behind him. To see who was on his tail. Was it Warren?

Evan took a shaky breath as his heartbeat quickened. This was a mistake. He'd just wanted to bump into Bill. He'd gone for a few drinks at the pub, left his car at home and now this.

'Evan.' The voice wasn't Warren's.

He froze and slowly turned around. In the dark shadows, it could have been Bill. But it wasn't. It was his dad.

'Sorry for sneaking up on you,' Craig said sans sorrow. 'I was on the other side of the street when I saw you leave the pub. I was wondering if we could have a little chat?'

He'd followed him from the pub? 'Okay.' Evan swallowed and his heart rate normalised. 'Is this about the drugs?'

Craig shook his head, now at arm's length. 'No.'

Was he laughing?

Discomfort clung heavily to the air. Why couldn't it have been Bill and not his dad? Evan wanted nothing more than the ground to swallow him whole. 'Well you know I'm sorry about that. I know I messed up.'

Craig studied Evan's gaze through the darkness. 'It's all right. It's not a big deal. Well, not compared to what I need to talk to you about.'

The hairs on the back of Evan's neck started to rise. 'What do you want to talk about?'

Craig stood in silence for a few moments, as if he was searching for the words. His stare remained strong. 'Evan, I know about you and Bill. I know everything.'

Evan felt his body stiffen. He couldn't help but exhale a gasp. 'What do you mean?' He almost choked on his words.

'Don't bother making up lies. It'll just waste both of our time.' Craig's tone had grown hostile.

'How?' Evan said. 'How did you find out?'

It was impossible to make out Craig's expression in the dark. 'A father finds out everything. One way or another.'

Evan opened his mouth to respond but withheld. He knew he'd have to tread carefully. What was Craig's intention of following him alone at night to speak to him about this? He suddenly found himself wishing it had been Warren.

'Where's your father, Evan?'

The question caught him off guard. He didn't feel like telling him, but he wanted this to end. 'He lives in Australia.'

Craig remained still. 'Got it. See, that could be part of the problem.'

Evan didn't follow. 'What do you mean?'

'A boy needs a father in his life, Evan. To show him good from bad. Right from… wrong.'

Evan didn't like where this was heading. He considered turning around and running, but he decided the better thing to do was to remain still. Humour him.

'As you know, Bill's gone without a mother. That has obviously had a huge effect on him, too.' Craig reached his hands into the pockets of his jacket. 'I'd say it's a mix of that, the drugs, and hanging around with you that's got him feeling confused.'

Evan could feel anger bubbling. 'Confused, how?'

Craig leaned in and whispered loud. 'My son isn't like you.' His thick hands grabbed the neck of Evan's hoodie and pulled him in close.

The rage Evan had felt was suddenly replaced with a different emotion. Fear.

Chapter Thirty-two

'What did they say exactly?' Collins' whisper was hoppy. Brooke's eyes darted the pub before she tilted in, matching her voice to his volume. 'They haven't seen Craig recently. They reckon because Bill's a suspect.' She squinted a touch. 'You remember what Bill said about his father?'

Collins gave a bob of the head. 'That he didn't want him to find out about his thing with Evan.'

'He also said that his dad hates gay people.' Brooke couldn't help but shudder as she whispered the words. 'Like we've said before, times have moved on in the world... in New Zealand... but not in Taonga. Homophobia is etched deep in the heart of this town.'

As her eyes scanned the pub, Brooke thought back to a girl who had come out at school. She remembered her sheer bravery, as she stood proud and shaven-headed, declaring her lesbianism. It had come as no surprise – she had always been different from the other girls. Less than a month later her parents had removed her from the school and left town. The bullying had been that bad.

Had Craig wanted to protect his son from a similar fate? Is that what this was? Had he gone to the ultimate length of sacrificing the boy for whom his son had fallen? The ultimate act of hatred and fear?

'Come on,' Collins said with his voice in full. 'Let's go speak to them.'

Before Brooke had time to contest, Collins had slipped behind the booth with his pint in hand. She hesitated for a moment, then followed. Her unfinished beer left behind.

On each side of the table sat two men, mirroring one another not only with their beer-clutching hunch, but their ruddy complexions, too. Collins had already positioned himself beside one, so Brooke settled next to the other. It only took a moment for her to recognise him. Harry Saunders' former sidekick, whose name she still couldn't remember.

'Thought it was you.' His croaky voice suggested he hadn't kicked the smokes, while the stale breath that followed confirmed it. That's when his name suddenly came.

'Glen Harris.' She examined him. The years had taken their toll on his chubby face, his liverish red nose exposing his fondness of the sauce. An addiction his friend incarcerated had the benefit of escaping. She found her mind wandering to the past. How Glen would follow Harry around like a lapdog. How they would taunt Jack without an ounce of empathy between them. Brooke felt her stomach churn as she sat inches away from the man who was once the best mate of her brother's killer. Had he been involved? It was never proven. And now he was a friend of Craig Henderson? Maybe she'd been too quick to assume Bill's dad was a good guy.

'You must be the famous Brooke then,' the other man said. She didn't recognise his weathered face.

'This is Tick.' Glen pointed at his friend. 'Gets his name from his lucky ticker.'

Tick gave a crooked grin. 'Stopped tickin' on me twice before but it always seems to kick back into gear.'

Glen shifted his eyes to Collins. 'And you're the detective workin' on the Wiley boy's case.'

Collins nodded and sipped his beer. 'Gold star for observation.'

Brooke steadied her breath.

'How can we help?' Tick said. 'I take it you're not just here to share a beer?'

Collins took another swig. 'We were hoping you'd let us join the little conversation you were just having.'

Glen side-eyed Brooke. 'You were eavesdroppin'?'

Brooke pulled her shoulders back and straightened her spine, as if to squash the younger, more intimidated version of herself. She wasn't here as a teenager talking to a school bully. She was here as an experienced detective on the brink of solving a homicide. She was the one in the driver's seat. 'Well, it was hard not to when I heard my name being mentioned.' She fixed her eyes fearlessly on Glen's. 'So Craig knew about Bill and Evan's relationship?'

Glen averted his stare to Tick.

'This is serious, and we know you have information,' Collins said. 'We can speak here or we can speak at the station. Your call.'

Glen's upper lip curled. 'Yeah, he knew. He heard they'd been gettin' into a bit of trouble 'round town, so he started checkin' up on him. Managed to get his hands on his phone and read a heap of messages between them. Worked it out pretty quick.'

Collins folded his arms and leaned back into the booth. 'Craig told you this?'

'Yeah, we were pretty shocked he told us.' Tick's smile seemed out of place. 'We don't normally talk about that sorta stuff. We were in my backyard one night drinkin', and he just blurted it out. He seemed pretty worked up about it.'

'Worked up how?' Brooke said, jumping on his words.

'I dunno. Like, he didn't know what to do. He had no idea his son was… y'know…'

'His son was what?' Collins chugged back the last of his beer. He clearly wasn't in the mood for small-town ignorance this afternoon, Brooke decided.

Tick searched for the words. 'That his son swings that way.'

Brooke shot both men a look. 'And how did you both react? When he told you?'

Glen threw back a splash of beer. 'We didn't really know what to say. We just said it's probably a phase and that he'd grow out of it. What else can you say?'

Collins rolled his eyes and unfolded his arms. 'Well, you could've told him to tell his son he'd love and support him no matter what.'

There was a thick silence as Glen and Tick absorbed the

foreign concept.

'So you think Craig's been laying low?' Brooke asked Tick. 'Because Bill's a suspect?'

Tick avoided her gaze. 'It was just a thought. 'Cause I haven't seen him around much.'

Brooke pretended she didn't see Glen shoot Tick a glare. 'You think Bill might be behind this then?'

Tick swigged his beer. 'Didn't say that.'

'Well, what are you saying?' Collins took his tone up a notch.

'He's just sayin' they're obviously stayin' outta your way,' Glen said. ''Til all this shit dies down.'

'Until someone else dies, you mean.' Brooke couldn't help herself.

Glen hesitated for a beat. His face had tightened into a grimace. 'You better be careful meddlin' in peoples' business. Last time you did that my best mate got locked up for life.'

Brooke's focus began to haze. She'd had enough of being blamed for Harry's sentence. 'Your best mate was a bloody murderer and got what he deserved.' She stood. 'Come on, Collins. We've heard all we need.'

Outside, the rain had subsided, but the dark had brought with it an even colder wind. Collins caught up with Brooke. 'You all right, Palmer?'

'I'm fine.' She wrapped her arms around herself to stay warm.

'How did you know that guy?' Collins threw a thumb over his shoulder.

Brooke considered telling him about her prison visit. About

coming face to face with the man she'd despised her entire adult life. But Collins had been through enough today. 'He's just another person I was happy to have left in the past.' She pulled her car keys from her coat pocket. 'Come on, we should get some rest. It's been a long day, especially for you. Let's go 'round to the Hendersons' first thing in the morning with fresh heads. Bill's dad has some explaining to do.'

Collins' tired eye managed a wink. 'You're the boss.'

Evan pulled out his pack of Fortunas. Just three left. He lit up and took a full drag as he thought about his encounter with Bill's dad. Evan could see now why Bill was afraid of him finding out. There was something intimidating about Craig Henderson.

'Just stay the fuck away from my son, okay?' he'd said in the park's pitch-dark. 'I heard you're planning on taking a little trip to Europe. The best thing you could do is pack your suitcase and book a one-way ticket.'

With what money? Evan had thought. He'd need a job first. And even then, it would take years to save what he'd spent. He wished more than anything he could turn back time. Quit the drugs. Even take up Bill's offer to work with him and his dad. Maybe he and Bill could have convinced Craig of their happiness. Perhaps he would have been more understanding if he could have just seen how good they were together. But no, the only thing Bill's dad could see was a threat to his son. A threat that he wanted gone. That much he'd made clear.

The vision of Craig Henderson was replaced by the now-approaching Warren Silvers. Their faces sharing the same look of malice, noticeable in Warren's eyes despite the darkness beneath the ramp. He crouched beside Evan and placed his phone on the ground, its screen carelessly cracked. 'I've been more than patient with you.'

'I know.' Evan kept his eyes low. 'I'm sorry.'

'I'll give you one more week. If you can't get me the money, you're gonna have to give me somethin' else. I'm sure your mum's got some real pretty jewellery. Nice bit of gold.'

'I'll get you the money.'

Warren's grin was grim. 'Or maybe just bring me your mum. She's real pretty. I've seen her around.'

Evan's throat grew dry. His fists were in tight balls. 'I said I'll get you the money.'

Warren's eyes stared at Evan, ignoring his own phone as it pinged to life on the ground. The crack on the screen drew Evan's attention to the camera icon in its corner. It was a sign. Selling his beloved DSLR was the only way. It would be more than enough to pay him back.

The phone lit up again, but this time it was vibrating. As Warren whipped the device to his ear, Evan just caught sight of the caller.

'Hello? Yeah, I'm in your hood now. I've got your stuff. Wanna meet at the usual place?'

It was in the gaps between Warren's words that confirmed to Evan who was on the other end of the line. He couldn't believe it. A devious smile broke across his face. Maybe he wouldn't need to sell his camera after all.

Warren hung up and flicked his eyes back to Evan. 'Gotta bounce.' He picked up his backpack. 'You're lucky I'm not gonna spit on you again. But it really is one more week. Last fuckin' chance.'

Evan nodded, but his mind was elsewhere.

With Warren gone, he must have typed the message out at least a dozen times. He wrote longer, more detailed versions. He tried short and punchy statements that got straight to the point and showed he meant business. Ultimately, he decided on the latter.

I know your secret. Don't worry, I'm good at keeping them. But I'm going to need a favour...

Evan took a deep breath and pressed send. His fate was sealed.

Chapter Thirty-three

Brooke had just finished her second coffee when she heard the car honk twice.

'He's early.' Gary pulled his newspaper from its cellophane and inspected the cover.

Brooke gave her hair a quick zhoosh in the mirror. 'We've got a big morning ahead. I'll tell you about it later.'

'Try and be here for dinner,' Barbara said through the steam of her cupped coffee. 'I'm roasting lamb tonight.'

Brooke slammed the door without answering. She was on a mission. She'd spent all night running through the facts in her mind, and she was sure she had it. Craig had lured Evan to the motel with the prospect of working for him. He would have told Evan to catch the bus to the motel, that he'd pick him up en route to Greymouth. But instead, he took him to the room he'd booked under a false name and beat him to death before dumping his body in a half-baked bid to make it look like suicide. All to get him out of his son's life. Brooke pictured Craig wiping his hands on that oily rag, only this time it was dripping with thick red blood. She blinked the thought from her mind. She needed to stay in control.

As she paced across the gravel, the freezing air cut through her. A reminder that it was still the peak of winter. The dull sun did nothing to warm her up.

'Morning.' She climbed into the passenger seat. 'How are you today?'

Collins pulled down his sunglasses a fraction to expose reddened eyes. 'Been better.'

She fastened her seatbelt and offered a sympathetic squint. 'I'm sorry.'

Collins reversed out the driveway with a jolt. 'No worries. I'll feel better once we get this guy.'

Brooke balmed her lips. 'Did you see Martin or June?'

'I actually checked into the hotel in town. It didn't seem right to keep staying at the Lucky Star.' Collins stopped at the intersection.

'I don't blame you.'

'I met their daughter when I checked out, though. Nice girl. Worried about her folks.'

Brooke gave a nod of the head. 'Understandable.' She thought back to June in the interview room. Her intense stare on Bill's picture. Had she recognised Craig in him?

'The press were buzzing around that place like flies, too.'

Brooke scanned the headlines on her phone. 'Yeah. They're having a field day with all this.'

'Let's hope we wrap this up so they bugger off and give the

Wileys some peace.'

Brooke gazed at the sky through the windscreen. It was a pristine blue; fringed with a white glow from the distant mountains' snow. 'Fingers crossed.'

Evan pulled on his hoodie and stared at his withdrawn face and sunken eyes in the mirror. Was he really going through with this? He unzipped the front of his bag and checked his smokes. Two left. Man, he'd been savouring those. He dropped them back into the front pocket and pulled out his lighter. He gave it a gentle shake and flicked it. Nothing. Just as he'd thought. Whatever, he'd pick one up on the way.

Evan slung his backpack over his shoulder and felt his camera inside. He hadn't been taking many pictures lately, but maybe today he'd feel inspired. After all, things were finally about to start looking up. He shot his reflection a final glance and stepped into the hallway.

Lana stood with a wash basket full of towels, as if she'd been lingering outside his room. 'Where are you off to?'

'A friend's.' Evan drifted past her with little eye contact.

'What friend's? It better not be Bill, Evan.'

He froze, before turning around to face his mum. 'I'm banned from seeing him, remember?'

Lana hardened her features. 'You only have yourself to blame for that.'

Evan backed his way down the hallway slow. 'I know. But I want to make it right. I still want to take that trip. Go see the world.'

'We don't always get what we want, Ev.'

He drew a sharp breath. 'I know that, but this is important to me. You know how much I need it. I just got a bit… distracted.'

Lana rolled her eyes. 'You spent your travel fund. All of it, just to show off to a pair of wasters. If you want to go see the world, you're going to have to go get a job.'

Evan daggered his eyes. 'Well, maybe I've found another way to get what I need.' He spun on his heels and made his way to the front door.

'What's that supposed to mean?'

He ignored the question. 'And I'd rather be around a pair of wasters than a selfish bitch like you.'

Lana slammed the basket on the floor and followed him to the front door. 'Who are you, Evan?'

In the doorway, he held his mother's stare, with nothing but vacancy in his eyes. 'That's what I want to find out.' As he left the house, he didn't need to look back to know he'd left her in tears.

A thick frost coated the overgrown front lawn of the Henderson home. Cold clouds exhaled from the detectives' mouths as they approached the front door. Rambo's bark rendered the doorbell redundant, although Collins still rang it.

'Let's hope we get the truth,' Brooke said through chattering teeth.

Collins removed his sunnies. 'Let's hope they've got the heating on.'

The door swung open to reveal a caught-off-guard Craig. 'Detectives.' He looked beyond them. 'How can I help?'

'Can we come in?' Collins rubbed his hands together. 'It's freezing out here.'

Craig shifted his eyes between them. 'Sure. As long as it won't take long. We need to get started on a big job this morning.'

The detectives followed him inside. Collins gave Brooke a wink as the heat enclosed them.

'Is Bill here too, then?' Brooke canvassed the living room.

'Yeah, he's in the shower. Is there a problem?'

Rambo torpedoed the room and Craig pointed an assertive index at him. 'No.'

The dog gingerly slowed his movement and slumped to the floorboards. Brooke noted the authority Craig held over the household as she and Collins took the sofa.

'We had an interesting conversation in the pub yesterday,' Collins said. 'With a couple of your mates.'

Craig stared him down and took the sofa opposite. 'What mates?'

'Glen and Tick,' Brooke said with a slither of stealth.

Craig kept his lips pinched for a beat. 'And what did they have to say for themselves?'

Collins leaned in. 'They told us you knew about Bill and Evan. That you knew all along.'

'What's going on?' Bill appeared at the doorway. His hair was combed to the side, still wet from the shower.

Craig didn't break his stare with Collins. 'Sit down, Son. We need to talk.'

Bill cautiously took the other end of the sofa from his dad. 'Okay…'

Collins ping-ponged his gaze between the father and son. 'I take it you haven't had this talk with Bill?'

Brooke winced at his lack of subtlety. 'We can give you a few minutes, if you'd like?'

'It's all right.' Craig clenched his jaw as he spoke. 'You might as well stay. Sooner we get this out in the open the better.' He turned to face his son and took in a deep breath. 'I knew about you and Evan. About your… thing.'

Bill shot Brooke a loaded look. 'You told him?'

'No, Son. I saw some messages on your phone.' Craig folded his arms. 'I'm sorry. I should've said something.'

Bill's chin started to tremble. His dampening eyes avoiding the contact of his dad's.

'It's okay, Bill,' Brooke said softly. 'You don't need to feel ashamed.'

'It was nothing.' Bill darted a glance at Craig. 'We were just messing around. Because we were high.'

Craig loosened his features and kept his focus on his son. 'It doesn't matter. None of that matters now.'

'But is that how you really feel?' Collins' tone had prickled.

Craig cocked his head a dash. 'What do you mean?'

Brooke stacked her spine and kept an eye on Bill. 'We're curious as to how accepting you are of your son's sexuality.'

'What do you mean my sexuality?' Bill's mannerisms had grown rigid. His already deep voice dropping another decibel.

'There's no need to feel ashamed, mate,' Collins said. 'With whoever you are.'

Craig's ears had reddened and a prominent line had appeared between his eyebrows. 'Look, what is your intention here? To give me tips on how to parent my son?'

Brooke looked at Bill intently. 'Bill. Do you want to tell your dad what you told us?'

He kept his eyes to the floor. 'About what?' His lips quivered as he spoke.

Collins shifted his attention to Bill. 'About the fact you thought he'd disown you if he found out you're gay.'

The silent room was filled with tension, and Brooke knew it was only going to get worse. She kept a hard stare on Craig.

He mocked a smile. 'What is this? Are you accusing me of something?'

Collins held out his outstretched hands. 'You tell us how this looks.'

Bill leaned forward a tad. 'My dad's not a killer. If that's what you're trying to say.'

'Don't worry, Son.' Craig held up a hand to signal that he could handle this. 'On what grounds are you making this accusation, Detectives?'

'We're not making any accusations,' Collins said calmly. 'The fact you knew about your son and Evan's relationship was news to us. And based on what we've been told…' He gave Bill a two-second look. 'I'm sure you can see why we're here.'

Craig leaned back, easing his defence. 'As you both already know, Bill and I were in Greymouth together on the night of–'

'It wouldn't be the first time a family member has falsified an alibi.' Collins' tone was matter-of-fact. 'Mr Henderson, what did you think when you found out about your son?'

Brooke side-eyed Collins. She knew what was coming.

'What do you mean?' Craig crouched forward again. Creases formed across his face as it tightened.

Collins kept a solid frown. 'I mean, how did it make you feel when you read the messages between Evan Wiley and your son?' He gestured towards Bill.

Craig's nostrils flared. 'I know what you're doing, Detective. It's not going to work.'

'Let me tell you how it made you feel.' This time, it was

Collins' assertive tone commanding the room. 'It made you feel ashamed. For whatever small-town, close-minded, ignorant reason… it made you feel like a failure. Like you'd somehow let down your son.'

Brooke noticed a vein pulse in Collins' neck.

'You don't know what you're talking about.' Craig bared his teeth to reveal a twisted grimace.

Collins returned his scowl. 'So you decided you wanted him gone. You decided that would be best. For Bill. For you. You knew from reading your son's texts that Evan needed money. So you offered him a way out of his predicament. A job. Told him to meet you at the motel–'

'That's not true!' Craig's face had flushed beetroot red.

'You beat him to death and threw his body in the back of your ute, and you drove him to Taonga Falls. Threw him over the edge.' Collins' tone turned patronising. 'Did you think we'd think he'd killed himself?'

'No!' Craig peered at Bill for a pulse and wiped his eyes.

Collins smiled and leaned back. 'Well, go on.'

'Look, I know you all think I'm some gay-hating monster. But that's not true. Sure, I grew up in a house where that sort of thinking was the norm. Guess I inherited some of that ignorance, I'll admit that. But I'm doing my best. I'm learning every day.' He turned his eyes to Collins and then Brooke. 'I didn't kill that boy. But I did make a stupid mistake. Right before.'

Bill's eyes were frozen open on his dad.

Craig lowered his head and avoided Brooke's focus. He kept silent a little longer, as if summoning the courage to speak. 'A few nights before Evan went missing, I saw him leaving the pub on his own. I followed him. Got halfway through the park before I caught up with him.'

Brooke leaned forward, so she was perched right on the edge of the sofa.

Tears streamed down Craig's cheeks. His steely expression had completely given way. 'I told him I knew about him and Bill. I told him to stay away from him. That I thought he should take his trip overseas.' He broke down, his face buried in the palms of his hands. 'I told him to book a one-way ticket.'

The room was quiet, but for the sound of a grown man sobbing.

Tears welled in Bill's eyes. He left the room, knocking into Rambo as he stomped. After a cluster of fleeting seconds, a door slammed.

It wasn't until Craig pulled his face from his hands that Brooke saw his bloodshot, puffy eyes. They solicited empathy.

'When I first heard Evan's body had been found at the falls, I thought he'd taken his own life,' Craig said. 'I thought it was my fault.' A short pause. 'When I found out it was murder… part of me was…' He wiped his nose with his sleeve, and a wet sniff followed. 'Part of me was relieved.'

Collins sighed and looked to Brooke with defeat.

She turned to Craig. 'Mr Henderson. Go talk to your son. Tell him how much you love him. That you'll love and accept him no matter what. You're lucky to be able to.' She stood up and signalled for Collins to follow.

Neither detectives said a word as they stepped outside. They both knew that Craig didn't have to tell them about his encounter with Evan. No one would have ever known. But he had, and that's how they knew he was telling the truth. As Brooke breathed in the frigid air, it stung her lungs. What now?

The motel sign glowed in the darkness, distorted by the unceasing stream of rain on the window. Up until now, all Evan could make out in the early dark was an occasional set of headlights soaring by, and the reflection of the bus' lit-up interior. Empty and insipidly green. A shadow had been cast across Taonga all day from the plume of grey that had rolled in overnight, but it wasn't until he'd changed services outside the dairy that the clouds finally let go of their swell. Evan pushed the red button and jumped to his feet. He'd been so deep in thought he'd almost missed the stop. He pulled his hood up, gave a brief nod to the driver and stepped off the bus.

Ducking beneath the shelter to avoid the rain, which was crashing loudly against its tin roof, Evan unpocketed his phone and glanced at the time. He still had ten minutes. He took a seat and pulled the Fortunas and lighter from his backpack. Holding a cigarette between his lips, he cupped his hands and lit up. As he blew a smoke cloud into the cold air, Santiago Pérez entered his mind. What would he think if he knew what he was doing right now? Evan imagined the disappointment. Sure, his number one student would still get to take that trip to Europe. To build his dream photography portfolio. But he'd be paying for it like this. With blackmail.

Evan exhaled the anguish and tipped his head forward, pressing his cigaretted hand into his temples. Did it even matter what he thought? He was just some teacher that had felt sorry for him. His bitter boyfriend would just be glad to see the back of him. He took another drag and thought of Bill next. What would he make of this new low? In another life, he'd be his. The pair of them would leave Taonga behind and discover a world where they could be exactly who they wanted. Evan's stomach turned. The butterflies he'd once felt for Bill now felt like venomous wasps.

Evan flicked what was left of his smoke into the rain. He watched the butt float along the glistening gutter before disappearing down the drain. He pulled the pack from the pocket of his hoodie and glanced inside. Just one left. Standing up, he drew the lone cigarette and stuffed it in his back pocket. He'd have that later. To celebrate. He threw the packet in the bin, waited for a car to pass and ran across the road.

Rain thrashed his front as he maintained a jog, as if trying to convince him to turn back. His saturated hoodie and jeans stuck uncomfortably to his skin. As he approached the Lucky Star, he watched the bus stop directly outside and contemplated abandoning his plan altogether. He'd be on the right side of the road now to go back home. He could say it was a stupid prank. Go ahead and get that job at Countdown like his mum had suggested. He couldn't lie to himself, he had thought he was better than that. But why? What he was doing now was far worse.

Before Evan had time to second-guess his plan any further, he'd reached the motel. Its neon sign beckoning passing cars with every flash of the word vacancy. He continued through the car park and began glancing at the numbers on the first set of rooms. Nope. None of them. He turned the corner and skimmed the next set. Nope. Must be the last batch. He made a dash opposite to the first of the final set of rooms. There it was. Number nineteen. And the light was on inside. A soft amber glow. He swivelled his gaze to the vehicle parked out front. It was definitely him.

Evan took a deep breath and knocked the door with a curled index finger.

Chapter Thirty-four

There was a soft knock on the door.

'Are you busy?' Barbara's voice was warm through the wood.

Brooke stared at the lack of progress she'd made packing her suitcase. It was the last thing she wanted to be doing, but she thought it best to get it out the way. That way she could spend her last few days in Taonga helping Collins with the case. She'd thought about requesting more time off, but the dead-end they'd reached gave her pause. Despite the promise she'd made to Lana – and herself – she knew she couldn't run from reality forever. And she knew she needed to get back to her own life. Besides, being home right now was too painful.

'No,' Brooke said loudly. 'Come in.'

Barbara opened the door two inches. 'I was wondering if you could come help me with a bit of organising? Amanda wants to go ahead with that Dress for Success event she postponed.'

Brooke gave in to a shrug. 'Sure.'

The morning sun lit Barbara and Gary's bedroom with a sharp white as dust danced in the air. The room was swamped with a sea of barely worn clothing, undoubtedly designer.

'Wow, you have been busy.' Brooke picked up a cream jumper she'd seen her mum wear once since she'd been home. 'Wish I was as motivated with my packing.'

Barbara beamed with pride. 'Yes, well. You know me. I like to keep busy.' She picked up an evening gown and rested it in the crook of her arm. 'Right, so… the pile on the bed is good enough to be auctioned and that one there is what I'm donating. What's no good, we'll just put in the corner here. And of course if there's anything you want, just take it.' She placed the gown on the bed pile.

Brooke half-smiled. 'Thanks. Although I shouldn't be adding anything more to my suitcase.'

Barbara searched for her daughter's gaze. 'How are you feeling about getting back? Mixed, I presume.'

Gingerly sifting through the mountain of knitwear beside her, Brooke gave a despondent nod. 'Yeah. I really don't want to be leaving without finding out what happened.' She took a deep inhale. 'But I'm not giving up hope just yet.'

Barbara kept a concerned stare on Brooke as she retrieved a small tower of shoeboxes from her walk-in. She placed them down and began sifting through. 'You've done so much for Lana and her family while you've been here. It's something none of them will ever forget.'

'I know.' Brooke twisted a silk scarf with a floral pattern

around her neck. 'It's just disheartening.'

Barbara kept quiet for a tick as she inspected a pair of heels. 'How's Detective Collins?'

'He's okay.' Brooke folded a chunky merino. 'Well, he's not really. He lost a custody battle for his daughter.'

'Oh?' Barbara held a look of intrigue and returned the heels to their box. 'I didn't know he has a daughter.'

'Yeah. His ex-wife will be moving her back to Auckland. Where she's from.' Brooke could feel her mother's eyes on her. She didn't need to return the look to know what she was thinking. She was that predictable.

'He seems like a good man. Dedicated to his work. Handsome.'

'Mum!' Once again, being home made Brooke feel like a teenager. 'That's the last thing on my mind right now.'

Barbara pursed her lips and shrugged.

Brooke kept quiet and carried an assortment of clothing to the donation pile.

'So, I was thinking we should have a nice dinner this weekend before you leave,' Barbara said as she disappeared back into the walk-in. 'Just the family. Hannah, Sean and the boys will join.' She reemerged, carrying a box of accessories. 'Any preference on what we eat?'

Brooke began building a new pile. 'I'm easy.'

Resting it on the ottoman, Barbara rummaged through the box. Belts. Sunglasses. Costume jewellery. 'I was thinking beef casserole. I know that's one of Sean's favourites.'

It wasn't until Barbara removed a pair of oversized sunglasses from the box that Brooke spotted it. Her heart began to pound in her ears. 'What's that?'

'Hm?' Barbara glanced at Brooke and then back to where she was pointing. 'What, this?' She picked it up. 'Oh, just a watch Gary let me have for the event. I think it's lovely, but he said it's not his style. It was a gift from a client or something. It's a good make. We'll definitely auction it.'

Brooke instinctively scrambled towards her mum and snatched the watch from her hands. Her heart was slamming against her chest now. She pulled her phone from her pocket and navigated to the photograph Collins had sent her. She carefully compared the watch to the photo. Identical.

'What's wrong?' Barbara's tone had arched.

Realising she was trembling, Brooke crouched beside her. 'Mum. You need to hear me out, okay?' She looked over her shoulder and kept her voice low.

'O… kay?'

'Where was Gary on the night of Evan's murder?'

Barbara's eyes amplified. They moved from her daughter to the watch and then back to Brooke again.

'Where was he?' The sharp timbre of Brooke's voice made it clear she wasn't joking.

Barbara pulled away her stare and thought for a long moment. She looked back at Brooke. 'He was away for business that night.' She looked to the ceiling and shrugged. 'Christchurch, presumably.'

Brooke's stomach plunged. She felt her skin go from prickly pale to flame red. Surely this couldn't be real. Why would it? What reason would Gary have had to kill Evan? It didn't make sense.

Barbara looked back at the watch in her daughter's hand. 'What's it got to do with that?'

Brooke took a big breath before she spoke. 'I didn't tell you guys at the time…' She stumbled over her words. 'I didn't want to keep going on about the case. But what led us to the motel was this picture on the dealer's phone of this watch.' She gave the watch a shake and outheld her phone. 'It was on Evan's wrist just before he was killed.'

Barbara's eyes narrowed on Brooke's phone. She examined the image closely. 'What makes you think it's the same watch?'

'Look at the grain.' She shoved both the phone and watch under her mum's nose. 'In the leather.'

Barbara did as she was told. After a few beats, her features became twisted. 'Oh, come on, Brooke. There must be a thousand of these watches.'

Brooke kept quiet, processing her thoughts.

'Have you thought about seeing who checked in to the motel that night?' Barbara was now standing with hipped hands, blissfully unaware of the smoking gun in the room. 'They might have their ID on file.'

Brooke exhaled a broken breath and placed the watch on the bed. 'They don't. Just the name. M Rivers.' She pulled the scarf away from her neck that she'd forgotten she was wearing. It suddenly felt like it was choking her.

She turned to her mum, who was now staring through the window. Searching for something in her mind.

'What is it?' Brooke said.

'It's not him. It's not him. It's not him.' Barbara spoke the words beneath her breath, as if repeating a mantra.

'Do you know something?'

After a drawn-out silence, Barbara formed her response and looked at Brooke with an unconvinced eye. 'It's probably nothing.' Her eyes turned to the television that hung on the wall. 'Rivers. I know that name.'

Brooke's heart felt like it was going to explode. 'You do?' She shared her mother's stare at the television. 'Something you watched on TV?'

Barbara twisted her features. 'Maybe.' A lengthy pause thickened the air. 'No.' She continued to look around the room.

Brooke tried to gather her thoughts. The name didn't matter. They had the watch, they could figure out the rest later. They needed to get out of the house. 'Where is he?'

Barbara didn't respond. She was lost in her own thoughts.

'Mum?' Brooke's voice was almost a shout now.

Barbara moved quickly towards the bedside table on Gary's side of the bed and picked up a well-read paperback. She began thumbing through, her jaw falling further with the flick of each page. She barely had the energy to pass it to Brooke, her face so pale it was almost translucent.

Brooke scanned through the book. There it was, written on every page. Almost every line. *Rivers. Rivers. Rivers.* She flipped the book to read its blurb. *Martin Rivers, a hedge fund manager, finds himself...* M Rivers. Mr M Rivers. It was like he was taunting her.

Brooke eyed her mother with some annoyance. 'Now do you believe?' She could see the answer on her mother's face as it nudged from ghost-white to blue.

'It just doesn't make sense,' Barbara said as she shook her

head. 'Why? Why would he do this?'

Brooke dropped the novel on the bed and paced the room anxiously. 'I don't know. Evan was desperate for money. Maybe he was going to pay him for...' Her mouth went dry. She tried to swallow before continuing, '...something.'

The pair fell silent and shared a glare. Brooke knew her mum was thinking the same as her. That acidic swirl in her stomach was back. The one she'd had when they'd smelled the bleach in the motel room. *I've found a way to get what I need.* The taste of bile reached her tongue as she attempted to push away the vision of her stepdad forcing himself on Evan. All for a fist-ful of cash. But there was no pushing it away. It was something her mind's eye couldn't unsee.

Brooke locked with Barbara's mortified gaze and finally spoke again. 'Did you ever... did you ever suspect anything?'

Her mum remained frozen, as if in a trance. She shook her head. 'No. Never.'

A pang of fear shot through Brooke. The man she thought she'd known all these years was suddenly a stranger. Worse. A monster. They needed to get out. 'Where is he?'

'He's out. Countdown I think.' Barbara's words came out stressed. 'He'll be back—'

She was cut off by the slam of the front door. Neither of them had even noticed the quiet hum of Gary's SUV as it had pulled into the driveway.

Brooke unlocked her phone and held it to her ear.

'Who are you calling?' Barbara said, tucking the watch away in a shoebox.

The phone clicked into voicemail. Brooke spoke with a

loud whisper after the beep. 'Collins. I don't have time to explain. But I know who did it. My stepdad. Gary killed Evan.' The words felt dirty as they came from her mouth. 'He just got home. We'll do our best to act normal, but I need backup.'

She'd just had time to hang up when the bedroom door creaked open.

For a beat, Evan considered turning and running. But he was here now. He had to follow through.

Gary's face remained blank. 'Come in.'

Inside, a small heater pushed out warm air that only appeared to be making a minor difference to the motel room's overall temperature. There was a musky smell. The curtains were pulled shut.

'Wait there,' Gary said with an assertive finger. 'I'll fetch you a towel.'

Evan watched him pad to the bathroom. A surge of guilt enclosed him. He'd known Gary his entire life. Was he really prepared to bribe him for the sake of a trip to Europe? Evan shook the thought away as he pulled down his hood. He had to do what he had to do. He wouldn't even give it a second thought once he boarded that flight.

Gary reappeared clutching what looked more like a rag. 'Here you go.' He threw it in Evan's direction. 'Take a seat.'

'Thanks.' Evan avoided eye contact as he unzipped and removed his drenched hoodie. He hung it over the back of the dated guest chair beside the bed, before sitting and patting his damp jeans, for what it was worth.

A minute or so passed and Gary paced around the room. He peered out the window. 'Where's your car?'

'I had to take the bus. I'm out of petrol. That's how skint I am. I'll get a taxi home once you've given me the money. I don't really want to carry it on the bus.'

Gary perched on the edge of the bed. 'Evan. How did you find out?'

Evan continued patting his jeans with the towel and kept his gaze to the floor. He couldn't tell him how he knew. He didn't want to risk losing Warren a loyal client only to end up even deeper in his dealer's bad books. 'It doesn't matter.'

Gary kept quiet, but Evan could feel his eyes on him. It made him feel uncomfortable.

'So, what's your poison?' Evan said, trying to make light of the situation.

There was a slow silence.

Evan met Gary's focus, in which he read confusion. 'Coke, speed?'

Gary's eyes widened a fraction. He remained quiet for a few more moments before he finally gave his response. 'Oh, prescription. Prescription drugs.' He couldn't contain his small laugh. 'I've got a very stressful job and need a bit of help relaxing.'

'Ah, okay.' Evan folded the towel and placed it neatly on the bedside table.

Gary straightened his stance. His demeanour had shifted a tad. 'Look. I haven't actually got the money on me today.' He looked around the room and then back to Evan. 'But I can give you something else in the meantime.'

As Gary ducked outside and into his car, Evan felt a rush of disappointment. He didn't have the money? Had this all been a waste of time?

Gary returned to the room carrying a small black box. 'Here. For you.'

Intrigued, Evan slowly opened it. A cream-faced watch with leather straps glared back at him.

'Here,' Gary said. 'Let me.' He removed the watch from the box and fastened it around Evan's wrist. 'There. It suits you.'

'Thanks.'

'No worries. Now, that's worth about half of what you asked for. So,

whether you sell it or keep it is completely up to you. I'll get you the rest soon.' Gary picked up the towel and returned it to the bathroom.

Evan pulled out his phone and took a photo of the watch on his wrist. Hopefully this would get Warren off his back for now. He sent the image through with a message. As he stuffed his phone back in his pocket, a barely visible bottle of bleach commanded his eye from beneath the bed. What was that doing there?

'I appreciate you keeping this between us, Evan,' Gary said as he reappeared. He sat back down, this time relaxing into his posture. 'You're a good kid. You don't want to have to spend your life watching your back.'

Evan kept quiet, his eyes wandering back to the bleach. Was that a threat? He racked his brain as to where he'd heard something similar recently.

That's when it hit him. The podcast. Watch your back. It was the note written in the back of Jack's schoolbook. Gary's stepson's schoolbook.

'So, you're after the money to take your trip overseas, right?' Gary went on. 'I'm surprised your mum or grandparents aren't willing to help you. You could have just asked me, you know. Without resorting to this. We're like family, remember?'

But Evan wasn't listening. He was thinking of Mick, how his dad had told him he didn't do it. Maybe he should have believed him.

'Evan?' Gary leaned in, his silver hair rusty in the light.

'What did you think I was talking about?' Evan was clumsy with his delivery. He was trembling now.

Gary squinted with confusion. 'What do you mean?'

'You thought I knew more,' Evan pressed. His desire to know the truth outweighed his urge to flee. 'That's why you brought me here, isn't it?' The bleach drew his focus again. 'You... you did it... didn't you? You killed Jack.'

Gary's face had grown white now. His eyes vacant. He stood up and marched to the door, turning the lock with a chilling click. He was built bigger than Evan had ever noticed.

Evan froze. He was picturing Jack's young face. His wide eyes. Toothy smile. Keeping his eyes on Gary, he reached for his phone.

'Don't you dare.' His words had stiffened. 'Hand me it.'

Evan felt weighed down. He couldn't move.

'I said, hand me your phone.'

This time, Evan didn't take any chances.

Gary slipped the phone into his pocket. 'I didn't want it to come to this, Evan. Once I realised you were talking about the drugs… I thought I could just let you go.'

'You can!' The desperation was clear in Evan's plea.

'No, I can't. You fucked it up.'

Evan swallowed. Straightening his back, he mustered the courage to ask the question burning inside him. 'Why did you do it?'

Gary grew still. His eyes transfixed with Evan's. There was a long silence until he finally spoke again. 'I didn't want to.'

Evan felt adrenaline surge through his veins. Nausea overcame him. He felt a shot of sadness for Brooke and her family. For Mick and his parents. He looked to the locked door. He just needed to distract him and make a run for it.

'I cared about Jack,' Gary continued. 'He was like a son. The same way Brooke and Hannah are like my daughters. They're the children I never had.'

'Then… why?' Evan had to know.

'It doesn't matter to you now.'

Gary launched forward and sent his clenched fist into the side of Evan's face. Stunned, Evan attempted to get up from the ground, but Gary was already on top of him, pinning him down with his all. Evan felt his ribs crack beneath Gary's weight, his arms trapped motionless. He had to get him off, before it was too late.

Evan attempted a deep breath, and with all his strength sent his knee into Gary's back. He barely nudged. Again. Nothing. It was as if he was possessed, his power unhuman.

He had to change tactics. Maybe he could talk him out of it. But when Evan went to speak, all that came out was a lost scream as Gary began swinging his tight fist into his head – knuckles wet with red. Evan's vision began to blur and his mind went to his mother. How he'd hurt her. If only he could apologise. Tell her he loved her. Another blow, and all he could see was black. His final thought was of Bill. Their first kiss. A warmth washed over him as the pain continued to intensify.

Until it stopped.

Chapter Thirty-five

'What's going on here?'

'Nothing,' Barbara responded too quickly. She lent her stare to Brooke and then fixed it back on Gary.

'Oh.' Gary's deep eyes skipped from one pile of clothes to another. 'Looks like you're moving out.' It was hard to tell whether or not he was joking. His tone was jovial, but the tightness of his expression said otherwise.

Brooke forced a laugh. 'I'm helping Mum with Amanda's charity event. Dress for Success.'

Gary stood broad, framed by the room's only exit. 'And who was that on the phone?' His gaze thinned.

'Just Collins. He wanted to give me an update on the case.'

'And?'

A bitter silence sliced the room. Brooke could see her mum in her eye's corner. Was she trembling? 'Nothing of importance.'

Gary honed in on Barbara, his face devoid of any emotion.

'What's wrong with you?'

'Nothing.' The crack in her voice disagreed.

There was another silence, this time almost too uncomfortable to stomach. Gary moved his tense stare between the pair and to the bed. The to-be-auctioned pile did nothing to hide the upturned book. 'What's that doing there?'

Brooke straightened her back and took a big breath. She couldn't keep the act up any longer. 'Gary, we know the truth. We know you killed Evan.'

Moments later, Gary's normal sandy complexion had turned blood red. Pulsing vessels cut across the whites of his eyes. 'What are you talking about?' He closed the bedroom door with a sharp thud.

'You disgust me.' It was Barbara who spoke this time. Her nervous voice had been replaced with one of conviction. 'How could you?'

Brooke's phone started to vibrate in her pocket. She ignored it. Collins, probably. Surely he'd be on his way by now.

Out of nowhere, Gary lunged forward and grabbed Barbara by her hair. She let out a desperate yell.

Brooke outstretched her hands and tried to keep calm. 'You don't need to do this.' Her heart was beating triple.

He forced Barbara's head beneath his arm. 'Stay where you are.' Fixed in a tight headlock, Gary dragged his wife towards his bedside table and hunted for something with his spare hand while keeping his eyes on Brooke.

She looked out the window. No backup. Shit. As she turned back to Gary and Barbara, her heart stood still. He was pointing the mouth of a black handgun to the base of her mum's skull. Her terrified gasp sounded more like a choke. Brooke hadn't even noticed her phone had stopped ringing.

'Call him back,' Gary barked. 'The detective. Make it a video call. Tell him that no one is to come near the house.'

Brooke closed her eyes and felt her entire body begin to sway. Who was this man? There was nothing about him she recognised.

'Do it!' His shout was brittle.

She opened her eyes and pulled the phone from her jean pocket. Nothing other than the missed call from Collins. She started to FaceTime him.

Collins was driving as he appeared on the screen. 'Palmer! Are you okay?'

'Point it at us!' As Gary yelled, a string of spittle glistened in the hard light. He didn't wipe it from his bottom lip.

Brooke spun the camera around. Gary had shifted the gun's position. Now the mouth was pressed against Barbara's right temple. Her eyes were desolate. Brooke fought to restrain her tears.

'Listen to me, Detective.' Gary took a deep breath to squash the shake in his voice. 'I want you and everyone else to stay away from my house. Okay?'

'Gary,' Collins began.

'Don't fuck with me.' He shifted Barbara up an inch, keeping his jaw clenched. 'I'm serious.'

'Okay. I'll tell them now. Don't do anything stupid, Gary.'

'Hang up.' Gary jerked his head to Brooke.

She obeyed. She couldn't take her eyes off the gun, his thick finger unsteady on its trigger. She'd never known him to own one. How long had he? And why? Her spine went cold with the thought. She pushed it away and attempted to compose herself. She had to remain strong. Both her and her mother's lives depended on it. 'You know the game's up, Gary. How do you want this to end?'

'How do *you* think this is going to end? Because I don't think any of us are getting out of this alive.'

Brooke heard the driveway's gravel crunch as one or two cars pulled up. Collins must have told them to keep the sirens off. Good move. She held her breath, expecting a raid to ensue.

'Get down,' Gary said. 'Keep your hands where I can see them.' He shoved Barbara to the floor. 'Both of you.'

Brooke slowly took to her knees. Her fingertips pressed against the beige carpet and her head bobbed as if in prayer.

Sirens appeared in the distance. More backup. But it didn't look like Gary had noticed. Instead, he was thumbing his phone. 'There.' He pocketed it. 'No one will get in without us knowing about it.'

Brooke winced. He'd activated the security system.

Gary paced over to Brooke and crouched beside her, close enough for her to feel his warm breath on her neck.

'Stay away from her!' Barbara's tone peaked with assertion.

Gary swerved the gun around so it was pointing at her. 'Quiet!' He twisted back to Brooke. 'I'm going to take your phone now. Which pocket?'

'The left one.'

He reached over, pulled it out and slipped it into his own. He then shifted to where Barbara was crouching and did the same.

'You won't get away with this,' she said.

The distant sound of a chopper grew closer. Gary strode back to the window and peered at the sky.

Brooke swallowed hard, wondering whether it was the police or the press. She scanned her eyes across the room in an attempt to refocus. The morning sun had now reached Barbara's dressing table. A family photo sat in a chunky, cut-glass frame. The old Gary with his arm around Barbara, a teenage Brooke and Hannah gleefully leaning in. How had he hidden this? How had she not noticed a change in him when she'd come home? She thought back to the drive from the airport. Sure, she'd been tired, but he hadn't been acting like someone who'd just killed someone for the first time. It wasn't until her eyes flicked to the next photo frame that she realised why.

Gary lowered his eyes from the sky to the driveway. 'Detective Collins,' he mused as his head nodded.

Brooke's eyes darted from the photo of Jack back to Gary. Harry Saunders' words played out in her head. *He told me to.* She held her tongue. *The lawyer.* She didn't even realise she was scrunching her fists so tight the crescents of her fingernails were cutting into her palms. *Said I wouldn't get as long a sentence.*

'You two were way off, weren't you?' Gary's words were designed to provoke. Not that Brooke needed it.

'Harry Saunders' lawyer,' Brooke said as the pieces started to fit. 'You paid him off to sabotage Harry's defence. To get him to confess to a crime he didn't commit. And you knew all along. He wasn't the one who killed Jack.' Her words were like glass. Seconds from shattering. '*You* were.' Her glare gave Gary the final stab.

After a series of increasingly uncontrolled breaths, Barbara let out an agonising wail.

Gary shifted his focus from Brooke to the floor, his up-un-til-now armoured stance loosening. He began pacing back and forth.

'Well?' Brooke could sense his unease. 'Are you going to tell us the truth? Don't you owe us that much?'

Gary stilled but maintained the gun on Brooke. 'Owe you that much? I've done everything for this family.' He clawed a black evening gown from the bed and flung it to the floor. It landed arm's length from the two women. 'Everything!'

Barbara controlled her sobs and spoke slow through gritted teeth. 'Did you kill my son?' No answer. This time she screamed the question: 'Did you kill my son?'

The pause gave Gary's eyes enough time to redden and well up. 'I didn't want to,' he whispered.

Barbara gave way. The tears came hard and fast. It was as if Brooke was watching her mum being told the news about Jack's murder for the first time all over again. All these years Gary had denied his wife the truth. And it wasn't just her he'd fooled. The entire world had lapped up his scam, episode by episode. That stupid podcast would definitely be getting its sequel now, Brooke thought.

'Why?' Barbara could barely get the word out of her dry mouth.

Gary wiped his eyes with the back of his gunned hand. 'I didn't have a choice. He found out. I didn't think anyone was home. I was on the phone and he heard something he shouldn't have. He was going to tell you.' His eyes were wet on Barbara. 'I couldn't let him.'

The sirens had stopped now. Just the sound of the helicopter circling overhead.

'What are you talking about?' Barbara's voice had grown glacial. It was clear she both wanted and didn't want to know.

There was a long pause, and at least three deep breaths before Gary spoke again. 'I was trying to protect you. You would have left me.' His eyes dropped. 'I should have just let you.'

'This isn't anyone's fault but yours.' Brooke wasn't falling for his self-pity.

'So, what was it?' Barbara pressed. 'An affair?'

'No.' He looked up and took in an abrupt breath. 'I got involved with some guys.' His eyes were skittish. 'Years ago. When business was bad. They were channelling money through the company. Cleaning it. I tried to stop it, but it just got worse and worse.' He shook his head. 'If it got out what I was doing… they would have—'

'Killed you?' Brooke finished his sentence. 'But instead, you decided Jack should take the fall. You're a coward.'

Barbara wiped the mascara smears from beneath her eyes. 'You bastard.' Her breath was heavy through her nostrils.

He turned to face her. 'That's not what you were saying when I bought you this house.' He waved the gun around the room. 'When I bought you all this shit.'

Brooke could almost taste her own disgust. She peered at her mum and felt her pain. All these years, she'd been married to a liar. A money-laundering monster that had killed her only son. She then felt a rush of guilt for Harry Saunders and his family. He'd been the perfect scapegoat.

'But,' Gary went on – a touch softer, 'I didn't want to kill him. Please know that. I didn't want it to turn out like that. Or with Evan.' Fresh tears were now streaming.

'He worked it all out, didn't he?' Brooke said. 'That's why you had to kill him.'

Gary answered with the smallest nod but kept silent.

Evan hadn't gone to the motel to sell his body, Brooke now knew. He'd gone to seek the truth. 'How did he figure it out?'

'He needed money.' Gary's voice cracked. 'Came to me about something else. Doesn't matter now. Wires got crossed and I slipped up.' He shook his head, a smile of disbelief on his face. 'To think after everything. The court case, that fucking podcast. *He* worked it out.' He cleared his throat. 'Clever kid.'

Brooke felt a sense of pride for Evan. She knew there'd been something special about him. He'd died in Jack's honour. She couldn't let it be in vain. 'Gary, it doesn't have to end like this.' She kept her voice soft.

'You're not getting it, are you?' Gary's tone had tightened and Brooke could now see the terror in his eyes. 'Jack knew. Evan found out. You know now. We all know.' He spun the gun around the room again. He fixed his desperate stare on Brooke. 'They'll kill us.'

She remained calm. 'Gary, there are ways to protect us from them.'

'You think a witness protection programme will save us?' Gary's laugh was nervous as he peered out the window. 'They're getting too close to the house.' He reached into his pocket and pulled out Brooke's phone. 'What's your code?' After she told him, he tapped it in and made a call. He held the phone so it was facing her. 'Tell them to move away from the house.'

Collins' face filled the screen. 'Palmer.'

Brooke took a shallow breath. 'Please… can you all move away from the house?'

He gave a quick nod.

Gary kept his eyes out the window. 'They're not moving back!'

Brooke took her chance. 'You guys need to move back right now, okay? He's going to watch until you do. He's got a gun.' Keeping her eyes on Gary, who was still looking outside, she held out her hands, her left outstretched and her right displaying her thumb and index finger. She then flicked her outstretched left hand twice, before presenting the peace sign and her lone index.

As Gary looked back, she turned her final gesture into a mock cheek scratch. She then returned it to the floor. He hung up and gave her a loaded glare.

Had she been clear enough? Would Collins understand? She hoped to God he would. It's all they had right now.

*

The feeble winter sun had moved halfway across the room by the time Brooke spoke again. She assumed it must have been close to noon. 'Let Mum go. Even if you want to keep me here.'

'I'm not leaving until you are,' Barbara said.

'Neither of you are leaving.' Gary's lips pressed so tight they turned white.

'Gary.' The woman's voice came from a loudspeaker. 'Can we please talk through the window? Or over the phone?'

'Fucking negotiator. Are these guys for real? Probably your stupid mate's idea.' He waved the gun at Brooke. She could sense he was growing impatient.

'Gary?' The woman's voice again. 'I'm calling you now.'

His phone began to ring its default tone. He pulled it from his pocket and threw it towards Brooke. 'Tell them I'm not interested, okay?'

She nodded and picked up the ringing phone from the carpet. As she swiped to answer the call, she drew a big breath and arched the small of her back. 'It's Brooke.'

'Loudspeaker!' Gary spat the word and his eyes darted from the window to Brooke and back again.

When the phone switched to its speaker, Collins' voice emitted. 'Brooke, it's Collins.'

'Gary doesn't want to speak to anyone. He's not going to negotiate.'

Collins gave a sigh. 'Understood. Just… don't do anything you'll regret, Gary. Okay?'

Gary hissed through pursed lips. 'You can't regret much when you're dead.'

Brooke flinched as he snatched the phone from her hand and threw it across the room.

'Right, both of you, lie facedown. Let's get this over with.'

Barbara's face was terrified. Humiliated, almost. But they both obeyed.

'You don't need to do this, Gary.' The thick carpet scratched

Brooke's cheek when she spoke.

'I do.' The fear was palpable in Gary's voice. He kissed Barbara on the back of her head. 'I love you, babe,' he whispered, before positioning the gun at the nape of her neck.

Brooke swore she heard movement in the hallway. She had to delay him. 'Wait.'

'What?'

'Start with me. I can't watch my own mother die.'

'No!' Barbara screamed in horror.

Gary thought hard and spun the gun in his hand. 'Fine.'

No sooner had he spoken the word than the door gave way to a deafening kick. The black-clad and helmeted Special Tactics Group swarmed the room with heavy feet, barking indistinct instructions. Brooke clocked the seeping canister as Gary regained control of his weapon.

'Close your eyes!' Brooke shouted to Barbara.

Within seconds, the room had filled with thick plumes of grey. All visibility was lost. Two shots were fired. Then a third.

Then it went quiet.

Chapter Thirty-six

Cold air whipped Brooke's cheek when the STG officer's heavy grip led her outside. Ahead of her, all she saw was a wavering white sheet, held aloft by two uniformed constables. A privacy screen from the bustle beyond. She twisted to look for her mum. 'Wait!'

'Keep moving,' the officer said gravely.

They finally reached one of three ambulances parked on the street, their doors open to the house. The officer helped a pair of paramedics lift Brooke into the vehicle's rear where they systematically checked her vitals. The pale, pilled blanket draped over her shoulders did nothing to mitigate her shiver.

'Is she okay?' Brooke asked to no response. She looked to the scene ahead. Her eyes still stung from the tear gas, but they managed to find the spray of crimson on the bedroom window. It turned her own blood cold. Please let it be his, she thought to herself as the paramedics reeled off a list of impossibly easy questions.

Moments later, the sheet was back. The chopper's blades caused it to quiver and flap while the constables remained stern. It wasn't until they reached the end of the drive that Brooke saw Barbara, safe and disorientated. She wailed her relief and tears rolled down her cheeks. 'Mum!'

The armoured officer dragged Barbara into the adjacent ambulance before she had time to respond.

'I want to see her,' Brooke bawled.

'Not yet,' one of the paramedics said, her coppery hair pulled back in a firm pony. 'We need to ensure you're not hurt.'

'I'm fine.' Brooke chewed a nail. 'I need to check she's okay.'

'I'll go check for you,' the other paramedic said in a warm American accent. He flashed Brooke a reassuring smile before slipping from the ambulance.

Just as Brooke watched two more paramedics sprint into the house, Collins blocked the view with his firm frown.

'Excuse me,' the woman said, tearing the cuff from Brooke's arm. 'You're not allowed in here.'

He proffered his badge without giving her his eyes, his attention solely on Brooke. 'You all right, Palmer?'

'Yeah, fine.' She continued to look past him, waiting for Gary to be taken from the house. 'What's happening?'

There was a second of stillness. Deep grooves contoured Collins' expression. 'He's dead, Palmer.'

Brooke clenched her eyes shut. Relief swelled in her chest, but it was topped with a dash of disappointment. She'd have liked them to have got him alive. Really made him pay. But at least it was over. At least his evil had been banished from the world forever. She opened her eyes and met Collins' stare. 'It was him. He killed Jack.'

Collins' eyes broadened. 'What?' A tick of silence. 'Why?'

The stretcher creaked and Brooke's body ached as she shifted. 'I'll explain later. I can barely think straight.' She turned away, unable to disguise her torment. 'I feel like I've let myself down. Not figuring it out earlier.'

'You can't think like that. He obviously knew how to cover his tracks.'

Brooke looked at Collins again, suddenly fear-stricken. 'Was anyone else hurt?'

'One of the STG guys took a bullet to his arm. He got lucky. Real lucky.'

The younger paramedic was back. 'Your mum's doing well. She's just in shock right now. The paramedics are calming her down. You're free to go see her once we're finished with you.'

The copper-haired woman gave him a glare.

'I'll leave you to it.' Collins offered a nod. 'We can catch up properly later.' He broke a small but warm smile. 'I'm glad you're okay, Palmer. That was some quick thinking back there. Signing the alarm code.'

'I'm glad you got it.'

'We're a good team.'

'You're all right, I suppose.' She winked.

The detectives swapped a short-lived grin.

'You rest up,' Collins said, buttoning his coat. 'The world needs you back on your feet.' With another nod, this time conclusive, he disappeared from sight.

Brooke gazed through the open doors of the ambulance as the helicopter circled above her family home. It looked completely different now. As did the world that framed it. She knew nothing would ever be quite the same. But at least there could be closure. Something both her family and the Wileys had rightfully earned.

Chapter Thirty-seven

It was missing this time. The excitement Brooke usually felt when she zipped up her suitcase to return to Auckland. Still crouched on the floor, she glanced at the photograph of her and Lana on the bedside table. Would either of them smile like that ever again? Her eyes grew wet at the thought of how distant Lana had been with her over the last fortnight. But she understood. Although she knew nothing was her fault, she couldn't help carry some of the blame. If Gary had never moved them to Taonga, if she'd never met Lana, she would never have brought him into her life. Evan would still be alive. The thought made her heart hurt.

Two knuckle-taps on the bedroom door. 'How's it going?' Barbara spoke softly.

'Come in.' Brooke was quick to smear away her warm tears.

Barbara entered the room and perched on the bed's edge. Rings framed her bleary eyes that had got used to crying. A fraction of grey roots were exposed at the parting of her bob. It was the first time Brooke had seen her allow this to happen. Her clothing was more casual than it had been in a long time, without a label in sight. 'You're all packed then?'

'Yep.' Brooke fixed on her mother's dewy gaze. 'But I'm not ready to go.'

Barbara mustered a meek smile. 'I'll be fine. Hannah's here. And the boys.'

'I know. It's just… everything's so different now. It's a lot to adjust to.' Brooke shifted her focus back to the photograph.

'Are you going to see her again before you go?' Barbara's tone was cautious.

Brooke gave a single shake of the head. 'I think she just needs time. Understandably.'

The room was filled with a large silence, but for the tiny sound of a ticking clock. Barbara hesitated before carefully selecting her words. 'She'll come around. It's a lot to process. For us all.'

Brooke veered back to her mother, her eyes once again laminated. 'How did we not see it? All these years?'

Barbara lowered her look to the floor. 'It will haunt me forever.' A single glistening tear traced her cheek. She instinctively flicked it away. 'We had our problems. All couples do. But I never doubted that he loved me. That he loved you kids.'

The thought made Brooke wince. Memories attempted to infest her mind of the years they'd spent with Gary as the figurehead of the family, but she blocked them out. It would be a technique she would have to spend a lifetime perfecting.

'Anyway, there are some positives to take from this.' Barbara folded her arms, which were hidden within merinoed sleeves.

Brooke looked at her mum through narrowed lids. 'Like what?'

Barbara surveyed the room. 'I'm finally ready to let go of this place. To downsize.'

'Really?'

'Really. It won't be easy. I still have precious memories here of when you were little. But it's been tarnished now.' She met her daughter's surprised stare and unfolded her arms. 'It's time to let go.'

Brooke managed a smile at how far her mother had come. She gripped her forearm. 'You don't have to do this alone. I'll be back soon. I'm going to start visiting much more often. And Hannah and Sean will always be happy to help.'

Barbara wiped another stray tear and returned the beam. 'I know. But some things you have to do on your own, right? This feels like one of those things.'

The faint chime of the doorbell. Barbara jumped and moved her eyes from the direction of Jack's bedroom to Brooke.

'It's okay,' Brooke said as she stood. 'I'll get it.' Meandering through the house, she thought about how fragile her mum had become. Getting on that flight tomorrow was going to be tough.

She swung open the front door to be met with Collins, his hands buried in the pockets of his faithful long coat. 'Palmer.' He tipped his head with a smile.

'Collins. What are you doing back in Taonga?'

'I had a couple of loose ends to tie up at the station. Thought I'd pop by, see if you're around.'

'Of course. Come in.'

Collins shuffled his shoes on the doormat and followed her inside. 'I've also got something exciting to share with you.'

'Now I'm intrigued,' Brooke said over her shoulder as they traced the hallway.

Barbara appeared in the living room, her weak arms cradling herself. 'Detective Collins. What a nice surprise.'

'Barbara. How are you going?'

She slumped forward and released her arms. They hung awkwardly on each side. 'Day at a time.'

Collins gave a single asserting nod. 'Well, if those FIU guys give you a hard time – give me a call.'

The Financial Intelligence Unit had spent hours in the days after the siege trawling through the house. Seizing evidence and quizzing a clueless Barbara. They'd traced the money back to a criminal organisation already known to the police. It would be a matter of months before they'd be dissolved, a forensic accountant had said as she flicked through bank statements with Barbara. The suggestion had helped her sleep if nothing else.

'Thank you,' Barbara managed. 'I'll leave you guys to it. Let me know if you need anything.' With a culminating half-smile, she disappeared down the hallway and closed her bedroom door.

Brooke gestured towards the plush sofa. 'Make yourself at home.'

Collins sat down heavily, as if he'd fallen into the seat. 'How's she really doing?' He signalled towards Barbara's room with his head.

Brooke hesitated before she spoke, taking a drawn-out breath. 'It's been rough. But she's actually doing a lot better than I expected. She was just talking about downsizing before you got here.'

Collins' eyebrows rose. 'That's great news.' A swollen pause. 'I assume you guys heard about Harry Saunders?'

Brooke still recoiled when she heard his name, despite her relief in knowing he'd been released. 'Yeah. I hope he and his family can find peace somehow.' She glanced out the window, watching the waves pick up their swell. She couldn't deny to herself she wouldn't spend her life checking her back. It was a small price to pay for justice. 'I know Harry and Tina will always hate my family and me. But I'm hoping Mick will be able to forgive us one day.'

Collins gave her a steady stare. 'From our brief time with the young man, I get the feeling he won't carry resentment.'

Brooke loosened her shoulders. 'Hopefully you're right. Maybe he's the new Taonga.'

'Maybe.' Collins gave his neck a satisfying click. 'So when are you heading back up north?'

'Tomorrow. I just finished packing.'

'I think I can already guess how you feel.'

'Yeah. It'll be good to get back to some shred of normality. But obviously it'll be hard to leave Mum and Hannah. And Lana.'

Collins' expression remained blank. 'Sometimes you've got to put yourself first, Palmer.'

Another silence, this time even more fleeting. Brooke fixed her tired eyes on his. 'What was your news?'

The room's mood instantly shifted as Collins puffed his chest and grinned. 'Thought you'd never ask. Well, I've done a lot of thinking over the last couple of weeks. Soul searching, I guess you could call it. I decided I want to be closer to my daughter. So I reached out to the team in Auckland and managed to get myself a transfer.'

Brooke's eyes grew as wide as her smile. 'Oh wow, congratulations.'

'Thanks – I'm excited. The whole team up there are. I told them how helpful you've been to me down here and how well we worked on the case together. They carved a role out for me. Who knows, maybe we'll even get to work together again sometime.'

The thought of Collins entering Brooke's world on a permanent basis was strangely comforting.

'Anyway, I better get a move on.' Collins rose to his feet. 'Can't say I'll be too upset to leave this town for the last time.'

'Hey, only I'm allowed to talk this place down.' Brooke halfed a smile when she stood. 'By the way, did you hear the Lucky Star closed down?'

'Sure did. That place will be knocked down and turned into apartments in a couple of years. Mark my words.'

Brooke shook her head. 'Poor couple. We knew what that place meant to them. But I don't think it would have ever fully recovered from that. Sounds like they've made the move to Melbourne now. Least they'll get to spend more time with their grandkids.'

Collins ambled towards the front door. 'I bet their kids are thrilled.' He gave a sarcastic smirk. 'Tell your mum goodbye, won't you?'

Brooke nodded and opened the door. 'I will. I'll be seeing

you soon then, partner.'

'You certainly will. Safe flight tomorrow.'

Brooke watched Collins crunch across the gravel, clamber into his SUV and meander onto the road. Once the car was completely out of sight, she grabbed her coat from its hook and buttoned it to the top. Although the sun was shining, the winter chill hadn't quite let up its grip.

Brooke called down the hallway to Barbara, telling her she'd be back soon, but she wasn't sure she even heard. Drifting into the cold air, she shivered, and instinctively followed the path towards the wooden steps. She wanted to feel close to Jack one last time before she left. But as she slowly made her descent to Little Taonga Bay, she realised something felt different this time. She wasn't leaving her brother behind, in the town they both hated. In the town that killed him. Taonga didn't kill Jack. And she no longer hated it.

Sinking each step into the familiar sand, Brooke now knew that wherever she went from here, Jack would be with her. Inside her heart, where he'd always been. She would also keep a special place for Evan. Every time she'd see someone clutching a camera, it would be he who'd click the shutter.

Acknowledgements

I wrote the majority of this book when the COVID-19 pandemic hit in March 2020 and it allowed me to disappear into another world when I needed it most. Reading and writing have always offered me an escape, so I was deeply grateful for both during such a turbulent time.

I want to thank literary agent Sarah McKenzie for believing in this story from the start. Your feedback and expertise truly helped to strengthen the manuscript.

I'm grateful to the various editors who read and provided valuable feedback for the book.

An eternal thank you to my parents and Nan for reading to me as a child. You always supported me and encouraged me to pursue my dreams.

Thank you to my sister, Vanessa, for your constant love and support. To my niece, Aria – I cannot wait to read to you. I hope books are as important to you growing up as they were to me.

To my extended family and friends, I thank all of you for your continuous encouragement and support.

Thanks to all my teachers and writing mentors over the years – you inspire me to keep picking up the pen (or tapping away at the keys).

To the indie bookstores and press who supported my last book, and to Lambda Literary Awards for making it a finalist. The opportunity found that story many extra eyeballs, which I am very grateful for.

A special thanks to all those who read and supported my last book, especially those who have been looking forward to this one. Thank you for being patient as I honed my craft and discovered the kind of writer I want to be. I hope you love this book.

And last, but never least, forever thank you to my husband and partner-in-creative-crime, Michael. As always, you were my first reader, editor and champion of the novel. Thanks again for the beautiful cover design – you always get my vision. It is hard to believe we created PRNTD Publishing over a decade ago, and I cannot think of a happier home for *Boy Fallen*. This book would not exist without you, so thank you for that. And for everything else.

About the Author

Chris Gill studied journalism at university and has worked as a copywriter for over a decade both in the UK and Australia. His novel *The Nowhere* was published in 2019 and went on to become a finalist in the Lambda Literary Awards the following year. Born in England to a British mother and New Zealander father, Chris now lives in Sydney with his husband.

@chrisgillbooks